GREAT SHORT STORIES ABOUT PARENTING

GREAT SHORT STORIES ABOUT PARENTING

Stories by **Jessamyn West,
Ray Bradbury, Shirley Jackson,
D.H. Lawrence** *and other great
writers which explore the world
of children and parents.*

EDITED BY **Philip Osborne** AND
Karen Weaver Koppenhaver

Good Books

Intercourse, PA 17534

"Mr. Parker," *Passion and Affect* by Laurie Colwin. Copyright © 1973 by Laurie Colwin. All rights reserved. Reprinted by permission of Viking Penguin, a division of Penguin Books USA, INC. Originally appeared in *The New Yorker*.

"Jack of Hearts," from *The Elizabeth Stories* by Isabel Huggan. Copyright © 1984 by Isabel Huggan. All rights reserved. Reprinted by permission of Viking Penguin, a division of Penguin Books USA, INC.

"The Rocking-Horse Winner," *The Complete Short Stories of D.H. Lawrence, Vol. III*, by D.H. Lawrence. Copyright © 1933 by the Estate of D.H. Lawrence. Copyright renewed © 1961 by Angelo Ravagli and C.M. Weekley, Executors of the Estate of Frieda Lawrence Ravagli. All rights reserved. Reprinted by permission of Viking Penguin, a division of Penguin Books USA, INC.

"Birthday Party" by Shirley Jackson, courtesy *Vogue*. Copyright © 1964 by the Conde Nast Publications, Inc.

"Bless Me, Father," from The *Times are Never So Bad* by Andre Dubus. Copyright © 1983 by Andre Dubus. Reprinted by permission of David R. Godine, Publisher, Boston.

"The Duchess and the Smugs," by Pamela Frankau; reprinted from the novel, *A Wreath for the Enemy*, copyright © 1952, 1954 by Pamela Frankau, copyright © renewed 1980 by the Estate of Pamela Frankau; by arrangement with McPherson & Company, Publishers.

"Going Ashore" by Mavis Gallant. Copyright © 1965 by Mavis Gallant. Reprinted with permission of Georges Burchardt, Inc. and the author.

"What Feels Like the World," from *Spirits* by Richard Bausch. Copyright © 1979, 1983, 1985, 1986, 1987 by Richard Bausch. Reprinted by permission of Linden Press, a division of Simon & Schuster, Inc.

"Winter II" from *Cress Delahanty*. Copyright © 1948 and renewed © 1976 by Jessamyn West. Reprinted by permission of Harcourt Brace Jovanovich, Inc. Previously appeared in *The New Yorker* as "Road to the Isles."

"Grass" is reprinted from *The Quest for Identity* by Allen Wheelis, by permission of W.W. Norton & Company, Inc. Copyright © 1958 by W.W. Norton & Company, Inc. Copyright renewed © 1986 by Allen Wheelis.

"The Forgiveness Trick," from *Time With Children* by Elizabeth Tallent. Copyright © 1986, 1987 by Elizabeth Tallent. Reprinted by permission of Alfred A. Knopf, Inc.

"The Veldt" by Ray Bradbury, reprinted by permission of Don Congdon Associates, Inc. Copyright © 1950 by Ray Bradbury; renewed © 1978 by Ray Bradbury.

"The Boy on the Train" by Arthur Robinson. Copyright © 1988. First published in *The New Yorker*. Reprinted by permission of the author.

"The Desert," from *Good Rockin' Tonight* (A Bantam Book, October 1988) by William Hauptman. Copyright © 1988 by William Hauptman. Reprinted by permission of Watkins/Loomis Agency, agents of the author.

"Simple Arithmetic" by Virginia Moriconi. First published in *The Transatlantic Review*, © Joseph McCrindle, 1963. Every effort has been made to contact the author. The publishers will be happy to arrange formal acknowledgement and customary payment if contacted by the author.

Design by Dawn J. Ranck
Cover design by Cheryl A. Benner

GREAT SHORT STORIES ABOUT PARENTING

International Standard Book Number: 1-56148-008-8
Library of Congress Catalog Card Number: 90-71116

Library of Congress Cataloging-in-Publication Data

Great short stories about parenting/edited by Philip Osborne and Karen Weaver Koppenhaver.
    p.   cm.
Includes bibliographical references.
ISBN 1-56148-008-8: $9.95
    1. Parent and child—Fiction. 2. Short stories, American. 3. Short stories, English. I. Osborne, Philip, 1943– . II. Koppenhaver, Karen Weaver.
PS648.P33G74   1990
813'.0108355—dc20

90-71116
CIP

Contents

ৼ

Acknowledgements

ᑲᘛ

Many persons have helped to make this book possible. Ruby Sawin, Prairie View Community Mental Health Center; Jackie Herrold, Hesston High School; Paul Friesen, Hesston College; Raylene Hinz-Penner, Bethel College; and Tom Oates, Georgetown University, suggested stories for our consideration.

A special word of thanks to those who reviewed the manuscript: Susan Bumbaugh, Bluffton College; Ed Zuercher, Hesston High School; and Joyce Sullentrop, Kansas Newman College. Their assistance was invaluable.

A collection of stories cannot be published, of course, without the consent of those who hold the copyrights. Thanks to the various publishing companies, literary agents and authors involved in this project, (especially Arthur Robinson).

Thanks to our own publisher, Merle Good, and editor, Phyllis Pellman Good, for their support of this project. We are grateful for their enthusiasm about the stories and the financial risk they have assumed to make the stories available to others. We are pleased that our story collection is among their publications which are consistently of such high quality.

We also acknowledge the contributions of our parents, Chester and Eva Troyer Osborne and Earl and Goldie Weaver, to our lives. The values underlying this book, including the love of reading, are theirs.

And finally, we want to acknowledge one of our teachers, Harold Schmidt, who made our eighth grade year such an important one and who is a great storyteller himself. This book is dedicated to you, Harold, with appreciation.

Philip Osborne and Karen Weaver Koppenhaver
Hesston College
Hesston, Kansas
Fall, 1990

A Word from the Editors

A friend of ours recently returned from a professional conference. "How were the sessions?" we inquired. "Good!" he reflected, "although I can't say I remember much about them. But I do remember a couple of stories the speakers told."

Most of us have had this experience. We enjoy and remember stories more than we remember formal talks.

Jerome Bruner (1986) observed that humans use two qualitatively different kinds of thought. One is what he calls *propositional thinking.* This is the logical, abstract, context-independent way of thinking upon which the scientific world rests. The other way of thinking Bruner calls *narrative thinking.* Narrative thinking is a description of reality based on personal experience. It requires imagination, an appreciation of the complexities of human interaction and intention, and an understanding of the time and place of the particular event.

In past times, people relied on the narrative mode for giving meaning to their existence. Stories about their origins, stories about their heroes and stories about ordinary people in ordinary dilemmas provided their perceptions about the world, their personal and group identities, and their ideals. They learned how to live through the narrative mode of thought.

As our modern world became increasingly developed, however, we began to rely more and more on propositional thought for formal education. Narrative thought became increasingly restricted to entertainment — visiting, watching movies and television, and reading for pleasure, particularly fiction. As formal education became less dependent on narrative thinking, we became less sure about how to live.

Such writers as Neil Postman (1989) remind us that personal, national and religious stories are needed to maintain vitality in our personal, national and religious identities. Postman writes:

Without stories as organizing frameworks we are swamped by the volume of our own experience, adrift in a sea of facts. . . . A story gives us direction by providing a kind of theory about how the world works — and how it needs to work if we are to survive. (p. 123)

It is not surprising, therefore, that we are witnessing a resurgence of interest in stories, jokes, anecdotes, legends, metaphors and other forms of narrative thought in many areas. Metaphors, stories and ceremonies are being used in psychotherapy (see **Narrative Means to Therapeutic Ends** by White and Epston, 1990). Robert Coles' work (for example, **The Call of Stories,** 1989) testifies to the importance of stories in the development of personal morality. Joseph Campbell's collections of myths illustrate the power of myths in belief systems (**Myths to Live By** by Campbell, 1984). Research into the importance of humor in emotional and physical healing is being investigated currently, stimulated in part by Norman Cousins' report of his recovery (Cousins, 1979, 1989). And in the field of religious eduction, we are witnessing an emphasis on stories (e.g., **Religion as Story,** edited by Wiggins, 1975).

The use of stories has far greater potential in parent education than has been realized. An enormous amount of "How-to" books for parents are used, of course, but there is much more to parenting than the theories described in books, just as there is much more to basketball than the fundamentals outlined in books. Stories, on the other hand, provide an almost lifelike description of the parenting dilemmas people actually experience. Through stories, the mind's eye sees parenting in action; the imagined scenarios are stored as templates in the memory, capable of guiding behavior.

I (Osborne) have been using stories in parent education classes for many years and have come to rely on them as an effective means of engaging students in discussion of ideals, goals, disappointments, inadequacies and common experiences, as well as theories and methods of parenting. I am convinced that students remember more lessons from stories than they remember from textbook assignments or my lectures.

Lessons are learned by observing the interaction of story char-

acters who are authentic, not necessarily faultless. The emphasis
in this collection, therefore, is on great *stories*, not great *parenting*.
The fifteen stories portray adult rejection ("Simple Arithmetic"),
insensitivity ("Jack of Hearts"), ineptness ("The Boy on the
Train"), manipulation ("Bless Me, Father"), punitiveness
("Grass"), immaturity ("Going Ashore") and materialism ("The
Rocking Horse Winner"). The stories are hauntingly effective —
haunting in that they linger in the mind; effective in that the
portrayal of parenting gone awry provokes questions about what
went wrong and how the parenting could be improved.

Some of the stories reveal parents who are relatively successful
("Winter II," "Birthday Party," "The Duchess and the Smugs"
and "What Feels Like the World"), but even these stories raise
questions about parenting styles and what makes them more or
less successful.

Preceding each story is an introduction to a parenting issue the
story depicts. Following each story is a brief sketch of the author's
life and work. Following this are questions to guide the reader's
movement from the concrete examples of the story to reflection
and propositional thought. Each set of questions begins with
factual review questions and ends with higher level interpretation
questions for group discussion and individual writing assignments.

Great Short Stories About Parenting serves as a book of
readings to supplement the parent education book, **Parenting for
the '90s** (Osborne, 1989). In the story collection we do not assume
that the reader is familiar with the other book. However, for the
convenience of those who use both, the 15 stories illustrate in
order each of the 15 chapters in **Parenting for the '90s.**

The stories were selected for their usefulness in parent education, but since few short fiction collections about family relationships exist, we believe the collection can be useful in other settings
as well: in high school family living and composition classes; in
college classes in communication and composition, counseling
psychology, personal growth and adjustment psychology, and
marriage and the family; in counseling centers; and in churches.

In whatever setting **Great Short Stories About Parenting** is
used, we are confident the book will provide pleasure for individual readers. I (Osborne) find that college students typically begin
their encounters with short fiction reluctantly ("Will it be on the
test?"), but as the term progresses and the students experience the

intellectual and emotional rewards of reading short stories, they come to class more and more eager to discuss what they have read.

All of the stories have been judged by critics and other anthologists as outstanding in quality. Many of the stories are award-winning. Authors include such notables as D. H. Lawrence and Jessamyn West, now deceased; and Richard Bausch, Andre Dubus, Mavis Gallant and Elizabeth Tallent, of contemporary fame. Stories range in type from science fiction ("The Veldt") to autobiography ("Grass" and "The Boy on the Train"), and in time from an earlier twentieth century setting ("Grass") to a contemporary setting ("The Forgiveness Trick"). One of the stories is novella-length ("The Duchess and the Smugs"); one consists of a series of letters ("Simple Arithmetic").

Our hope is that these stories provide pleasure, provoke thought and discussion, and prod readers to better parenting in their own lives.

Philip Osborne and Karen Weaver Koppenhaver
Fall, 1990

Parenting Issue:

Maintaining Balance

Maintaining balance among all the requirements of the parent-hood role is not easy. Effective parents need to be able to develop a sense of family caring and togetherness, while simultaneously being able to foster the autonomy of individual family members and manage conflict among them. They need to be able to comfort and encourage and also to confront and demand. Furthermore, parents need patience in the day-to-day challenges of life together since children mature slowly. The task of parenting is a long-term one, and responses to daily struggles need to be kept in balance with long-term goals.

"Winter II," which takes place over a two-day period, shows a father, mother and daughter coping the best they can with their individual problems and the conflicts they feel with each other, while at the same time attempting to be supportive of each other.

1.
Winter II
Jessamyn West

It was the last Thursday in January, about nine in the evening, cold and raining. The three Delahantys sat close about the living-room fireplace — Mr. Delahanty at the built-in desk working on his schedule, Mrs. Delahanty on the sofa reading, and between them, crosswise in the wing chair, their fourteen-year-old daughter, Crescent. Cress was apparently studying the program of the folk-dance festival in which she was to appear the next evening. For the most part, however, she did not even see the program. She saw, instead, herself, infinitely graceful, moving through the figures of the dance that had been so difficult for her to master.

The high-school folk-dancing class was made up of two kinds of performers — those with natural ability, who had themselves elected the class, and those who, in the language of the physical-education department, were "remedials." The remedials had been sent into the class willy-nilly in an effort to counteract in them defects ranging from antisocial attitudes to what Miss Ingols, the gym teacher, called "a general lack of grace." Cress had achieved the class under this final classification but now, at midterm, had so far outgrown it as to be the only remedial with a part in the festival.

The first five numbers on the program, "Tsiganotchka," "Ladies' Whim," "Meitschi Putz Di," "Hiawatha," and "Little Man in a Fix," Cress ignored. It was not only that she was not in these but that they were in no way as beautiful as "Road to the Isles," in which Mary Lou Hawkins, Chrystal O'Conor, Zelma Mayberry, Bernadine Deevers, and Crescent Delahanty took part. The mere sight of her name beside that of Bernadine Deevers, Tenant High School's most gifted dancer — most gifted *person*, really—instantly called up to Cress a vision of herself featly footing it in laced kirtle and starched skirts, a vision of herself dancing not only the outward steps of "Road to the Isles" but its inner meaning: what Miss Ingols had called "the achievement of the impossible."

Cress thought that she was particularly adapted to dancing that meaning because she had so recently come that way herself. If she had been given three wishes when school opened in September, two of them would have been that Bernadine be her friend and that she herself succeed in the folk-dancing class. Both had then seemed equally impossible. Now not only did she have a part in the festival but Bernadine was her dear friend and coming to spend the weekend with her. At the minute the evening reached what she considered its peak of mellowness, she intended to speak to her father and mother about the festival and Bernadine's visit. She was exceedingly uncertain about their performances on both these occasions.

The rain suddenly began to fall harder. Cress's father, hearing it on the roof, watched with gratification as the water streamed across the dark windowpanes. "Just what the oranges have been a-thirsting for," he said.

Mrs. Delahanty closed her book. "How's the schedule coming?" she asked her husband.

"O.K., I guess," said Mr. Delahanty.

Cress looked up from the festival program with embarrassment. The schedule was one of the things she wanted to speak to her father about. She hoped he wouldn't mention it while Bernadine was visiting them. Every winter, as work on the ranch slackened, he drew up a schedule for the better ordering of his life. And every spring, as work picked up, he abandoned it as easily as if it had never been. Last winter, he had made a plan called "A Schedule of Exercises to Ensure Absolute Fitness," which included not only the schedule of exercises and the hours at which he proposed to practice them but a list of the weaknesses they were to counteract. He had even gone so far, last winter, as to put on a pair of peculiar short pants and run six times around the orchard without stopping, arms flailing, chest pumping—a very embarrassing sight, and one that Cress could not possibly have explained to Bernadine.

This winter, the subject of her father's schedule-making was not in itself so unsuitable. He had bought a new encyclopedia set and was mapping out a reading program that would enable him, by a wise use of his spare time, to cover the entire field of human knowledge in a year. The name of the schedule, written at the top of a sheet of Cress's yellow graph paper, was, in fact, "Human Knowledge in a Year." There was nothing about this plan that would call for embarrassing public action, like running around the orchard in shorts, but it was so incredibly naïve and dreamy that Cress hoped her father would not speak of it. Bernadine was far too sophisticated for schedules.

"Where are you now on your schedule, John?" Mrs. Delahanty asked.

Mr. Delahanty, who liked to talk about his plans almost as much as he liked to make them, put down his pen and picked up the sheet of paper on which he had been writing. "I've got all the subjects I want to read up about listed, and the times I'll have free *for* reading listed. Nothing left to do now but decide what's the best time for what. For instance, if you were me, Gertrude, would you spend the fifteen minutes before breakfast on art? Or on archeology, say?"

"You don't ever have fifteen minutes before breakfast," Mrs. Delahanty said.

Mr. Delahanty picked up his pen. "I thought you wanted to discuss this."

"Oh, I do!" said Mrs. Delahanty. "Well if *I* had fifteen minutes before breakfast, *I'd* read about archeology.

"Why?" asked Mr. Delahanty.

"It's more orderly that way," Mrs. Delahanty said.

"Orderly?" asked Mr. Delahanty.

"A-r-c," Mrs. Delahanty spelled, "comes before a-r-t."

Mr. Delahanty made an impatient sound. "I'm not going at this alphabetically, Gertrude. Cut and dried. What I'm thinking about is what would make the most interesting morning reading. The most interesting and inspiring."

"Art is supposed to be more inspiring," Mrs. Delahanty told him. "If that's what you're after."

This seemed to decide Mr. Delahanty. "No, I think science should be the morning subject," he said, and wrote something at the top of a sheet—"Science," Cress supposed. "That's better," he said. "That leaves art for the evening, when I'll have time to read aloud to you."

"Don't change your schedule around for my sake, John," said

Mrs. Delahanty, who hated being read to about anything.

"I'm not. All personal consideration aside, that's a more logical arrangement. Now the question is, which art?"

This seemed to Cress the moment for which she had been waiting. "Dancing is one of the earliest and most important of the arts," she said quickly.

"Oho!" said her father. "I thought you were in a coma."

"I've been rehearsing," said Cress.

"Rehearsing!" exclaimed Mr. Delahanty.

"In my mind," Cress said.

"So that's what was going on—'Ladies' Whim,' 'Tsiganotchka'—"

"Father," Cress interrupted, "I've told you and told you the t's silent. Why don't you take the program and practice the names? I'll help you." Cress got up and took the program across to her father.

"Practice them," said Mr. Delahanty with surprise, reading through the dances listed. "What do I care how they're pronounced? 'Korbushka,' 'Kohanotchka,' " he said, mispronouncing wildly. "I'm not going to Russia."

"But you're going to the folk-dance festival," Cress reminded him.

"I don't *have* to go. If you don't want—"

"I do, Father. You know I want you to go. Only I don't want you to mispronounce the names."

"Look, Cress," Mr. Delahanty said. "I promise you I'll keep my mouth shut the whole time I'm there. No one will know you have a father who can't pronounce. Mute I'll come and mute I'll go."

"I don't want you to be mute," Cress protested. "And even if I did, you couldn't very well be mute the whole time Bernadine's here. And Bernadine's the star of the program."

"To Bernadine," said Mr. Delahanty, referring to the program once again, "I shall speak of 'Badger,' and 'The Lumberman's Two Step.' I can pronounce them fine and they ought to hold Bernadine. She's not going to be here long, is she?"

"Friday to Monday," said Mrs. Delahanty.

"In that case," said Mr. Delahanty, "maybe I should find another one. How about 'The Irish Jollity,' Cress? Do I say that all right?"

"Now, John!" Mrs. Delahanty reproved her husband.

"It's all right for him to joke about it to me, Mother. But he mustn't before Bernadine. Bernadine's serious about dancing. She's going to be a great artist."

"A great dancer?" Mrs. Delahanty asked.

"She hasn't decided what kind of an artist yet," Cress said. "Only to be great in something."

"Well, well," said Mr. Delahanty. "I'm beginning to look forward to meeting Bernadine."

"You already have," Cress told him. "Bernadine was one of the girls who rode with us to the basketball game."

Mr. Delahanty squinted his eyes, as if trying to peer backward to the Friday two weeks before when he had provided Cress and four of her friends with transportation to an out-of-town game. He shook his head. "Can't recall any Bernadine," he said.

"She was the one in the front seat with us," Cress reminded him.

"That girl!" exclaimed Mr. Delahanty, remembering. "But her name wasn't Bernadine, was it?"

No," Cress told him. "That's what I wanted to explain to you, because tomorrow's Friday, too."

Mr. Delahanty left desk and schedule and walked over in front of the fireplace. From this position, he could get a direct view of his daughter.

"What's this you're saying, Cress?" he asked. "Her name isn't Bernadine because tomorrow's Friday. Is that what you said?"

"Yes, it is," Cress told him, seriously. "Only it's not just tomorrow. Her name isn't Bernadine on any Friday."

Mr. Delahanty appealed to his wife. "Do you hear what I hear, Gertrude?"

"Mother," Cress protested, "this isn't anything funny. In fact, it's a complete tragedy."

"Well, Cress dear," her mother said reasonably, "I haven't said a word. And your father's just trying to get things straight."

"He's trying to be funny about a tragedy," Cress insisted obstinately.

Now, Cress," Mr. Delahanty urged, "you're jumping to conclusions. Though I admit I think it's queer to have a name on Fridays you don't have the rest of the week. And I don't see anything tragic about it."

"That's what I'm trying to tell you, only you keep acting as if it's a joke."

"What is Bernadine's name on Fridays, Cress?" asked her

mother.

"Nedra," said Cress solemnly.

Mr. Delahanty snapped his fingers. "Yes, sir," he said, "that's it! That's what they called her, all right."

"Of course," said Cress. "Everyone does on Fridays, out of respect for her sorrow."

"Just what *is* Bernadine's sorrow, Cress?" her mother asked.

"Bernadine never did say—out and out, that is. Once in a while she tries to. But she just can't. It overwhelms her. But we all know what, generally speaking, must have happened."

"What?" asked Mr. Delahanty. "Generally speaking?"

Cress looked at her father suspiciously, but his face was all sympathetic concern.

"On some Friday in the past," she said, "Nedra had to say no to someone. Someone she loved."

"How old is Berna—Nedra?" Mrs. Delahanty asked.

"Sixteen," Cress said. "Almost."

"Well, it couldn't have been too long ago then, could it?" her mother suggested.

"Was this person," Mr. Delahanty ventured, "this person Nedra said no to, a male?"

"Of course," said Cress. "I told you it was a complete tragedy, didn't I? His name was Ned. That much we know."

"Then the Nedra is in honor of—Ned?" asked her mother.

"In honor and loving memory," Cress told her. "On the very next Friday, Ned died."

Mr. Delahanty said nothing. Mrs. Delahanty said, "Poor boy!"

"I think he was probably more than a boy," Cress said. "He owned two drugstores."

After the elder Delahantys had thought about this for a while Mr. Delahanty asked, "This 'no' Bernadine—Nedra—said, was it to a proposal of marriage?"

"We don't ever ask about that," Cress told her father disapprovingly. "It doesn't seem like good taste to us."

"No, I don't suppose it is," Mr. Delahanty admitted.

"Anyway," Cress said, "that's Bernadine's tragedy and we all respect it and her wish to be called Nedra on Fridays. And tomorrow is a Friday, and it would be pretty awful to have her upset before the festival."

Mr. Delahanty stepped briskly back to his desk. "Don't you worry for a second, Cress," he said. "As far as I'm concerned, the girl's name is Nedra."

"Thank you, Father," Cress said. "I knew you'd understand. Now I'd better go to bed." At the door to the hallway, she turned and spoke once again. "If I were you, Father, I wouldn't say anything about your schedule to Bernadine."

"I hadn't planned on talking to her about it. But what's wrong with it?" Mr. Delahanty sounded a little testy.

"Oh, nothing," Cress assured him. "I think it's dear and sweet of you to make schedules. Only," she explained, "it's so idealistic."

After Cress left the room, Mr. Delahanty said, "What the hell's wrong with being idealistic?"

Cress thought that her friend, in her costume for "Fado Blanquita," the Spanish dance in which she performed the solo part, looked like the queen of grace and beauty. And she said so.

"This does rather suit my type," Bernadine admitted. She was leaning out from the opened casement window of Cress's room into the shimmering, rain-washed air. She tautened her costume's already tight bodice, fluffed up its already bouffant skirt, and extended her hands in one of the appealing gestures of the dance toward the trees of the orange orchard upon which the window opened.

"Is your father a shy man?" she asked.

Mr. Delahanty, who had been working near the driveway to the house when the two girls got off the school bus an hour before, had, instead of lingering to greet them, quickly disappeared behind a row of trees. Now, in rubber boots, carrying a light spade that he was using to test the depth to which the night before's rain had penetrated the soil, he came briefly into sight, waved his spade, and once again disappeared.

"No," said Cress, who thought her father rather bold, if anything. "He's just busy. After the rain, you know."

"Rain, sunshine. Sunshine, rain," Bernadine said understandingly. She moved her hands about in the placid afternoon air as if scooping up samples. "Farming is an awfully elemental life, I expect. My father" — Bernadine's father, J. M. Deevers, was vice-president of the Tenant First National Bank — "probably doesn't known one element from another. I expect your father's rather an elemental type, too, isn't he? Fundamentally, I mean?"

"I don't know, Nedra," Cress said humbly.

"He's black-haired," Bernadine said. "It's been my experience that black-haired men are very elemental." She brought her expressive hands slowly down to her curving red satin bodice. "You must have a good deal of confidence in your family to let them go tonight," she went on briskly.

"Let them!" Cress repeated, amazed at the word.

"Perhaps they're different from my family. Mine always keep me on pins and needles about what they're going to say and do next."

"Mine, too," Cress admitted, though loyalty to her father and mother would not permit her to say how greatly they worried her. She never went anyplace with them that she was not filled with a tremulous concern lest they do or say something that would discredit them all. She stayed with them. She attempted to guide them. She hearkened to every word said to them, so that she could prompt them with the right answers. But *let* them! "They always just take it for granted that where I go, they go," she said. "There's not much question of letting."

"Mine used to be that way," Bernadine confided. "But after what happened at the festival last year, I put my foot down. 'This year,' I told them, 'you're not going.'"

"What happened last year?" asked Cress, who had not then been a dancer.

"After the program was over last year, Miss Ingols asked for parent participation in the dancing. And my father participated. He danced the 'Hopak,' and pretty soon he was lifting Miss Ingols off the floor at every other jump."

"Oh, Nedra," Cress said. "How terrible! What did Ingols do?"

"Nothing," said Bernadine. "That was the disgusting part. As a matter of fact, she seemed to enjoy it. But you can imagine how I suffered."

Cress nodded. She could. She was thinking how she would suffer if her father, in addition to mispronouncing all the dances, went out on the gymnasium floor and, before all her friends, misdanced them.

"Are your parents the participating type?" Bernadine asked.

Cress nodded with sad conviction. "Father is. And Mother is if encouraged."

"You'd better warn them right away," Bernadine said. "Your father just came in the back door. You could warn him now."

Cress walked slowly down the hallway toward the kitchen. Before the evening was over, her father, too, would probably be jouncing Miss Ingols around, and even calling Bernadine Bernadine–then all would be ruined completely, all she had looked forward to for so long. In the kitchen, she noted signs of the special supper her mother was cooking because of Bernadine: the cole-slaw salad had shreds of green peppers and red apples mixed through it tonight to make it festive; the party sherbet glasses, with their long, icicle stems, awaited the lemon pudding. But her mother was out of the kitchen — on the back porch telling her father to hurry, because they would have to have dinner early if they were to get to the festival in time. "Festival!" Cress heard her father say. "I wish I'd never heard of that festival. How did Cress ever come to get mixed up in this dancing business, any-way?" he asked. "She's no dancer. Why, the poor kid can hardly get through a room without knocking something over. Let alone dance!"

"That's *why* she's mixed up with it," her mother explained. "To overcome her awkwardness. And she *is* better."

"But is she good enough?" asked her father. "I'd hate to think of her making a spectacle of herself — to say nothing of having to sit and watch it."

"Now, John," Cress heard her mother say soothingly. "You're always too concerned about Cress. Will she do this right? Will she do that right? Stop worrying. Cress'll probably be fine."

"Maybe fall on her ear, too," her father said morosely. "They oughtn't to put so much responsibility on kids. Performing in public. Doesn't it worry you any?"

"Certainly it worries me. But all parents worry. And remember, we'll have the star of the performance with us. You can concen-trate on Nedra if watching Cress is too much for you."

"That Nedra! The only dance I can imagine that girl doing is one in which she would carry somebody's head on a platter."

Cress had started back down the hall before her father finished this sentence, but she had not gone so far as to miss its final word. She stopped in the bathroom to have a drink of water and to see how she looked in the mirror over the washbasin. She looked different. For the first time in her life, she saw herself through other eyes than her own. Through her parents' eyes. Did parents worry about the figures their *children* cut? Were they embarrassed for *them*, and did they wonder if they were behaving suitably, stylishly, well? Cress felt a vacant, hollow space beneath her heart, which another glass of water did nothing to fill. Why, *I'm* all right, Cress thought. *I* know how to behave. I'll get by. *They're* the ones . . . but she looked at her face again and it was wavering, doubtful—not the triumphant face she had imagined, smiling in sureness as she danced the come-and-go figures of "Road to the Isles."

She went back to her room full of thought. Bernadine was changing her costume, and her muffled voice came from under all her skirts. "Did you tell them?" this muffled voice asked.

"No," said Cress, "I didn't."

"Why not? Won't you be worried?"

"They're the ones who are worrying. About me."

"About you?"

"Father thinks I may fall on my ear."

Bernadine, clear of her skirts, nodded in smiling agreement. "It's a possibility that sometimes occurs to *me*, Cress dear."

Cress gazed at her friend speculatively. "They're worried about you, too," she said.

"Me?" asked Bernadine, her smile fading.

"Father said the only dance he could imagine you doing was one with a head on a platter."

"Salome!" Bernadine exclaimed with pleasure. "Your father's imaginative, isn't he? Sympathetically imaginative?"

"I guess so," Cress said, and in her confusion told everything. "He keeps schedules."

"Schedules?"

"For the better ordering of his life."

Bernadine laughed again. "How precious!" she said.

Then, as if remembering after too long a lapse the day and her bereavement, she said, "Neddy was like that, too."

"Neddy," repeated Cress, pain for the present making Bernadin's past seem not only past but silly. "Oh, shut up about Neddy, *Bernadine!*"

Bernadine gave a little gasp. "Have you forgotten it's Friday?"

"I don't care what day it is," Cress said. She walked over to her bed, picked up the pillow, and lay down. Then she put the pillow over her face.

&

About the Author

Jessamyn West was born in 1907. She began writing while confined to bed for a period of time with tuberculosis, and eventually published numerous novels, short stories, screenplays and poems. She wrote of Indiana, where she was born, and of California, where she was educated at Whittier College and the University of California and where she lived as an adult. She died in 1984.

West's family was Quaker; her first novel and best-known work, *The Friendly Persuasion,* consists of stories told with a gentle humor about a Quaker family living in Indiana during the Civil War. Most of her heroes and heroines exhibit the Quaker virtues of industry, patience and, especially, integrity.

Cress Delahanty is a collection of stories about an adolescent girl of that name. Like other West characters, Cress exhibits the idealism of the 19th century rather than the disillusionment of the 20th. In "Winter II" (from *Cress Delahanty* and originally titled "Road to the Isles") the author does not set Cress in moral contrast to her adult world, as many modern authors do their teenage protagonists (see Isabel Huggans's "Jack of Hearts"). Cress's accidental entre to and acceptance of her parents' perspective is shown as a step in her maturation.

Questions for Thought and Discussion

1. About how old is Cress? Why was she enrolled in the dance class?

2. What do you think of the way the family interacted during the evening they were home together?

3. How does Cress's father respond to her concerns? Why does he offer not to go to the dance festival?

4. Until the end of the story, Cress is patronizing to her parents. She assumes she is more sophisticated than they and is embarrassed by them. How is this revealed?

5. How is Bernadine's view of Cress's father different from Cress's view of him? Why do you think this is? What is the importance of what Cress learns when Bernadine tells her about the prior year's dance festival?

6. What does Cress discover about her parents when she over-

hears their conversation? Could the parents have handled the situation differently?

7. As Cress looks in the mirror at the end of the story, she appears to herself to be different. What has changed?

8. Do you think Cress and her father might be quite alike, even though they react negatively to each other? What are the similarities between her dance fantasies and her father's "schedules"?

9. What makes Cress and John and Gertrude Delahanty believable characters? Do you know persons like them?

10. People commonly use the word discipline to mean correction or even punishment. But discipline is more than this, as illustrated by this story. How do the events of both days contribute to Cress's discipline, even though her parents do not overtly correct or punish her? How do you define discipline?

Parenting Issue:

Individual Differences and
Male-Female Differences of Parents

All parents differ in the array of personal strengths and weaknesses they bring to the parenting situation. They hear conflicting advice about these individual differences. Behavioral psychologists advise them to be "consistent." Humanistic psychologists advise them to be "real." Family systems theorists advise them to be "differentiated."

In regard to sex differences, conservative Christian authorities argue that husbands should be dominant and wives should be "submissive." Traditional sex role advocates prefer that husbands be "instrumental" and wives be "expressive," whereas proponents of nontraditional sex roles urge them to be "egalitarian."

Perhaps the most important issue in regard to these differences is the extent to which the parents are mutually supportive in carrying out their parental responsibilities, however the responsibilities are divided. This requires at least some acceptance of their differences and a willingness to share their children's affections, rather than compete for them. "The Forgiveness Trick" shows, through their interactions in a brief incident, one couple's struggle with this issue.

2.

The Forgiveness Trick

Elizabeth Tallent

ᐒ

In London, Nicholas, who was nearly five and had never been afraid of the dark before, began to need his father at night. Barefoot on the pricklish Oriental rug, Nicholas would feel his way through the sitting room, which was dark except for six high, fogged-over windows that smelled of cold rainy glass and dirty painted mullions — he knew because he liked to lean his forehead against them in the afternoon. At night, a sudden dappling of lights on the ceiling meant a taxi in the street below, passing the hotel where black cabs often idled; his mother liked to catch them there. These lights wavered, flared very white, then flying-saucered around the walls, taking the corners fast, dipping when they hit the plush back of an aged armchair. The taxi's sound was a sticky unreeling like a long, long strand of tape being pulled free from something; there were deep puddles the tire had gone through. Then it was quiet. London was quiet.

The thing that worried him most was when the cat came into the room. The cat belonged to two old English people who had gone away, leaving it, and their flat, in the care of the Americans — Nicholas and his mother and father. The cat knew when Nicholas was awake: at the rug's far side it would fold itelf into a crouch, steer its ears forward, and turn its sharpened attention, its small vexed mouth and round eyes, entirely on the child. Neither moved; this was hatred. Nicholas taunted it softly, "Fleas, fleas, fleas." The cat shied around antique-chair legs and was gone, leaving Nicholas alone.

At the door of his parents' room, he bumped his back rhythmically against the doorjamb in relief. The old radiator on the wall croaked and fluted as its metal pipes contracted; it was warmer in there than it had been downstairs, and he could see his mother's head behind his father's shoulder, and hear their different breathing. Going in, he stood by the bed until his father opened his eyes.

Nicholas's face, when touched in the dark by his father, had that charged, freshened feel it had after tears. All Charlie was aware of in that moment of sleepy chaos was fear, a wrench of hard alertness, which lasted until, his slightly more sensible self dawning, he realized that this had happened before, that this was only a night like the others when Nicholas had waked him because of a dream; it wasn't the surreal, sudden wrong Charlie believed could invade his life—his son hurt. If Charlie had felt what he felt on waking and not had Nicholas right before him, he would have gone crazy. He would have had to run until he found Nicholas, if it meant running ten miles. So he was grateful that there was just enough distance between them for his arm to stretch comfortably across. He loved the fit of his son's cheek in his hand. He caught some of the fine hair, tugged his son's head sideways, and said, "You and me, buddy."

Charlie conducted his son to the little bathroom, clicked the light on, and Kyra in the bed heard her husband whisper, "Niagara Falls," and then the patter of Nicholas's pee, followed by silence as they went back through the flat, then down the stairs, to Nicholas's room.

And Kyra, for whom sleep had vanished, didn't know what to do. She imagined herself sitting on the edge of a bed, sheltering Nicholas, rocking and murmuring through the first caught breaths and the hard hiccups, stroking the hair back from his hot forehead, wiping his nose, then cleverly eliciting the details of the dream, but that couldn't happen now that Nicholas wanted his *father*. In an excess of loneliness for them, she lay heeding the cranky radiator's groans (this place cost too much, and the nagging letters from its distant owners irritated her immensely. All those questions about their darling cat, when they had regarded Nicholas with the fastidious suspicion of the elderly and childless, and almost not rented the place to Charlie and Kyra, giving in at the last possible—). When Charlie wanted something, he started right in: London was this, London was that; the year's apprenticeship to an English publisher meant recognition of his worth. Then he went for her weaknesses: "New York is getting scarier, Ky. When Jay and Linda lived on Hampstead Heath, they let their three-year-old wander anywhere, and he says they felt perfectly safe. How long since we felt perfectly safe? He says London's sane. Think what it will mean to Nicholas to have one year of childhood when we're not watching him every sec." How could she have known to say no? She'd have felt selfish, one of the things she least liked feeling.

She cast her leg across Charlies's side. His absence was nice. Now she could think. There was so little thinking in families, such a ruckus of needy feeling. It seemed to her that Nicholas's dreams had to be her fault, that there was something she was capable of — some insight, some decision — and the dreams would be fanned away. She pushed her foot down to the cold bottom of the bed and found the cat there; he worked up a small, protesting yawn. She scooped him off the bed — a silkenslack sack, unresisting, that met the cold floor with a thump. The responsibility for Nicholas's nightmares was making her resentful, and she wanted to know what Charlie was doing. Going down the stairs she heard his voice. She didn't listen closely, but guessed from his intonation he wasn't getting anywhere.

In Nicholas's doorway, she got an update: "Something was in here," Charlie explained from the edge of the bed.

Kyra pushed her hair from her face. All she could think of to say was "What?" so she said, "What?" guiltily, to her husband and her small son.

"Tell me what," Charlie urged. Nicholas shook his head. He could go stubborn like that, on her, on his sitter, or on anyone. During the week, Charlie sealed himself away in that gray suite of Bedford Square offices; his lunches lasted all afternoon, his afternoons lasted until long after dark. Most of his precious year was up, and he tended to come home so exhausted that he hadn't yet picked up on something that should have been obvious: his son's head-shaking resistance was part of a phase, and basically had nothing to do with him. If he didn't watch out, Charlie was going to turn into the sort of father who pretended closeness but who really relied on briefings from his wife about their son's emotions. Kyra hated fathers like that.

Charlie insisted. "Can you start with what it looked like?"

Nicholas made a soft hissing, tongue to his front teeth: a child's embarrassment at being asked a question so far off the mark, so devoid of any intuition about the child's situation, that he is forced — briefly but with urgency — to wonder at the poverty of comprehension, which seems to imply that he is not at the heart of his father's world. Nicholas would have forgotten it completely in a minute, Kyra knew, but she didn't like that he had had to feel it. She imagined that her eyes were firing tiny red darts into Charlie's big, dense back.

He didn't turn. He said, "Nicky, you got me out of bed because of it. Don't you think I deserve to know something about it?"

Blackmail, Kyra thought. Wrong wrong wrong. Blackmail was the last thing that worked with Nicholas.

Her son's head shook fiercely, No, no, no. He fitted his shoulders more closely against the wall, put his chin on his kneecap, and gripped his ankles painfully hard. What he wanted to do now, Kyra was sure, was to distract his father from this course of questioning. He was trying to make his feet turn white. He gazed intently at his toes, waiting for the blood to be cut off.

"He doesn't want to talk about it yet," Kyra offered from the doorway.

"Ky, that's good. That's great. Undo what I've done. We were getting somewhere."

"You were not; look at him."

"I needed two more minutes; that's just like you."

"Stop it, then." She thought, *Pig.* She was amazed to have thought that about Charlie. *Pig?*

"What are you smiling about?" he demanded. "Have you got a lover?"—a question so astonishing, so out of the blue, that Charlie froze where he was, looking over his shoulder at her, and she froze where she was, neither of them immediately believing, but both then hearing, far too clearly, the unforgiving automatic inner replay of his words. She knew it was one of those things that just slip out; she knew that Charlie would never forget that it had slipped out in front of Nicholas; she knew that Charlie was going to worry the possible future psychological complexities of that for a long time. Thus far, they'd been so cunning in keeping their problems to themselves, even the affair Charlie had strayed into and out of in New York last March. They'd wished into place over Nicholas a rainbowed security, and neither had ever before let the tremors between them trouble it. She did a quick mother's scan: Nicholas didn't look as if he'd heard a thing. "Lover"—what could that conceivably mean to four-and-a-half? Nothing. He was staring, with satisfaction, at his toes. More than anything, Kyra wished to pry his fingers from his feet.

To Nicholas, Charlie said in a stricken tone, "You won't talk to me."

His voice was hoarse. It was too much emotion to address a child with; it could only confuse Nicholas more. In a protective rush, Kyra said, "Hey, no more tonight, guys."

Charlie slid from the bed and knelt. He covered his face and said through his fingers, "Why won't you?" Frightened, Kyra thought: He's going to cry. But he only said, "What am I doing that changed you?" He couldn't see the startled glance his son gave him.

Kyra could. "Up, Charlie," she said. "Back to bed now. Come on, old bear."

Nicholas said to her over his father's head, "No, *you* go." When she didn't move, he bounced against the wall in irritation and shouted, "You go! You go!"

"Nicholas," she pleaded, "I—"

"Nicholas Chinaman Cincinnati," Charlie said, lifting his head, the purifying light of nonsense in his eye. "In the morning, see, you and I are going to get down to business. I love you, and that's it. That's all you need to know before you start talking to me, because I get this feeling more and more lately like something's wrong, and I'm your father, and I'm going to make it stop being wrong, see, because that's my job." Charlie kissed his son's forehead, though Nicholas, still scrunched up against the wall, tried to duck to the side. "God, he still smells great," Charlie said to Kyra. "Let's do it again. Let's have a baby in grotty old, gray old London. His hair's wonderful. I can't believe it. I love every cell of you," he said to Nicholas. "I love every atom in your body and the spaces between atoms—don't be frightened, they're just little spaces—and I love your fingernails, even bitten down to nothing, and the backs of your hands that're so chapped, and the insides of your ears, and your eardrums, and I love your brain, and your teeth, and the way your tongue looks—stick it out, ah, that's ugly, that's pathetic. I love your elbows and your knees and your navel. Did I leave anything out?"

"My penis," Nicholas said. He was giggling wildly. "My *penis*."

"Nothing wrong with you," Charlie said. "That's the life force speaking up. When you were inside your mom—listen to this— the doctor said you had the strongest heartbeat she'd heard in twelve years of listening to babies."

"Me?" Nicholas said. "In Mom? I was the strongest?"

"Out of a lot of babies listened to, yes, you were. You really were. Now, are you O.K. to be left?"

He was; suddenly he was. Charlie climbed the stairs behind Kyra, and his hands framed her bottom as it ascended, bracketed it lightly on either side, though he didn't touch her. "What do you think the dream was?" he asked, when they were in their own bed. The room seemed to have gotten much colder in their absence. She shook her head softly in the dark, knowing he could feel the movement, and then said, "What do you think?"

"Whatever it was, if he was scared, why would he want you to go away?"

"I don't know that either." Then she remembered. "Charlie, why did you ask me if I had a lover?"

"Christ, in front of him."

"I know. So why?"

"I know you don't have a lover."

"Then why did you open your mouth and have that come out?"

"Crazy."

"I wanted to kill you," she said.

"You should have. London was never what you wanted, right? So it's been strange, us being in England because of me, with nothing here for you. It could have come between us."

"It could have."

"In the office lately, I wonder, 'What is she doing right now?' In New York, I don't know, I was beginning to feel remote from you. Now it's back the way it used to be."

"Why? Why now, Charlie?"

"Dunno, sweet. Do not know."

"Sweet" was an old endearment, possibly their first. It meant that Charlie was a senior at the University of Michigan, she a green-eyed girl who'd glanced up from a coffee cup to find, directed her way across the jammed cafeteria, a scrutiny she'd rather theatrically returned. Now she was grateful no such look was possible. He could find things out only through her voice. She kept it calm. "But why not have loved me like that in New York? Why now?"

"That's what I ask myself. And I don't know, so I haven't brought it up before. I just want us to get through these last months and be back in New York still us. I meant I need you."

In the dark her mouth went round, considering, then indented at the corners in a smile, because she had felt that swift internal tug, deep as instinct, by which she knew the truth when any of three people told it: Charlie, or Nicholas, or—not least useful—herself. She was still smiling when he rolled over and caught the point of her chin between his teeth. They were breathing each other's breath. "Away," she said. "I have to yawn." He let go, and she yawned. She still felt a dazzling white spot of hatred for him, which she wouldn't have been conscious of if he hadn't insisted on being so close to her—but the thing he had done was a huge thing.

He rested his cheek against her shoulder, she rested her chin against his head and, flicking his dark hair very lightly with her fingertips, she said, "Sleep," and pushed him away.

She had an irritated sense of their straining to be silent together, each aware of how the least movement might, this far into the night, prove unbearable to the other, and of how stranded they were, really, with sleep receding farther and farther from probability. Yet she must have been napping, because she was snatched awake when she heard, "I can't sleep."

"You feel so bad."

"Yes."

Her dislike was so great she couldn't fashion a question for him. She simply said, "About."

"Christ, in front of him. I mean you and I, we can understand, we're equipped—"

"He's all right," she said. "He's a child. They have—they have some kind of protection. I mean we all had childhoods, and we turned out all right. Look at us."

"Comforting," he said.

She was exhausted. "It is and isn't," she said.

But she was awake enough to pity Charlie, feeling for him the insinuation of guilt into his future, guilt toward his son, and her heart did its forgiveness trick. Often after the very worst moments in their marriage, she had experienced a blithe instant in which she was all lightness, all reckless tenderness toward Charlie, as if nothing he did was beyond her power to understand and endure, yet as if those things were suddenly immensely easy to forgive, far easier than it could ever have looked from outside—but there was nobody outside, of course. It was a marriage. There had been somebody outside, but there wouldn't be, after tomorrow.

∽

About the Author

Elizabeth Tallent was born in 1954 in Washington, D.C., and was educated at the University of Illinois at Normal. She is married and the author of a collection of essays, a novel and two collections of short stories. "The Forgiveness Trick" is from the collection *Time With Children*, published in 1986.

Tallent's stories move by description and accumulation of detail, both surface and internal, rather than by narrative action or plot. (Contrast this story to those by Huggans and Bausch, for example, where plot or "story" is much more important.)

Tallent's use of vivid imagery and exacting description, as well as her ability to render thoughts and feelings, have enabled her to capture one significant moment in the life of a family, as in a snapshot. In "The Forgiveness Trick" she reveals the emotional electricity that flows among family members in moments of interaction.

Questions for Thought and Discussion

1. To review some of the facts of the story, where does it take place? How long have they lived there? For what reason? Where are they from? How was the year going for Charlie? For Kyra?

2. What do you think is the reason Nicholas goes to his parents' room? Does this seem to happen often?

3. How does Charlie deal with Nicholas in this situation? Is there anything he does which you like? How does Kyra deal (or how would she deal) with Nicholas? Is there anything about her manner which impresses you?

4. Why are the interpersonal dynamics so intense the moment Nicholas says, "No, you go"? What do you think each of them is feeling at that moment?

5. What do you think is the truth which brings a smile to Kyra's face like an "internal tug"?

6. How do you interpret "the forgiveness trick" in the final paragraph? Who is being forgiven? Of what? To whom do you think the final sentence refers? To Charlie's former lover? Does it hint that Kyra might have a lover, as Charlie wondered aloud? Or perhaps it refers to nobody in particular?

7. Although you have only this brief incident on which to form

an opinion, what would you guess to be Charlie's strengths as a parent? His weaknesses? What do you think Kyra's strengths would be? Her weaknesses?

8. Over time, how do you think each would tend to react to the other, given their differences?

9. How typical of father-mother differences do you think their differences are?

10. In this household, would you say that one parent tends to be "dominant" and the other "submissive"? Do you think one parent tends to be "instrumental" and the other "expressive"? Do they seem to you to be "egalitarian" in their parenting roles?

11. What do you think determines parenting success when two parents are as different as Charlie and Kyra seem to be?

The Duchess and the Smugs   Pamela Frankau

Parenting Issue:

Philosophies of Parenting

Parenting style is determined in part by skills and in part by parents' beliefs. Beliefs of parents — about the nature of child-hood, about appropriate and inappropriate behavior, and about life-style values and long-term goals — determine the way "discipline" is defined in their home.

"The Duchess and the Smugs" shows two contrasting philosophies of parenting in action. As you read, look for differences in what the parents believe about children and about discipline. Also look for the differences in the children which result from the two parenting styles.

3.
The Duchess and the Smugs
Pamela Frankau

༄

There had been two crises already that day before the cook's husband called to assassinate the cook. The stove caught fire in my presence; the postman had fallen off his bicycle at the gate and been bitten by Charlemagne, our sheep dog, whose policy it was to attack people only when they were down.

Whenever there were two crises my stepmother Jeanne said, *"Jamais deux sans trois."* This morning she and Francis (my father) had debated whether the two things happening to the postman could be counted as two separate crises and might therefore be said to have cleared matters up. I thought that they were wasting their time. In our household things went on and on and on happening. It was a hotel, which made the doom worse: it would have been remarkable to have two days without a crisis and even if we did, I doubted whether the rule would apply in reverse, so that we could augur a third. I was very fond of the word augur.

I was not very fond of the cook. But when I was sitting on the terrace in the shade working on my Anthology of Hates, and a man with a bristled chin told me in *patois* that he had come to kill her, I thought it just as well for her, though obviously disappointing for her husband, that she was off for the afternoon. He carried a knife that did not look particularly sharp; he smelt of licorice, which meant that he had been drinking Pernod. He stamped up and down, making speeches about his wife and Laurent the waiter, whom he called a *salaud* and many other words new to me and quite difficult to understand.

I said at last, "Look, you can't do it now, because she has gone over to St. Raphael in the bus. But if you wait I will fetch my father." I took the Anthology with me in case he started cutting it up.

I went down the red rock steps that sloped from the garden to the pool. The garden looked the way it always looked, almost as brightly colored as the post cards of it that you could buy at the desk. There was purple bougainvillaea splashing down the white walls of the hotel; there were hydrangeas of the exact shade of pink blotting paper; there were huge silver-gray cacti and green umbrella pines against a sky that was darker blue than the sky in England.

I could not love this garden. Always it seemed to me artificial, spiky with color, not quite true. My idea of a garden was a green lawn and a little apple orchard behind a gray stone house in the Cotswolds. I saw that garden only once a year, in September. I could conjure it by repeating inside my head—

> And autumn leaves of blood and gold
> That strew a Gloucester lane.

Then the homesickness for the place that was not my home would make a sharp pain under my ribs. I was ashamed to feel so; I could not talk about it; not even to Francis, with whom I could talk about most things.

I came to the top of the steps and saw them lying around the pool, Francis and Jeanne and the two novelists who had come from Antibes for lunch. They were all flat on the yellow mattresses, talking.

I said, "Excuse me for interrupting you, but the cook's husband has come to assassinate the cook."

Francis got up quickly. He looked like Mephistopheles. There were gray streaks in his black hair; all the lines of his face went upward and the pointed mustache followed the lines. His body was dark brown and hairy, except that the scars on his back and legs, where he was burned when the airplane was shot down, did not tan with the sun.

"It's a hot afternoon for an assassination," said the male novelist as they ran up the steps together.

"Perhaps," said Francis, "he can be persuaded to wait until the evening."

"He will have to," I said, "because the cook is in St. Raphael. I told him so."

"Penelope," said my stepmother, sitting up on the yellow mattress, "you had better stay with us."

"But I am working on my book."

All right, *chérie;* work on it here."

The lady novelist, who had a sparkling, triangular face like a cat, said, "I wish you would read some of it to us. It will take our minds off the current bloodcurdling events."

I begged her to excuse me, adding that I did not anticipate any bloodcurdling events because of the battered look of the knife.

Jeanne said that the cook would have to go in any case, but that her love for Laurent was of a purely spiritual character.

I said, "Laurent is a smoothy, and I do not see how anybody could be in love with him."

"A certain smoothness is not out of place in a headwaiter," said the lady novelist.

I did not tell her my real reason for disliking Laurent; he made jokes. I hated jokes more than anything. They came first in the Anthology: they occupied whole pages: I had dozens and dozens: it was a loose-leaf book, so that new variations of hates already listed could be inserted at will.

Retiring from the conversation, I went to sit on the flat rock at the far end of the pool. Francis and the male novelist returned very soon. Francis came over to me. I shut the loose-leaf book.

"The cook's husband," he said, "has decided against it."

"I thought he would. I imagine that if you are really going to murder somebody you do not impart the intention to others."

"Don't you want to swim?" said Francis.

"No, thank you. I'm working."

"You couldn't be sociable for half an hour?"

"I would rather not."

"I'll write you down for RCI," he threatened.

RCI was Repulsive Children Incorporated, an imaginary foundation which Francis had invented a year before. It came about because a family consisting mainly of unusually spoiled children stayed at the hotel for two days, and were asked by Francis to leave on the third, although the rooms were booked for a month. According to Francis, RCI did a tremendous business and there were qualifying examinations wherein the children were tested for noise, bad manners, whining, and brutal conduct. I tried to pretend that I thought this funny.

"Will you please let me work for a quarter of an hour?" I asked him. "After all, I was disturbed by the assassin."

"All right. Fifteen minutes," he said. "After which you qualify."

In fact I was not telling him the truth. I had a rendezvous at this hour every day. At four o'clock precisely I was sure of seeing the people from the next villa. I had watched them for ten days and I knew how Dante felt when he waited for Beatrice to pass him on the Ponte Vecchio. Could one, I asked myself, be in love with four people at once? The answer seemed to be Yes. These people had become a secret passion.

The villa was called La Lézardière; a large, stately pink shape with green shutters; there was a gravel terrace, planted with orange trees and descending in tiers, to a pool that did not sprawl in a circle of red rocks as ours did, but was a smooth gray concrete. At the tip of this pool there was a real diving board. A long gleaming speedboat lay at anchor in the deep water. The stage was set and I waited for the actors.

They had the quality of Vikings; the father and mother were tall, handsome, white-skinned, and fair-haired. The boy and girl followed the pattern. They looked as I should have preferred to look. (I was as dark as Francis, and, according to the never-ceasing stream of personal remarks that seemed to be my lot at this time, I was much too thin. And not pretty. If my eyes were not so large I knew that I should be quite ugly. In Francis' opinion, my face had character. "But this, as Miss Edith Cavell said of patriotism," I told him, "is not enough.")

Oh, to look like the Bradleys; to be the Bradleys, I thought, waiting for the Bradleys. They were fair, august, and enchanted; they wore the halo of being essentially English. They were Dad and Mum and Don and Eva. I spied on them like a huntress, strained my ears for their words, cherished their timetable. It was regular as the clock. They swam before breakfast and again at ten, staying beside the pool all the morning. At a quarter to one the bell would ring from the villa for their lunch. Oh, the beautiful punctuality of those meals! Sometimes we did not eat luncheon until three and although Jeanne told me to go and help myself from the kitchen, this was not the same thing at all.

In the afternoon the Bradleys rested on their terrace in the shade. At four they came back to the pool. They went fishing or waterskiing. They were always doing something. They would go for drives in a magnificent gray car with a white hood that folded back. Sometimes they played a catching game beside the pool; or they did exercises in a row, with the father leading them. They had cameras and butterfly nets and fieldglasses. They never seemed to lie around and talk, the loathed recreation in which I was expected to join.

I took Don and Eva to be twins; and perhaps a year younger than I. I was just fourteen. To be a twin would, I thought, be a most satisfying destiny. I would even have changed places with the youngest member of the Bradley family, a baby in a white perambulator with a white starched nurse in charge of it. If I could be the baby, I should at least be sure of growing up and becoming a Bradley, in a white shirt and gray shorts.

Their magic linked with the magic of my yearly fortnight in England, when, besides having the gray skies and the green garden, I had acquaintance with other English children not in the least like me: solid, pink-cheeked sorts with ponies; they came over to tea at my aunt's house and it was always more fun in anticipation than in fact, because I seemed to make them shy. And I could never tell them that I yearned for them.

So, in a way, I was content to watch the Bradleys at a distance. I felt that it was hopeless to want to be friends with them; to do the things that they did. I was not only different on the outside, but different on the inside, which was worse. On the front page of the Anthology I had written: "I was born to trouble as the sparks fly upward," one of the more consoling quotations because it made the matter seem inevitable.

Now it was four o'clock. My reverie of the golden Bradleys became the fact of the golden Bradleys, strolling down to the water. Dad and Don were carrying the water-skis. I should have only a brief sight of them before they took the speedboat out into the bay. They would skim and turn far off, tantalizing small shapes on the shiny silky sea. Up on the third tier of the terrace, between the orange trees, the neat white nurse was pushing the perambulator. But she was only faintly touched with the romance that haloed the others. I mourned.

Then a most fortunate thing happened. There was a drift of strong current around the rocks and as the speedboat moved out toward the bay, one of the water-skis slipped off astern, and was carried into the pool under the point where I sat. Don dived in after it; I ran down the slope of rock on their side, to shove it off from the edge of the pool.

"Thanks most awfully," he said. He held on to the fringed seaweed and hooked the water-ski under his free arm. Now that he was so close to me I could see that he had freckles; it was a friendly smile and he spoke in the chuffy, English boy's voice that I liked.

"It's rather fun, water-skiing."

"It looks fun. I have never done it."

"Would you like to come out with us?" he jerked his head towards the boat: "Dad's a frightfully good teacher."

I groaned within me, like the king in the Old Testament. Here were the gates of Paradise opening and I must let them shut again, or be written down for RCI.

"Painful as it is to refuse," I said, "my father has acquired visitors and I have sworn to be sociable. The penalty is ostracism." (Ostracism was another word that appealed to me.)

Don, swinging on the seaweed, gave a gurgle of laughter.

"What's funny?" I asked.

"I'm terribly sorry. Wasn't that meant to be funny?"

"Wasn't what meant to be funny?"

"The way you talked."

"No, it's just the way I talk," I said, drooping with sadness.

"I like it awfully," said Don. This was warming to my heart. By now the speedboat was alongside the rock point. I could see the Viking heads; the delectable faces in detail. Mr. Bradley called: "Coming aboard?"

"She can't," said Don. "Her father has visitors; she'll be ostracized." He was still giggling and his voice shook.

"Oh, dear, that's too bad," said Mrs. Bradley. "Why don't you ask your father if you can come tomorrow?"

"I will, most certainly," I said, though I knew that I need never ask permission of Jeanne or Francis for anything that I wanted to do.

I felt as though I had been addressed by a goddess. Don gurgled again. He flashed through the water and they pulled him into the boat.

I had to wait for a few minutes alone, hugging my happiness, preparing a kind of vizor to pull down over it when I went back to the group on the yellow mattresses.

"Making friends with the Smugs?" Francis greeted me.

"What an enchanting name," said the lady novelist.

"It isn't their name; it's what they are," said Francis.

I heard my own voice asking thinly: "Why do you call them that?" He shocked me so much that my heart began to beat heavily and I shivered. I tried to conceal this by sitting crouched and hugging my knees. I saw him watching me.

"Well, aren't they?" he said gently. I had given myself away. He had guessed that they meant something to me.

"I don't know. I don't think so. I want to know why you think so."

"Partly from observation," said Francis. "Their gift for organized leisure; their continual instructions to their children; the expressions on their faces. And the one brief conversation that I've conducted with Bradley — he congratulated me on being able to engage in a commercial enterprise on French soil. According to Bradley, you can never trust the French." He imitated the chuffy English voice.

"Isn't 'commercial enterprise' rather an optimistic description of Chez François?" asked the lady novelist, and the male novelist laughed. Francis was still looking at me.

"Why do you like them, Penelope?"

I replied with chilled dignity: "I did not say that I liked them. They invited me to go water-skiing with them tomorrow."

Jeanne said quickly: "That will be fun. You know, Francis, you are becoming too intolerant of your own countrymen: it is enough in these days for you to meet an Englishman to make you dislike him." This was comforting; I could think this and feel better. Nothing, I thought, could make me feel worse than for Francis to attack the Bradleys. It was another proof that my loves, like my hates, must remain secret, and this was loneliness.

II

I awoke next morning full of a wild surmise. I went down early to the pool and watched Francis taking off for Marseilles in his small, ramshackle seaplane. He flew in a circle over the garden as he always did, and when the seaplane's long boots pointed for the west, I saw Don and Eva Bradley standing still on the gravel terrace to watch it. They were coming down to the pool alone. Offering myself to them, I went out to the flat rock. They waved and beckoned and shouted.

"Is that your father flying the seaplane?"

"Yes."

"Does he take you up in it?"

"Sometimes."

"Come and swim with us," Don called.

I ran down the rock slope on their side. I was shy now that we stood together. I saw that Eva was a little taller than Don; that she also was freckled; and that they had oiled their skins against sunburn as the grownups did. Don wore white trunks and Eva a white swimming suit. They laughed when I shook hands with them, and Don made me an elaborate bow after the handshake. Then they laughed again.

"Are you French or English?"

That saddened me. I said, "I am English, but I live here because my stepmother is a frenchwoman and my father likes the Riviera."

"We know that," said Don quickly. "He was shot down and taken prisoner by the Germans and escaped and fought with the Resistance, didn't he?"

"Yes. That is how he met Jeanne."

"And he's Francis Wells, the poet?

"Yes."

"And the hotel is quite mad, isn't it?"

"Indubitably," I said. It was another of my favorite words. Eva doubled up with laughter. "Oh, that's wonderful. I'm *always* going to say indubitably."

"Is it true," Don said, "that guests only get served if your father likes the looks of them, and that he charges nothing sometimes, and that all the rooms stay empty for weeks if he wants them to?"

"It is true. It does not seem to me the most intelligent way of running an hotel, but that is none of my business."

"Is he very rich?" asked Eva.

Don said quickly: "Don't, Eva, that's not polite."

"He isn't rich or poor," I said. I could not explain our finances to the Bradleys any more than I could explain them to myself. Sometimes we had money. When we had not, we were never poor in the way that other people were poor. We were "broke," which, as far as I could see, meant being in debt but living as usual and talking about money.

"Do you go to school in England?"

"No," I said, handing over my chief shame. "I am a day boarder at a convent school near Grasse. It is called Notre Dames des Oliviers."

"Do you like it?"

"I find it unobjectionable," I said. It would have been disloyal to Francis and Jeanne to tell these people how little I liked it.

"Do they teach the same things as English schools?"

"Roughly."

"I expect you're awfully clever," said Eva, "and tops at everything."

How did she know that? Strenuously, I denied it. Heading the class in literature, composition, and English poetry was just one more way of calling attention to myself. It was part of the doom of being noticeable, of not being like Other People. At Les Oliviers, Other People were French girls, strictly brought up, formally religious, cut to a foreign pattern. I did not want to be they, as I wanted to be the Bradleys: I merely envied their uniformity.

God forbid that I should tell the Bradleys about winning a special prize for a sonnet; about being chosen to recite Racine to hordes of parents; about any of it. I defended myself by asking questions in my turn. Eva went to an English boarding school in Sussex; Don would go to his first term at public school this autumn. I had guessed their ages correctly. They were just thirteen. "Home" was Devonshire.

"I would greatly love to live in England," I said.

"I'd far rather live in an hotel on the French Riviera. Lucky Penelope."

"I am not lucky Penelope; I am subject to dooms."

"How heavenly. What sort of dooms?"

"For example, getting an electric shock in science class, and finding a whole nest of mice in my desk," I said. "And being the only person present when a lunatic arrived believing the school to be Paradise."

"Go on. Go on," they said. "It's wonderful. Those aren't dooms, they are adventures."

"Nothing that happens all the time is an adventure," I said. "The hotel is also doomed."

They turned their heads to look up at it; from here, through the pines and the cactus, we could see the red crinkled tiles of its roof, the bougainvillaea, the top of the painted blue sign that announced *"Chez François."*

"It can't be doomed," Don said. "Don't famous people come here?"

"Oh yes. But famous people are more subject to dooms than

ordinary people."

"How?"

"In every way you can imagine. Important telegrams containing money do not arrive. Their wives leave them; they are recalled on matters of state."

"Does Winston Churchill come?"

"Yes."

"And Lord Beaverbrook and Elsa Maxwell and the Duke of Windsor and Somerset Maugham?"

"Yes. Frequently. All their signed photographs are kept in the bar. Would you care to see them?"

Here I encountered the first piece of Bradley dogma. Don and Eva, who were splashing water on each other's hair ("Dad is most particular about our not getting sunstroke"), looked doubtful.

"We *would* love to."

"I'm sure it's all right, Eva; because she lives there."

"I don't know. I think we ought to ask first. It is a bar, after all."

Ashamed, I hid from them the fact that I often served in the bar when Laurent was off duty.

"Oh, do let's chance it," said Don.

"I don't believe we ought to."

Mr. and Mrs. Bradley had gone over to Nice and would not return until the afternoon, so a deadlock threatened. The white starched nurse appeared at eleven o'clock with a Thermos-flask of cold milk and a plate of buns. I gave birth to a brilliant idea; I told her that my stepmother had invited Don and Eva to lunch with us.

It was a little difficult to convince them after the nurse had gone, that Jeanne would be pleased to have them to lunch without an invitation. When I led them up through our garden, they treated it as an adventure, like tiger shooting.

Jeanne welcomed them, as I had foretold, and the lunch was highly successful, although it contained several things, such as *moules*, which the Bradleys were not allowed to eat. We had the terrace to ourselves. Several cars drove up and their owners were told politely that lunch could not be served to them. This delighted Don and Eva. They were even more delighted when Jeanne told them of Francis' ambition, which was to have a notice: "Keep Out; This Means You," printed in seventeen languages. One mystery about the Bradleys was that they seemed to like jokes. They thought that I made jokes. When they laughed at my phrases they did not laugh as the grownups did, but in the manner of an appreciative audience receiving a comedian. Eva would hold her stomach and cry: "Oh *stop!* It hurts to giggle like this; it really hurts."

I took them on a tour of the hotel. The salon was furnished with some good Empire pieces. The bedrooms were not like hotel bedrooms, but more like rooms in clean French farmhouses, with pale walls and dark wood and chintz. All the rooms had balconies where the guests could eat their breakfast. There were no guests.

"And Dad says people *clamor* to stay here in the season," Don said, straddled in the last doorway.

"Yes, they do. Probably some will be allowed in at the end of the week," I explained, "but the Duchess is arriving from Venice at any moment and Francis always waits for her to choose which room she wants, before he lets any. She is changeable."

Eva said, "I can't get over your calling your father Francis. Who is the Duchess? "

"The Duchessa di Terracini. She is half Italian and half American."

"Is she very beautiful? "

"Very far from it. She is seventy and she looks like a figure out of a waxworks. She was celebrated for her lovers but now she only loves roulette." I did not wish to be uncharitable about the Duchess, whose visit was to be dreaded, and these were the nicest things that I could make myself say. The only thing in her favor was that she had been a friend of my mother, who was American and utterly beautiful and whom I did not remember.

"Lovers? " Eva said, looking half pleased and half horrified. Don flushed and looked at his feet. I had learned from talks at school that reactions to a mention of the facts of life could be like this. I knew also that Francis despised the expression, "the facts of life," because, he said, it sounded as though all the other things that happened in life were figments of the imagination.

"A great many people loved the Duchess desperately," I said. "She was engaged to an Austrian Emperor; he gave her emeralds, but somebody shot him."

"Oh well, then, she's practically history, isn't she? " Eva said, looking relieved.

III

I might have known that the end of the day would bring doom.

It came hard upon the exquisite pleasure of my time in the speedboat with the Bradleys. This was even better than I had planned it in anticipation, a rare gift. I thought that the occasion must be under the patronage of a benign saint or what the Duchess would call a favorable aura; the only worry was Mrs. Bradley's worry about my having no dry clothes to put on after swimming; but with typical Bradley organization there were an extra white shirt and gray shorts in the boat. Dressed thus I felt like a third twin.

The sea changed color; the sea began to be white and the rocks a darker red.

"Would you like to come back and have supper with us, Penelope?"

I replied, "I can imagine nothing that I would like more."

"She *does* say wonderful things, doesn't she?" said Eva. I was drunk by now on Bradley admiration and almost reconciled to personal remarks.

"Penelope speaks very nice English," said Mrs. Bradley.

"Will you ask your stepmother then?" she added as we tied up the boat. I was about to say this was unnecessary when Don gave my ribs a portentous nudge; he said quickly, "Eva and I will walk you up there." It was obvious that the hotel exercised as much fascination for them as they for me.

When the three of us set off across the rocks Mr. Bradley called, "Seven o'clock sharp, now!" and Eva made a grimace. She said, "Wouldn't it be nice not to have to be punctual for anything?"

"I never have to be," I said, "except at school, and I think that I prefer it to having no timetable at all."

"Oh, my goodness! Why?"

"I like days to have a shape," I said.

"Can you just stay out to supper when you want to? Always? Without telling them?"

"Oh, yes."

"What would happen if you stayed away a whole night?"

I said that I had never tried. And now we went into the bar because Don said that he wanted to see the photographs again. Laurent was there; straw-colored and supercilious in his white coat. He began to make his jokes: *"Mesdames, monsieur, bon soir. What may I serve you? A Pernod? A champagne cocktail?"* He flashed along the shelves, reading out the name of each drink, muttering under his breath, *"Mais non; c'est terrible; we have* nothing that pleases our distinguished visitors." I saw that the Bradleys were enchanted with him.

We walked all round the gallery of photographs and were lingering beside Winston Churchill when the worst thing happened. I heard it coming. One could always hear the Duchess coming. She made peals of laughter that sounded like opera; the words came fast and high between the peals.

And here she was, escorted by Francis. She cried, "Ah my love, my love," and I was swept into a complicated, painful embrace, scratched by her jewelry, crushed against her stays, and choked with her scent before I got a chance to see her in perspective. When I did, I saw that there were changes since last year and that these were for the worse. Her hair, which had been dyed black, was now dyed bright red. Her powder was whiter and thicker than ever; her eyelids were dark blue; she had new false eyelashes of greater length that made her look like a Jersey cow.

She wore a dress of dark blue chiffon, sewn all over with sequin stars, and long red gloves with her rings on the outside; she tilted back on her heels, small and bony, gesticulating with the gloves.

"Beautiful—beautiful—beautiful!" was one of her slogans. She said it now; she could not conceivably mean me; she just meant everything. The Bradleys had become awed and limp all over. When I introduced them they shook hands jerkily, snatching their hands away at once. Francis took from Laurent the bottle of champagne that had been on ice awaiting the Duchess; he carried it to her favorite table, the corner table beside the window. She placed upon the table a sequin bag of size, a long chiffon scarf, and a small jeweled box that held *bonbons au miel,* my least favorite sweets, reminding me of scented glue.

Francis uncorked the champagne.

"But glasses for all of us," the Duchess said. "A glass for each." The Bradleys said, "No thank you very much," so quickly that they made it sound like one syllable and I imitated them.

"But how good for you," cried the Duchess. "The vitalizing, the magnificent, the harmless grape. All children should take a little to combat the lassitude and depressions of growth. My mother used to give me a glass every morning after my fencing lesson. *Et toi,* Penelope? More than once last year you have taken your *petit verre* with me."

"Oh, didn't you know? Penelope is on the water wagon," said Francis, and the Duchess again laughed like opera. She cried,

"Santé, santé!" raising her glass to each of us. Francis helped himself to a Pernod and perched on the bar, swinging his legs. The Bradleys and I stood in a straight, uncomfortable row.

"Of youth," said the Duchess, "I recall three things. The sensation of time seeming endless, as though one were swimming against a current; the insipid insincerity of one's teachers; and bad dreams, chiefly about giants."

Sometimes she expected an answer to statements of this character; at other times she went on talking: I had known her to continue without a break for fifteen minutes.

"I used to dream about giants," said Eva.

"How old are you, Miss?"

"Thirteen."

"At fifteen the dreams become passionate," said the Duchess, sounding lugubrious about it.

"What do you dream about now?" asked Don, who had not removed his eyes from her since she came.

"Packing, missing airplanes; losing my clothes," said the Duchess. "Worry—worry—worry; but one is never bored in a dream, which is more than can be said for real life. Give me your hand," she snapped at Eva. She pored over it a moment, and then said briskly, "You are going to marry very young and have three children; an honest life; always be careful in automobiles." Don's hand was already stretched out and waiting. She gave him two wives, a successful business career, and an accident "involving a horse between the ages of twenty and twenty-three."

"That is tolerably old for a horse," Francis interrupted.

"Sh-h," said the Duchess, "perhaps while steeple-chasing; it is not serious." She blew me a little kiss: "Penelope I already know. She is as clear to me as a book written by an angel. Let me see if there is any change," she commanded, a medical note in her voice: "Beautiful—beautiful—beautiful! Genius and fame and passion are all here."

"Any dough?" asked Francis.

"I beg your pardon," said the Duchess, who knew perfectly well what dough meant, but who always refused to recognize American slang.

"I refer to cash," said Francis looking his most Mephistophelean; "My ambition for Penelope is that she acquire a rich husband, so that she may subsidize Papa in his tottering old age."

"Like so many creative artists, you have the soul of a fishmonger," said the Duchess. She was still holding my hand; she planted a champagne-wet kiss on the palm before she let it go. "I have ordered our dinner, Penelope. It is to be the *écrevisses au gratin* that you like with small *goûters* of caviar to begin with and *fraises des bois* in kirsch afterward."

I had been anticipating this hurdle; she always insisted that I dine with her on her first evening, before she went to the Casino at nine o'clock.

"I am very sorry, Duchessa; you must excuse me. I am having supper with Don and Eva." I saw Francis raise one eyebrow at me. "I really didn't know you were coming tonight," I pleaded.

"No, that is true," said the Duchess, "but I am very disappointed. I have come to regard it as a regular tryst." She put her head on one side. "Why do you not all three stay and dine with me? We will make it a *partie carrée*. It could be managed, Francis? Beautiful—beautiful—beautiful! There. That is settled."

"I'm most awfully sorry; we'd love to," Eva said. "But we couldn't possibly. Supper's at seven and Mum's expecting us."

"Thank you very much, though," said Don, who was still staring at her. "Could we do it another time?"

"But of course! Tomorrow; what could be better? Except tonight," said the Duchess. "I was looking to Penelope to bring me good luck. Do you remember last year, how I took you to dine at the Carlton and won a fortune afterward?"

"And lost it on the following afternoon," said Francis. The Duchess said an incomprehensible Italian word that sounded like a snake hissing. She took a little ivory hand out of her bag and pointed it at him.

"I thought one never could win at roulette," said Don. "According to my father, the game is rigged in favor of the Casino."

"Ask your father why there are no taxes in Monaco," said the Duchess. "In a game of this mathematic there is no need for the Casino to cheat. The majority loses naturally, not artificially. And tell him further that all European Casinos are of the highest order of probity, with the possible exception of Estoril and Budapest. Do you know the game?"

When the Bradleys said that they did not, she took from her bag one of the cards that had upon it a replica of the wheel and the cloth. She embarked upon a roulette lesson. The Bradleys were fascinated and of course we were late for supper. Francis delayed me further, holding me back to speak to me on the terrace: "Do you have to have supper with the Smugs?"

"Please don't call them that. Yes, I do."

"It would be reasonable, I should think, to send a message saying that an old friend of the family had arrived unexpectedly."

Of course it would have been reasonable; Mrs. Bradley had expected me to ask permission. But nothing would have made me stay.

"I'm extremely sorry, Francis; I can't do it."

"You should know how much it means to her. She has ordered your favorite dinner. All right," he said, "I see that it is useless to appeal to your better nature. Tonight you qualify for RCI." He went back to the bar, calling, "The verdict can always be withdrawn if the candidate shows compensating behavior."

"Didn't you want to stay and dine with the Duchess?" asked Don, as we raced through the twilit garden.

"I did not. She embarrasses me greatly."

"I thought she was terrific. I do hope Mum and Dad will let us have dinner with her tomorrow."

"But *don't* say it's *écrevisses*, Don, whatever you do. There's always a row about shell fish," Eva reminded him.

"I wouldn't be such an ass," Don said. "And the only thing that would give it away would be if you were ill afterward."

"Why should it be me?"

"Because it usually is," said Don.

I awoke with a sense of doom. I lay under my mosquito curtain, playing the scenes of last evening through in my mind. A slight chill upon the Viking parents, due to our being late; smiles pressed down over crossness, because of the visitor. Don and Eva pouring forth a miscellany of information about the Duchess and the signed photographs; myself making mental notes, a devoted sociologist studying a favorite tribe: grace before supper; no garlic in anything; copies of *Punch* and the English newspapers; silver napkin rings; apple pie. That secret that I found in the Cotswold house was here, I told myself; the house in Devonshire took shape; on the walls there were photographs of it; a stream ran through the garden; they rode their ponies on Dartmoor; they had two wirehaired terriers called Snip and Snap. I collected more evidence of Bradley organization: an expedition tomorrow to the Saracen village near Brignoles; a Current-Affairs Quiz that was given to the family by their father once a month.

No, I said to myself, brooding under my mosquito net, nothing went wrong until after the apple pie. That was when Eva had said, "The Duchess told all our fortunes." The lines spoken were still in my head:

Don saying, "Penelope's was an absolute fizzer; the Duchess says she will have genius, fame, and passion." Mr. Bradley's Viking profile becoming stony; Mrs. Bradley's smooth white forehead puckering a little as she asked me gently, "Who is this wonderful lady?"

Myself replying, "The Duchessa de Terracini," and Mrs. Bradley remarking that this was a beautiful name. But Mr. Bradley's stony face growing stonier and his officer-to-men voice saying, "Have we all finished?"; then rising so that we rose too and pushed in our chairs and bowed our heads while he said grace.

After that there was a spirited game of Monopoly. "But the atmosphere," I said to myself, "went on being peculiar." I had waited for Don and Eva to comment on it when they walked me home, but they were in a rollicking mood and appeared to have noticed nothing.

"Indubitably there is a doom," I thought while I put on my swimming suit, "and since I shall not see them until this evening because of the Saracen village, I shall not know what it is."

As I crossed the terrace, the Duchess popped her head out of the corner window above me; she leaned like a little gargoyle above the bougainvillaea; she wore a lace veil fastened under her chin with a large diamond.

"Good morning, Duchessa. Did you win?"

"I lost consistently, and your friends cannot come to dine tonight, as you may know; so disappointing, though the note itself is courteous." She dropped it into my hands. It was written by Mrs. Bradley; fat, curling handwriting on paper headed

CROSSWAYS
CHAGFORD
DEVON

It *thanked* the Duchess and regretted that owing to the expedition Don and Eva would not be able to accept her kind invitation to supper.

I knew that the Bradleys would be back by six.

IV

I spent most of the day alone working on the Anthology. I had found quite a new Hate, which was headed "Characters." People called the Duchess a character and this was said to others who came here. I made a brief description of each and included some of their sayings and habits.

There was the usual paragraph about the Duchess in the *Continental Daily Mail;* it referred to her gambling and her emeralds and her *joie-de-vivre. Joie-de-vivre* seemed to be a worthy subject for Hate and I entered it on a separate page, as a subsection of Jokes.

At half-past-four, to my surprise, I looked up from my rock writing desk and saw the Bradley's car sweeping in from the road. Presently Eva came running down the tiers of terrace alone. When she saw me she waved, put her finger to her lips, and signaled to me to stay where I was. She came scrambling up.

"I'm so glad to see you. There's a row. I can't stay long. Don has been sent to bed."

"Oh, dear. I was conscious of an unfavorable aura," I said. "What happened?"

Eva looked miserable. "It isn't anything against you, of course. They like you terribly. Mum says you have beautiful manners. When Don and I said we wanted you to come and stop a few days with us at Crossways in September, it went down quite *well.* Would you like to?" she asked, gazing at me, "or would it be awfully boring?"

I was momentarily deflected from the doom and the row. "I cannot imagine anything that would give me greater pleasure," I said. She wriggled her eyebrows as usual, at my phrases.

"That isn't just being polite?"

"I swear by yonder horned moon it isn't."

"But of course it may not happen now," she said in melancholy, "although it wasn't *your* fault. After all you didn't make us meet the Duchess on purpose."

"Was the row about the Duchess?"

"Mm — m."

"Because of her telling your fortunes and teaching you to play roulette? I did have my doubts, I admit."

"Apparently they were quite cross about that, but of course they couldn't say so in front of you. Daddy had *heard* of the

Duchess, anyway. And they cracked down on the dinner party and sent a note. And Don kept on asking why until he made Daddy furious; and there seems to have been something in the *Continental Mail,* which we are not allowed to read."

"Here it is," I said helpfully. She glanced upward over her shoulder. I said, "Have no fear. We are invisible from the villa at this angle."

She raised her head from the paper and her eyes shone; she said, "Isn't it wonderful?" I had thought it a pedestrian little paragraph, but I hid my views.

"Mummy said that the Duchess wasn't at all the sort of person she liked us to mix with, and that no lady would sit in a bar drinking champagne when there were children present, and that we shouldn't have gone into the bar again anyway. And Don lost his temper and was quite rude. So that we came home early instead of having tea out; and Dad said that Don had spoiled the day and asked him to apologize. And Don said a word that we aren't allowed to use and now he's gone to bed. Which is awful for him because he's too big to be sent to bed. And I'll have to go back. I'm terribly sorry."

"So am I," I said. "Please tell your mother that I deplore the Duchess deeply, and that I always have."

As soon as I had spoken, I became leaden inside myself with remorse. It was true that I deplored the Duchess because she was possessive, overpowering, and embarrassing, but I did not disapprove of her in the way that the Bradleys did. I was making a desperate effort to salvage the thing that mattered most to me.

In other words, I was assuming a virtue though I had it not, and while Shakespeare seemed to approve of this practice, I was certain that it was wrong. (And I went on with it. I added that Francis would not have dreamed of bringing the Duchess into the bar if he had known that we were there. This was an outrageous lie. Francis would have brought the Duchess into the bar if the Archbishop of Canterbury were there—admittedly an unlikely contingency.)

When Eva said that this might improve matters and might also make it easier for Don to apologize, because he had stuck up for the Duchess I felt lower than the worms.

Which is why I quarreled with Francis. And knew that was why. I had discovered that if one were feeling guilty one's instinct was to put the blame on somebody else as soon as possible.

Francis called to me from the bar door as I came up onto the terrace. I had been freed from RCI on the grounds of having replaced Laurent before lunch at short notice. He grinned at me. "Be an angel and take these cigarettes to Violetta's room, will you, please? I swear that woman smokes two at a time."

"I am sorry," I said. "I have no wish to run errands for the Duchess just now."

Francis, as usual, was reasonable. "How has she offended you?" he asked.

I told him about the Bradleys, about the possible invitation to Devonshire; I said that, thanks to the Duchess cutting such a petty figure in the bar, not to mention the *Continental Mail,* my future was being seriously jeopardized. I saw Francis' eyebrows twitching.

He said, "Penelope, you are a thundering ass. These people are tedious *petits bourgeois,* and there is no reason to put on their act just because you happen to like their children. And I see no cause to protect anybody, whether aged seven or seventy, from the sight of Violetta drinking champagne."

"Mrs. Bradley said that no lady would behave in such a way."

"Tell Mrs. Bradley with my love and a kiss that if she were a tenth as much of a lady as Violetta she would have cause for pride. And I am not at all sure," he said, "that I like the idea of your staying with them in Devonshire."

This was, as the French said, the *comble.*

"Do you mean that you wouldn't let me go?" I asked, feeling as though I had been struck by lightning.

"I did not say that. I said I wasn't sure that I liked the idea."

"My God, why not?"

"Do not imagine when you say, 'My God,'" said Francis, "that you add strength to your protest. You merely add violence."

He could always make me feel a fool when he wanted to. And I could see that he was angry; less with me than with the Bradleys. He said, "I don't think much of the Smugs, darling, as you know. And I think less after this. Violetta is a very remarkable old girl, and if they knew what she went through in Rome when the Germans were there, some of that heroism might penetrate even their thick heads. Run along with those cigarettes now, will you please?"

I was trembling with rage; the worst kind of rage, hating me as well as everything else. I took the cigarettes with what I hoped was a dignified gesture, and went.

The Duchess was lying on the chaise longue under her window; she was swathed like a mummy in yards of cyclamen chiffon trimmed with marabou. She appeared to be reading three books at once; a novel by Ignazio Silone, Brewer's *Dictionary of Phrase and Fable,* and a *Handbook of Carpentry for Beginners.*

The room, the best of the rooms, having two balconies, had become unrecognizable. It worried me with its rampaging disorder. Three wardrobe trunks crowded it: many dresses, scarves, and pairs of small pointed shoes had escaped from the wardrobe trunks. The Duchess always brought with her large unexplained pieces of material; squares of velvet, crepè de chine, and damask, which she spread over the furniture. The writing table had been made to look like a table in a museum; she had put upon it a black crucifix and two iron candlesticks, a group of ivory figures, and a velvet book with metal clasps.

Despite the heat of the afternoon the windows were shut; the room smelled of smoke and scent.

"Beautiful — beautiful — beautiful!" said the Duchess, holding out her hands for the cigarettes. "There are the *bonbons au miel* on the bedside table. Help yourself liberally, and sit down and talk to me."

"No, thank you very much. If you will excuse me, Duchess, I have to do some work now."

"I will not excuse you, darling. Sit down here. Do you know why I will not excuse you?"

I shook my head.

"Because I can see that you are unhappy, frustrated, and restless." She joined her fingertips and stared at me over the top of them. "Some of it I can guess," she said, "and some of it I should dearly like to know. Your mother would have known."

I was silent; she was hypnotic when she spoke of my mother, but I could not make myself ask her questions.

"Genius is not a comfortable possession. What do you want to do most in the world, Penelope?"

The truthful reply would have been, "To be like other people. To live in England; with an ordinary father and mother who do not keep a hotel. To stop having dooms; never to be told that I am a genius, and to have people of my own age to play with so that I need not spend my life listening to grownups."

I said, "I don't know."

The Duchess sighed and beat a tattoo with her little feet inside the marabou; they looked like clockwork feet.

"You are, beyond doubt, crying for the moon. Everybody at your age cries for the moon. But if you will not tell me which moon, I cannot be of assistance. What is the book that you are writing?"

"It is an Anthology of Hates," I said, and was much surprised that I had told her because I had not told anybody.

"Oho," said the Duchess. "Have you enough Hates to make an anthology?"

I nodded.

"Is freedom one of your hates?"

I frowned; I did not want to discuss the book with her at all and I could not understand her question. She was smiling in a maddening way that implied more knowledge of me than I myself had.

"Freedom is the most important thing that there is. You have more freedom than the average child knows. One day you will learn to value this and be grateful for it. I will tell you why." Her voice had taken on the singsong, lecturing note that preceded a fifteen-minute monologue. I stared at the figures on the writing table. She had let her cigarette lie burning in the ash tray, and a small spiral of smoke went up like incense before the crucifix; there was this, there was the hot scented room and the sound of her voice: "It is necessary to imprison children to a certain degree, for their discipline and their protection. In schools, they are largely hidden away from life, like bees in a hive. This means that they learn a measure of pleasant untruth; a scale of simple inadequate values that resemble the true values in life only as much as a plain colored poster of the Riviera resembles the actual coastline.

"When they emerge from the kindly-seeming prisons, they meet the world of true dimensions and true values. These are unexpectedly painful and irregular. Reality is always irregular and generally painful. To be unprepared for its shocks and to receive the shocks upon a foundation of innocence is the process of growing up. In your case, Penelope, you will be spared many of those pains. Not only do you have now a wealth of freedom which you cannot value because you have not experienced the opposite, but you are also endowing yourself with a future freedom; freedom from the fear and shock and shyness which make the transition from youth to maturity more uncomfortable than any other period of existence. Francis is bringing you up through the looking-glass, back-to-front. You are learning what the adult learns, and walking through these lessons toward the light-heartedness that is usually to be found in childhood but lost later. I wonder how long it will take you to find that out." She sat up on her elbows and stared at me again. "Do you know what I think will happen to your Anthology of Hates when you do find it out? You will read it through and find that these are not Hates any more."

By this last remark she had annoyed me profoundly, and now she clapped her hands and cried, "If young people were only allowed to gamble! It takes the mind off every anxiety. If I could take you to the Casino with me tonight, Penelope! Wouldn't that be splendid? Disguised as a young lady of fashion!" She sprang off the chaise longue, snatched the square of velvet from the bed and flung it over my shoulders. Its weight almost bore me to the ground, it was heavy as a tent and it smelled musty. "Look at yourself in the mirror!" cried the Duchess. "Beautiful — beautiful — beautiful! A Principessa!" She scuttled past me. "We will place this silver girdle here." She lashed it so tightly that it hurt my stomach; I was stifled; it felt like being dressed in a carpet. "Take this fan and these gloves." They were long white kid gloves, as hard as biscuits; she forced my fingers in and cajoled the gloves up my arms as far as the shoulders.

"The little amethyst circlet for your head."

She caught some single hairs as she adjusted it and put one finger in my eye. Sweat was trickling all over me.

"Now you have a very distinct resemblance to your mother," said the Duchess, standing before me and regarding me with her head on one side.

"This is the forecast of your womanhood. Will you please go downstairs at once and show yourself to Jeanne?"

I said that I would rather not. She was peevishly disappointed. I struggled out of the ridiculous costume; hot, dispirited, no fonder of myself than before, I got away.

V

My bedroom was on the ground floor, with a window that opened onto the far end of the terrace. It was late, but I was still awake and heard Francis and Jeanne talking outside. I did not mean to listen, but their voices were clear and when I heard the name "Bradley" I could not help listening.

"I agree with you," Jeanne said, "that it is all an outrageous fuss. But these Bradleys mean a great deal to Penelope."

"Wish I knew why," said Francis. "They represent the worst and dullest aspect of English 'county'; a breed that may soon become extinct and no loss, either."

"They are the kind of friends that she has never had; English children of her own age."

Their footsteps ceased directly outside my window. I heard Francis sigh. "*Ought* we to send her to school in England, do you think?"

"Perhaps next year."

"That will be too late, beloved."

I had heard him call Jeanne "beloved" before, but tonight the word touched my heart, perhaps because I was already unhappy; it made me want to cry. "She will be fifteen," Francis said. "First she'll kill herself trying to fit into the pattern and if she succeeds in the task, we shall never see her again. God knows what we'll get but it won't be Penelope."

"She will change in any case, whether she stays or goes, darling; they always do."

"Perhaps I've done a poor job with her from the beginning," Francis said: he spoke my mother's name. And then I was so sure I must listen no more, that I covered my ears with my hands. When I took them away Jeanne was saying, "You are always sad when your back is hurting you. Come to bed. Tomorrow I'll invite the Bradley children for lunch again; on Thursday when Violetta's in Monte Carlo."

"Why should we suck up to the Smugs?" Francis grumbled, and Jeanne replied, "Only because of Penelope, *tu le sais*," and they walked away down the terrace.

I wept because they destroyed my defenses; my conscience still troubled me for the speeches of humbug that I had made to Eva, for quarreling with Francis, and for being uncivil to the Duchess. It was a weary load. If the Bradleys accepted the invitation to lunch, it would seem that God was not intending to punish me for it, but exactly the reverse, and that was a bewildering state of affairs.

By morning, however, God's plan became clear. Jeanne brought me my breakfast on the terrace. She sat with me while I ate it. I thought, as I had thought before, that she looked very young; more an elder sister than a stepmother, with her short, flying dark hair, the blue eyes in the brown face, the long slim brown legs. She smoked a *caporal* cigarette.

I could hardly wait for her to tell me whether she had healed the breach with the Bradleys. But I dared not ask. Their talk on the terrace had been too intimate for me to admit that I had heard it. She said, "Penelope, the situation with your friends at La Lézardière has become a little complex."

My heart beat downward heavily and I did not want to eat any more.

"I thought that it would give you pleasure if I asked them to lunch and would perhaps clear up any misunderstanding. But I have been talking to Mrs. Bradley and apparently she would prefer them not to visit the hotel."

I did not know whether I was blushing for the hotel, for my own disappointment, or for the Bradleys; I was only aware of the blush, flaming all over my skin, most uncomfortably.

"Mrs. Bradley was friendly and polite, you must not think otherwise. She wants you to swim with them as much as you like; she said that she hoped you would go out in the speedboat again. But her exact phrase was, 'We feel that the hotel surroundings are just a little too grown-up for Don and Eva.'"

I was silent.

"So, I thought that I would tell you. And ask you not to be unhappy about it. People are entitled to their views, you know, even when one does not oneself agree with them."

"Thank you, Jeanne: I am not at all unhappy," I said, wishing that my voice would not shake. "And if the Bradleys will not come to me, I am damned if I am going to them." And I rose from the table. She came after me, but when she saw that I was near to tears she gave me a pat on the back and left me alone.

This was the point at which I discovered that hate did not cast out love, but that it was, on the contrary, possible to hate and love at the same time. I could not turn off my infatuation for the Bradleys, much as I longed to do so. They were still the desirable Vikings. The stately pink villa above the orange trees, the gray rocks where the diving board jutted and the speedboat lay at anchor, remained the site of romance, the target of forlorn hopes. It hurt me to shake my head and retire from the flat rock when Don and Eva beckoned me. They seemed to understand quickly enough, more quickly than their parents did. Mr. Bradley still called, "Coming aboard?" and Mrs. Bradley waved to me elaborately on every possible occasion. The children turned their heads away. For two days I saw them all like figures set behind a glass screen; only the echo of their voices reached me; I gave up haunting the beach and worked in a corner of the garden; the regularity of their timetable made it easy to avoid the sight of them. I told myself that they were loathsome, that they were the Smugs, that Don and Eva were both candidates for RCI. I even considered including them in the Anthology of Hates, but I found it too difficult. Now they had indeed become the moon that the Duchess told me I cried for. I cherished dreams of saving Don's life or Eva's at great risk to myself, and being humbly thanked and praised by their parents. Then I hoped that they would all die in a fire, or better still that I would die and they would come to my funeral.

In these two days, I found myself looking at my home differently; seeing it in Bradley perspective. I had been plagued by the crises and irregularities but never ashamed of them. Was I ashamed now? I could not be sure; the feeling was one of extra detachment and perception; I was more than ever aware of the garden's bright colors, of the garlic smells from the kitchen, of the dusky coolness in the bar; every time that I walked through the salon I looked at it with startled visitors' eyes; Bradleys' eyes:

"It's pretty, of course; it's like a little room in a museum, but it isn't the sort of place where one wants to *sit*." The terrace with the blue and white umbrellas above the tables, the stone jars on the balustrade, the lizards flickering along the wall, seemed as temporary as the deck of a ship on a short voyage. I felt as though I were staying here, not living here. And there was no consolation in my own room with my own books because here the saddest thoughts came and they seemed to hang in the room waiting for me, as palpable as the tented mosquito net above the bed.

I found that I was seeing Francis, Jeanne, and the Duchess through a grotesque lens; they were at once complete strangers and people whom I knew intimately. I could place them in a Bradley context, thinking, "That is Francis Wells, the poet, the poet who keeps the mad hotel. He always seems to wear the same red shirt. He looks like Mephistopheles when he laughs. And that is his wife, his *second* wife; younger than he is; very gay always, isn't she? What very *short* shorts. And there goes the Duchessa de

Terracini, rather a terrible old lady who gambles at the Casino and drinks champagne; doesn't she look ridiculous in all that make-up and chiffon?" And then I would be talking to them in my own voice and with my own thoughts and feeling like a traitor.

I knew that they were sorry for me; that Francis above all approved my defiant refusal. I was aware of their hands held back from consoling gestures, to spare me too much overt sympathy. Even the Duchess did not speak to me of the Bradleys.

For once I welcomed the crises as diversion. And these two days naturally were not free from crisis; a British ambassador and his wife found themselves *en panne* at our gates. All the entrails of their car fell out upon the road and we were obliged to give them rooms for the night.

This would not of itself have been other than a mechanical crisis, because the ambassador and Francis were old friends. Unfortunately the ambassador and the press baron from Cap d'Ail, who was dining with the Duchess, were old enemies. So a fierce political fight was waged in the bar, with both elderly gentlemen calling each other poltroon, and they would have fought a duel had not the electric current failed and the hotel been plunged in darkness till morning. (My only grief was that Don and Eva had missed it. All roads led to the Bradleys.)

On the third morning, which was Thursday, doom accelerated. I woke to find Francis standing beside my bed.

"Sorry, darling; trouble," he said. "A telephone call just came through from Aix; Jeanne's mother is very ill and I'm going to drive her over there now. Can you take care of you for today?"

He never asked me such questions: this was like a secret signal saying, "I know you are miserable and I am sorry."

"But of course. Please don't worry."

"There are no guests, thank God. Violetta's going over to Monte Carlo; Laurent will be in charge tonight. You might see that he locks up, if I'm not back."

"I will do that."

"But don't let him lock Violetta out, for Heaven's sake."

"I will see that he does not. Can I help Jeanne or do anything for you?"

"No, my love. We are off now. I'll telephone you later." He ducked under the mosquito curtain to kiss me.

"You must pray rather than worry," the Duchess said to me, standing on the doorstep. For her expedition to Monte Carlo, she wore a coat and skirt of white shantung, a bottle-green frilly blouse, and the usual chiffon scarf. She was topped by a bottle-green tricorn hat with a green veil descending from it. "Death is a part of life," she added, pulling on her white gloves.

I could feel little emotion for my stepgrandmother who lived in seclusion near Aix-en-Provence, but I was sorry for Jeanne.

"The best thing that you could do, Penelope," said the Duchess, grasping her parasol like a spear, "would be to come over with me to Monte Carlo. We will lunch delightfully on the balcony of the Hotel de Paris; then you shall eat ices while I am at the tables; then a little stroll and a little glass and we could dine on the port at Villefranche and drive home under the moon. The moon is at the full tonight and I look forward to it. *Viens, chérie, ça te changera les idées,*" she added, holding out her hand.

I thanked her very much and said that I would rather stay here.

When she was placed inside the high purple Isotta-Fraschini, I thought that she and her old hooky chauffeur looked like a Punch-and-Judy show. The car was box-shaped with a fringed canopy under the roof and they swayed as it moved off. I waved good-by.

The first part of the day seemed endless. I sat in the garden on a stone bench under the largest of the umbrella pines. That way I had my back to La Lézardière. I could hear their voices and that was all. When the bell rang for their lunch, I went down to the pool and swam. I swam for longer than usual; then I climbed to the flat rock and lay in the sun. I was almost asleep when I heard Eva's voice. "Penelope!"

She was halfway up the rock; she said, "Look; we are so miserable we've written you this note. I have to go back and rest now." She was like a vision out of the long past; the freckles, the sunburn, and the wet hair. I watched her scuttle down and she turned to wave to me from the lowest tier of the terrace. I gave her a half-wave and opened the note.

It said:

Dear Penelope,
    Please don't be cross with us. Mum and Dad are going out to supper tonight. Don't you think that you could come? They have asked us to ask you.

Always your friends,
Don and Eva.

I wrote my reply at the *écritoire* in the salon. I wrote:

> Much as I appreciate the invitation, I am unable to accept it. Owing to severe illness in the family my father and stepmother have left for Aix. I feel it necessary to stay here and keep an eye on things.
>
> Penelope.

To run no risk of meeting them, I went into the bar and asked Laurent if he would be so kind as to leave this note at La Lézardière.

Laurent was in one of his moods; he replied sarcastically that it gave him great pleasure to run errands and do favors for young ladies who had not the energy to perform these for themselves. I echoed the former cook's husband, the assassin, and said, "*Salaud,*" but not until he was gone.

After I had answered the note, I alternated between wishing that I had accepted and wishing that I had given them more truthful reasons for my refusal.

Later, I sought comfort by writing to my aunt in England; I sat there conjuring the fortnight as it would be and putting in the letter long descriptions of the things that I wanted to see and do again. It helped. I had covered twelve pages when the telephone rang.

Francis' voice spoke over a bad line: "Hello, Child of Confusion. Everything all right?"

"Yes, indeed. Nothing is happening at all. What is the news?"

"Better," he said. "But Jeanne will have to stay. I may be very late getting back. See that Laurent gives you the cold lobster. Jeanne sends her love."

Nothing would have induced me to ask Laurent for my dinner, but I was perfectly capable of getting it myself and the reference to cold lobster had made me hungry. No reason why I should not eat my dinner at six o'clock. I was on my way to the kitchen by way of the terrace when I heard a voice calling me:

"Penelope!"

I turned, feeling that horrible all-over blush begin. Mrs. Bradley stood at the doorway from the salon onto the terrace. She looked golden and statuesque in a white dress with a scarlet belt. The sight of her was painful. It seemed as though I had forgotten how lovely she was.

"May I talk to you a moment, my dear?"

"Please do," I said, growing hotter and hotter.

"Shall we sit here?" She took a chair beneath one of the blue and white umbrellas. She motioned to me to take the other chair. I said, "Thank you, but I prefer to stand."

She smiled at me. I could feel in my heart the alarming collision of love and hate and now I could see her in two contexts; as a separate symbol, the enemy; as a beloved haunting of my own mind, the Mrs. Bradley of the first days, whom I had made my private possession. Her arms and hands were beautifully shaped, pale brown now against the white of her dress.

"Can't we be friends, Penelope? I think we can, you know, if we try. Don and Eva are so sad and it all seems such a pity."

I said, "But, Mrs. Bradley, you made it happen."

"No, dear. That is what I want to put right. When I talked to your stepmother, I made it quite clear that we all hoped to see much more of you."

"But," I said, "that Don and Eva couldn't come here. As though it were an awful place."

She put her hand on mine; she gave a soft low laugh. "Penelope, how foolish of you. Of course it isn't an awful place. You have just imagined our thinking that, you silly child."

"Did I imagine what you said about the Duchess?"

Still she smiled and kept her hand on mine. "I expect that what I said about the Duchess was quite a little exaggerated to you by Eva and Don. That was an uncomfortable day for all of us. We don't often quarrel in our family; I don't suppose that you do, either. Quarrels are upsetting to everybody and nobody likes them."

"Certainly," I said, "I don't like them."

"Let's try to end this one, Penelope."

Did she guess how badly I wanted to end it? I could not tell.

"Supposing," she said, "that you let me put my point of view to you, as one grown-up person to another. You are very grown-up for your age, you know."

"I do know, and I deplore it."

She gave another little low laugh. "Well, I shouldn't go on deploring it if I were you. Think what a dull world it would be if we were all made alike."

I winced inside at the cliché because Francis had taught me to wince at clichés. But I pretended that she had not said it. She went on: "Listen, dear. Just because you are so grown-up and this place is your home, you have a very different life from the life that Don and Eva have. I'm not saying that one sort of life is right and the other wrong. They just happen to be different. Now, my husband and I have to judge what is good for Don and Eva, don't we? You'll agree? Just as your father and stepmother have to judge what is good for you."

"Yes. I agree to that." It sounded reasonable; the persuasion of her manner was beginning to work.

"Well, we think that they aren't quite grown-up enough yet to understand and appreciate all the things that you understand and appreciate. That's all. It's as though you had a stronger digestion and could eat foods that might upset them. Do you see?"

When I was still silent, she added, "I think you should. Your stepmother saw perfectly."

"I suppose I see."

"Do try."

In fact I was trying hard; but the struggle was different from the struggle that she imagined. I felt as though I were being pulled over the line in a tug of war. Inside me there was a voice saying, "No, no. This is wrong. Nothing that she says can make it right. It is not a matter of seeing her point of view; you *can* see it; she has sold it to you. But you mustn't surrender." Oddly, the voice seemed to be the voice of the Duchess. I felt as though the Duchess were inside me, arguing.

I looked into the lovely, smiling face. "Do try," Mrs. Bradley repeated. "And do please come and have supper with the children tonight. Let's start all over again; shall we?"

When she held out both hands to me, she had won. I found myself in her arms and she was kissing my hair. I heard her say, "Poor little girl."

VI

Only the smallest shadow stayed in my heart and I forgot it for long minutes. We talked our heads off. It was like meeting them again after years. I found myself quoting in my head: "And among the grass shall find the golden dice wherewith we played of yore." They still loved me; they still laughed at everything I said. When I ended the description of the ambassador fighting the press baron and the failure of the electric lights, they were sobbing in separate corners of the sofa.

"Go on; go on. What did the Duchess do?"

"I think she enjoyed it mightily. She had an electric torch in her bag and she flashed it over them both like a searchlight."

"You do have the loveliest time," said Eva.

"Where is the Duchess tonight?" asked Don.

"In fact I think I heard her car come back about ten minutes ago." I began to describe the car and the chauffeur.

"*Older* than the Duchess? He can't be. I'd love to see them bouncing away under the fringe. Let's go out and look."

"Too late," I said. "At night he takes the car to the garage in Théoule."

"Hark, though," Don said. "There's a car now." He ran to the window; but I knew that it wasn't the Isotta-Fraschini. It was the putt-putt noise of Laurent's little Peugeot.

"How exactly like Laurent," I said. "As soon as the Duchess gets home, he goes out for the evening. And Francis has left him in charge."

It occurred to me now that I should go back. I reminded myself that Charlemagne was an effective watchdog. But I was not comfortable about it.

"D'you mean you ought to go and put the Duchess to bed? Undo her stays; help her off with her wig?"

"It isn't a wig; it's her own hair, and she requires no help. But I do think I should go back. The telephone may ring."

"Well then, the Duchess will answer it."

"She will not. She claims that she has never answered a telephone in her life. She regards them as an intrusion upon privacy."

"Isn't there anybody else in the hotel?"

"No."

"Oh you *can't* go yet," said Eva.

I sat on a little longer. Then I knew that it was no good. "I shall have remorse if I don't," I said, "and that is the worst thing."

"All right, then. We'll go with you."

"Oh, Don—" said Eva.

"Mum and Dad won't be back yet awhile," said Don, "and we'll only stay ten minutes."

"They'll be furious."

"We won't tell them."

Eva looked at me. I said, "I cannot decide for you. I only know I must go."

"Of course if you want to stay behind," Don said to Eva.

"Of course I don't. What shall we say to Nanny?"
"We can say we went down to the beach."

We crept out, silent in the spirit of adventure. The moon had risen, the full moon, promised by the Duchess, enormous and silver and sad; its light made a splendid path over the sea; the palms and the orange trees, the rock shapes on the water, were all sharp and black.

"Here we go on Tom Tiddler's ground," Eva sang. We took the short cut, scrambling through the oleander hedge instead of going round by the gate. I could hear Don panting with excitement beside me. Almost, their mood could persuade me that the hotel was an enchanted place. We came onto the terrace and darted into the empty bar; Laurent had turned off the lights; I turned them up for the Bradleys to look at the photographs.

"What'll we drink?" said Don facetiously, hopping onto a stool.

"Champagne," said Eva.

"If the Duchess was still awake, she'd give us some champagne."

"You wouldn't drink it," said Eva.

"I would."

"You wouldn't."

"I jolly well would."

"She's probably in the salon," I said. "She never goes to bed early."

I put out the lights again and led them to the salon by way of the terrace. The salon lights were lit. We looked through the windows.

"There she is," said Don. "She's lying on the sofa."

They bounded in ahead of me. I heard Don say, "Good evening, Duchessa," and Eva echoed it. There was no reply from the Duchess. With the Bradleys, I stood still staring at her. She was propped on the Empire sofa; her red head had fallen sideways on the stiff satin cushion. Her little pointed shoes and thin ankles stuck out from the hem of her shantung skirt and the skirt, which was of great width, drooped down over the edge of the sofa to the floor. On the table beside her she had placed the green tricorn hat, the green scarf, and her green velvet bag. A bottle of champagne stood in an ice pail; the glass had fallen to the floor; since one of her arms dangled limply, I thought that she must have dropped the glass as she went off to sleep.

"Please wake up, Duchessa; we want some champagne," said

Don.

He took a step forward and peered into her face, which was turned away from us.

"She looks sort of horrid," he said; "I think she's ill."

For no reason that I could understand I felt that it was impertinent of him to be leaning there so close to her. When he turned back to us, I saw that his face was pale; the freckles were standing out distinctly on the bridge of his nose.

"She is ill, I'm sure," he said. "She's unconscious." He looked at the bottle of champagne. "She must be —" He stopped. I saw that he thought that the Duchess was intoxicated and that he could not bring himself to say so.

"Let's go," Eva said in a thin scared voice. She grabbed Don's hand. "Come on, Penelope. Quick."

"But of course I'm not coming."

They halted. "You can't stay here," Don said. Eva was shivering. There was no sound nor movement from the figure on the sofa. I said, "Certainly I can stay here. What else can I do? If she is ill, I must look after her."

I saw them straining against their own panic. Suddenly they seemed like puppies, very young indeed.

"But *we* can't stay here," Eva said. "Oh, please, Penelope, come with us."

"No indeed. But you go," I said. "It's what you want to do isn't it?"

"It's what we ought to do," Eva stammered through chattering teeth. Don looked a little more doubtful. "Look here, Penelope, you needn't stay with her. When they — they get like that, they sleep it off."

Now I was angry with him. "Please go at once," I said. "This is my affair. And I know what you mean and it isn't true." I found that I had clapped my hands to shoo them off; they went; I heard the panic rush of their feet on the terrace. I was alone with the Duchess.

Now that they were gone, I had no hesitation in approaching her. I said softly, "Hello, Duchessa. It's only me," and I bent above her as Don had done. I saw what he had seen; the shrunken look of the white face with the false eyelashes. Indeed she looked shrunken all over, like a very old doll.

I lowered my head until my ear touched the green frilled

chiffon at her breast. I listened for the beat of her heart. When I could not hear it, I lifted the little pointed hand and felt the wrist. There was no pulse here that I could find.

I despised myself because I began to shiver as Eva Bradley had shivered. My fingers would not stay still; it was difficult to unfasten the clasp of the green velvet bag. I thought that there would be a pocket mirror inside and that I must hold this to her lips. Searching for the mirror I found other treasures; the ivory hand that she had aimed at Francis, a cut-glass smelling-bottle, some colored plaques from the Casino, a chain holding a watch, and a cluster of seals.

The mirror, when I found it, was in a folding morocco case with visiting cards in the pocket on the other side. I said, "Excuse me, please, Duchessa," as I held it in front of her face. I held it there a long time; when I took it away the bright surface was unclouded. I knew that the Duchess was dead.

A profound curiosity took away my fear. I had never seen a person lying dead before. It was so strange to think of someone I knew well, as having stopped. But the more I stared at her, the less she looked as though she had stopped; rather, she had gone. This was not the Duchess lying here; it was a little old doll, a toy thing of which the Duchess had now no need. Where, I wondered, had she gone? What had happened to all the things that she remembered, the fencing lessons, and the child's dreams, and the Emperor? What happened, I wondered, to the memories that you carried around in your head? Did they go on with your soul or would a soul not want them? What did a soul want? Did the Duchess's soul like roulette? Theology had never been my strongest subject and I found myself baffled by the rush of abstract questions flowing through my mind.

Then I became aware of her in relation to me. It was impossible to believe that I would not talk to her again. I was suddenly deeply sorry that I had not dined with her on the first evening, that I had not gone down in the fancy-dress to show myself to Jeanne. She had asked me to do this; she had asked me to Monte Carlo with her. *"Viens, chérie, ça te changera les idées."* Always she had been kind. I had not. I had never been nice to her because she embarrassed me and now I should never have another chance to be nice to her.

Automatically I began to perform small meaningless services. I covered her face with the green scarf, drawing it round her head so that it made a dignified veil. I fetched a rug and laid it across her feet; I did not want to see the little shoes. I carried the untouched champagne back to the bar. I lifted her tricorn hat, her bag and gloves off the table; I took them up to her room. It was more difficult to be in her room, with the bed turned down and the night clothes laid there, than it was to be in the salon with her body. I put the hat, bag, and gloves down on the nearest chair and I was running out when I saw the crucifix on the table. I thought that she might be pleased to have this near her ("Although," I said to myself, "she isn't there any more, one still goes on behaving as if she is"), and I carried it down; I set it on the table beside her. There seemed to be too many lights here now. I turned off all but one lamp; this room became a suitable place for her to lie in state, the elegant little shell of a room with the Empire furnishings. I pulled a high-backed chair from the wall, set it at the foot of the sofa, and sat down to watch with her.

Outside the windows the moonlight lay in the garden. I heard her saying, "The moon is at the full tonight. I look forward to it." I heard her saying, "Naturally, you cry for the moon." I heard her saying, "Death is a part of life," as she pulled on her white gloves.

At intervals I was afraid again; the fear came and went like intermittent seasickness. I did not know what brought it. She was so small and still and gone that I could not fear her. But I felt as though I were waiting for a dreadful thing to walk upon the terrace, and the only poem that would stay in my head was one that had always frightened me a little, "The Lykewake Dirge":

> This ae nighte, this ae nighte,
> Everye nighte and alle,
> Fire and sleet and candlelyte,
> And Christe receive thy saule.

It made shivers down my back. I would have liked to fetch Charlemagne from his kennel, but I had heard that dogs howled in the presence of the dead and this I did not want.

Sitting there so stiffly I became terribly tired: "But it is a vigil," I said to myself, "and it is all that I can do for her." It was not much. It was no true atonement for having failed her in kindness; it could not remit my having betrayed her to the Bradleys. It seemed hours since I had thought of the Bradleys. Now I wondered whether the parents had returned, and with the question there came incredulity that Don and Eva should not have come back. They had simply run off and left me, because they were afraid. The memory of their scared faces made them small and silly in my mind. Beside it, I uncovered the memory of my talk with Mrs. Bradley: the talk that had left a shadow. I admitted the shadow now: it was the note of patronage at the end of all the spellbinding. She had called me "poor little girl."

"You never called me poor little girl," I said in my thoughts to the Duchess. She had called me fortunate and a genius. She had spoken to me of the world, of freedom and maturity. That was truly grown-up conversation. In comparison the echo of Mrs. Bradley saying, "As one grown-up person to another," sounded fraudulent. Some of the magic had left the Bradleys tonight.

I was so tired. I did not mean to sleep, because this was vigil. But I found my head falling forward and the moonlight kept vanishing and the Duchess's voice was quite loud in my ears. "Of death," she said, "I remember three things; being tired, being quiet, and being gone. That's how it is, Penelope." She seemed to think that I could not hear her. She went on calling, "Penelope! Penelope!"

I sat up with a start. Somebody was in fact calling "Penelope": a man's voice from the terrace. I climbed down stiffly from the chair. "Who's that?" I asked, my voice sounding cracked and dry. Mr. Bradley stood against the moonlight.

"Are you there, child? Yes, you are. Come along out of this at once." He looked large and golden and worried; he seized my hand; then he saw the Duchess on the sofa.

"Lord," he said. "She's still out, is she?" He started again. "Did you cover her up like that?"

"Yes. Please talk quietly," I said. "She is dead."

He dropped my hand, lifted the scarf a little way from her face, and put it back. I saw him looking at the crucifix.

"I put it there. I thought that she would like it. I am watching by her," I said.

He looked pale, ruffled, not the way, I thought, that grown-up people should look. "I'm terribly sorry," he said in a subdued voice. "Terribly sorry. Young Don came along to our room, said he couldn't sleep for knowing you were over here with her. Of course he didn't think —"

"I know what he thought, Mr. Bradley," I said coldly. "Don and Eva are only babies really. Thank you for coming, just the same."

He said, in his officer-to-men voice, "Out of here now. There's a good girl."

"I beg your pardon?"

"You're coming to our house. I'll telephone the doctor from there." He took my hand again; I pulled it free.

"I'll stay with her, please. You telephone the doctor."

He looked down at me, amazed, almost smiling. He dropped his voice again. "No, no, no, Penelope. You mustn't stay."

I said, "I must."

"No, you mustn't. You can't do her any good."

"It is a vigil."

"That's just morbid and foolish. You're coming over to our house now."

"I am not."

"Yes, you are," he said, and he picked me up in his arms. To struggle in the presence of the Duchess would have been unseemly. I remained tractable, staying in his arms until he had carried me onto the terrace. He began to put me down and at once I twisted free.

"I'm not coming with you. I'm staying with her. She is my friend and she is not your friend. You were rude about her, and stupid," I said to him.

He grabbed me again and I fought: he imprisoned me with my arms to my sides. For the moment he did not try to lift me. He simply held me there.

"Listen, Penelope, don't be hysterical. I'm doing what's best for you. That's all. You can't possibly sit up all night alone with the poor lady; it's nearly one o'clock now."

"I shall stay with her till dawn; and she is not a poor old lady, just because she is dead. That is a ridiculous cliché."

I was aware of his face close to mine, the stony, regular features, the blue eyes and clipped mustache in the moonlight. The face seemed to struggle for speech. Then it said, "I don't want insolence any more than I want hysteria. You just pipe down and come along. This is no place for you."

"It is my home," I said.

He shook me gently. "Have some sense, will you? I wouldn't let my kids do what you're doing and I won't let you do it."

"Your children," I said, "wouldn't want to do it anyway; they are, in vulgar parlance, a couple of sissies."

At this he lifted me off my feet again and I struck at his face. I had the absurd idea that the Duchess had come to stand in the doorway and was cheering me on. And at this moment there came the miracle. The noise of the car sweeping in from the road was not the little noise of Laurent's car, but the roaring powerful engine that meant that Francis had come home.

The headlights swung yellow upon the moonlit garden. Still aloft in Mr. Bradley's clutch I said, "That is my father, who will be able to handle the situation with dignity."

He set me down as Francis braked the car and jumped out.

"That you, Bradley?" said Francis. "What, precisely, are you doing?"

Mr. Bradley said, "I am trying to make your daughter behave in a sensible manner. I'm very glad to see you."

Francis came up the steps onto the terrace. He sounded so weary that I knew his back hurt him: "Why should it be your concern to make my daughter behave in any manner what-soever?"

"Really, Wells, you'll have to know the story. There's been a tragedy here tonight, I'm afraid. Just doing what I could to help."

"I will tell him," I said. I was grateful for Francis' arm holding me; my legs had begun to feel as though they were made of spaghetti.

"You let me do the talking, young woman," said Mr. Bradley.

"If you don't mind, I'd prefer to hear it from Penelope," said Francis.

I told him. I told him slowly, leaving out none of it; there seemed less and less breath in my lungs as I continued. "And Mr. Bradley called it morbid and foolish and removed me by force," I ended.

"Very silly of you, Bradley," said Francis.

"Damn it, look at the state she's in!"

"Part of which might be due to your methods of persuasion, don't you think? All right, Penelope, easy now." I could not stop shivering.

"Leaving her alone like that in a place like this. You ought to be ashamed of yourself," Mr. Bradley boomed.

"Quiet, please," said Francis in his most icy voice.

"Damned if I'll be quiet. It's a disgrace and I don't want any part of it."

"Nobody," I said, "asked you to take any part in it, Mr. Bradley."

"Hush," said Francis. "Mr. Bradley meant to be kind and you must be grateful."

"I am not in the least."

"Fine manners you teach her," said Mr. Bradley.

"Quiet, please," said Francis again. "Penelope has perfect manners, mitigated at the moment by perfect integrity and a certain amount of overstrain." Looking up at him, I could see the neat Mephistophelean profile, the delicate shape of his head. I loved him more than I had ever loved him. Mr. Bradley, large and blowing like a bull, was outside this picture, nothing to do with either of us.

Suddenly he looked as though he realized this. He said: "I don't want my wife or my kids mixed up in it either."

"Mixed up in what, precisely?" Francis asked.

I said, "It is possible that he is referring to the inquest. Or do you mean mixed up with me? Because if you do, no problem should arise. After tonight I have not the slightest wish to be mixed up with them or you."

It would have been more effective had I been able to stop shivering; I was also feeling rather sick, never a help when attempting to make dignified speeches.

Mr. Bradley faded away in the moonlight.

Francis said gently, "Did you mean it? It is easy to say those things in anger."

"I think I meant it. Was the vigil, in your opinion, the right thing to do?"

"It was. I am very pleased with you."

I said, "But I am not sure that I can continue with it for a moment. I feel funny."

Francis took me into the bar; he poured out a glass of brandy and a glass of water, making me drink them in alternate swallows.

"Of course," he said gloomily, "it may make you sick. In which event the last state will be worse than the first."

But it did not; it made me warm.

"They can't *help* being the Smugs, can they?" I said suddenly, and then for the first time I wanted to cry.

"They're all right," said Francis. "They are merely lacking in imagination."

I managed to say, "Sorry," and no more. I knew that he disliked me to cry. This time he said, watching me, "On some occasions it is better to weep."

I put my head down on the table and sobbed, "If only she could come back; I would be nice."

Francis said, "You gave her great pleasure always."

"Oh, not enough."

"Nobody can give anybody enough."

"Not ever?"

"No, not ever. But one must go on trying."

"And doesn't one ever value people until they are gone?"

"Rarely," said Francis.

I went on weeping; I saw how little I had valued him; how little I had valued anything that was mine. Presently he said, "Do you think that you can cry quite comfortably by yourself for a few minutes because I must telephone the doctor?"

Though I said, "Yes, indeed," I stopped crying immediately. As I sat waiting for him, I was saying good-by, to my first dead, to a love that was ended, and to my dream of being like other people.

The next day I tore the Anthology of Hates into pieces and cast the pieces into the sea. I did not read through the pages first, so certain was I that I had done with hating.

About the Author

British novelist Pamela Frankau was born in London in 1908. After 1945 she also lived in France, the time and place of this story, and the United States. She died in 1967.

Like Penelope, the main character of this story, Frankau was a precocious writer. Her first novel was published when she was only 19 and was a huge popular success. She went on to write over 30 novels in her career. "The Duchess and the Smugs" was first published as a short story in *Harpers* in 1952; it then appeared in 1954 as the first of three sections of the novel *Wreath for an Enemy.*

Frankau's fiction is divided in both content and form by World War II and her conversion to Catholicism. Her earlier works are about love affairs or superficial examinations of British high society, characterized by witty dialogue and minimal plot. In contrast, much of her work after the war has an overt, heavy-handed religious message. "Duchess" is one of the best pieces of her mature work, using plain English to convincingly portray a young girl's search for values.

Questions for Thought and Discussion

1. Answer the first few questions to set the story in time and place and to review some of the other facts about the story. How old is Penelope? Assuming the story takes place about 1950 (after World War II ended in 1945, and before the story's publication in 1952), when would Penelope have been born?

2. What connection does the Duchess have with World War I? How old would she have been then? How old is she in the story?

3. What is the nationality of Penelope's father? Her mother? Her step-mother? How did her father and step-mother meet? What are her father's occupations? Where (specifically) does the story take place? (Why is this location important to the story?)

4. What kind of school does Penelope attend? If you were her classmate, how do you think you would describe her?

5. Why did Penelope need to write an "Anthology of Hates"? Why do you think the Duchess made the prediction she made about the book (which turned out to be accurate)?

7. Describe the parenting style of Penelope's parents and the family's daily routine. Describe the parenting style of the twins' parents and the daily routine of their family.

8. Why did Penelope find the twins so attractive at first? Why were the twins initially so fascinated by Penelope?

9. Would you prefer that your own children be more like Penelope or more like the twins? Explain their differences and why you prefer one pattern over the other.

10. How do you think the two sets of parents would define "discipline"? Were their children well disciplined? In what ways?

11. What do you like about each style of parenting? Refer to parental reactions to specific incidents.

12. What do you perceive to be lacking or weak in each style?

The Desert   William Hauptman

Parenting Issue:

Parents as Role Models

As children grow up by their parents' sides they learn how to live by listening to what their parents say, watching what they do, and by observing their parents' emotional reactions — their facial expressions, tones of voice, silence and so on. This means that parents sometimes teach values and attitudes which they are not aware of teaching or which they do not intend to teach.

Parents' success in passing on the values which they profess to have depends on the extent to which their "values" are genuinely held. It depends also on the extent to which children perceive their parents as worthy of being imitated, since parents are always somewhat adequate and somewhat inadequate in the ways they respond to life.

"The Desert" is a story about a father, told through the eyes of a son. It consists of memories, especially the events of the summer of his fourteenth year, a formative time in his development. That summer he learned more about his father's character, both the admirable qualities and the flaws, and grew to love his father in spite of the flaws.

4.
The Desert
William Hauptman

೧೪

My father was a petroleum geologist. Today, they've got a lot of help — they look for oil with dynamite charges and geophones, exploding the charges and recording the shock wave as it moves through the layers of rock. Then this information goes into a computer.

But my father didn't have all this technology. He studied the surface formations. From what he could see, he tried to imagine what he could not. Slowly, he built up a picture of the landscape as it had existed through time, layer after layer for millions of years.

When he thought he'd found oil, he told them where to drill. Sometimes he was right, and sometimes wrong. But people thought he was good — some people thought he was the best geologist they'd ever worked with.

We lived in Texas, but his early jobs took us all over the country. As he drove, he pointed out geologic features. Other families looked at landmarks from the history of the United States; we looked at landmarks from the history of the world. When I was six years old, we drove to Wyoming in a yellow Chrysler. I rode in the backseat, too little to understand much of what my parents said. But I knew we were happy — my father because he had a good job, my mother because now we could buy a house, and me because on the radio Vaughn Monroe was singing my favorite song, "Ghost Riders in the Sky."

It got dark. Then, fifty miles ahead, we saw a light. When we got closer, it was a big yellow torch.

"A rig's on fire," my father said.

He pulled off the road to get a closer look and lifted me onto the hood of the Chrysler. The air trembled, and I could feel heat on my face.

He explained how oil was found in underground pools. Something had ignited the oil, and now it might burn for months. But won't it all burn up? I wanted to know.

"Yes, Sonny," my father said. "Someday it will all be gone."

At first I thought of my father as a soldier. When I was very young, he showed me a photograph of himself, wearing a helmet and fatigues, holding a machine gun, and standing in front of his jeep, somewhere in Belgium.

He was there when Patton's Third Army relieved the airborne at the Battle of the Bulge; he crossed the Remagen Bridge three days after it was captured and helped trap the German Army in the Ruhr Pocket. He was a captain and avoided General Patton, who was hard on officers. Once, when Patton arrived at a farmhouse command post, my father, along with several other officers, climbed out a rear window. He brought back a Bronze Star, his decoration for valor, a Nazi ceremonial dagger, and a pistol taken from a German prisoner. Sometimes he brought his footlocker down from the attic and I was allowed to look at these things. The Bronze Star was in a blue plush case. The dagger had a chrome blade. Best of all was the pistol, black and deadly.

Then something went wrong. My father changed. He got frighteningly angry for reasons I couldn't understand, and I fell out of love with him. Suddenly he seemed to have a lot of enemies. Every night he watched the Army–McCarthy hearings on television. "Maybe old Georgie Patton was right," he said. "When we finished with the Germans, we should have taken on the Reds."

He became very suspicious. There were floodlights in our backyard so he could cook outside. Sometimes, without warning, he would turn them on.

"What's wrong?" I would say.

"Nothing. I just thought I heard somebody in the backyard."

For years my father went along, never earning much money. Meanwhile, his friends were making their pile, moving into big offices downtown and hiring younger geologists to work for them.

Then he did make money. He found an overlooked deposit of oil only thirty miles away. It was brilliant geology. Everyone said so. But instead of moving downtown, my father built an office in the garage. Money bought freedom, but what did he do with it? He bought a big Steinway piano.

My father loved the piano. As a boy in Lincoln, Nebraska, he had taught himself to play; had earned pocket money in high school by playing for a movie theater that still showed silent pictures. Now he practiced all the time. Instead of making more money, he learned to play Chopin.

But it got so I hated to come home and hear him playing. It meant he'd been drinking. Sometimes I would go in his office and look at his maps. Before he made money, he had spent long hours working on them. Each contour line was lovingly inked in; there were overlays of colored tissue paper for each geologic age. Now they were ignored.

My father was trying to decide what to do. He thought about it longer and longer, staying up all night at the piano and sleeping all day.

Once, when he was cleaning the pistol, my mother said it was dangerous and he should throw it away. To prove that an unloaded pistol was not dangerous, my father aimed it out the back door and pulled the trigger. The bullet made a small hole in the screen.

When my father was in his early forties, he began doing field work again. That summer he took us to Chambers, Arizona. There was no town, just the yellow cinderblock motel, where we lived, in the middle of nowhere. Ten miles west was the Painted Desert. Across the highway was the Navajo Reservation.

Every morning my father's Navajo driver knocked on the door of my parents' room. He drove my father off into the desert, leaving my mother and me behind. While she read the *Ladies' Home Journal* under the roaring air-conditioner, I watched the other guests leave. Most were on their way to California. Night had surprised them on this long, empty stretch between Gallup and Flagstaff. They got in late and left early the next day.

Sometimes I walked around behind the motel, where a big landfill, full of garbage, sloped down to the Puerco River. A girl stood in the back door of the café adjoining the motel. She was a year or so older than I was. "What's your name?" she said.

"Bill."

"Where you from, Billy?"

"Texas." I tried to sound tough. Girls who called you Billy didn't take you seriously.

"I got a horse. Maybe we can ride it sometime."

"Maybe."

She disappeared into the cafe. Then I walked along the highway, past the corral and her horse and an old Airstream trailer, my loafers filling with hot sand.

I was fourteen years old. My grades were not very good. I sketched in my notebook instead of writing down the things my teachers said. When I was younger, I had suffered from terrifying nightmares about the atomic bomb. I had seen our house, standing alone in the Nevada desert like the houses on the television programs. There was a flash, and the shingles ignited; then there was only flying debris as the shock wave rolled over it, like surf.

"Learn everything about what frightens you," my father had said, "and you can overcome it." I had taken his advice and had learned everything there was to know about protons, neutrons, electrons. The nightmares had stopped. Now I had only one problem — talking to girls.

Ahead, I heard singing. Three Navajos sat under a highway bridge. They wore robes and big hats and passed a bottle. There was a fire, the flames almost invisible in the glare. The singing faded in and out as the wind shifted. I crouched down and watched them for a long time.

Later, when they were gone, I went closer. Empty bottles of Gallo Thunderbird lay on the sand. I poked the ashes of the fire with a long stick. What sort of people, I wondered, would sit around a fire on a day like this, drinking, wearing those hot clothes? A big semi boomed over the bridge. I got nervous and walked back to the motel.

My father returned about the time the neon sign out front began to glow. He wore a clean white shirt to dinner, and a string tie with a turquoise clasp. After closing time, the couple who owned the motel sat in our booth and talked to my parents. Everyone was friendly here. I watched their daughter, whom I'd spoken to that morning, working in the kitchen with two Navajo girls. Later, her boyfriend came for her in a pickup. Wearing charcoal-gray slacks, a pink shirt, and a thin gray plastic belt, I dropped nickel after nickel in the jukebox, playing a song I didn't even like, Pat Boone's "Love Letters in the Sand."

From the day we came to Chambers, we heard about Hank Luscombe, who ran the trading post — he had lived with a Navajo woman, had tried peyote. He sounded like the most interesting person around. One evening, my father and I drove over to see him.

The trading post was on the old, bypassed highway, a mile north. It was a long, low building, part log, part adobe. Navajos sat on the front porch, ignoring us and drinking Orange Crush.

Hank had a sly, dishonest look. As he talked to my father, his eye kept roving around and finding me. I felt uncomfortable and walked away through rooms that got smaller and smaller. In the last room of all, I found the paintings.

They were of birds, deer, Navajo. Painted in bright primary colors, they showed a world of stylized light. The moon was a silver crescent, the clouds a glowing, scalloped line. The most beautiful, to my mind, was of an impossibly blue horse.

"You buy?"

A big Navajo was standing at my shoulder, his hair in a pigtail. "Fifty dollars," he said.

Hank, followed by my father, came into the room. "This is Jimmy Begay," he said. "He painted all those pictures."

"Fifty dollars. Good price."

"We're not looking for a painting," my father said.

"Hank," the Navajo said, "you got something for me?"

They went in the other room. Through the window, a moment later, we watched him leave. In one hand he carried a can of tomatoes; in the other, a bottle wrapped in a papper sack.

Hank returned and told us about Jimmy Begay. He had joined the Marines at fourteen, lying about his age. When he came back, he started to paint. Among collectors of Indian art he was famous; but he hadn't sold a major painting for two years.

"I thought liquor was illegal on the reservation," my father said.

"I give Jimmy a bottle now and then. He does me a favor, bringing me those paintings, so I do him one. Jimmy's my friend."

He showed us the largest one — a Navajo in a Marine uniform, floating in a thundercloud and staring off over golden mesas with a look of tragic, helpless love.

"He says this is his masterpiece. But he wants five hundred dollars for it, and it's so gloomy nobody will buy it."

Hank was right. Nobody ever bought the painting. But I was

inspired and began sketching the horse in the corral behind the motel. This should have been easy, since it stood motionless for hours. Sometimes I almost got the proportions right. But I always gave up and went back to my room. The motel was silent at noon except for the droning, singsongy chants on Radio Gallup, which I could half hear on the maid's transistor radio. Under my bed I kept a copy of *Playboy* I had found on the landfill. It was years old, but its pages had been preserved by the dry desert air. I stared at it for hours. There was one photograph of Marilyn Monroe, her skin the color of honey, lying naked on a spill of red velvet. Sometimes it seemed afterwards I had actually made love to her.

One Saturday we drove to Gallup. While my parents went shopping, I went to see a movie I'd heard a lot about, *Rebel Without a Cause*.

For two hours, I became the boy on the screen—had a knife fight, wore a red nylon windbreaker, screamed at my parents, *You're tearing me apart*, tried to save Plato by emptying his gun of shells. When I came out, I stared into the blue mirror covering the facade of the building next door and was shocked to see I was still myself. Staring back was the same confused face of my yearbook photo.

The building was a hock shop. I went inside and bought a switchblade with a transparent handle—when it was turned just the right way, you could see a naked girl, her pubic hair covered by the ace of spades.

All the way back to Chambers, I stared out the car window, having grim, enjoyable visions of being misunderstood for the rest of my life. "What's wrong with you?" my mother said.

"Nothin'," I mumbled.

"For God's sake, Sonny, speak up!" my father said. "I can't understand a word you're saying."

But I didn't answer. I was busy perfecting my impersonation of James Dean, teenager from the moon.

After dinner that night, I sat at the counter, rolling one toothpick after another out of the dispenser, until the girl leaned across the Formica top and said, "Billy, is something wrong?"

"No," I said, rolling out another toothpick.

"Come back in the kitchen, so we can talk."

I followed her. She wore a papery skirt and shoes with red crepe soles. The Navajo girls dropped silverware and giggled at us. "Billy," she said with some concern, "are you In Trouble?"

This was the fifties, and being In Trouble could mean anything from being pregnant to stealing hubcaps. I made up a story on the spot, borrowing from the movie. "I go to a pretty tough school. They get rough with you if you don't belong. . . . Sometimes they fight with knives. If you don't they think you're chicken."

I showed her my knife. She seemed to like what she heard. The movie had confirmed something I had long suspected: Girls didn't go for nice guys. They liked the guys who got In Trouble; liked the guys they said they didn't like.

"Let's go out to my uncle's trailer," she said. "He's got a radio."

Her uncle was a ham operator. The walls of the trailer were covered with postcards. She tuned his big Zenith to a commercial station, and from far-off Chicago I heard the Coasters singing "Searchin'." "Come on," she said, holding out her hand, "pretend I'm your big sister."

"I don't feel like it."

I looked instead at postcards from Dayton, Ohio, and Anchorage, Alaska. Most of my dancing had been done with myself, in front of a mirror. Dancing with a girl seemed almost as impossible as going all the way with her.

"You are a strange boy. I watch you sometimes. What are you doing out there all day long?"

"Sketching."

"You going to be an artist?"

"Maybe."

"Dancing's against our religion," she said. "We're Latter-Day Saints. But sometimes my boyfriend takes me. The Navajo girls showed me some steps."

She opened a cabinet. Inside was a bottle. "Maybe someday I'll stop going to church, like my uncle did. He drinks and plays poker all night long with his railroad friends.

"Say," she said, looking at me, "how about drinking some of this?"

My mouth had the metallic taste that goes along with doing all dangerous things for the first time; but there was never any doubt I was going to drink it.

After we had some, she took the bottle to the sink. "I'll just put some tap water in it and he'll never know the difference," she said. "It's always worked before." She left the bottle on the table.

Together we sat on the couch, and she told me about going to

Gallup with her boyfriend. "Maybe you and me can drive to Gallup sometime."

"I can't. I mean, my parents took away my license when I got In Trouble."

We had another one. I thought it was doing nothing to me and wondered why my father liked it. While we talked she extended one leg, pointing it at the bottle, dangling her shoe from one toe like a little girl. I got up to put the bottle away, but found myself in the bathroom, staring at my reflection in the dirty mirror. Did my face show any change? My lips no longer had any feeling in them.

Now the Five Satins were singing a sad, ghostly song, "In the Still of the Night." "Won't you try dancing with me?" she said. "Just once."

I held her, no big sister now, and we circled slowly on the linoleum floor, grains of sand scratching underfoot. Dancing was easier than I'd thought. I just shifted my weight from one foot to the other.

"You got a girlfriend?"

"Yeah, she's the only one who really understands me."

"What's she look like?"

"I can't describe her. There's this big ol' haunted house, and we go there sometimes and pretend our parents are dead, and we're all we've got."

"You're so strange, Billy."

"Don't call me Billy."

"Bill, Billy," she said. "Who cares? There's billions of Bills, a billion boys."

Silence fell, full of the singing of blood in my ears. Then the screen door was jerked open. I was grabbed and thrust outside; I fell on my hands and knees. I heard a slap; then she ran past me, sobbing. "You've been drinking," her father said to me, righteous as Charlton Heston in *The Ten Commandments*.

"Nosir."

"Don't nosir me. The bottle's right there on the table."

He shoved me along to the door of my parents' room and knocked. the door opened. There they were. "They were dancing," he said, "and drinking her uncle's liquor."

"You don't have to get rough with the boy," my father said apologetically. "I'll discipline him myself."

"See that you do."

The door slammed behind me. My mother said, "You have

disappointed me today in more ways than one."

She opened my door, and to my horror I saw the *Playboy* lying on the bed. The maid must have left it there when she made up my room.

My father was taking off his belt. "I haven't punished you like this since you were a boy," he said, "but I guess you need it."

There was only one thing to do. Screaming, *You're tearing me apart*, I ran off into the night.

For hours I sat on the landfill. There was no place else to go, although I considered hopping a freight to Los Angeles. Secretly, I was very proud of myself. With a long stick I wrote several Love Letters in the Sand. When my parents' lights went out, I slipped back into my room and my bed, trying not to think about tomorrow.

From a great distance, I heard a groaning sound. Struggling up out of sleep, I realized somebody was trying to start my father's jeep.

Just as I got to the window, my father burst from the door of their room, wearing only Jockey shorts, pistol in hand, and fired into the air.

The shots woke the whole motel. Whoever was trying to steal the Jeep ran off. My father called the police. Sleep was impossible. We sat around in bathrobes. At least my trouble was forgotten.

"I've wished a thousand times you'd throw that old thing away," my mother said.

"If I hadn't had the pistol," my father said, "I would have lost the Jeep."

At daybreak, the Navajo tribal police brought back my father's driver, who had tried to hot-wire the Jeep. They'd caught him hitchhiking, miles down the highway. My father talked to them, then walked away from their car, whose spinning red lights lit up the courtyard. "I didn't press charges," he said. "That boy wasn't worth a goddamn. A year in jail's not going to make him any better."

For a moment he sat, his head in his hands, then looked up. "Sonny, I've got to finish this job, and I don't want to hire another Navajo. Do you think you can help me?"

"Yessir."

"Then I'll give you another chance."

In the desert, I fell back in love with my father. The first day we gassed up at Hank's trading post. I heard a Navajo say, "Where are you going in that Jeep?" It was Jimmy Begay.

"Over toward Black Knoll," my father said, "looking for oil."

"You got a cigarette?" My father gave him one of his Viceroys and they looked at each other.

"You'll get lost out there."

"I don't think so," my father said.

"You be careful, you get lost." He added something in Navajo, and the Indians on the porch laughed. Then he walked off down the road to Wide Ruins.

My father and I drove south, across the Puerco River, onto a ranch belonging to Mr. Paulson. Ahead was a frozen sea — not of ice but of bentonite, yellow desert clay.

My father had to know the elevation of certain beds. He drove me to the foot of a hill and dropped me off. Then I climbed to the top, carrying the surveyor's rod that unfolded in sections, like a carpenter's rule.

Holding the rod upright, I stared off into a world of silent light. To the west was Black Knoll; to the south, the shimmering outline of the White Mountains, fifty miles off. To the east, I could see the tiny figure of my father. He stared back at me through the telescopic sight of his transit, which was mounted on a tripod that stood by the Jeep.

Finally, he walked away from the tripod, waving his hat; a moment later, I heard a faint cry. This was the signal that he was finished. Folding the rod, I climbed down and waited for him to pick me up.

One afternoon at the end of the first week, I noticed my father was in pain. He had injured his back jumping into a ditch in Belgium under fire, and it had given him trouble ever since. "Sonny," he said, "why don't you drive?"

"Are you serious?"

"Go ahead, it's about time you learned."

So I drove the thirty miles back to the motel, learning to coordinate clutch and gas pedal. Maybe that was when I began to love my father again. Knowing I could drive, I looked forward to going back to school in September and perhaps getting my beginner's license, so I could take the car on dates.

In the desert, we told time by light. In the morning, the rocks were pink and gray. At noon, when the sun was overhead, they looked white as plaster. The heat was too great to work. My father parked the Jeep in the shade of a cedar, and we ate lunch.

Then, while he took a nap, I explored the nearby arroyos, keeping my eyes to the ground, looking for pottery left by the tribe the Navajo called the Anasazi, or Old Ones.

As I walked, I thought of the first time my father had taken me into the country. That summer in Wyoming, when I was six years old, we had driven across the prairie, pronghorn antelope scattering from the Jeep. In an arroyo like this, he had found two stones, covered with tiny cracks, and placed them in my hands.

"They're dinosaur eggs," he said. "They've been here so long they've turned to stone."

This country, he told me, was the greatest in the world for fossils. Back there, along the ridgeline, he'd found the thighbone of a brontosaurus.

Couldn't we go get it, take it home? I thought it must be very valuable and was in agony, afraid somebody else would find it.

"They'd walk right past it and not even notice," he said, laughing. "They wouldn't know what to look for." That was the day I had learned what a geologist did.

I liked the way my father looked at this country. Sitting on a petrified log, holding the map on his knees, he stared off at the exposed layers of sandstone: Kayenta, Kaibab, Coconino, Chinle: My father was seeing the memory of the earth.

At the top of the arroyo, I looked out over the whole bentonite sea. After a long time I let my eyes fall on my father sleeping by the Jeep, seemingly at my feet. I had never seen him so happy. In the desert, my father never drank, never wondered what to do. He belonged there.

Later, the light changed again, and the rocks were golden-looking, almost soft. I climbed down the arroyo to wake my father. But he was up before I reached him, as if even in his sleep he had sensed the change. Then we worked another range of hills, until we lost the light entirely.

Once, he dug a bit of yellow rock out from under a ledge with his pocketknife, and I asked him what it was.

"Carnotite. A not-very-pure sample of uranium ore."

"Can't we stake a claim or something?"

"No, there's nothing here. The big beds are across the highway, on the Navajo Reservation."

"Well, then, let's go there."

"Even if you found it, it would belong to the Navajos."

I put the rock in the knapsack. "Let's look around," I said. "Maybe there's more."

For a moment I was angry again. This was like the dinosaur bone: another example of my father's knowledge that he could not, or somehow refused to, profit by.

In August, Clint Yarborough came, my father's boss, landing his Beechcraft Bonanza on the dirt strip behind the trading post. He was a gray-haired, handsome man who wore a beautifully tailored blue suit and cowboy boots. When my father showed him the map, he said, "I don't see the structure."

"Right here, along this bed."

"Forget it, you're the geologist. Come on, I'll take y'all to dinner."

Afterwards, back in my parents' room, he propped his expensive boots on the desk. He was paying the bills. "Boy," he said, "why don't you get some ice?" He opened his suitcase and took out a bottle of Wild Turkey.

My father talked geologic theory. "Clint, there's no doubt about it, the younger geologists are right. The continents are in motion."

"I hope Africa doesn't float up next to Padre Island. I got some property there."

My mother forced a laugh, and I hated Clint Yarborough.

"No, Clint, I'm talking about millions of years—"

"Millions? What kind of football team are the Longhorns going to have next year, that's all I care about. You're going to join us for the Cotton Bowl, aren't you? I got a suite at the Adolphus Hotel. You can play the piano and tell all your good stories. Goddamn, you tell a better story than Arthur Godfrey, you know that?"

I went to my room. Later, listening through the walls, I heard Clint say, "People back in North Texas say you're the best geologist there is. They also say you got a drinking problem."

"It's not a problem, Clint, so long as I don't drink."

"You had some tough experiences in the war. That probably had something to do with it. But that's none of my business. I'm proud to employ you."

"Thanks, Clint."

"There's only one thing I want to know: Have we got a well here or not?"

A long silence.

"Just give me your professional opinion."

"You've got a well. The question is, where?"

"All right," Clint said. "When you're absolutely certain, you give me the word. Can you do that?"

"Can do."

"Good." I heard Clint get to his feet. "When it comes in, I'll put you on salary. There's going to be some government reserves turned over to private corporations soon, and Lyndon's a good friend of mine. Yarborough Oil is going places . . . and you could be going places with it."

My father worked more slowly after that. In his silences, as he stared off at the distant beds, I sensed confusion.

One day, there was a thunderstorm. I watched the clouds carefully — the surveyor's rod could attract lightning. From the Jeep my father and I watched the gray broom of rain hitting the desert floor, one hundred, then only fifty yards away. Solid drops struck the roof of the Jeep, like shot. The arroyos were filled with floodwater that looked like moving concrete. Afterwards, the desert was not a world of light but was all in tones of gray, like a photograph. The clouds pressed right down on our heads. The crows always seemed bolder on days like that; they followed us, silently, everywhere we went.

"There's nothing more to do today," my father said. "Let's go home."

Driving back, I decided to take a shortcut up one of the arroyos. My father didn't think I could do it. "The hell I can't," I said.

Halfway up, I got stuck. The Jeep rocked back and forth, wheels spinning in the wet sand. My father told me to get out and push. Nothing worked. Finally, he turned off the ignition.

"We'll walk," he said.

"Walk?"

"Do you want to spend the night here? The road runs right along the top of this arroyo. It's only about seven miles. Here, you take the knapsack."

At the top of the arroyo, we walked through big boulders. "You couldn't have gotten through here anyway," he said. "I shouldn't have let you try. Here's the road. Put a pebble in your mouth."

"What for?"

"So you won't get thirsty."

We walked. At first, I went ahead. When I got a blister and

slowed down, my father caught up with me. "What's your hurry?" he said. He took the knapsack. At sunset the sky cleared, and every little stone cast a pencil of violet shadow. Then the sun was gone, and the air was losing its warmth.

At the Puerco Ford, my father was far ahead. He stopped. Against the afterglow, he looked like a silhouette cut out of blotting paper. When I reached him, I said, "What's wrong?"

"There's a fire."

Just ahead was a sandstone outcrop. It was full of caves, hollowed by the wind out of solid rock. Their roofs were blackened by the smoke of countless campfires, their walls scratched everywhere with the petroglyphs of the Anasazi.

Sitting in one were three Navajos. They were drinking Thunderbird around a fire they'd built with one of Mr. Paulson's fenceposts.

"You get lost?" one said. It was Jimmy Begay.

"No," my father said. "We're not lost."

"Come over here and give me a cigarette."

To the north, I could see the lights of the motel. "We're almost home," I said. "It's only another mile or so." But my father sat down by the fire. "That feels good," he told them. "We were getting cold."

He passed around cigarettes; they offered him the bottle, but he refused. "What are you looking for out there?" Jimmy said.

"Oil."

"There's no oil here."

"Oh, yes," my father said, "you have lots of oil here, underground." He explained how, millions of years ago, this was a forest. They'd seen the petrified wood on Black Knoll? Some of the trees had turned to stone; others had sunk into the ground and turned into coal and oil. He loved to talk geology, even when the people listening couldn't understand a word.

Then a long silence fell, broken only by the pop of sticks in the fire.

One of the Navajos looked at us and said something. My father asked Jimmy to translate. "He says he doesn't like you Anglos," Jimmy said.

The Navajos seemed to pull together in the firelight. Let's go, I kept thinking. Let's get out of here.

"He says you're always trying to take something from the Navajos."

"This isn't your land," my father said. "It belongs to Mr. Paulson. And you're burning one of his fenceposts."

I got ready to leap up—not to defend my father but to go for help. If I could outrun them.

"Once all this land belonged to the Navajos," Jimmy said. "Then you Anglos took it."

"That's right," my father said. "Kit Carson took it from you at the battle of Canyon de Chelly. You were great fighters. But you didn't have rifles. He took you prisoner and sent you to Fort Sumner. But your whole people walked back here together."

Jimmy spoke with one of the other Navajos; then he said, "You're right. He says his great-grandfather was on the Long Walk, and told him all about it."

The Navajos seemed impressed. They nodded several times and a more comfortable silence fell, while I wondered where my father had learned all this.

"It's hard for Navajos," Jimmy said. "Sometimes it seems like you Anglos got everything. All the Navajo has is his land. It's holy—every rock means something. Hank says you fought."

"Fought?" my father said. "Yes, I fought."

"I fought the Japs. I killed one of them with my bare hands. Maybe I shouldn't have done it. When I got back, I found my life was shortened. I started drinking. I really hated people and spent my time alone somewhere. You fought."

"Yes," my father said.

"So you know." Jimmy lit a cigarette from a glowing stick and took another drink.

"My father was what you call a medicine man. He told me the sickness I had was well-known and would get me in a lot of trouble. I believe in some of the Navajo religion and some of the Anglo religion. He took me to a holy place. I breathed in and out four times, and every time I could feel the sickness leaving me. There was a storm coming. I painted a picture of this. That ceremony really blessed me. I sang all night long, and everything was beautiful."

He stood and tossed the empty bottle away. I heard it explode on the rocks, somewhere beyond the firelight.

"But now, I don't know. Things are not what I thought they'd be. I'm not a good farmer. All I want to do is paint. They"—he indicated the other Navajos—"think I'm stupid. I owe Hank a lot of money. But I don't make money painting, and sometimes I get sick again."

Another silence fell. Then one of the Navajos said something else.

"He wants to know if you're working for Washington, "Jimmy said. "He thinks you're looking for this blasting powder the government uses to make the atomic bomb."

My father took the carnotite from the knapsack. "It looks like this," he said.

The Navajos passed it from hand to hand.

"Yes," Jimmy said, examining it carefully, "I've seen rock like this, long time ago—I don't remember the year. I was a boy, herding sheep near Sanhosteen. I went up a blind canyon and there was rock like this, lots of yellow rock."

He sounded like my father. It was strange to think your father looked at the world like an Indian.

Jimmy started to give it back. Their hands touched. "Keep it," my father said.

Before we left, the two of them stood for a moment, saying things I couldn't hear. Jimmy put his arms around my father and slapped his back. Boy, I thought, he's really loaded. The air outside the circle of firelight was cold. The other Navajos were still staring into the glowing fire, motionless as painted figures. Then we were walking again, toward the lights of the motel.

"Where'd you learn all that about Kit Carson?"

"At Fort Leavenworth Staff and Command School, when I was studying to get my captain's bars. I learned something in the army, Sonny; I didn't leave it a complete fool."

"What did he say to you?"

"Hell if I know. These Indians are the most sentimental people on the face of the earth. They should never let them drink. Do you know that boy is only thirteen years older than you? Terrible thing, what drinking does to them."

"I'm sorry about the Jeep."

"Don't worry about that," he said. "My work is done. I figured out where they should drill. Somewhere back along that road, the whole structure just sort of fell into place in my head."

We were getting close to the highway. Ahead, I could hear the soft roar of cars. "I was getting worried," I said. "For a while I thought we were going to have to spend the night out there."

"I slept in plenty of ditches in Europe," my father said.

A rig was brought in. By the second week, they reached the reservoir sandstone. The drill was stopped and samples brought up. Under ultraviolet light they were the yellow color of oil. But everyone already knew the well was going to be a big producer. The air around the rig was full of the odor of petroleum.

My father phoned Clint, who promised a big bonus. We drove to Gallup, and traded in our old car on a new Oldsmobile Rocket 88. It was turquoise and silver, like a piece of Navajo jewelry. Then we drove to Las Vegas, to meet Clint Yarborough for a big celebration. Before we left, my father went to the trading post and bought me the painting of the blue horse. The price had gone up to one hundred dollars.

In Las Vegas we stayed at the Desert Inn. It was like a big motel, with palm trees and a golf course. The bars were serving Atomic Cocktails. There was going to be a shot at the proving grounds the next morning. The papers said it was going to be one of the largest atomic bombs set off in the United States.

Clint Yarborough brought along a strange woman. He announced he was going to get a divorce and marry her. My mother took this hard. They took me to see Jack Benny and Gisele MacKenzie, then dropped me off and went out to party all night long. Sometime during the night, there was a terrible argument. My mother told me about it when they got back. I was already up and standing by the pool in my bathrobe, waiting for the bomb to go off.

"Your father told Clint Yarborough he didn't want to work for him," she said. She walked off toward their room. I saw my father coming slowly toward me, looking down at the ground.

The last seconds ticked off as we stood there together. In the flash, I saw on my father's face the same look of despair it always wore when he made money. To the north, what looked like the sun rose over the hills. People were shouting all over Las Vegas, but I stared at it calmly. I saw it as the release of billions of electron volts of energy, and felt no fear, only intense interest. My father had been right. Learn everything about what you feared, and you no longer feared it. In time, you could even learn to love it.

About the Author

William Hauptman was born in 1942 in Wichita Falls, Texas. He received a B.F.A. degree from the University of Texas and an M.F.A. from the Yale University of Drama. He is twice married and the father of a daughter and son.

Hauptman is best known as a playwright whose works have won many awards, including an Obie Award for his play "Domino Courts" and a Tony Award for his play "Big River." He is also a writer of short stories. "The Desert" appeared in a collection called *Good Rockin' Tonight,* which was published in 1988.

The characters in Hauptman's plays and short stories are almost always working-class, although the father in "The Desert" is a professional geologist, as was Hauptman's real father.

Many of the themes in his plays are also evident in "The Desert": an awareness of the land and the forces of nature, an alternation of scenes between "natural" and "civilized" places, friendships between two men, and characters in search of their identities.

Like his plays, "The Desert" is constructed episodically; that is, internal action moves through a series of loosely connected scenes rather than through a tightly structured plot.

Questions for Thought and Discussion

1. The story is told through the eyes of a son who, like the author himself, was called Bill and was a teenager during the 1950s. In order to set the story in time, list some of the many references which connect the story to the 1950s. In what specific year do you think the desert summer takes place? On what information do you base your calculation?

2. One of the story's episodes is a Saturday afternoon and evening described in memorable detail: the son sees the movie "Rebel Without a Cause"; he is caught drinking and dancing with the girl in the trailer; and his *Playboy* magazine is discovered. These events are followed immediately by the attempted theft of the Jeep. How was his relationship with his father affected by this series of events?

3. Imagine that you met this young teenager. How would you describe him? Do you think he is "strange," as the girl in the motel stated? Or do you think he is as ordinary as other teenagers would

be in similar circumstances?

4. The father advised the son to "learn everything about what frightens you." The obvious reference in the story is to the son's fear of the atomic bomb; by the end of the story he seems to have conquered this fear. But the implicit reference is to the changes in the son's feelings towards his father. What did Bill learn about his father that helped him to love him again?

5. How did you respond emotionally to the father? When were you sympathetic with him? What seemed to trigger his episodes of happiness and unhappiness? Why do you think he reported to his company the location to drill? How did you feel when he did?

6. What attitudes/values did the son observe in his father's life regarding:

war	the land and its resources
guns	the Navajos
drinking	work
money/material possessions	music

7. How do you think the son will be influenced in the long term by his father's life?

Parenting Issue:

Taking Advantage of
"No Problem" Moments

Although discipline is commonly thought to be correcting the misbehavior of children, it is actually much broader than this. What parents do when children are not misbehaving (the "no problem" times) is equally important. Being a parent also includes developing a sense that family members care about each other and enjoy being together. This sense of belonging to a caring family is generated by celebrating birthdays, holidays and special achievements; playing and working together; conversing at the table, in the bedtime routine or at other times; and supporting one another in times of crisis.

In this story, a family celebrates a birthday and, in doing so, enriches their life together. A deposit is made into their family relationships account from which happy memories later can be withdrawn.

5.
Birthday Party
Shirley Jackson

It was planned by Jannie herself. Jannie even went so far as to say that if she could have a pajama party she would keep her room picked up for one solid month, a promise so far beyond the realms of possibility that I could only believe that she wanted the pajama party more than anything else in the world. My husband thought it was a mistake. "You are making a terrible, an awful mistake," he said to me. "And don't try to say I didn't tell you so." My older son Laurie told me it was a mistake. "Mommy-O," he said, "*this* you will regret. For the rest of your life you will be saying to yourself 'Why did I let that dopey girl ever, *ever* have a pajama party that night?' For the rest of your life. When you're an old lady you will be saying . . . "

"What can I do?" I said. "I promised." We were all at the breakfast table, and it was seven-thirty on the morning of Jannie's eleventh birthday. Jannie sat unhearing, her spoon poised blissfully over her cereal, her eyes dreamy with speculation over what was going to turn up in the packages to be presented that evening after dinner. Her list of wanted birthday presents had included a live pony, a pare of roller scates, high-heeled shoes of her very own, a make-up kit with reel lipstick, a record player and records, and a dear little monkey to play with, and any or all of these things might be in the offing.

"You know of course," Laurie said to me, "I have the room right next to her? I'm going to be sleeping in there like I do every night? You know I'm going to be in my bed trying to sleep?" He shuddered. "Giggle," he said. "Giggle, giggle, giggle, giggle, giggle, giggle. Two, three o'clock in the morning—giggle, giggle, giggle. A human being can't bear it."

Jannie focused her eyes on him. "Why don't we burn up this boy's birth certificate?" she asked.

"Giggle giggle," Laurie said.

Barry spoke, waving his toast. "When Jannie gets her birthday presents can I play with it?" he asked. "If I am very careful can I play with just the . . . "

Everyone began to talk at once to drown him out. "Giggle giggle," Laurie shouted. "Don't say I didn't warn you," my husband said loudly. "Anyway I promised," I said. "Happy birthday dear sister," Sally sang. Jannie giggled.

"There," Laurie said. "You hear her? All night long—five of them." Shaking his head as one who has been telling them and telling them and *telling* them not to bring that wooden horse through the gates of Troy, he stamped off to get his schoolbooks and his trumpet. Jannie sighed happily. Barry opened his mouth to speak and his father and Sally and I all said "Shhh."

Jannie had to be excused from her cereal, because she was too excited to eat. It was a cold frosty morning, and I forced the girls into their winter coats. Laurie, who believes that he is impervious to cold, came downstairs, said "Mad, I tell you, mad," sympathetically to me, "Bye, cat," to his father, and went out the back door toward his bike, ignoring my insistence that he put on at least a sweater.

I told the girls to hold Barry's hand crossing the street, told Barry to hold the girls' hands crossing the street, put Barry's midmorning cookies into his jacket pocket, reminded Jannie for the third time about her spelling book, held the dogs so they could not get out when the door was opened, told everyone goodbye and happy birthday again to Jannie, and watched from the kitchen window while they made their haphazard way down the driveway, lingering, chatting. I opened the door once more to call to them to move along, they would be late for school, and they disregarded me. I called to hurry *up*, and for a minute they moved more quickly, hopping, and then came to the end of the driveway and onto the sidewalk where they merged at once into the general traffic going to school. I came back to the table and sat down wearily, reaching for the coffeepot. "Five of them are too many," my husband explained. "One would have been quite enough."

"You can't have a pajama party with just one guest," I said sullenly. "And anyway no matter who she invited the other three would have been offended."

By lunchtime I had set up four cots, two of them borrowed from a neighbour who was flatly taken aback when she heard what I wanted them for. "I think you must be crazy," she said. Jannie's bedroom is actually two rooms, one small and one, which she calls her library because her bookcase is in there, much larger. I put one cot in her bedroom next to her bed, which left almost no room in there to move around. The other three cots I lined up in her library, making a kind of dormitory effect. Beyond Jannie's library is the guest room, and all the other bedrooms except Laurie's are on the other side of the guest room. Laurie's room is separated by only the thinnest wall from Jannie's library.

When Jannie came home from school I told her to lie down and rest, pointing out in one of the most poignant understatements of my life that she would probably be up late that night. In fifteen minutes she was downstairs asking if she could get dressed for her party. I said her party was not going to start until eight o'clock and to take an apple and go lie down again. In another ten minutes she was down to explain that she would probably be too excited to dress later and it would really be only common sense to put her party dress on now. I said if she came downstairs again before dinner was on the table I would personally call her four guests and cancel the pajama party. She finally rested for half an hour or so in the chair by the upstairs phone, talking to her friend Carole.

She was, of course, unable to eat her dinner, although she had chosen the menu. She nibbled at a piece of lamb, rearranged her mashed potatoes, and told her father and me that she could not understand how we had endured as many birthdays as we had. Her father said that he personally had gotten kind of used to them, and that as a matter of fact a certain quality of excitement did seem to go out of them after — say — thirty, and Jannie sighed unbelievingly.

"One more birthday like this would *kill* her," Laurie said. He groaned. "Carole," he said, as one telling over a fearful list. "Kate. Laura. Linda. Jannie. You must be *crazy*," he said to me.

"I suppose your friends are so much?" Jannie said. "I suppose Joey didn't get sent down to Miss Corcoran's office six times today for throwing paper wads? I suppose Billy . . . "

"You didn't seem to think Billy was so terrible, walking home from school," Laurie said. "I guess that wasn't *you* walking with . . . "

Jannie turned pink. "Does my own brother have any right to

insult me on my own birthday?" she asked her father.

In honor of Jannie's birthday Sally helped me clear the table, and Jannie sat in state with her hands folded, waiting. When the table was cleared we left Jannie there alone, and assembled in the study. While my husband lighted the candles on the pink and white cake, Sally and Barry took from the back of the hall closet the gifts they had chosen themselves and lovingly wrapped. Barry's gift was clearly a leathercraft set, since his most careful wrapping had been unable to make the paper go right around the box, and the name showed clearly. Sally had three books. Laurie had an album of records he had chosen himself. ("This is for my *sister*," he had told the clerk in the music store, most earnestly, with an Elvis Presley record in each hand, "for my sister — not *me*, my *sister*.")

Laurie also had to carry the little blue record player which my husband and I had decided was a more suitable gift for our elder daughter than a dear little monkey or even a pair of high-heeled shoes. I carried the boxes from the two sets of grandparents, one holding a flowered quilted skirt and a fancy blouse, and the other holding a stiff, lacy, beribboned crinoline petticoat. With the cake leading, we filed into the dining room where Jannie sat. "Happy birthday to you," we sang, and Jannie looked once and then leaped past us to the phone. "Be there in a minute," she said, and then "Carole? Carole, listen, I *got* it, the record player. Bye."

By a quarter to eight Jannie was dressed in the new blouse and skirt over the petticoat, Barry was happily taking apart the leathercraft set, the record player had been plugged in and we had heard, more or less involuntarily, four sides of Elvis Presley. Laurie had shut himself in his room, dissociating himself utterly from the festivities. "I was willing to *buy* them," he explained, "I even spent good money out of my bank, but no one can make me *listen*."

I took a card table up to Jannie's room and squeezed it in among the beds; on it I put a pretty cloth and a bowl of apples, a small dish of candy, a plate of decorated cupcakes, and an ice bucket in which were five bottles of grape soda embedded in ice. Jannie brought her record player upstairs and put it on the table and Laurie plugged it in for her on condition that she would not turn it on until he was safely back in his room. With what Laurie felt indignantly was a complete and absolute disregard for the peace of mind and healthy sleep of a cherished older son I put a deck of fortunetelling cards on the table, and a book on the meaning of dreams.

Everything was ready, and Jannie and her father and I were sitting apprehensively in the living room when the first guest came. It was Laura. She was dressed in a blue party dress, and she brought Jannie a small package containing a charm bracelet which Jannie put on. Then Carole and Linda arrived together, one wearing a green party dress and the other a fancy blouse and skirt, like Jannie. They all admired Jannie's new blouse and skirt, and one of them had brought her a book and the other had brought a dress and hat for her doll. Kate came almost immediately afterward. She was wearing a wide skirt like Jannie's, and she had a crinoline, too. She and Jannie compared crinolines, and each of them insisted that the other's was much, *much* prettier. Kate had brought Jannie a pocketbook with a penny inside for luck. All the girls carried overnight bags but Kate, who had a small suitcase. "You'll think I'm going to stay for a month, the stuff I brought," she said, and I felt my husband shudder.

Each of the girls complimented, individually, each item of apparel on each of the others. It was conceded that Jannie's skirt, which came from California, was of a much more advanced style than skirts obtainable in Vermont. The pocketbook was a most fortunate choice, they agreed, because it perfectly matched the little red flowers in Jannie's skirt. Laura's shoes were the prettiest anyone had *ever* seen. Linda's party dress was of Orlon, which all of them simply *adored*. Linda said if she *did* say it herself, the ruffles never got limp. Carole was wearing a necklace which no one could *possibly* tell was not made of real pearls. Linda said we had the *nicest* house, she was always telling her mother and father that she wished they had one just like it. My husband said he would consider any reasonable offer. Kate said our dogs were just *darling*, and Laura said she *loved* that green chair. I said somewhat ungraciously that they had all of them spent a matter of thousands of hours in our house and the green chair was no newer or prettier than it had been the last time Laura was here, when she was bouncing up and down on the seat. Jannie said hastily that there were cupcakes and Elvis Presley records up in her room, and they were gone. They went up the back stairs like a troop of horses, saying "Cupcakes, cupcakes."

Sally and Barry were in bed, but permitted to stay awake because it was Friday night and Jannie's birthday. Barry had taken

Jannie's leathercraft set up to his room, planning to make his dear sister a pair of moccasins. Because Sally and Barry were not invited to the party I took them each a tray with one cupcake, a glass of fruit juice, and three candies. Sally asked if she could play *her* phonograph while she read fairy tales and ate her cupcake and I said certainly, since I did not think that in the general air of excitement even Barry would fall asleep for a while yet. As I started downstairs Barry called after me to ask if *he* could play *his* phonograph, and of course I could hardly say no.

When I got downstairs my husband had settled down to reading freshman themes in the living room. "Everything seems . . . " he said; I believe he was going to finish "quiet," but Elvis Presley started then from Jannie's room. There was a howl of fury from Laurie's room, and then *his* phonograph started; to answer Elvis Presley he had chosen an old Louis Armstrong record, and he was holding his own. From the front of the house upstairs drifted down the opening announcement of "Peter and the Wolf," from Sally, and then, distantly, from Barry's room, the crashing chords which heralded (blast off!) "Space Men on the Moon."

"What did you say?" I asked my husband.

"Oh, when the saints come marching in . . . "

"I said it seemed quiet," my husband yelled.

"The cat, by a clarinet in a loooow register . . . "

"I want you, I need you . . . "

"Prepare for blast: five — four — three — two — "

"The golden trumpets will begin . . . "

"It sure does," I yelled back.

"BOOM." Barry's rocket was in space.

Jannie had switched to "Hound Dog," and Laurie called on his reserves and took out his trumpet. He played without a mute, which is ordinarily forbidden in the house, so for a few minutes he was definitely ascendant, even though a certain undeniable guitar beat intruded from Jannie's room, but then Jannie and her guests began to sing and Laurie faltered, lost "the Saints," fell irresistibly into "Hound Dog," cursed, picked up "the Saints," and finally conceded in time for four — three — two — one — BOOM. Peter's gay strain came through clearly for a minute and then Jannie finished changing records and our house rocked to its foundations with "Heartbreak Hotel."

Laurie's door slammed and he came pounding down the back

stairs and into the living room. "Dad," he said pathetically.

His father nodded bleakly. "I'll stop them," I said, and went to the back stairs; in the kitchen I could only hear a kind of steady combined beat which shivered the window frames and got the pots and pans crashing together softly where they hung on the wall. I waited till the record was finished and then called up to Jannie that it was time for Sally and Barry to go to sleep and she must turn off the record player for the night.

She agreed amiably, saying that they had played every record three times anyway, and the phonograph stopped. Since it was close to nine-thirty I went up to Sally's room, and found that Sally had turned off *her* phonograph because she was getting sleepy. I went on to Barry's room, where Barry had fallen asleep in his space suit somewhere on the dim craters of the moon, fragments of leather all over his bed. I came back to the living room to find my husband back at his freshman themes and Laurie sprawled all over the couch reading *Downbeat*.

"See?" I said. "They were very nice about quieting down."

"Yeah," Laurie said. "*Suuuure.*"

I took up my book and sat down. It was so quiet I could almost hear the kitten purring on Sally's bed.

"I hope you notice," I said to my husband, "that—*just* as I said—it is perfectly possible for a group of five girls to have a quiet, almost grown-up party overnight. I used to do it all the time when I was a girl, and I can't remember that we ever made much of a disturbance."

"The trouble with girls," Laurie said in a tone of dire foreboding, "is that as soon as you don't know what they're doing, it's probably something no one in their right minds would ever think of."

"That's not the *only* trouble with girls," his father said.

We read peacefully in a silence broken only by Laurie's whistling between his teeth and an occasional remark from my husband or myself to the effect that if Laurie was unable to control that infuriating racket he could take himself off to bed. After a while Laurie went into the kitchen and consumed three cold cube steaks, a quart of milk, and two cupcakes. When he came back to the living room I said I hoped he was already regretting his unkind words about his sister and her friends, because—

Laurie lifted his head. "Now it starts," he said.

He was right.

After about half an hour I went to the foot of the back stairs and tried to call up to the girls to be quiet, but they could not hear me. They were apparently using the fortunetelling cards, because I could hear someone calling on a tall, dark man and someone else remarking bitterly upon jealously from a friend. I went halfway up the stairs and shouted, but they still could not hear me. I went to the top and pounded on the door and I could have been banging my head against a stone wall. I could hear the name of a young gentleman of Laurie's acquaintance being bandied about lightly by the ladies inside, coupled with Laura's name and references to a certain cake-sharing incident at recess, and insane shrieks, presumably from the maligned Laura. I banged both fists on the door, and there was silence for a second until someone said, "Maybe it's your *brother*," and then there was a great screaming of "Go away! Stay out! Don't come in!"

"Joanne," I said, and there was absolute silence.

"Yes, Mother?" said Jannie at last.

"May I come in?" I asked gently.

"Oh, yes," said all the little girls.

I opened the door and went in. They were all sitting on the two beds in Jannie's room. The needle arm had been taken off the record but I could see Elvis Presley going around and around. All the cupcakes and soda were gone, and so was the candy. The fortunetelling cards were scattered over the two beds. Jannie was wearing her pink shortie pajamas, which were certainly too light for that cold night. Linda was wearing blue shortie pajamas. Kate was wearing a college-girl-type ski pajama. Laura was wearing a lace-trimmed nightgown, white with pink roses. Carole was wearing yellow shortie pajamas. Their hair was mussed, their cheeks were pink, they were crammed uncomfortably together onto the two beds, and they were clearly awake long after their several bedtimes.

"Don't you think," I said, "that you had better get some sleep?"

"Oh, noooo," they all said, and Jannie added, "The party's just *beginning*." They looked incredibly pretty and happy, and so I said, with a deplorable lack of firmness, that they could stay up for just five minutes more, if they were very, very quiet.

"Dickie," Kate whispered, clearly referring to some private joke and the little girls dissolved into helpless giggles, all except Carole, who cried out indignantly, "I did not, I never *did*, I *don't*."

Downstairs again, I said nostalgically to my husband and

Laurie, "I can remember, when *I* used to have pajama parties
. . ."

"Mommy," Jannie said urgently from the darkness of the dining room. Startled, I hurried in.

"Listen," she said, "something's gone *terribly* wrong."

"What's the matter?"

"Shhh," Jannie said. "It's Kate and Linda. I thought they would
both sleep in my library but now Kate isn't talking to Linda
because Linda took her lunch box today in school and said she
didn't and wouldn't give it back so now Kate won't sleep with
Linda."

"Well then, why not put Linda . . ."

"Well, you see, I was going to have Carole in with me because
really only don't tell the others, but really she's my *best* friend of
all of them only now I can't put Kate and Linda together and
. . ."

"Why not put one of them with you?"

"Well, I *can't* put Carole in with Laura."

"Why not?" I was getting tired of whispering.

"Well, because they *both* like Jimmie *Watson*."

"Oh," I said.

"And anyway Carole's wearing a shortie and Kate and Laura
aren't."

"Look," I said, "how about my sneaking up right now through
the front hall and making up the guest-room bed? Then you can
put someone in there. Jimmie Watson, maybe."

"*Mother*." Jannie turned bright red.

"Sorry," I said. "Take a pillow from one of the beds in your
library. Put someone in the guest room. Keep them busy for a few
minutes and I'll have it ready. I just hope I have two more sheets."

"Oh, *thank* you." Jannie turned, and then stopped. "Mother?"
she said. "Don't think from what I said that *I* like Jimmie Watson."

"The thought never crossed my mind," I said.

I raced upstairs and found two sheets; they were smallish, and
not colored, which meant that they were the very bottom of the
pile, but as I closed the guest-room door behind me I thought
optimistically that at least Jannie's problems were solved, if I
excepted Jimmie Watson and the dangerous rivalry of Carole,
who is a natural platinum blonde.

Jannie came down to the dining room again in about fifteen
minutes. "Shhh," she whispered when I came in to talk to her.

"Kate and Linda want to sleep together in the guest room."

"But I thought you just said that Kate and Linda . . . "

"But they made up and Linda apologized for taking Kate's lunch box and Kate apologized for thinking she did, and they're all friends now, except Laura is kind of mad because now Kate says she likes Harry Benson better."

"Better than Laura?" I asked stupidly.

"Oh, *Mother*. Better than Jimmie Watson, of course. Except *I* think Harry Benson is goony."

"If he was the one on patrol who let your brother Barry go across the street by himself he certainly *is* goony. As a matter of fact, if there is one word I would automatically and instinctively apply to young Harry Benson it would surely be . . . "

"Oh, *Mother*. He is *not*."

I had been kept up slightly past my own bedtime. "All right," I said. "Harry Benson is not goony and it is fine with me if Kate and Carole sleep in the guest room if they will only . . . "

"Kate and *Linda*."

"Kate and Linda. If they will only *only* go to *sleep*."

"*Thank* you. And may I sleep in the guest room too?"

"What?"

"It's a big bed. And we wanted to talk very quietly about . . . "

"Never mind," I said. "Sleep anywhere, but *sleep*."

In about ten minutes Jannie was back downstairs again. "Listen," she said, when I came wearily into the dining room, "can Kate sleep in the guest room, too?"

"I don't care where Kate sleeps," I said. "I don't care where any of you sleep."

"Anyway, Kate and I are sleeping in the guest room, because now everyone is mad at Kate. And Carole is mad at Linda so Carole is sleeping in my room and Linda and Laura are sleeping in my library. Except I just really don't know *what* will happen," she sighed, "if anyone tells Laura what Linda said about Jerry. Jerry Harper."

"Why can't Carole change with Linda and sleep with Laura?"

"Oh, *Mother*. You *know* about Carole and Laura and Jimmie Watson."

"I guess I just forgot for a minute," I said.

"Well," Jannie said, "I only wanted to let you know where everyone was."

It was perhaps twenty minutes later when Laurie held up his hand and said "Listen." I had been trying to identify the sensation, and thought it was like the sudden lull in a heavy wind which has been beating against the house for hours.

I went up the back stairs in my stocking feet, not making a sound, and opened the door to Jannie's room, easing it to avoid even the slightest squeak.

Jannie was peacefully asleep in her own bed. The other bed in her room and the three beds in her library were empty. Reflecting upon the sorcery of Jimmie Watson's name, I found the other four girls all asleep on the guest-room bed. None of them were covered, but there was no way of putting a blanket over them without smothering somebody. I closed the window, and tiptoed away, called softly downstairs to let my husband and Laurie know that all was quiet, and got myself to my own bed and fell into it. I slept soundly until seventeen minutes past three by the bedroom clock, when I was awakened by Jannie.

"Kate feels sick," she said. "You've got to get up right away and take her home."

About the Author

Shirley Jackson was born in 1919 in San Francisco. She graduated from Syracuse University, married author and critic S.E. Hyman and was the mother of four children. She died in 1965.

Jackson authored numerous novels and short stories, many of which were adapted for film or stage. Her most famous work, "The Lottery," published in 1948, exhibits her theme of the dark side of human nature and society: most of humankind is profoundly misguided, perhaps incapable of enlightenment. Jackson was a master of the modern gothic tale. She brought a touch of the supernatural to a genre which traditionally requires a victimized protagonist (usually a young female), a brooding house or castle, madness, cruelty and terror.

But Jackson wrote in two styles. She could also write of the delight and humor of family life. Her novel *Life Among the Savages*, 1953, and "The Birthday Party," first published in *Vogue* in 1962, are wonderful examples of that.

Questions for Thought and Discussion

1. To review the setting of the story, list the interests of the children and other terms which associate the story with its original publication date of 1962.

2. The story is full of humorous comments family members make about (and to) each other, most of which are understatement by the parents and exaggeration by the children. How do you think their relationships were affected by their humor?

3. What impressed you about relationships within the family? What did not impress you?

4. The mother does many things to make the birthday a happy, memorable event. Why does she do this? Do you think she is resentful?

5. What role does the father play in the events of the evening? How typical of mothers and fathers are these parents in the ways they perform their mothering and fathering roles? How different would the birthday party (and the parents, themselves) be if the story took place today rather than in the late '50s or early '60s?

6. What is Jannie likely to remember about this birthday?

7. What birthday memories do you have?

Parenting Issue:

The Effects of Heavy Television Viewing

There exists today a substantial body of research literature documenting the effects of heavy television viewing. We know that viewing television displaces other activities; because of TV people today sleep less, read less, talk less and spend less time in religious activities and in other leisure activities. Children spend less time in outdoor play, since air conditioning keeps them inside and TV occupies their time.

We know that viewers become "narcotized" while watching television; they resist efforts to get them to stop and when they are forced to stop, they are irritable and restless.

We also know that television programming distorts the perceptions of viewers and affects their behavior. Heavy viewers, compared with light viewers, are more fearful of being personally assaulted, are less likely to intervene when someone else is being assaulted and are more aggressive themselves when experiencing conflict with others.

Such values as commitment to long-term relationships, cooperation, humility and respect for the dignity of others are undermined by television programming just like the value of nonviolence is distorted and weakened.

"The Veldt" is science fiction, a fantasy. But the "nursery" and its effects on the Hadley family, in Bradbury's story, are disturbingly similar to the effects of television.

6.
The Veldt
Ray Bradbury

ᴄᴡᴐ

"George, I wish you'd look at the nursery."

"What's wrong with it?"

"I don't know."

"Well, then."

"I just want you to look at it, is all, or call a psychologist in to look at it."

"What would a psychologist want with a nursery?"

"You know very well what he'd want." His wife paused in the middle of the kitchen and watched the stove busy humming to itself, making supper for four.

"It's just that the nursery is different now than it was."

"All right, let's have a look."

They walked down the hall of their soundproofed Happylife Home, which had cost them thirty thousand dollars installed, this house which clothed and fed and rocked them to sleep and played and sang and was good to them. Their approach sensitized a switch somewhere and the nursery light flicked on when they came within ten feet of it. Similarly, behind them, in the halls, lights went on and off as they left them behind, with a soft automaticity.

"Well," said George Hadley.

They stood on the thatched floor of the nursery. It was forty feet across by forty feet long and thirty feet high; it had cost half again as much as the rest of the house. "But nothing's too good for our children," George had said.

The nursery was silent. It was empty as a jungle glade at hot high noon. The walls were blank and two dimensional. Now, as George and Lydia Hadley stood in the center of the room, the walls began to purr and recede into crystalline distance, it seemed, and presently an African veldt appeared, in three dimensions, on all sides, in color, reproduced to the final pebble and bit of straw. The ceiling above them became a deep sky with a hot yellow sun.

George Hadley felt the perspiration start on his brow.

"Let's get out of this sun," he said. "This is a little too real. But I don't see anything wrong."

"Wait a moment, you'll see," said his wife.

Now the hidden odorophonics were beginning to blow a wind of odor at the two people in the middle of the baked veldtland. The hot straw smell of lion grass, the cool green of the hidden water hole, the great rusty smell of animals, the smell of dust like a red paprika in the hot air. And now the sounds: the thump of distant antelope feet on grassy sod, the papery rustling of vultures. A shadow passed through the sky. The shadow flickered on George Hadley's upturned, sweating face.

"Filthy creatures," he heard his wife say.

"The vultures."

"You see, there are the lions, far over, that way. Now they're on their way to the water hole. They've just been eating," said Lydia. "I don't know what."

"Some animal." George Hadley put his hand up to shield off the burning light from his squinted eyes. "A zebra or a baby giraffe, maybe."

"Are you sure?" His wife sounded peculiarly tense.

"No, it's a little late to be sure," he said, amused. "Nothing over there I can see but cleaned bone, and the vultures dropping for what's left."

"Did you hear that scream?" she asked.

"No."

"About a minute ago?"

"Sorry, no."

The lions were coming. And again George Hadley was filled with admiration for the mechanical genius who had conceived this room. A miracle of efficiency selling for an absurdly low price. Every home should have one. Oh, occasionally they frightened you with their clinical accuracy, they startled you, gave you a twinge, but most of the time what fun for everyone, not only your own son and daughter, but for yourself when you felt like a quick jaunt to a foreign land, a quick change of scenery. Well, here it was!

And here were the lions now, fifteen feet away, so real, so feverishly and startlingly real that you could feel the prickling fur on your hand, and your mouth was stuffed with the dusty uphol-stery smell of their heated pelts, and the yellow of them was in your eyes like the yellow of an exquisite French tapestry, the yellows of lions and summer grass, and the sound of the matted lion lungs exhaling on the silent noontide, and the smell of meat from the panting, dripping mouths.

The lions stood looking at George and Lydia Hadley with terrible green-yellow eyes.

"Watch out!" screamed Lydia.

The lions came running at them.

Lydia bolted and ran. Instinctively, George sprang after her. Outside, in the hall, with the door slammed, he was laughing and she was crying, and they both stood appalled at the other's reaction.

"George!"

"Lydia! Oh, my dear poor sweet Lydia!"

"They almost got us!"

"Walls, Lydia, remember; crystal walls, that's all they are. Oh, they look real, I must admit—Africa in your parlor—but it's all dimensional, superreactionary, supersensitive color film and metal tape film behind glass screens. It's all odorophonics and sonics, Lydia. Here's my handkerchief."

"I'm afraid." She came to him and put her body against him and cried steadily. "Did you see? Did you *feel*? It's too real."

"Now, Lydia . . . "

"You've got to tell Wendy and Peter not to read any more on Africa."

"Of course—of course." He patted her.

"Promise?"

"Sure."

"And lock the nursery for a few days until I get my nerves settled."

"You know how difficult Peter is about that. When I punished him a month ago by locking the nursery for even a few hours—the tantrum he threw! And Wendy too. They *live* for the nursery."

"It's got to be locked, that's all there is to it."

"All right." Reluctantly he locked the huge door. "You've been working too hard. You need a rest."

"I don't know—I don't know," she said, blowing her nose,

sitting down in a chair that immediately began to rock and comfort her. "Maybe I don't have enough to do. Maybe I have time to think too much. Why don't we shut the whole house off for a few days and take a vacation?"

"You mean you want to fry my eggs for me?"

"Yes." She nodded.

"And darn my socks?"

"Yes." A frantic, watery-eyed nodding.

"And sweep the house?"

"Yes, yes — oh, yes!"

"But I thought that's why we bought this house, so we wouldn't have to do anything?"

"That's just it. I feel like I don't belong here. The house is wife and mother now, and nursemaid. Can I compete with an African veldt? Can I give a bath and scrub the children as efficiently or quickly as the automatic scrub bath can? I cannot. And it isn't just me. It's you. You've been awfully nervous lately."

"I suppose I have been smoking too much."

"You look as if you didn't know what to do with yourself in this house, either. You smoke a little more every morning and drink a little more every afternoon and need a little more sedative every night. You're beginning to feel unnecessary too."

"Am I?" He paused and tried to feel into himself to see what was really there.

"Oh, George!" She looked beyond him, at the nursery door. "Those lions can't get out of there, can they?"

He looked at the door and saw it tremble as if something had jumped against it from the other side.

"Of course not," he said.

At dinner they ate alone, for Wendy and Peter were at a special plastic carnival across town and had televised home to say they'd be late, to go ahead eating. So George Hadley, bemused, sat watching the dining-room table produce warm dishes of food from its mechanical interior.

"We forgot the ketchup," he said.

"Sorry," said a small voice within the table, and ketchup appeared.

As for the nursery, thought George Hadley, it won't hurt for the children to be locked out of it awhile. Too much of anything isn't good for anyone. And it was clearly indicated that the children had been spending a little too much time on Africa. That *sun*. He could feel it on his neck, still, like a hot paw. And the *lions*. And the smell of blood. Remarkable how the nursery caught the telepathic emanations of the children's minds and created life to fill their every desire. The children thought lions, and there were lions. The children thought zebras, and there were zebras. Sun — sun. Giraffes — giraffes. Death and death.

That *last*. He chewed tastelessly on the meat that the table had cut for him. Death thoughts. They were awfully young, Wendy and Peter, for death thoughts. Or, no, you were never too young, really. Long before you knew what death was you were wishing it on someone else. When you were two years old you were shooting people with cap pistols.

But this — the long, hot African veldt — the awful death in the jaws of a lion. And repeated again and again.

"Where are you going?"

He didn't answer Lydia. Preoccupied, he let the lights glow softly on ahead of him, extinguish behind him as he padded to the nursery door. He listened against it. Far away, a lion roared.

He unlocked the door and opened it. Just before he stepped inside, he heard a faraway scream. And then another roar from the lions, which subsided quickly.

He stepped into Africa. How many times in the last year had he opened this door and found Wonderland, Alice, the Mock Turtle, or Aladdin and his Magical Lamp, or Jack Pumpkinhead of Oz, or Dr. Doolittle, or the cow jumping over a very real-appearing moon — all the delightful contraptions of a make-believe world. How often had he seen Pegasus flying in the sky ceiling, or seen fountains of red fireworks, or heard angel voices singing. But now, this yellow hot Africa, this bake oven with murder in the heat. Perhaps Lydia was right. Perhaps they needed a little vacation from the fantasy which was growing a bit too real for ten-year-old children. It was all right to exercise one's mind with gymnastic fantasies, but when the lively child mind settled on *one* pattern . . . ? It seemed that, at a distance, for the past month, he had heard lions roaring, and smelled their strong odor seeping as far away as his study door. But, being busy, he had paid it no attention.

George Hadley stood on the African grassland alone. The lions looked up from their feeding, watching him. The only flaw to the illusion was the open door through which he could see his wife, far down the dark hall, like a framed picture, eating her dinner abstractedly.

"Go away," he said to the lions.

They did not go.

He knew the principle of the room exactly. You sent out your thoughts. Whatever you thought would appear.

"Let's have Aladdin and his lamp," he snapped.

The veldtland remained; the lions remained.

"Come on, room! I demand Aladdin!" he said.

Nothing happened. The lions mumbled in their baked pelts.

"Aladdin!"

He went back to dinner. "The fool room's out of order," he said. "It won't respond."

"Or—"

"Or what?"

"Or it *can't* respond," said Lydia, "because the children have thought about Africa and lions and killing so many days that the room's in a rut."

"Could be."

"Or Peter's set it to remain that way."

"Set it?"

"He may have got into the machinery and fixed something."

"Peter doesn't know machinery."

"He's a wise one for ten. That I.Q. of his—"

"Nevertheless—"

"Hello, Mom. Hello, Dad."

The Hadleys turned. Wendy and Peter were coming in the front door, cheeks like peppermint candy, eyes like bright blue agate marbles, a smell of ozone on their jumpers from their trip in the helicopter.

"You're just in time for supper," said both parents.

"We're full of strawberry ice cream and hot dogs," said the children, holding hands. "But we'll sit and watch."

"Yes, come tell us about the nursery," said George Hadley.

The brother and sister blinked at him and then at each other. "Nursery?"

"All about Africa and everything," said the father with false joviality.

"I don't understand," said Peter.

"Your mother and I were just traveling through Africa with rod and reel; Tom Swift and his Electric Lion," said George Hadley.

"There's no Africa in the nursery," said Peter simply.

"Oh, come now, Peter. We know better."

"I don't remember any Africa," said Peter to Wendy. "Do you?"

"No."

"Run see and come tell."

She obeyed.

"Wendy, come back here!" said George Hadley, but she was gone. The house lights followed her like a flock of fireflies. Too late, he realized he had forgotten to lock the nursery door after his last inspection.

"Wendy'll look and come tell us," said Peter.

"She doesn't have to tell *me*. I've seen it."

"I'm sure you're mistaken, Father."

"I'm not, Peter. Come along now."

But Wendy was back. "It's not Africa," she said breathlessly.

"We'll see about this," said George Hadley, and they all walked down the hall together and opened the nursery door.

There was a green, lovely forest, a lovely river, a purple mountain, high voices singing, and Rima, lovely and mysterious, lurking in the trees with colorful flights of butterflies, like animated bouquets, lingering in her long hair. The African veldtland was gone. The lions were gone. Only Rima was here now, singing a song so beautiful that it brought tears to your eyes.

George Hadley looked in at the changed scene. "Go to bed," he said to the children.

They opened their mouths.

"You heard me," he said.

They went off to the air closet, where a wind sucked them like brown leaves up the flue to their slumber rooms.

George Hadley walked through the singing glade and picked up something that lay in the corner near where the lions had been. He walked slowly back to his wife.

"What is that?" she asked.

"An old wallet of mine," he said.

He showed it to her. The smell of hot grass was on it and the smell of a lion. There were drops of saliva on it, it had been chewed, and there were blood smears on both sides.

He closed the nursery door and locked it, tight.

In the middle of the night he was still awake and he knew his wife was awake. "Do you think Wendy changed it?" she said at last, in the dark room.

"Of course."

"Made it from a veldt into a forest and put Rima there instead of lions?"

"Yes."

"Why?"

"I don't know. But it's staying locked until I find out."

"How did your wallet get there?"

"I don't know anything," he said, "except that I'm beginning to be sorry we bought that room for the children. If children are neurotic at all, a room like that—"

"It's supposed to help them work off their neuroses in a healthful way."

"I'm starting to wonder." He stared at the ceiling.

"We've given the children everything they ever wanted. Is this our reward—secrecy, disobedience?"

"Who was it said, 'Children are carpets, they should be stepped on occasionally'? We've never lifted a hand. They're insufferable —let's admit it. They come and go when they like; they treat us as if we were offspring. They're spoiled and we're spoiled."

"They've been acting funny ever since you forbade them to take the rocket to New York a few months ago."

"They're not old enough to do that alone, I explained."

"Nevertheless, I've noticed they've been decidedly cool toward us since."

"I think I'll have David McClean come tomorrow morning to have a look at Africa."

"But it's not Africa now, it's *Green Mansions* country and Rima."

"I have a feeling it'll be Africa again before then."

A moment later they heard the screams.

Two screams. Two people screaming from downstairs. And then a roar of lions.

"Wendy and Peter aren't in their rooms," said his wife.

He lay in his bed with his beating heart. "No," he said. "They've broken into the nursery."

"Those screams—they sound familiar."

"Do they?"

"Yes, awfully."

And although their beds tried very hard, the two adults

couldn't be rocked to sleep for another hour. A smell of cats was in the night air.

"Father?" said Peter.

"Yes."

Peter looked at his shoes. He never looked at his father any more, nor at his mother. "You aren't going to lock up the nursery for good, are you?"

"That all depends."

"On what?" snapped Peter.

"On you and your sister. If you intersperse this Africa with a little variety — oh, Sweden perhaps, or Denmark or China — "

"I thought we were free to play as we wished."

"You are, within reasonable bounds."

"What's wrong with Africa, Father?"

"Oh, so now you admit you have been conjuring up Africa, do you?"

"I wouldn't want the nursery locked up," said Peter coldly. "Ever."

"Matter of fact, we're thinking of turning the whole house off for about a month. Live sort of a carefree one-for-all existence."

"That sounds dreadful! Would I have to tie my own shoes instead of letting the shoe tier do it? And brush my own teeth and comb my hair and give myself a bath?"

"It would be fun for a change, don't you think?"

"No, it would be horrid. I didn't like it when you took out the picture painter last month."

"That's because I wanted you to learn to paint all by yourself, son."

"I don't want to do anything but look and listen and smell; what else *is* there to do?"

"All right, go play in Africa."

"Will you shut off the house sometime soon?"

"We're considering it."

"I don't think you'd better consider it any more, Father."

"I won't have any threats from my son!"

"Very well." And Peter strolled off to the nursery.

"Am I on time?" said David McClean.

"Breakfast?" asked George Hadley.

"Thanks, had some. What's the trouble?"

"David, you're a psychologist."

"I should hope so."

"Well, then, have a look at our nursery. You saw it a year ago when you dropped by; did you notice anything peculiar about it then?"

"Can't say I did; the usual violences, a tendency toward a slight paranoia here or there, usual in children because they feel persecuted by parents constantly, but, oh, really nothing."

They walked down the hall. "I locked the nursery up," explained the father, "and the children broke back into it during the night. I let them stay so they could form the patterns for you to see."

There was a terrible screaming from the nursery.

"There it is," said George Hadley. "See what you make of it."

They walked in on the children without rapping.

The screams had faded. The lions were feeding.

"Run outside a moment, children," said George Hadley. "No, don't change the mental combination. Leave the walls as they are. Get!"

With the children gone, the two men stood studying the lions clustered at a distance, eating with great relish whatever it was they had caught.

"I wish I knew what it was," said George Hadley. "Sometimes I can almost see. Do you think if I brought high-powered binoculars here and —"

David McClean laughed dryly. "Hardly." He turned to study all four walls. "How long has this been going on?"

"A little over a month."

"It certainly doesn't *feel* good."

"I want facts, not feelings."

"My dear George, a psychologist never saw a fact in his life. He only hears about feelings; vague things. This doesn't feel good, I tell you. Trust my hunches and my instincts. I have a nose for something bad. This is very bad. My advice to you is to have the whole damn room torn down and your children brought to me every day during the next year for treatment."

"Is it that bad?"

"I'm afraid so. One of the original uses of these nurseries was so that we could study the patterns left on the walls by the child's mind, study at our leisure, and help the child. In this case, however, the room has become a channel toward — destructive thoughts, instead of a release away from them."

"Didn't you sense this before?"

"I sensed only that you had spoiled your children more than most. And now you're letting them down in some way. What way?"

"I wouldn't let them go to New York."

"What else?"

"I've taken a few machines from the house and threatened them, a month ago, with closing up the nursery unless they did their homework. I did close it for a few days to show I meant business."

"Ah, ha!"

"Does that mean anything?"

"Everything. Where before they had a Santa Claus now they have a Scrooge. Children prefer Santas. You've let this room and this house replace you and your wife in your children's affections. This room is their mother and father, far more important in their lives than their real parents. And now you come along and want to shut it off. No wonder there's hatred here. You can feel it coming out of the sky. Feel that sun. George, you'll have to change your life. Like too many others, you've built it around creature comforts. Why, you'd starve tomorrow if something went wrong in your kitchen. You wouldn't know how to tap an egg. Nevertheless, turn everything off. Start new. It'll take time. But we'll make good children out of bad in a year, wait and see."

"But won't the shock be too much for the children, shutting the room up abruptly, for good?"

"I don't want them going any deeper into this, that's all."

The lions were finished with their red feast.

The lions were standing on the edge of the clearing watching the two men.

"Now *I'm* feeling persecuted," said McClean. "Let's get out of here. I never have cared for these damned rooms. Make me nervous."

"The lions look real, don't they?" said George Hadley. "I don't suppose there's any way—

"What?"

"—that they could *become* real?"

"Not that I know."

"Some flaw in the machinery, a tampering or something?"

"No."

"I don't imagine the room will like being turned off," said the father.

"Nothing ever likes to die — even a room."

"I wonder if it hates me for wanting to switch it off?"

"Paranoia is thick around here today," said David McClean. "You can follow it like a spoor. Hello." He bent and picked up a bloody scarf. "This yours?"

"No." George Hadley's face was rigid. "It belongs to Lydia."

They went to the fuse box together and threw the switch that killed the nursery.

The two children were in hysterics. They screamed and pranced and threw things. They yelled and sobbed and swore and jumped at the furniture.

"You can't do that to the nursery, you can't!"

"Now, children."

The children flung themselves onto a couch, weeping.

"George," said Lydia Hadley, "turn on the nursery, just for a few moments. You can't be so abrupt."

"No."

"You can't be so cruel."

"Lydia, it's off, and it stays off. And the whole damn house dies as of here and now. The more I see of the mess we've put ourselves in, the more it sickens me. We've been contemplating our mechanical, electronic navels for too long. My God, how we need a breath of honest air!"

And he marched about the house turning off the voice clocks, the stoves, the heaters, the shoe shiners, the shoe lacers, the body scrubbers and swabbers and massagers, and every other machine he could put his hand to.

The house was full of dead bodies, it seemed. It felt like a mechanical cemetery. So silent. None of the humming hidden energy of machines waiting to function at the tap of a button.

"Don't let them do it!" wailed Peter at the ceiling, as if he was talking to the house, the nursery. "Don't let Father kill everything." He turned to his father. "Oh, I hate you!"

"Insults won't get you anywhere."

"I wish you were dead!"

"We were, for a long while. Now we're going to really start living. Instead of being handled and massaged, we're going to *live*."

Wendy was still crying and Peter joined her again. "Just a moment, just one moment, just another moment of nursery," they wailed.

"Oh, George," said the wife, "it can't hurt."

"All right—all right, if they'll just shut up. One minute, mind you, and then off forever."

"Daddy, Daddy, Daddy!" sang the children, smiling with wet faces.

"And then we're going on a vacation. David McClean is coming back in half an hour to help us move out and get to the airport. I'm going to dress. You turn the nursery on for a minute, Lydia, just a minute, mind you."

And the three of them went babbling off while he let himself be vacuumed upstairs through the air flue and set about dressing himself. A minute later Lydia appeared.

"I'll be glad when we get away," she sighed.

"Did you leave them in the nursery?"

"I wanted to dress too. Oh, that horrid Africa. What can they see in it?"

"Well, in five minutes we'll be on our way to Iowa. Lord, how did we ever get in this house? What prompted us to buy a nightmare?"

"Pride, money, foolishness."

"I think we'd better get downstairs before those kids get engrossed with those damned beasts again."

Just then they heard the children calling, "Daddy, Mommy, come quick—quick!"

They went downstairs in the air flue and ran down the hall. The children were nowhere in sight. "Wendy? Peter!"

They ran into the nursery. The veltland was empty save for the lions waiting, looking at them. "Peter, Wendy?"

The door slammed.

"Wendy, Peter!"

George Hadley and his wife whirled and ran back to the door.

"Open the door!" cried George Hadley, trying the knob. "Why, they've locked it from the outside! Peter!" He beat at the door. "Open up!"

He heard Peter's voice outside, against the door.

"Don't let them switch off the nursery and the house," he was saying.

Mr. and Mrs. George Hadley beat at the door, "Now, don't be

ridiculous, children. It's time to go. Mr. McClean'll be here in a minute and . . ."

And then they heard the sounds.

The lions on three sides of them, in the yellow veldt grass, padding through the dry straw, rumbling and roaring in their throats.

The lions.

Mr. Hadley looked at his wife and they turned and looked back at the beasts edging slowly forward, crouching, tails stiff.

Mr. and Mrs. Hadley screamed.

And suddenly they realized why those other screams had sounded familiar.

"Well, here I am," said David McClean in the nursery doorway. "Oh, hello." He stared at the two children seated in the center of the open glade eating a little picnic lunch. Beyond them was the water hole and the yellow veldtland; above was the hot sun. He began to perspire. "Where are your father and mother?"

The children looked up and smiled. "Oh, they'll be here directly."

"Good, we must get going." At a distance Mr. McClean saw the lions fighting and clawing and then quieting down to feed in silence under the shady trees.

He squinted at the lions with his hand up to his eyes.

Now the lions were done feeding. They moved to the water hole to drink.

A shadow flickered over Mr. McClean's hot face. Many shadows flickered. The vultures were dropping down the blazing sky.

"A cup of tea?" asked Wendy in the silence.

About the Author

Ray Bradbury was born in 1920 in Waukegan, Illinois. He attended schools in Illinois and California. After working as a newsboy for three years, he became a full-time writer, mostly of fantasy and science fiction. He is married and the father of four.

Bradbury is a prolific author of novels, short stories, plays, poems and scripts, whose work has won many awards and is represented in over 700 anthologies. He is best known for the novel, *The Martian Chronicles* (1950), and the short stories, "The

Illustrated Man" (1951) and "Fahrenheit 451" (1953), published in short story collections of the same names. The television series, "The Ray Bradbury Theatre," has helped make his name a household word.

Bradbury is considered one of America's best science fiction writers, although his work concerns itself not so much with technological wizardry as with the moral implications of scientific development. In "The Veldt," first published as a play in *The Wonderful Ice-Cream Suit* (1972), he warns of the potential human cost of improperly used technology.

Questions for Thought and Discussion

1. To review the facts of the story, list the mechanical services provided by the Happylife Home.

2. What was the genius and tragedy in the way the nursery worked?

3. What did the psychologist, David McClean, say was the cause of the problem in the nursery? What did he recommend? Do you agree with him?

4. Do you think the parents contributed to the tragedy? What do you think they could have done differently to have prevented it from happening?

5. How could this story be prophetic?

6. How are television, VCRs, and videogames similar to the nursery in the risks they pose? How are they different?

Parenting Issue:

Nurturing the Parent-Child Relationship

A parent-child relationship is like a savings account. Each gesture of support, expression of affection, word of encouragement and enjoyable moment together is like a deposit into the account which enriches the relationship. Relationships not nurtured in this way have less to draw on in times of stress and eventually become bankrupt of emotional connectedness. "Simple Arithmetic" is an example of this.

Letters between a son at a boarding school and his parents reveal a family torn apart, emotionally and physically. The son concludes dejectedly, ". . . you see that you are supposed to have your life and your parents are supposed to have their lives, and you have lost the connection."

7.
Simple Arithmetic
Virginia Moriconi
∽

Geneva, January 15

Dear Father:

Well, I am back in School, as you can see, and the place is just as miserable as ever. My only friend, the one I talked to you about, Ronald Fletcher, is not coming back any more because someone persuaded his mother that she was letting him go to waste, since he was extremely photogenic, so now he is going to become a child actor. I was very surprised to hear this, as the one thing Ronnie liked to do was play basketball. He was very shy.

The flight wasn't too bad. I mean nobody had to be carried off the plane. The only thing was, we were six hours late and they forgot to give us anything to eat, so for fourteen hours we had a chance to get quite hungry but, as you say, for the money you save going tourist class, you should be prepared to make a few little sacrifices.

I did what you told me, and when we got to Idlewild I paid the taxi driver his fare and gave him a fifty-cent tip. He was very dissatisfied. In fact he wouldn't give me my suitcase. In fact I don't know what would have happened if a man hadn't come up just while the argument was going on and when he heard what it was all about he gave the taxi driver a dollar and I took my suitcase and got to the plane on time.

During the trip I thought the whole thing over. I did not come to any conclusion. I know I have been very extravagant and unreasonable about money and you have done the best you can to explain this to me. Still, while I was thinking about it, it seemed to me that there were only three possibilities. I could just have given up and let the taxi driver have the suitcase, but when you realize that if we had to buy everything over again that was in the suitcase we would probably have had to spend at least five hundred dollars, it does not seem very economical. Or I could have gone on arguing with him and missed the plane, but then we would have had to pay something like three hundred dollars for another ticket. Or else I could have given him an extra twenty-five cents which, as you say, is just throwing money around to create an impression. What would you have done?

Anyway I got here, with the suitcase, which was the main thing. They took two week-end privileges away from me because I was late for the opening of School. I tried to explain to M. Frisch that it had nothing to do with me if the weather was so bad that the plane was delayed for six hours, but he said that prudent persons allow for continjensies of this kind and make earlier reservations. I don't care about this because the next two week-ends are skiing week-ends and I have never seen any point in waking up at six o'clock in the morning just to get frozen stiff and endure terrible pain even if sports are a part of growing up, as you say. Besides, we will save twenty-seven dollars by having me stay in my room.

In closing I want to say that I had a very nice Christmas and I apreciate everything you tried to do for me and I hope I wasn't too much of a bother. (Martha explained to me that you had had to take time off from your honeymoon in order to make Christmas for me and I am very sorry even though I do not think I am to blame if Christmas falls on the twenty-fifth of December, especially since everybody knows that it does. What I mean is, if you had wanted to have a long honeymoon you and Martha could have gotten married earlier, or you could have waited until Christmas was over, or you could just have told me not to come and I would have understood.)

I will try not to spend so much money in the future and I will keep accounts and send them to you. I will also try to remember to do the eye exercises and the exercises for fallen arches that the doctors in New York prescribed.

Love,
Stephen

New York, January 19

Dear Stephen:

Thank you very much for the long letter of January fifteenth. I was very glad to know that you had gotten back safely, even though the flight was late. (I do not agree with M. Frisch that prudent persons allow for "continjensies" of this kind, now that air travel is as standard as it is, and the service usually so good, but we must remember that Swiss people are, by and large, the most meticulous in the world and nothing offends them more than other people who are not punctual.)

In the affair of the suitcase, I'm afraid that we were both at fault. I had forgotten that there would be an extra charge for luggage when I suggested that you should tip the driver fifty cents. You, on the other hand, might have inferred from his argument that he was simply asking that the tariff—i.e. the fare, plus the overcharge for the suitcase—should be paid in full, and regulated yourself accordingly. In any event you arrived, and I am only sorry that obviously you had no time to learn the name and address of your benefactor so that we might have paid him back for his kindness.

I will look forward to going over your accounting and I am sure you will find that in keeping a clear record of what you spend you will be able to cut your cloth according to the bolt and that, in turn, will help you to develop a real regard for yourself. It is a common failing, as I told you, to spend too much money in order to compensate oneself for a lack of inner security, but you can easily see that a foolish purchase does not insure stability, and if you are chronically insolvent you can hardly hope for peace of mind. Your allowance is more than adequate and when you learn to make both ends meet you will have taken a decisive step ahead. I have great faith in you and I know you will find your anchor to windward in your studies, in your sports, and in your companions.

As to what you say about Christmas, you are not obliged to "apreciate" what we did for you. The important thing was that you should have had a good time, and I think we had some wonderful fun together, the three of us, don't you? Until your mother decides where she wants to live and settles down, this is your *home* and you must always think of it that way. Even though I have remarried, I am still your father, first and last, and Martha is very fond of you too, and very understanding about your problems. You may not be aware of it but in fact she is one of the best friends you have. New ideas and new stepmothers take a little getting used to, of course.

Please write me as regularly as you can, since your letters mean a great deal to me. Please try too, at all times, to keep your marks up to scratch, as college entrance is getting harder and harder in this country, and there are thousands of candidates each year for the good universities. Concentrate particularly on spelling. "Contingency" is difficult, I know, but there is no excuse for only one "p" in "appreciate"! And *do* the exercises.

Love,
Father

Geneva, January 22

Dear Mummy:

Last Sunday I had to write to Father to thank him for my Christmas vacation and to tell him that I got back all right. This Sunday I thought I would write to you even though you are on a cruze so perhaps you will never get my letter. I must say that if they didn't make us write home once a week I don't believe that I would ever write any letters at all. What I mean is that once you get to a point like this, in a place like this, you see that you are supposed to have your life and your parents are supposed to have their lives, and you have lost the connection.

Anyway I have to tell you that Father was wonderful to me and Martha was very nice too. They had thought it all out, what a child of my age might like to do in his vacation, and sometimes it was pretty strenuous, as you can imagine. At the end the School sent the bill for the first term, where they charge you for the extras which they let you have here and it seems that I had gone way over my allowance and besides I had signed for a whole lot of things I did not deserve. So there was a terrible scene and Father was very angry and Martha cried and said that if Father always made such an effort to consider me as a person I should make an effort to consider him as a person too and wake up to the fact that he was not Rockefeller and that even if he was sacrificing himself so that I could go to one of the most expensive schools in the world it did not mean that I should drag everybody down in the mud by my reckless spending. So now I have to turn over a new leaf and keep accounts of every penny and not buy anything which is out of proportion to our scale of living.

Except for that one time they were very affectionate to me and did everything they could for my happiness. Of course it was awful without you. It was the first time we hadn't been together and I couldn't really believe it was Christmas.

I hope you are having a wonderful time and getting the rest you need and please write me when you can.

All My Love,
Stephen

Geneva, January 29

Dear Father:

Well it is your turn for a letter this week because I wrote to Mummy last Sunday. (I am sure I can say this to you without hurting your feelings because you always said that the one thing you and Mummy wanted was a civilized divorce so we could all be friends.) Anyway Mummy hasn't answered my letter so probably she doesn't aprove of my spelling any more than you do. I am beginning to wonder if maybe it wouldn't be much simpler and much cheaper too if I didn't go to college after all. I really don't know what this education is for in the first place.

There is a terrible scandal here at School which has been very interesting for the rest of us. One of the girls, who is only sixteen, has gotten pregnant and everyone knows that it is all on account of the science instructer, who is a drip. We are waiting to see if he will marry her, but in the meantime she is terrifically upset and she has been expelled from the School. She is going away on Friday.

I always liked her very much and I had a long talk with her last night. I wanted to tell her that maybe it was not the end of the world, that my stepmother was going to have a baby in May, although she never got married until December, and the sky didn't fall in or anything. I thought it might have comforted her to think that grownups make the same mistakes that children do (if you can call her a child) but then I was afraid that it might be disloyal to drag you and Martha into the conversation, so I just let it go.

I'm fine and things are just the same.

Love,
Stephen

New York, February 2

Dear Stephen:

It would be a great relief to think that your mother did not "aprove" of your spelling either, but I'm sure that it's not for that reason that you haven't heard from her. She was never any good as a correspondent, and now it is probably more difficult for her than ever. We did indeed try for what you call a "civilized divorce" for all our sakes, but divorce is not any easy thing for any of the persons involved, as you well know, and if you try to put yourself in your mother's place for a moment, you will see that she is in need of time and solitude to work things out for herself. She will certainly write to you as soon as she has found herself again, and meanwhile you must continue to believe in her affection for you and not let impatience get the better of you.

Again, in case you are really in doubt about it, the purpose of your education is to enable you to stand on your own feet when you are a man and make something of yourself. Inaccuracies in spelling will not *simplify* anything.

I can easily see how you might have made a parallel between your friend who has gotten into trouble, and Martha who is expecting the baby in May, but there is only a superficial similarity in the two cases.

Your friend, is, or was, still a child, and would have done better to have accepted the limitations of the world of childhood—as you can clearly see for yourself, now that she is in this predicament. Martha, on the other hand, was hardly a child. She was a mature human being, responsible for her own actions and prepared to be responsible for the baby when it came. Moreover I, unlike the science "instructer," am not a drip, I too am responsible for *my* actions, and so Martha and I are married and I will do my best to live up to her and the baby.

Speaking of which, we have just found a new apartment because this one will be too small for us in May. It is right across the street from your old school and we have a kitchen, a dining alcove, a living room, two bedrooms—one for me and Martha, and one for the new baby—and another room which will be for you. Martha felt that it was very important for you to feel that you had a place of your own when you came home to us, and so it is largely thanks to her that we have taken such a big place. The room will double as a study for me when you are not with us, but we will move all my books and papers and paraphernalia whenever you come, and Martha is planning to hang the Japanese silk screen you liked at the foot of the bed.

Please keep in touch, and *please* don't forget the exercises.

Love,
Father

Geneva, February 5

Dear Father:

There is one thing which I would like to say to you which is that if it hadn't been for you *I* would never have heard of a "civilized divorce," but that is the way you explained it to me. I always thought it was crazy. What I mean is, wouldn't it have been better if you had said, "I don't like your mother any more and I would rather live with Martha," instead of insisting that you and Mummy were always going to be the greatest friends? Because the way things are now Mummy probably thinks that you still like her very much, and it must be hard for Martha to believe that she was chosen, and I'm pretty much confused myself, although it is really none of my business.

You will be sorry to hear that I am not able to do any of the exercises any longer. I cannot do the eye exercises because my roommate got so fassinated by the stereo gadget that he broke it. (But the School Nurse says she thinks it may be just as well to let the whole thing go since in her opinion there was a good chance that I might have gotten more cross-eyed than ever, fidgeting with the viewer.) And I can not do the exercises for fallen arches, at least for one foot, because when I was decorating the Assembly Hall for the dance last Saturday, I fell off the stepladder and broke my ankle. So now I am in the Infirmary and the school wants to know whether to send the doctor's bill to you or to Mummy, because they had to call in a specialist from outside, since the regular School Doctor only knows how to do a very limited number of things. So I have cost a lot of money again and I am very very sorry, but if they were halfway decent in this School they would pay to have proper equipment and not let the students risk their lives on broken stepladders, which is something you could write to the Bookkeeping Department, if you felt like it, because I can't, but you could, and it might do some good in the end.

The girl who got into so much trouble took too many sleeping pills and died. I felt terrible about it, in fact I cried when I heard it. Life is very crewel, isn't it?

I agree with what you said, that she was a child, but I think she knew that, from her point of view. I think she did what she did because she thought of the science instructer as a grownup, so she imagined that she was perfectly safe with him. You may think she was just bad, because she was a child and should have known better, but I think that it was not entirely her fault since here at School we are all encouraged to take the teachers seriously.

I am very glad you have found a new apartment and I hope you won't move all your books and papers when I come home, because that would only make me feel that I was more of a nuisance than ever.

Love,
Stephen

New York, February 8

Dear Stephen:

This will have to be a very short letter because we are to move into the new apartment tomorrow and Martha needs my help with the packing.

We were exceedingly shocked by the tragic death of your friend and very sorry that you should have had such a sad experience. Life can be "crewel" indeed to the people who do not learn how to live it.

When I was exactly your age I broke my ankle too — I wasn't on a defective stepladder, I was playing hockey — and it hurt like the devil. I still remember it and you have all my sympathy. (I have written to the School Physician to ask how long you will have to be immobilized, and to urge him to get you back into the athletic program as fast as possible. The specialist's bill should be sent to me.)

I have also ordered another stereo viewer because, in spite of the opinion of the School Nurse, the exercises are most important and you are to do them *religiously.* Please be more careful with this one no matter how much it may "fassinate" your roommate.

Martha sends love and wants to know what you would like for your birthday. Let us know how the ankle is mending.

Love,
Father

Geneva, February 12

Dear Father:

I was very surprised by your letter. I was surprised that you said you were helping Martha to pack because when you and Mummy were married I do not ever remember you packing or anything like that so I guess Martha is reforming your character. I was also surprised by what you said about the girl who died. What I mean is, if anyone had told me a story like that I think I would have just let myself get a little worked up about the science instructer because it seems to me that he was a villan too. Of course you are much more riserved than I am.

I am out of the Infirmary and they have given me a pair of crutches, but I'm afraid it will be a long time before I can do sports again.

I hope the new apartment is nice and I do not want anything for my birthday because it will seem very funny having a birthday in School so I would rather not be reminded of it.

Love,
Stephen

New York, February 15

Dear Stephen:

This is not an answer to your letter of February twelfth, but an attempt to have a serious discussion with you, as if we were face to face.

You are almost fifteen years old. Shortly you will be up against the stiffest competition of your life when you apply for college entrance. No examiner is going to find himself favorably impressed by "charactor" or "instructer" or "villan" or "riserved" or similar errors. You will have to face the fact that in this world we succeed on our merits, and if we are unsuccessful, on account of sloppy habits of mind, we suffer for it. You are still too young to understand me entirely, but you are not too young to recognize the importance of effort. People who do not make the grade are desperately unhappy all their lives because they have no place in society. If you do not pass the college entrance examinations simply because you are unable to spell, it will be nobody's fault but your own, and you will be gravely handicapped for the rest of your life.

Every time you are in doubt about a word you are to look it up in the dictionary and *memorize* the spelling. This is the least you can do to help yourself.

We are still at sixes and sevens in the new apartment but when Martha accomplishes all she has planned it should be very nice indeed and I think you will like it.

Love,
Father

Geneva, February 19

Dear Father:

I guess we do not understand each other at all. If you immagine for one minute that just by making a little effort I could imaggine how to spell immaggine without looking it up and finding that actually it is "imagine," then you are all wrong. In other words, if you get a letter from me and there are only two or three mistakes well you just have to take my word for it that I have had to look up practically every single word in the dictionary and that is one reason I hate having to write you these letters because they take so long and in the end they are not at all spontainious, no, just wait a second, here it is, "spontaneous," and believe me only two or three mistakes in a letter from me is one of the seven wonders of the world. What I'm saying is that I am doing the best I can as you would aggree if you could see my dictionary which is falling apart and when you say I should *memmorize* the spelling I can't because it doesn't make any sence to me and never did.

Love,
Stephen

New York, February 23

Dear Stephen:

It is probably just as well that you have gotten everything off your chest. We all need to blow up once in a while. It clears the air.

Please don't ever forget that I am aware that spelling is difficult for you. I know you are making a great effort and I am very proud of you. I just want to be sure that you *keep trying.*

I am enclosing a small check for your birthday because even if you do not want to be reminded of it I wouldn't want to forget it and you must know that we are thinking of you.

Love,
Father

Geneva, February 26

Dear Father:

We are not allowed to cash personal checks here in the School, but thank you anyway for the money.

I am not able to write any more because we are going to have the exams and I have to study.

Love,
Stephen

New York, March 2

NIGHT LETTER
BEST OF LUCK STOP KEEP ME POSTED EXAM RESULTS LOVE
FATHER.

Geneva, March 12

Dear Father:

Well, the exams are over. I got a C in English because aparently I do not know how to spell, which should not come as too much of a surprise to you. In Science, Mathematics, and Latin I got A, and in French and History I got a B plus. This makes me first in the class, which doesn't mean very much since none of the children here have any life of the mind, as you would say. I mean they are all jerks, more or less. What am I supposed to do in the Easter vacation? Do you want me to come to New York, or shall I just stay here and get a rest, which I could use?

Love,
Stephen

New York, March 16

Dear Stephen:

I am *immensely* pleased with the examination results. Congratulations. Pull up the spelling and our worries are over.

Just yesterday I had a letter from your mother. She has taken a little house in Majorca, which is an island off the Spanish coast, as you probably know, and she suggests that you should come to her for the Easter holidays. Of course you are always welcome here —and you could rest as much as you wanted—but Majorca is very beautiful and would certainly appeal to the artistic side of your nature. I have written to your mother, urging her to write to you immediately, and I enclose her address in case you should want to write yourself. Let me know what you would like to do.

Love,
Father

Geneva, March 19

Dear Mummy:

Father says that you have invited me to come to you in Majorca for the Easter vacation. Is that true? I would be very very happy if it were. It has been very hard to be away from you for all this time and if you wanted to see me it would mean a great deal to me. I mean if you are feeling well enough. I could do a lot of things for you so you would not get too tired.

I wonder if you will think that I have changed when you see me. As a matter of fact I have changed a lot because I have become quite bitter. I have become bitter on account of this School.

I know that you and Father wanted me to have some experience of what the world was like outside of America but what you didn't know is that Geneva is not the world at all. I mean, if you were born here, then perhaps you would have a real life, but I do not know anyone who was born here so all the people I see are just like myself, we are just waiting not to be lost any more. I think it would have been better to have left me in some place where I belonged even if Americans are getting very loud and money conscious. Because actually most of the children here are Americans, if you come right down to it, only it seems their parents didn't know what to do with them any longer.

Mummy I have written all this because I'm afraid that I have spent too much money all over again, and M. Frisch says that Father will have a crise des nerfs when he sees what I have done, and I thought that maybe you would understand that I only bought these things because there didn't seem to be anything else to do and that you could help me some how or other. Anyway, according to the School, we will have to pay for all these things.

Concert, Segovia (Worth it)	16.00 (Swiss Francs)
School Dance	5.00
English Drama (What do they mean?)	10.00
Controle de l'habitant (?)	9.10
Co-op purchases	65.90
Ballets Russes (Disappointing)	47.00
Librairie Prior	59.30
Concert piano (For practicing)	61.00
Teinturie (They ruined everything)	56.50
Toilet and Medicine	35.00

Escalade Ball	7.00
Pocket Money	160.00
77 Yoghurts (Doctor's advice)	42.40
Book account	295.70
Total	869.90 (Swiss Francs)

Now you see the trouble is that Father told me I was to spend about fifty dollars a month, because that was my allowance, and that I was not to spend anything more. Anyway, fifty dollars a month would be about two hundred and ten Swiss Francs, and then I had fifteen dollars for Christmas from Granny, and when I got back to School I found four Francs in the pocket of my leather jacket and then I had seventy-nine cents left over from New York, but that doesn't help much, and then Father sent me twenty-five dollars for my birthday but I couldn't cash the check because they do not allow that here in School, so what shall I do?

It is a serious situation as you can see, and it is going to get a lot more serious when Father sees the bill. But whatever you do, I imploar you not to write to Father because the trouble seems to be that I never had a balance foreward and I am afraid that it is impossible to keep accounts without a balance foreward, and even more afraid that by this time the accounts have gone a little bizerk.

Do you want me to take a plane when I come to Majorca? Who shall I say is going to pay for the ticket?

Please do write me as soon as you can, because the holidays begin on March 30 and if you don't tell me what to do I will be way out on a lim.

Lots and lots of love,
Stephen

Geneva, March 26

Dear Father:

I wrote to Mummy a week ago to say that I would like very much to spend my Easter vacation in Majorca. So far she has not answered my letter, but I guess she will pretty soon. I hope she will because the holidays begin on Thursday.

I am afraid you are going to be upset about the bill all over again, but in the Spring term I will start anew and keep you in touch with what is going on.

Love,
Stephen

P.S. If Mummy doesn't write what shall I do?

About the Author

Virginia Moriconi is something of a mystery. Two of her short stories written in first person suggest she had intimate knowledge of a privileged New England childhood, a failed American marriage with at least one child, an escape to Italy and a second Italian marriage.

"Simple Arithmetic" was written in 1963 and is included in a collection titled *The Mark of St. Crispin.* These short stories, written between 1953–77, were published in 1978 by an English publisher.

"Simple Arithmetic" is written in the epistolary form, highly unusual for a short story, but one which well documents this child's reactions to his parents.

Questions for Thought and Discussion

1. Describe Stephen's life at the boarding school.

2. Why was Stephen sent to boarding school?

3. What are his father's interests and concerns? And what are Stephen's?

4. List the undesirable traits which, according to his father's letters, Stephen is in danger of adopting. How appropriate do you think his father's concerns are?

5. The letters from Stephen's father are full of platitudes which are meant to teach Stephen how to live. One example: "Sports are a part of growing up." List other examples. Why is the advice so counterproductive?

6. Although intended to be so, the letters of the father are not uplifting. Why not? What is missing? What do you think Stephen needs?

7. Although the story doesn't tell us the reasons for the parents'

divorce, what do you think the problems in their relationship might have been?

8. Why do you think Stephen did not hear from his mother?

9. How do Stephen's letters change from the beginning to the end of the story? What do you think will happen to him in the next few years?

Parenting Issue:

The Need for Listening Skills

When children are bothered about something and feeling discouraged, humiliated, afraid, confused or weary (to name a few
examples of feelings), the most important task of parents is to
listen. This requires that they respond in ways which invite
children to talk about their feelings and that they be respectful of
their children's feelings when they do so. Few parents do this
well. Instead of showing interest and acceptance, they respond by
moralizing, criticizing, ridiculing, shaming, lecturing or ordering
the child to deal with the problem in a particular way, as the
parents of eleven-year-old Elizabeth do in this story.

8.
Jack of Hearts
Isabel Huggan
❧

People never expect me to be good at poker, probably because I have such an open face. (My mother used to say she could read me like a book. Her mistake, my advantage.) But what people don't know is that I've been playing poker since I turned eleven, and I play the game very well. I may appear flushed and agitated, but my excitement is impersonal, abstract. How can I explain this? What I love about poker is the tension, not the actual winning or losing but the tension between random chance and changeless numbers. Slap, slap, slap, slap, cards dealt and destiny beckons, two-and-a-half million different hands in a deck. It's the chance to play around with fate a little, that's what draws me in. It's what you do with what you've got; in every encounter with pure, immutable kings and queens and their rough and tumble shuffle with luck, you get the chance to make it work for you. There is no certainty anywhere, but in poker that's part of the game.

Sometimes strangers, especially men, are surprised by my lack of compunction in taking their money after I've bluffed my way to the pot. But as Aunt Eadie used to say, *If you can take 'em by surprise, then take 'em for everything they've got.* It was Aunt Eadie who first taught me how to play, strengthening in me a toughness that, sadly, only shows itself at cards. But then, poker isn't life, after all. I think Aunt Eadie said that, too. And of course that's what I first loved about the game. It wasn't like life at all.

Eadie was a friend of my mother's, not really an aunt. They'd worked together in Toronto when they were young, and even when they were 45 or 46 they seemed girlish when they were together. Eadie was still a secretary there, although not just any secretary, my mother was quick to point out, but an executive secretary to one of the top brokers in the whole stock exchange. I had no idea what a stock exchange was. The only exchange I knew was the one at Medley Sports where you traded in skates.

But it was easy to see that Aunt Eadie was important from the way she held herself, as if she were much taller than she actually was, and from the glamorous clothes she brought in her matching leather luggage. In winter she'd arrive in mink or in fox, and those first hellos at the door were wonderful for the smells — sweet fur and perfume and smoke. "You bring the city with you, Ead," my mother would say, and it was true; there was a roar of traffic and glitter of lights just in the way she smelled. Beneath her coat there was bound to be something bright and silky, for Eadie loved passionate, tropical colours. The image still lingering in my mind is of feathers and flowers, palm leaves and hibiscus, brilliant and foreign. In her lectures to me about the importance of appearance, my mother often used Eadie as an example of someone who bought the very best quality, someone whose handbag and shoes were always the same colour. But she'd usually end with a proviso such as "although Eadie does use a trifle too much rouge" or "of course, she is a little over-fond of jewellery." Nevertheless, her friend from the city had a flair for fashion that no woman in Garten could match, and she wanted me to take note. Perhaps she hoped that I might see in Eadie what she had been, before her life required only cotton housedresses and navy crêpe for going out.

As much as my mother admired her friend, my father disparaged her. He was critical not only of the way she dressed ("flashy") and looked ("hair is never that colour in nature"), but even of the way she laughed ("she has a loose laugh, Mavis, loose!"). She was, in a word, flamboyant — the epitome of all that Frank Kessler loathed and feared.

Their mutual interest in money, rather than giving them common ground, kept them apart, for my father had such distrust of the stock market that he lumped Eadie in with "all those crooks who make their money by speculation." Banking, on the other hand, he regarded as good solid business; careful investment and guaranteed interest, twenty-year bonds and steady growth. The money in *his* bank, he said, was clean.

"She's no better than a gambler," he'd say after one of Eadie's visits in which she had described her latest killing on the market. "Never was and never will be." He'd known her nearly as long as he'd known my mother. They had all met while working on Bay

Street during the thirties. Those years of Depression influenced the course of their lives not only by changing them, but by compressing and intensifying the qualities they already had. So Frank became more heavy and solid, weighed down by the metal in his soul, and Eadie hardened under the pressure to diamond-like sharpness. Mavis stayed, as she had always been, carefully in between, but when the chips were down, her money was on solidity. The house, the husband, the child.

Eadie had never married, and that too was a flaw that incurred my father's wrath. He thought that she "ran around" and that my mother oughtn't to invite her to the house in case I, his impressionable young daughter, be corrupted. Once, when they were arguing and didn't know I was listening from behind the kitchen door, he said, "She may be smart but she's still a tart!" and I nearly gave my hiding place away by laughing out loud.

"Don't worry so much, Frank," my mother would say on these occasions. "Elizabeth has no idea what Eadie's private life entails, nor need she ever. Eadie's got a lot of goodness in her, no matter what you say. I think it's just lovely to see her with a child after all she's been through. These visits are good for them both."

In fact, I was never so fond of Aunt Eadie as either of them seemed to think. After the preliminary questions about how school was going, she didn't have the slightest notion of what to talk to me about. Not until the night she taught me how to play poker did she ever give me anything of value.

It must have been sometime in early March, for there was still snow and it was the week after my disgrace at the ballet recital. Looking back I can see how lucky I was that Eadie and her cards came along when they did, offering me salvation and self-preservation. Somehow, when you're a child, you simply accept each turn of events as it comes, as if there is no other way for the world to be. And perhaps that *is* the right way to look at life. But looking back you can see how coincidence created your character, like coral atolls in the Pacific, building themselves slowly, moment upon moment.

By all odds, I should have been dragged down by the life I led as a child in Garten. I should still be there, or somewhere like it, forced under by my upbringing and all the expectations around me. But luck was with me, and small pockets of defiance multiplied beneath my surface, keeping me afloat, preparing me for that final escape.

Our ballet teacher, Mrs. Verser, always chose to hold the recital in the bleak weeks of late winter because it was then, she said, that most people needed an escape, a promise of springtime. What better harbingers of spring than the daughters of Garten leaping across the stage? Along with most of my friends, I had been enrolled in Saturday morning classes at the age of seven. We were beginning that long process of instillation, the steady drip, drip, drip of Values onto our skulls and into our brains. If our parents could only control our lives long enough, we would eventually achieve grace, tidiness and frugality.

But it wasn't for the social graces alone that Mavis Kessler sent her only child to dancing class. She hoped to combat my natural inelegance. I had inherited her face but my father's shape, with such large, heavy bones it became apparent early that I would be close to six feet when I grew up. In another time or place my body might have been prized for its usefulness in the fields. Unlucky soul, I was born generations away from where I should have been; and my sturdy peasant legs, which would have been well employed plodding down the turnip rows, were instead engaged in vain exercise at the barre. "Heels down!" Mrs. Verser would cry as we'd do our *demi-pliés,* lined up along the stage at the end of the high school gymnasium. Sharon's father was manager of the ironworks factory and had produced a portable barre of pipe for the class, to which we clung white-knuckled as we tried to bend and stretch without wobbling.

Strangely, I grew to like ballet, and looked forward to those sessions of music and movement, learning to hold my arms and legs just so, as careful of my body as if it were glass. Mrs. Verser had an assistant who gave tap lessons as well, but I was in full agreement with Mavis on this point; tap was crude and showy, ballet was *élégant.* There were no French phrases in tap, it was all just brush, brush, slide, step, hop. But in ballet there was the marvellous beauty and authority of Mrs. Verser calling out, *"Battements tendus! Maintenant, ronds de jambes! Changement de pieds!"* Across the floor we would go, obedient automatons responding to her clear high voice. *"Glissade jeté, assemblé, entrechat royale . . ."* She was a small woman who had been at Sadler's Wells (no-one knew for what or for how long), with a straight back and a snappy manner, and a sense of mission that made it possible for her to teach dance in Garten, year after year, without ever descending into self-pity or cynicism. She was like a small bright bird chirping

"Plus haut! Plus haut!"

The recital we worked toward was an event that beckoned with the same inviting gleam as the annual trip to the city hockey arena to see *The Nutcracker*. My mother and I always went with her friend June, whose daughter Trudy was in my ballet class. High up in the cavernous building we'd sit on wooden benches and pass my father's field glasses back and forth. I liked the music, its easy slippery flow, and I liked the predictable patterns of the dance. But best of all I liked the costumes, and would take away with me visions of velvet and satin and sparkling lace in which to clothe my own fantasies for another year. Even in the early years of our own recitals, when the junior classes only got to dress up as tulips or bunnies, I felt my heart would burst with excitement once I was zipped and buttoned into a new being. I would become, for the duration of the dance, whatever my costume dictated and thus discovered a release from the confines of Garten, transient but intense.

Ordinarily, Mrs. Verser made a big thing out of the story in each number she choreographed for us, and exhorted us to let our faces tell the tale. She made us practise various expressions — grief, joy, anticipation — along with the corresponding arm and leg movements, which we eventually interpreted as "up is happy, down is sad." But this year she put off telling us intermediate girls what our recital piece would be about, because she wasn't sure she could get the right costumes from Malabar's, and if she had to make changes at the last minute she didn't want any of us to be disappointed. So for the first few weeks of preparation she simply put us through specific drills and we learned step after step. I liked this way of doing it, having the movement clean and devoid of meaning; the purity of *des battements dégagés, des battements tendus.* I would have preferred to dance like that always, to let my own mood determine the way I rendered the steps. Often we danced without any sort of music, just Mrs. Verser on the side, steadily counting time.

There were five of us for this number — myself and Trudy, Sharon, Amy and Janet. Trudy and I kept up the pretence of liking each other for our mothers' sakes because they seemed so pleased to see their friendship extend into the next generation. But in truth we were bitterly jealous, especially in ballet class, each convinced she was better than the other. And so it was with open exultation that I noted, as we began fitting the various steps of the dance together, I was always in the middle. Trudy said it was only because I was the tallest, but I was sure I detected Mrs. Verser's subtle plan. She had been watching us practise and now it was clear to her that it was I, Elizabeth, who would be the star. I imagined what our costumes might be, and foresaw something for myself in glistening white satin and tulle. The other girls would be my handmaidens, circling around, perhaps bringing wreaths of flowers for me to wear in my hair. Twisted silk lilies would be perfect, I decided.

Still, I felt confused by some of Mrs. Verser's directions as the weeks wore on, and it became apparent that the movements required of me were much less intricate than the other girls'. And it struck me as a little odd, if I were indeed the best, that I should not be given the most difficult steps to execute, a series of *entrechats quatres*, perhaps. Nevertheless, I was completely unprepared for the letter that Mrs. Verser waved at us, that February morning, and I could barely absorb her words.

"And Malabar's have exactly what we need for our number, and in all the right sizes, at such reasonable cost I know your parents won't mind paying a little extra so that we can give a really *professional* show. And so this morning, girls, at long last, we can begin our rehearsal for *Jack of Hearts*, and you'll see now how all our steps go together to make a story. Quickly, let's get ourselves up on stage. Come, Elizabeth! We'll have to call you Jack from now on!" A smile, a wave of the hand, a clucking noise made to gather up the other four around me.

My heart fell like a stone. I stood there blinking, hardly able to breathe or think, with Mrs. Verser holding my elbow, ready to guide me across the stage in the opening steps.

"Now we can put our expression in, as we see what is happening in the dance. You, Jack, enter with the skipping step, a one-and-two-and-one, lightly and gaily, we must see you for what you are, a rogue, a knave, a stealer of hearts. You'll have a lovely red velvet heart, here on your arm. You must make these girls think you wear your heart on your sleeve, but really, you have no heart at all, you are the fellow who loves them and leaves them." She stopped for a moment, looking at my sad and bewildered face. She took my expression for puzzlement, and gave her tinkling, ballet-mistress laugh. "But of course, you are too young to know about the cruel ways of love. Well then, you must learn about life through the dance. You will see how, in the end, because you wouldn't choose *one* you are left alone by them all, broken-hearted." She made an extravagant gesture, hand to breast, head bowed.

I heard Trudy and Janet giggling, and knew they weren't laughing at Mrs. Verser the way we usually did. They were laughing at me because I was being humiliated, and they knew it, even if silly Mrs. Verser didn't. What worse shame than to play the part of a boy? It meant you were too ugly to be a girl, that's what it meant. I dreaded the mockery and teasing I knew would come as soon as we were changing in the dressing-room.

Somehow I got through the hour of rehearsal, noting at each turn how stupid I had been not to have seen before why I needed only *promenade* behind the other girls, as each one did her *pirouettes* and *arabesques.* Of couse, that's why I was left alone at the end. My body had never felt so thick and lumpish, so unable to extend itself through the air. Around me danced Trudy and Janet and Sharon and Amy, more daintily than ever, making little comments whenever they came near. When we joined hands or I had to touch them in any way, they shrank away with giggles. "Don't get fresh with me," Trudy whispered as we crossed the stage in our brief *pas de deux.* "You boy, you!"

Finally, out in the cold grey noon, I ran home by myself, able to give vent at last to pent-up tears. I was still crying when I let myself in the back door. My mother heard me and came from the kitchen, holding a saucepan by its handle. "You're late, Elizabeth, your father and I went ahead with lunch. I'll just put your soup on the tab . . . goodness' sake, Elizabeth, what's wrong?" Her forehead furrowed with sympathetic concern. That's all I needed to start a fresh flow of tears and I sobbed out my story with emphasis on the awful injustice of it all. As we so seldom met on any level where we could communicate, I think my mother entered my crisis eagerly. Here was something she could feel too. "What a shame," she kept saying, sensing only my disappointment about the costumes and not the very thing that made it unbearable. The shame, the shame. I wanted her to hold me in her arms and stroke my hair, but she just stood there with the saucepan between us, tears filling her eyes.

My noisy grief brought my father from the living-room, the Saturday *Globe* in his hand. "I have to be a boy in the recital, Daddy," I said. "I have to be a boy just because I'm the tallest." More tears, and the waiting for his sympathy to fall down around my shoulders like silk scarves, the way my mother's had. But not a chance. No coddling from Frank Kessler.

"Nothing wrong with being a boy," he said, folding the newspaper into a narrow roll. "Be proud of it. All the other girls will look the same, you'll be different. Right, Mavis? Whoever remembers the corps de ballet, eh? No sir, you be glad, Elizabeth. A chance to show character. A chance to shine. Nothing wrong with being a boy. You be glad." He tapped his open palm with the paper for emphasis and smiled down at me. I had an excruciating opening of the heart like the wrenching up of a window. I saw clearly and absolutely how much he had wanted me to be a son. And what he had was a daughter who wasn't even very good at being a girl.

I knew all about humiliation and I coped as I always did, by clenching myself in a corner of my closet, safe in the wool-smelling dark. I tried to work out for myself what meaning there might be in what had happened, but it seemed as if there were too many things to think of at once, and my mind became more and more jumbled. The conventions of dressing up were familiar enough to me, and yet I felt so confused. What did it *mean* to be a girl or a boy, and why did I feel like such a failure? It was as if I had touched with my toe a hidden switch that suddenly made visible, as far as my eye could see, limits and lines and boundaries over which one could not transgress without great danger and pain. There it was for the first time; the minefield of sex.

The night before the recital we all met in the gymnasium for the dress rehearsal. The costumes, some made by mothers, and some ordered from Toronto, were placed on tables along the walls with crayoned signs above them. Under *Jack of Hearts* lay the Malabar boxes; I felt their unopened threat from across the room. As I crossed the floor the babble of voices around me became nightmarish, filling my head as if ten insane radio stations were screaming through at the same spot on the dial. I couldn't move, I held back as my mother went on ahead. She was determined to show me how to make the best of things.

"Ginny, stand still, the waist needs tucking." "Where are the wings, the blue wings?" "All tulips, on stage, five minutes." "Tell Susan to hitch up, her ankles are wrinkled." "Ruthie, leave Judy alone, get your slippers on." At the centre of the madness, Mrs. Verser, resplendent in sapphire silk, her small body arched with a thrilling tension. She loved the dress rehearsal, she told us, possibly even more than the actual performance night itself. This was it, the glamour of the dance in all its potential. Perhaps here she could still imagine that her girls would, with the donning of their costumes, materialize into lithe, graceful dancers. There was still a chance, there was still a hope.

Once Malabar's boxes were opened, I lost all hope. Out of the tissue paper wrappings came pastel dresses, pale green and apricot, lemon and lavender, just as Mrs. Verser had promised. And then mine; short grey velvet pants caught with an elastic band at the thigh so that they looked full and blousy, and a matching long-sleeved jacket with padded shoulders which would, as one mother noted, help to make me look "even more boyish." I was to wear high red knee socks to accent the red velvet heart, and to top it all off, a jaunty velvet hat with a red feather, to pull down over my head at one side.

"If Elizabeth's hair were just a teensie bit shorter, Mrs. Kessler, I think the whole effect would be so much more, ah, professional," suggested Mrs. Verser in that tone that implied there were no options. My hair was already bobbed at my ears, thick straight brown hair that stuck out oddly from beneath the cap. I could tell from my mother's silence, as I tried various angles, that she would have me on the high stool in the kitchen for a trim before Mrs. Verser set eyes on me again.

I went off to the dressing-room to try on the costume, and then regarded myself in the mirror above the row of sinks. I did, I looked like a big fat boy. I took off my glasses and was met by a blessed blur of grey and red. That was better. If only that was how the rest of the world would see me, I thought, a grey blur on stage. We were never allowed to wear our glasses at the recital, and dress rehearsal was usually the first time the more myopic of us danced blind. It meant there was lots of bumping and joking backstage and I could manage to avoid looking at the jeering faces of my dancing partners as we waited for our turn. But once out on the brightly lit stage, I could not help but see the glint in Trudy's eyes.

At the end of our number I was flushed with hope that once Mavis had seen her daughter being made a fool of, she would make Mrs. Verser change the dance, even at this late moment. But no, she was caught up in my father's enthusiasm for teaching me to face the challenge, and she was bound now to help me be brave. "This will help form your character," she told me on the way home, her voice all cheery. But I could tell from her expression that she was as devastated as I, and would have been much happier as the mother of Trudy, whose blond curls were perfectly set off by the apricot dress. Or Amy, who had a solo toe number to *The Surrey With the Fringe on Top* in the second half of the program. These were the daughters she should have had. For unlike Frank, she had wanted a girl; she told me she had prayed all during her pregnancy that I would be a girl.

She was 35 when I was born, as late to motherhood as she had been to marriage seven years before. She had met my father when he was starting his bank career at the Imperial's main office, long before he was near any kind of managerial level. When they wed, the Depression had the country in its grip, and perhaps they put off parenthood until they could save a little money. That's the kind of sensible move I would expect them to have made. Or perhaps they tried and tried, and I was the result of diligence and perseverance. Or perhaps she had planned to keep on working, as Eadie did, and I was a mistake that altered her expectations. I have no idea. The whole matter was so closely allied to sex that it was never possible to ask questions. It was all part of my mother's private life to which I only had secret access—rifling through her bureau drawers or eavesdropping on telephone conversations.

As soon as I wake the next morning I determine I will get out of the recital if I can. I complain of stomach cramps and a headache immediately upon rising, and later tell my mother I feel feverish. I drink hot water out of the bathroom tap before asking her to take my temperature. The thermometer registers 106 degrees, and Mavis has the presence of mind to make me lie down where she can keep an eye on me for an hour before she takes it again. Then she cuts my hair. I try to find the courage to throw myself down the cellar stairs, but each time I lunge forward my hand always goes involuntarily out to the railing. It's no good, there is no way out.

After lunch my mother announces that she and I are going to go downtown and that she is going to buy me a surprise. I feel I've had enough surprises lately but she has a sprightly look that means she has decided to be nice to me and I know there's no point in resisting. In our bare feet I am as tall as Mavis, but she is wearing her high-heeled winter boots that have a ruff of black fur around the ankle, and so I feel smaller and daughter-like as we walk along. She is wearing her black Persian lamb jacket with its matching hat and she looks very smart and important. My mother always dresses to go downtown, even though the shopping district is only four blocks from our house. It is a matter of pride with her to keep up her city habits; she does not expect to be in Garten forever, she says.

She tells me repeatedly not to scuff my feet and to walk properly but I keep forgetting and let my feet slide and drag along the sandy ice on the pavement. I have begun to feel curious about what she is going to buy. I know full well that her idea of a good surprise and mine are entirely different. I would like a cream-filled long-john from Bauman's Bakery, or a *Photoplay* magazine, or a box of coloured pencils, and I expect to be disappointed. We walk the full length of the street, my mother nodding and waving to several acquaintances, until we reach my father's bank standing squarely up to the corner, like a great ship anchored in the harbour.

We turn down the street there and stop outside. The Beverly Shoppe, Lingerie and Women's Apparel. My mother and her friends always call it The Beverly Shop-pay, making fun of the pretensions of its owner, a widow with whom they all play bridge on Wednesday afternoons, her half-day closing. Her name is Beverly Mutch, and she is a tall, dry stick of a woman with whom my mother loves to talk about quality. They will stand together fingering cloth and murmuring until my skin crawls and itches and I stand before the trio of mirrors in whatever sensible outfit my mother is buying for me. I loathe this store. It is where my mother buys my navy blue jumpers and bloomers, and all my wool and cotton underwear and starchy blouses. Nothing she ever buys here is beautiful or nice, it is always just good quality, meant to last.

Mavis bends toward me at the door of the shop, her voice a low, conspiratorial whisper. "Here's where we go for the surprise," she says, smiling at me in a flushed, earnest way. "I'm going to buy you a brassière. I think it's time."

She steps back and looks at me, hoping for some reaction on my part. I am stunned. She really *has* surprised me. All the blood in my body seems to be rushing to my head and I feel very hot and red around the eyes. I am still blushing when we go into the store, hating as always the little chime that rings ding-ding-dong when the door opens and closes. I would go crazy if I worked in a place where there was a bell like that, I think. No wonder Mrs. Mutch always seems so edgy and can never settle her eyes on your face.

"Ah, Elizabeth!" She comes from behind her small counter where she has been smoking a cigarette and reading a magazine. She clasps her hands and smiles at me, intimate, benevolent. "So this is the big day."

I know right away that she does not mean the ballet recital, that my mother has phoned ahead and made an appointment. It has all been plotted behind my back. I am trapped. I do not want a brassière. Nobody else in my grade has one and I do not want to be first. If I am first I will suffer for it. I would much rather be third.

"Just take off your parka, dear, and we'll go to the back for a fitting," says Mrs. Mutch. My mother gives me a little push with her hand on the place between my shoulderblades that means "behave yourself" and so I obediently follow the other woman to the room separated from the rest of the shop by a heavy pink curtain. "Take off your blouse," Mrs Mutch says, as she unrolls a frayed yellow tape measure, holding it out straight, ready to "do" me. The curtain moves aside and my mother's face appears, anxious to be involved in every step of the project.

"What do you think, Bev?" she asks, as Mrs. Mutch's thin fingers pull the tape tightly around my chest.

"Oh yes, Mavis, by all means," she says, appraising my breasts through the woven cotton undershirt. "Now, Elizabeth," she continues, turning back to me, "I'm going to bring you a number of bras to try on. I think you'd like to try them on yourself, wouldn't you?" She smiles, aware of how alert and sensitive she is being. "After you have each one on, your mother and I will come have a look. Like a little fashion show." A final cigarette-stained smile, and she ducks through the curtain, to join my mother in preserving my modesty.

I hear their whispered voices. "At the rehearsal," my mother is saying. "Just hadn't noticed before . . . bouncing up and down . . . in this costume especially . . . really kind of funny, but . . . I knew you could help, Bev . . . probably more puppy fat than anything else, but still . . ."

I run my hands over the coarse undershirt and think how much I have always complained about wearing it, and how much now I don't want to part with it. There is nowhere to turn. Even my mother thinks I'm laughable.

The brassières are all stiff and unkind, digging into my skin along the edges. White cotton, pointy, harsh, unnatural. My discomfort grows with each attempt and with Mrs. Mutch's professional prodding and poking. She and my mother are having a lovely time, laughing and reminiscing, perhaps trying to make me feel a part of their charmed circle of womanhood. I don't know.

"They really don't feel very nice," I finally say to Mrs. Mutch as she is hooking me up at the back.

"Oh dear, it's only because they're new," she says. "You'll get used to the feeling in no time. But say now, I do have a junior in satin, maybe that will be more comfy. Just a minute now."

Mutterings from behind the curtain, little murmurs and "ahs" from them both, then a blue satin brassière is thrust in. "Try this, dear," she says, and I do. It feels cool and costume-like, it is at least bearable.

"Now then, Elizabeth, isn't this a special surprise?" asks my mother as we stand at the cash register.

"Do I have to wear it all the time now?" I inquire in my most plaintive tone, hoping against hope for a no.

"Support is terribly important for big girls," Mrs. Mutch assures us, and goes on to warn of the horrors of sag and droop. "Once you get used to this one, dear, we'll get you into a nice everyday cotton and you'll feel just fine."

"You'll wear it tonight for a start," says Mavis as we head back home. She is not cross but she is very decisive. She will not have her daughter's breasts bouncing on stage, not for anything.

Right after supper I walk to the school, dreading the taunts I am sure will come. But the other girls are far too absorbed in their powdering and rouging to notice my newly short hair or the shiny blue brassière. I hunch in a corner, pulling on the heavy velvet suit. It makes me sweat before I even move. I get a little brown pancake rubbed on by one of the mothers, who tells me I look like a perfect little man, a real heartbreaker. I tell her I feel like throwing up, and she tells me to go to the washroom and be careful not to spatter the velvet. I go, but I can't make myself vomit even by sticking a finger down my throat. I wonder about falling against the porcelain toilet bowl and knocking myself out, but there's not enough room in the cubicle and I give up. I feel desperate but there are no choices. I am in a nightmare out of which I cannot wake.

Even when we have to run across the snow outside to get in the side door of the stage, the bright cold March night can't clear away the colours of the dream. We crowd together behind the curtain and make little peepholes to look out. The gymnasium is full, all of Garten seems to be there, restless on their metal folding chairs. I can't find my parents, I can't see farther than the first row where Mr. Willie, editor of the weekly *Enterprise*, sits with his camera and flash on his knee. Mrs. Verser has made him promise not to take pictures during the performance but he is there at the front just the same.

Then, lowered lights, darkness, a spotlight on Mrs. Verser introducing the junior class and *The Coming of Spring*. We mass together in the wings, waiting our turns, listening to the clatter of applause. *Spanish Dancers* follow on the heels of *Southern Belles*, and after *Anchors Aweigh* there we are, out in the warm bath of light, the phonograph needle falls down on the record and the music swells up and out of the loudspeakers and I am skipping, hands on my hips, across the stage. I think I hear a murmur from the audience but it is such an anonymous sound I have no way of judging what it means. The girls in their frothy dresses weave around me and I dance with each one, and with them all, trying to smile and wink the way Mrs. Verser showed me, putting expression in. My face is very hot from the exertion of the dance and from the effort of not crying. I am weighted down by the velvet suit, and the brassière cuts and binds along my midriff and under my arms. When I raise my arms the straps dig into my shoulders. I think no one in the world knows how unhappy I am, and somehow that helps. There is comfort in solitude.

Before I can believe it the music is over and we are joining hands for a curtain call. Trudy smiles at me in an open and friendly way and I know it is because our mothers are watching. She and Sharon and Amy and Janet all make sweeping, graceful curtsies, their heads bent low over their pointed toes, and I give my bobbing bow, then fall to one knee in the centre so that they can cluster around me. Suddenly, unrehearsed, Trudy jumps up and perches on my extended knee and fluffs her skirt, and Mr. Willis springs up and snaps a picture. The flash leaves little green explosions in my eyes, and the sound of applause is now mixed with laughter. I am feeling very odd, as if I am swelling up. But I get to my feet with the others, retreat back ten steps, and see Mrs. Verser in the wings urging us forward for one last curtain call. As we skip forward to the footlights, I can feel it, I can feel the pressure building. The summoning of the dark abyss. The others step back and I lean forward, on the edge of the stage. Into the darkness, driven.

"I'm really a girl," I shout, my voice horribly high and tinny. The noise in the gym lulls and I shout again, as loud as I can, into the startled silence. "I'm really a girl, I'm really a girl!"

My parents' scoldings that night were probably tempered by some instinctive sympathy, but it still seemed to me that my mother's major concern was *her* humiliation, not mine. My father's theme was his great disappointment at the weakness of my character. "Hysteria, Elizabeth, that's what that was! No self-control! No call for such a display, none at all!"

What could I say to explain myself? Nothing. I sat, redfaced and weeping as they reproached me, unable to tell them why I had called out, unable to understand myself why I had done it. All I knew was that I had disgraced not only myself and our household but the entire ballet school, and the next day was made to write a letter of apology to Mrs. Verser. I didn't care, I was past caring, no further punishment could equal the dance itself.

Surprisingly, the matter was never spoken of again. Mr. Willis, whether through my father's intervention or his own kindly intuition, did not publish the photograph in the paper, and used a full-length picture of Amy *en pointe* with his recital review. I was so relieved I felt no envy of Amy at all. She and Trudy and the others no longer called me "Jack" at school; it seemed as if everyone had set about forgetting the incident. It was almost as if I had frightened them all with the intensity of my pain.

My mother might have made more of the whole thing if there had not been the lucky diversion of a visit from Eadie, who arrived on Monday for a four-day visit. Normally she only stayed one or two days, but this time, for some reason I was not allowed to know, Aunt Eadie needed a nice long rest away from the city. As usual, she brought gifts: a lacy slip for Mavis, silver cufflinks for Frank, and for me a box of discarded costume jewellery and scarves, last season's accessories but a gift that never failed to please me. Once, these things had all gone in my dressing-up box, but now they had a more immediate appeal. I found a ring of rhinestone chips set in red enamel, and put it on my fourth finger. A little loose, but spectacular.

My mother and her friend settled into a routine of secretive, girlish behaviour that produced in my father a more clipped and

aloof manner than usual. He contrived to be out at meetings both
Tuesday and Wednesday evenings, which suited my mother just
fine. She and Aunt Eadie sat at the kitchen table, smoking Black
Cat cigarettes and drinking tea and endlessly, endlessly talking.
Sometimes they would laugh so hard they'd lean back in their
chairs, gulping air and wiping away tears, and sometimes they
seemed really to be crying, but in a soft, resigned sort of way.
They'd barely notice my coming or going in the kitchen after
supper, and if they did I was always told to get along up to my
room. But my mother always said it nicely, and would slip her arm
around my waist for a moment before giving me a little push off.
She looked rosy and happy. She was always nicer when Eadie
was there; the lines that had begun to pucker her small mouth into
a tight purse seemed, suddenly, not to be there.

On the Thursday night there was a "coffee and dessert" meeting at the church, being given by the Couples' Club for the new
minister. It was the kind of social event that neither Frank nor
Mavis could resist, but it was also not the sort of thing they could
take Eadie to—nor would she have gone. She waved them out
the door, reassuring them that she looked forward to some time
alone with me. I felt nervous and embarrassed, wondering
whether I was now obliged to stay down in the living-room with
her all evening.

As soon as they disappeared, Aunt Eadie said, "Well, let's get
out the cards, Elizabeth, we'll pass the time with a little poker."

I was relieved that she wasn't intending to talk to me, but
worried because the only card games I knew were Rummy and
Fish. I found the good deck my parents used at their Bridge Club,
and confessed my ignorance. She had brought down her purse
from her bedroom, and opened the clasp slowly as she spoke.

"Okay, then," she said. "We'll make a deal. I'll teach you how
to play poker, and you'll keep a little secret." She took from her
purse a flat silver flask engraved with flowers and fancy scroll-
work. "Your Aunt Eadie is going to have a drink or two. God
knows after three days in Garten I deserve it. And you're not
going to tell a soul. How's that for an idea?" She flashed the same
kind of warm smile she gave my mother when they were whispering, and I felt a terrific pleasure spreading all through me. I
nodded, speechless, watching her fingers working, undoing the
lid of the flask. It was a large cap,meant to be used as a measure,
and she poured the amber liquid into it with a slow, steady hand.

"Whisky," she said, looking at me. "Here's to you, Elizabeth."

She put the silver jigger to her lips and drained it, then poured another. She smiled and gave an enormous, happy sigh. "I'll just set this here beside the couch. You be careful now, the last thing we want to do is spill it. Now get a little table for us while I shuffle."

I could hardly move I was so fascinated by this revelation. I had never seen anyone drink openly before, and the air seemed charged with wickedness and endless possibility. Once, I had seen my father pouring drinks for a party, but he was huddled over the kitchen counter to shield my eyes from his sinning, and I was told to leave. Alcohol was a vice, to be indulged in carefully and privately, never in front of the children. I didn't have any idea that people might carry liquor with them or drink alone, and the sheer nerve of what Aunt Eadie was doing made me quiver with excitement. What if they came home and she got caught? But she seemed not even to consider that, and with each emptying of the cap grew more relaxed and easy. I could see at last what my father really hated about her—because she didn't care, she was safe.

Her painted nails flashed as she cut the deck, all the while outlining the basic rules of the game. "Get someting for us to bet with, Elizabeth," she said, and I ran to the sewing closet and brought back the button jar, pleased with myself for doing something to make her laugh. And she did, she laughed and laughed, her head thrown back, her hands still busy flicking the cards out onto the table. "Okay, look sharp now," she said. "There's a lot to learn here."

Right from that moment I loved it, loved the simplicity and quickness of the game, the wonderful formality that was almost like a dance. Aunt Eadie and I were to play poker together many times in the years that followed, but I don't remember any other evening as vividly as that. I asked questions and she answered, instructing me in matters of technique and terminology. What we both sought we found in the cards—the solace of rules ("three of a kind always beats two of a kind") and the thrill of tampering with chance. Here, at last, I could exert some influence over whatever fate dealt me. My head felt as clear as if a cold wind had blown through.

By ten o'clock I had a pile of buttons in front of me and she had only a scattering. She seemed not as interested in the game as she had been, and her face had a slackness that made me feel a little uneasy. "One last hand and off to bed," she said, and dealt. I looked her straight in the eye and bluffed so that I won the whole pot, every last button she had, with a crummy pair of jacks.

"You're good," she said. "You're going to be okay, Elizabeth. Put the cards away now, and remember this is our little secret. Nighty-night." She leaned back on the couch and smiled at me, her arms spread out like wings. A bird of paradise, as out of place in that pale beige and green living-room as the joker in the deck. The wild card that meant I now had the means of escape. Even that night I began what was to become a ritual whenever I wanted to make myself feel calm. By flashlight in my closet I would lay out hand after hand, figuring out all the possibilities.

I was still in the closet when I heard my parents come in downstairs. I went to the door of my room to listen, heard a rustle of voices and then father's heavy exclamations, and my mother's voice, all warm and forgiving. "Eadie, Eadie, what have you been doing?" And my father's, "Did the child see you like this?" Then Aunt Eadie's low laughter, and the words "bed early" and then silence. I crept away from the door and into my bed as I heard their feet on the stairs. My stomach and legs didn't stop shaking for a very long time but finally I slept, dreaming of face-cards.

At breakfast the next morning Aunt Eadie was still asleep, and all my mother said in reference to the night before was, "What time did you get to bed, Elizabeth?" And I said, "Gee, I went up to my room about 8:30, I guess. Aunt Eadie and I couldn't think of much to talk about."

When I came home for lunch she had gone. My mother's eyes were red and she let me have two bowls of fruit cocktail for dessert. At dinner that night my father told me to take off that ridiculous rhinestone ring, he didn't want to see me wearing that trash. My mother pursed her lips tightly and said, "Be a good girl, Elizabeth. Do as you're told."

About the Author

Canadian Isabel Huggan was born in 1943 in Kitchener, Ontario. She is married and the mother of a daughter. "Jack of Hearts" is from her collection of short stories called *The Elizabeth Stories*, published in 1984.

The Elizabeth Stories is a series of related stories which document one young girl's experience of growing up female in a provincial small town in the 1950s, the time period in which Huggan herself grew up. They vividly portray small rebellions which helped the character Elizabeth escape some of the repression she felt. Huggan uses the uncompromising honesty of an adolescent perspective and the selective humor of an adult narrator to expose the self-righteous attitudes and insensitive acts she so disagrees with.

"Jack of Hearts" has been adapted for Canadian television.

Questions for Thought and Discussion

1. Answer the first few questions to review some of the facts of the story. Approximately when and where did the story take place? How had Frank, Mavis and Eadie met? What were their occupations then? What were their occupations at the time of the story?

2. How did the dynamics of the household change when Eadie was present? What did Mavis get out of her friendship with Eadie? What did Frank react to? What did Eadie do for Elizabeth?

3. In Elizabeth's mind, why did Mavis send her to dance classes? What about dancing did Elizabeth come to enjoy?

4. What did Mavis want for her own future? What did Elizabeth want for her future? Was there a connection? What was the nature of Mavis's influence on Elizabeth?

5. Find examples in the story of parental moralizing, criticizing, ridiculing, shaming, lecturing, ordering and other poor responses to feelings.

6. When Elizabeth came home from dance rehearsal the Saturday she found out she was to be Jack, how could her parents have responded to the situation more effectively?

7. How could Mavis have handled the bra incident better?

8. How could Mavis and Frank have responded better the night of Elizabeth's humiliating performance?

9. The Kessler family seems to be more inclined to mutual mistrust and secrecy than to mutual trust and openness.

How did Frank deal with the alcohol issue?

What did Mavis tell Elizabeth to do when she and Eadie were visiting?

How does Elizabeth find out about Mavis's personal life and

feelings?

How do Frank and Mavis deal with their worries about Eadie's influence?

How does Elizabeth respond to their questions the night Eadie taught her to play poker?

Where does Elizabeth go for comfort and what does she do there? How healthy do you think this pattern is? How common do you think it is?

10. The author uses card-playing as a theme throughout the story. The story title also comes from the name of the ballet which Elizabeth was in. More importantly, we find out in the opening paragraphs that a deck of cards represents for Elizabeth something about life itself.

Why does she like cards so well? What is the connection between her affection for cards and the family interaction patterns? Between cards and the female experience?

Parenting Issue:

Encouraging Autonomy

The task of helping children cope with their problems is never easy. Some parents become too involved in their children's struggles and take over their children's problems as their own. Other parents are indifferent, too uninvolved, and leave their children on their own. The challenge is to be sensitive and supportive, without being highly anxious and reactive. This balance is not easily maintained, but in this story the grandfather makes an admirable effort to do so.

9.
What Feels Like the World
Richard Bausch

Very early in the morning, too early, he hears her trying to jump rope out on the sidewalk below his bedroom window. He wakes to the sound of her shoes on the concrete, her breathless counting as she jumps — never more than three times in succession — and fails again to find the right rhythm, the proper spring in her legs to achieve the thing, to be a girl jumping rope. He gets up and moves to the window and, parting the curtain only slightly, peers out at her. For some reason he feels he must be stealthy, must not let her see him gazing at her from this window. He thinks of the heartless way children tease the imperfect among them, and then he closes the curtain.

She is his only granddaughter, the unfortunate inheritor of his big-boned genes, his tendency toward bulk, and she is on a self-induced program of exercise and dieting, to lose weight. This is in preparation for the last meeting of the PTA, during which children from the fifth and sixth grades will put on a gymnastics demonstration. There will be a vaulting horse and a mini-trampoline, and everyone is to participate. She wants to be able to do at least as well as the other children in her class, and so she has been trying exercises to improve her coordination and lose the weight that keeps her rooted to the ground. For the past two weeks she has been eating only one meal a day, usually lunch, since that's the meal she eats at school, and swallowing cans of juice at other mealtimes. He's afraid of anorexia but trusts her calm determination to get ready for the event. There seems no desperation, none of the classic symptoms of the disease. Indeed, this project she's set for herself seems quite sane: to lose ten pounds, and to be able to get over the vaulting horse — in fact, she hopes that she'll be able to do a handstand on it and, curling her head and shoulders, flip over to stand upright on the other side. This, she has told him, is the outside hope. And in two weeks of very grown-up discipline and single-minded effort, that hope has mostly disappeared; she's still the only child in the fifth grade who has not even been able to propel herself over the horse, and this is the day of the event. She will have one last chance to practice at school today, and so she's up this early, out on the lawn, straining, pushing herself.

He dresses quickly and heads downstairs. The ritual in the mornings is simplified by the fact that neither of them is eating breakfast. He makes the orange juice, puts vitamins on a saucer for them both. When he glances out the living-room window, he sees that she is now doing somersaults in the dewy grass. She does three of them while he watches, and he isn't stealthy this time but stands in the window with what he hopes is an approving, unworried look on his face. After each somersault she pulls her sweat shirt down, takes a deep breath, and begins again, the arms coming down slowly, the head ducking slowly under; it's as if she falls on her back, sits up, and then stands up. Her cheeks are ruddy with effort. The moistness of the grass is on the sweat suit, and in the ends of her hair. It will rain this morning—there's thunder beyond the trees at the end of the street. He taps on the window, gestures, smiling, for her to come in. She waves at him, indicates that she wants him to watch her, so he watches her. He applauds when she's finished—three hard, slow tumbles. She claps her hands together as if to remove dust from them and comes trotting to the door. As she moves by him, he tells her she's asking for a bad cold, letting herself get wet so early in the morning. It's his place to nag. Her glance at him acknowledges this.

"I can't get the rest of me to follow my head," she says about the somersaults.

They go into the kitchen, and she sits down, pops a vitamin into her mouth, and takes a swallow of the orange juice. "I guess I'm not going to make it over that vaulting horse after all," she says suddenly.

"Sure you will."

"I don't care." She seems to pout. This is the first sign of true discouragement she's shown.

He's been waiting for it. "Brenda—honey, sometimes people aren't good at these things. I mean, I was never any good at it."

"I bet you were," she says. "I bet you're just saying that to make me feel better."

"No," he says, "really."

He's been keeping to the diet with her, though there have been times during the day when he's cheated. He no longer has a job, and the days are long; he's hungry all the time. He pretends to her that he's still going on to work in the mornings after he walks her to school, because he wants to keep her sense of the daily balance of things, of a predictable and orderly routine, intact. He believes this is the best way to deal with grief — simply to go on with things, to keep them as much as possible as they have always been. Being out of work doesn't worry him, really: he has enough money in savings to last awhile. At sixty-one, he's almost eligible for Social Security, and he gets monthly checks from the girl's father, who lives with another woman, and other children, in Oregon. The father has been very good about keeping up the payments, though he never visits or calls. Probably he thinks the money buys him the privilege of remaining aloof, now that Brenda's mother is gone. Brenda's mother used to say he was the type of man who learned early that there was nothing of substance anywhere in his soul, and spent the rest of his life trying to hide this fact from himself. No one was more upright, she would say, no one more honorable, and God help you if you ever had to live with him. Brenda's father was the subject of bitter sarcasm and scorn. And yet, perhaps not so surprisingly, Brenda's mother would call him in those months just after the divorce, when Brenda was still only a toddler, and she would try to get the baby to say things to him over the phone. And she would sit there with Brenda on her lap and cry after she had hung up.

"I had a doughnut yesterday at school," Benda says now.

"That's lunch. You're supposed to eat lunch."

"I had spaghetti, too. And three pieces of garlic bread. And pie. And a big salad."

"What's one doughnut?"

"Well, and I didn't eat anything the rest of the day."

"I know," her grandfather says. "See?"

They sit quiet for a little while. Sometimes they're shy with each other — more so lately. They're used to the absence of her mother by now — it's been almost a year — but they still find themselves missing a beat now and then, like a heart with a valve almost closed. She swallows the last of her juice and then gets up and

moves to the living room, to stand gazing out at the yard. Big
drops have begun to fall. It's a storm, with rising wind and, now,
very loud thunder. Lightning branches across the sky, and the
trees in the yard disappear in sheets of rain. He has come to her
side, and he pretends an interest in the details of the weather,
remarking on the heaviness of the rain, the strength of the wind.
"Some storm," he says finally. "I'm glad we're not out in it." He
wishes he could tell what she's thinking, where the pain is; he
wishes he could be certan of the harmlessness of his every word.
"Honey," he ventures, "we could play hooky today. If you want
to."

"Don't you think I can do it?" she says.

"I know you can."

She stares at him a moment and then looks away, out at the
storm.

"It's terrible out there, isn't it?" he says. "Look at that lightning."

"You don't think I can do it," she says.

"No. I know you can. Really."

"Well, I probably can't."

"Even if you can't. Lots of people—lots of people never do
anything like that."

"I'm the only one who can't that I know."

"Well, there's lots of people. The whole thing is silly, Brenda. A
year from now it won't mean anything at all—you'll see."

She says nothing.

"Is there some pressure at school to do it?"

"No." Her tone is simple, matter-of-fact, and she looks directly
at him.

"You're sure."

She's sure. And of course, he realizes, there *is* pressure; there's
the pressure of being one among other children, and being the
only one among them who can't do a thing.

"Honey," he says lamely, "it's not that important."

When she looks at him this time, he sees something scarily
unchildlike in her expression, some perplexity that she seems to
pull down into herself. "It is too important," she says.

He drives her to school. The rain is still being blown along the
street and above the low roofs of the houses. By the time they
arrive, no more than five minutes from the house, it has begun to

let up.

"If it's completely stopped after school," she says, "can we walk home?"

"Of course," he says. "Why wouldn't we?"

She gives him a quick wet kiss on the cheek. "Bye, Pops."

He knows she doesn't like it when he waits for her to get inside, and still he hesitates. There's always the apprehension that he'll look away or drive off just as she thinks of something she needs from him, or that she'll wave to him and he won't see her. So he sits here with the car engine idling, and she walks quickly up the sidewalk and into the building. In the few seconds before the door swings shut, she turns and gives him a wave, and he waves back. The door is closed now. Slowly he lets the car glide forward, still watching the door. Then he's down the driveway, and he heads back to the house.

It's hard to decide what to do with his time. Mostly he stays in the house, watches television, reads the newspapers. There are household tasks, but he can't do anything she might notice, since he's supposed to be at work during these hours. Sometimes, just to please himself, he drives over to the bank and visits with his old co-workers, though there doesn't seem to be much to talk about anymore and he senses that he makes them all uneasy. Today he lies down on the sofa in the living room and rests awhile. At the windows the sun begins to show, and he thinks of driving into town, perhaps stopping somewhere to eat a light breakfast. He accuses himself with the thought and then gets up and turns on the television. There isn't anything of interest to watch, but he watches anyway. The sun is bright now out on the lawn, and the wind is the same, gusting and shaking the window frames. On television he sees feasts of incredible sumptuousness, almost nauseating in the impossible brightness and succulence of the food: advertisements from cheese companies, dairy associations, the makers of cookies and pizza, the sellers of seafood and steaks. He's angry with himself for wanting to cheat on the diet. He thinks of Brenda at school, thinks of crowds of children, and it comes to him more painfully than ever that he can't protect her. Not any more than he could ever protect her mother.

He goes outside and walks up the drying sidewalk to the end of the block. The sun has already dried most of the morning's rain, and the wind is warm. In the sky are great stormy Matterhorns of cumulus and wide patches of the deepest blue. It's a beautiful day, and he decides to walk over to the school. Nothing in him voices this decision; he simply begins to walk. He knows without having to think about it that he can't allow her to see him, yet he feels compelled to take the risk that she might; he feels a helpless wish to watch over her, and, beyond this, he entertains the vague notion that by seeing her in her world he might be better able to be what she needs in his.

So he walks the four blocks to the school and stands just beyond the playground, in a group of shading maples that whisper and sigh in the wind. The playground is empty. A bell rings somewhere in the building, but no one comes out. It's not even eleven o'clock in the morning. He's too late for morning recess and too early for the afternoon one. He feels as though she watches him make his way back down the street.

His neighbor, Mrs. Eberhard, comes over for lunch. It's a thing they planned, and he's forgotten about it. She knocks on the door, and when he opens it she smiles and says, "I knew you'd forget." She's on a diet too, and is carrying what they'll eat: two apples, some celery and carrots. It's all in a clear plastic bag, and she holds it toward him in the palms of her hands as though it were piping hot from an oven. Jane Eberhard is relatively new in the neighborhood. When Brenda's mother died, Jane offered to cook meals and regulate things, and for a while she was like another member of the family. She's moved into their lives now, and sometimes they all forget the circumstances under which the friendship began. She's a solid, large-hipped woman of fifty-eight, with clear, young blue eyes and gray hair. The thing she's good at is sympathy; there's something oddly unspecific about it, as if it were a beam she simply radiates.

"You look so worried," she says now, "I think you should be proud of her."

They're sitting in the living room, with the plastic bag on the coffee tale before them. She's eating a stick of celery.

"I've never seen a child that age put such demands on herself," she says.

"I don't know what it's going to do to her if she doesn't make it over the damn thing," he says.

"It'll disappoint her. But she'll get over it."

"I don't guess you can make it tonight."

"Can't," she says. "Really. I promised my mother I'd take her to the ocean this weekend. I have to go pick her up tonight."

"I walked over to the school a little while ago."

"Are you sure you're not putting more into this than she is?"

"She was up at dawn this morning, Jane. Didn't you see her?"

Mrs. Eberhard nods. "I saw her."

"Well?" he says.

She pats his wrist. "I'm sure it won't matter a month from now."

"No," he says, "that's not true. I mean, I wish I could believe you. But I've never seen a kid work so hard."

"Maybe she'll make it."

"Yes," he says. "Maybe."

Mrs. Eberhard sits considering for a moment, tapping the stick of celery against her lower lip. "You think it's tied to the accident in some way, don't you?"

"I don't know," he says, standing, moving across the room. "I can't get through somehow. It's been all this time and I still don't know. She keeps it all to herself — all of it. All I can do is try to be there when she wants me to be there. I don't know — I don't even know what to say to her."

"You're doing all you can do, then."

"Her mother and I . . . " he begins. "She — we never got along that well."

"You can't worry about that now."

Mrs. Eberhard's advice is always the kind of practical good advice that's impossible to follow.

He comes back to the sofa and tries to eat one of the apples, but his appetite is gone. This seems ironic to him. "I'm not hungry now," he says.

"Sometimes worry is the best thing for a diet."

"I've always worried. It never did me any good, but I worried."

"I'll tell you," Mrs. Eberhard says. "It's a terrific misfortune to have to be raised by a human being."

He doesn't feel like listening to this sort of thing, so he asks her about her husband, who is with the government in some capacity that requires him to be both secretive and mobile. He's always off to one country or another, and this week he's in India. It's strange to think of someone traveling as much as he does without getting hurt or killed. Mrs. Eberhard says she's so used to his being gone all the time that next year, when he retires, it'll take a while to get used to having him underfoot. In fact, he's not a very likable man;

there's something murky and unpleasant about him. The one time Mrs. Eberhard brought him to visit, he sat in the living room and seemed to regard everyone with detached curiosity, as if they were all specimens on a dish under a lens. Brenda's grandfather had invited some old friends over from the bank — everyone was being careful not to let on that he wasn't still going there every day. It was an awkward two hours, and Mrs. Eberhard's husband sat with his hands folded over his rounded belly, his eyebrows arched. When he spoke, his voice was cultivated and quiet, full of self-satisfaction and haughtiness. They had been speaking in low tones about how Jane Eberhard had moved in to take over after the accident, and Mrs. Eberhard's husband cleared his throat, held his fist gingerly to his mouth, pursed his lips, and began a soft-spoken, lecture-like monologue about his belief that there's no such thing as an accident. His considered opinion was that there are subconscious explanations for everything. Apparently, he thought he was entertaining everyone. He sat with one leg crossed over the other and held forth in his calm, magisterial voice, explaining how everything can be reduced to a matter of conscious or subconscious will. Finally his wife asked him to let it alone, please, drop the subject.

"For example," he went on, "there are many collisions on the highway in which no one appears to have applied brakes before impact, as if something in the victims had decided on death. And of course there are the well-known cases of people stopped on railroad tracks, with plenty of time to get off, who simply do not move. Perhaps it isn't being frozen by the perception of one's fate but a matter of decision making, of will. The victim decides on his fate."

"I think we've had enough, now," Jane Eberhard said.

The inappropriateness of what he had said seemed to dawn on him then. He shifted in his seat and grew very quiet, and when the evening was over he took Brenda's grandfather by the elbow and apologized. But even in the apology there seemed to be a species of condescension, as if he were really only sorry for the harsh truth of what he had wrongly deemed it necessary to say. When everyone was gone, Brenda said, "I don't like that man."

"Is it because of what he said about accidents?" her grandfather asked.

She shook her head. "I just don't like him."

"It's not true, what he said, honey. An accident is an accident."

She said, "I know." But she would not return his gaze.

"Your mother wasn't very happy here, but she didn't want to leave us. Not even—you know, without . . . without knowing it or anything."

"He wears perfume," she said, still not looking at him.

"It's cologne. Yes, he does—too much of it."

"It smells," she said.

In the afternoon he walks over to the school. The sidewalks are crowded with children, and they all seem to recognize him. They carry their books and papers and their hair is windblown and they run and wrestle with each other in the yards. The sun's high and very hot, and most of the clouds have broken apart and scattered. There's still a fairly steady wind, but it's gentler now, and there's no coolness in it.

Brenda is standing at the first crossing street down the hill from the school. She's surrounded by other children yet seems separate from them somehow. She sees him and smiles. He waits on his side of the intersection for her to cross, and when she reaches him he's careful not to show any obvious affection, knowing it embarrasses her.

"How was your day?" he begins.

"Mr. Clayton tried to make me quit today."

He waits.

"I didn't get over," she says. "I didn't even get close."

"What did Mr. Clayton say?"

"Oh—you know. That it's not important. That kind of stuff."

"Well," he says gently, "*is* it so important?"

"I don't know." She kicks at something in the grass along the edge of the sidewalk—a piece of a pencil someone else had discarded. She bends, picks it up, examines it, and then drops it. This is exactly the kind of slow, daydreaming behavior that used to make him angry and impatient with her mother. They walk on. She's concentrating on the sidewalk before them, and they walk almost in step.

"I'm sure I could never do a thing like going over a vaulting horse when I was in school," he says.

"Did they have that when you were in school?"

He smiles. "It was hard getting everything into the caves. But sure, we had that sort of thing. We were an advanced tribe. We had fire, too."

"Okay," she's saying, "okay, okay."

"Actually, with me, it was pull-ups. We all had to do pull-ups. And I just couldn't do them. I don't think I ever accomplished a single one in my life."

"I can't do pull-ups," she says.

"They're hard to do."

"Everybody in the fifth and sixth grades can get over the vaulting horse," she says.

How much she reminds him of her mother. There's a certain mobility in her face, a certain willingness to assert herself in the smallest gesture of the eyes and mouth. She has her mother's green eyes, and now he tells her this. He's decided to try this. He's standing, quite shy, in her doorway, feeling like an intruder. She's sitting on the floor, one leg outstretched, the other bent at the knee. She tries to touch her forehead to the knee of the out-stretched leg, straining, and he looks away.

"You know?" he says. "They're just the same color—just that shade of green."

"What was my grandmother like?" she asks, still straining.

"She was a lot like your mother."

"I'm never going to get married."

"Of course you will. Well, I mean—if you want to, you will."

"How come you didn't ever get married again?"

"Oh," he says, "I had a daughter to raise, you know."

She changes position, tries to touch her forehead to the other knee.

"I'll tell you, that mother of yours was enough to keep me busy. I mean, I called her double trouble, you know, because I always said she was double the trouble a son would have been. That was a regular joke around here."

"Mom was skinny and pretty."

He says nothing.

"Am I double trouble?"

"No," he says.

"Is that really why you never got married again?"

"Well, no one would have me, either."

"Mom said you liked it."

"Liked what?"

"Being a widow."

"Yes, well," he says.

"Did you?"

"All these questions," he says.

"Do you think about Grandmom a lot?"

"Yes," he says. "That's—you know, we remember our loved ones."

She stands and tries to touch her toes without bending her legs. "Sometimes I dream that Mom's yelling at you and you're yelling back."

"Oh, well," he says, hearing himself say it, feeling himself back down from something. "That's—that's just a dream. You know, it's nothing to think about at all. People who love each other don't agree sometimes—it's—it's nothing. And I'll bet these exercises are going to do the trick."

"I'm very smart, aren't I?"

He feels sick, very deep down. "You're the smartest little girl I ever saw."

"You don't have to come tonight if you don't want to," she says. "You can drop me off if you want, and come get me when it's over."

"Why would I do that?"

She mutters. "*I* would."

"Then why don't we skip it?"

"Lot of good *that* would do," she says.

For dinner they drink apple juice, and he gets her to eat two slices of dry toast. The apple juice is for energy. She drinks it slowly and then goes into her room to lie down, to conserve her strength. She uses the word *conserve*, and he tells her he's so proud of her vocabulary. She thanks him. While she rests, he does a few household chores, trying really just to keep busy. The week's newspapers have been piling up on the coffee table in the living room, the carpets need to be vacuumed, and the whole house needs dusting. None of it takes long enough; none of it quite distracts him. For a while he sits in the living room with a newspaper in his lap and pretends to be reading it. She's restless too. She comes back through to the kitchen, drinks another glass of apple juice, and then joins him in the living room, turns the television on. The news is full of traffic deaths, and she turns to one of the local stations that shows reruns of old situation comedies. They both watch *M*A*S*H* without really taking it in. She bites the cuticles of her nails, and her gaze wanders around the room. It comes to him that he could speak to her now, could make his way through to her grief — and yet he knows that he will do no such thing; he can't even bring himself to speak at all. There are regions of his own sorrow that he simply lacks the strength to explore, and so he sits there watching her restlessness, and at last it's time to go over to the school. Jane Eberhard makes a surprise visit, bearing a handsome good-luck card she's fashioned herself. She kisses Brenda, behaves exactly as if Brenda were going off to some dangerous, faraway place. She stands in the street and waves at them as they pull away, and Brenda leans out the window to shout goodbye. A moment later, sitting back and staring out at the dusky light, she says she feels a surge of energy, and he tells her she's way ahead of all the others in her class, knowing words like *conserve* and *surge*.

"I've always known them," she says.

It's beginning to rain again. Clouds have been rolling in from the east, and the wind shakes the trees. Lightning flickers on the other side of the clouds. Everything seems threatening, relentless. He slows down. There are many cars parked along both sides of the street. "Quite a turnout," he manages.

"Don't worry," she tells him brightly. "I still feel my surge of energy."

It begins to rain as they get out of the car, and he holds his sport coat like a cape to shield her from it. By the time they get to the open front doors, it's raining very hard. People are crowding into the cafeteria, which has been transformed into an arena for the event — chairs set up on four sides of the room as though for a wrestling match. In the center, at the end of the long, bright-red mat, are the vaulting horse and the mini-trampoline. The physical-education teacher, Mr. Clayton, stands at the entrance. He's tall, thin, scraggly-looking, a boy really, no older than twenty-five.

"There's Mr. Clayton," Brenda says.

"I see him."

"Hello, Mr. Clayton."

Mr. Clayton is quite distracted, and he nods quickly, leans toward Brenda, and points to a doorway across the hall. "Go on ahead," he says. Then he nods at her grandfather.

"This is it," Brenda says.

Her grandfather squeezes her shoulder, means to find the best thing to tell her, but in the next confusing minute he's lost her; she's gone among the others and he's being swept along with the crowd entering the cafeteria. He makes his way along the walls behind the chairs, where a few other people have already gathered and are standing. At the other end of the room a man is speaking from a lectern about old business, new officers for the fall. Brenda's grandfather recognizes some of the people in the crowd. A woman looks at him and nods, a familiar face he can't quite place. She turns to look at the speaker. She's holding a baby, and the baby's staring at him over her shoulder. A moment later, she steps back to stand beside him, hefting the baby higher and patting its bottom.

"What a crowd," she says.

He nods.

"It's not usually this crowded."

Again, he nods.

The baby protests, and he touches the miniature fingers of one hand — just a baby, he thinks, and everything still to go through.

"How is — um . . . Brenda?" she says.

"Oh," he says, "fine." And he remembers that she was Brenda's kindergarten teacher. She's heavier than she was then, and her hair is darker. She has a baby now.

"I don't remember all my students," she says, shifting the baby to the other shoulder. "I've been home now for eighteen months, and I'll tell you, it's being at the PTA meeting that makes me see how much I *don't* miss teaching."

He smiles at her and nods again. He's beginning to feel awkward. The man is still speaking from the lectern, a meeting is going on, and this woman's voice is carrying beyond them, though she says everything out of the side of her mouth.

"I remember the way you used to walk Brenda to school every morning. Do you still walk her to school?"

"Yes."

"That's so nice."

He pretends an interest in what the speaker is saying.

"I always thought it was so nice to see how you two got along together — I mean these days it's really rare for the kids even to know who their grandparents *are*, much less have one to walk them to school in the morning. I always thought it was really something." She seems to watch the lectern for a moment, and then speaks to him again, this time in a near whisper. "I hope you won't take this the wrong way or anything, but I just wanted to say how sorry I was about your daughter. I saw it in the paper when Brenda's mother. . . . Well. You know, I just wanted to tell you how sorry. When I saw it in the paper, I thought of Brenda, and how you used to walk her to school. I lost my sister in an automobile accident, so I know how you feel—it's a terrible thing. Terrible. An awful thing to have happen. I mean it's much too sudden and final and everything. I'm afraid now every time I get into a car."

She pauses, pats the baby's back, then takes something off its ear. "Anyway, I just wanted to say how sorry I was."

"You're very kind," he says.

"It seems so senseless," she murmurs. "There's something so senseless about it when it happens. My sister went through a stop sign. She just didn't see it, I guess. But it wasn't a busy road or anything. If she'd come along one second later or sooner nothing would've happened. So senseless. Two people driving two different cars coming along on two roads on a sunny afternoon and they come together like that. I mean—what're the chances, really?"

He doesn't say anything.

"How's Brenda handling it?"

"She's strong," he says.

"I would've said that," the woman tells him. "Sometimes I think the children take these things better than the adults do. I remember when she first came to my class. She told everyone in the first minute that she'd come from Oregon. That she was living with her grandfather, and her mother was divorced."

"She was a baby when the divorce—when she moved here from Oregon."

This seems to surprise the woman. "Really," she says, low. "I got the impression it was recent for her. I mean, you know, that she had just come from it all. It was all very vivid for her, I remember that."

"She was a baby," he says. It's almost as if he were insisting on it. He's heard this in his voice, and he wonders if she has, too.

"Well," she says, "I always had a special place for Brenda. I always thought she was very special. A very special little girl."

The PTA meeting is over, and Mr. Clayton is now standing at the far door with the first of his charges. They're all lining up outside the door, and Mr. Clayton walks to the microphone to announce the program. The demonstration will commence with the mini-trampoline and the vaulting horse: a performance by the fifth- and sixth-graders. There will also be a break-dancing demonstration by the fourth-grade class.

"Here we go," the woman says. "My nephew's afraid of the mini-tramp."

"They shouldn't make them do these things," Brenda's grandfather says, with a passion that surprises him. He draws in a breath. "It's too hard," he says, loudly. He can't believe himself. "They shouldn't have to go through a thing like this."

"I don't know," she says vaguely, turning from him a little. He has drawn attention to himself. Others in the crowd are regarding him now — one, a man with a sparse red beard and wild red hair, looking at him with something he takes for agreement.

"It's too much," he says, still louder. "Too much to put on a child. There's just so much a child can take."

Someone asks gently for quiet.

The first child is running down the long mat to the mini-trampoline; it's a girl, and she times her jump perfectly, soars over the horse. One by one, other children follow. Mr. Clayton and another man stand on either side of the horse and help those who go over on their hands. Two or three go over without any assistance at all, with remarkable effortlessness and grace.

"Well," Brenda's kindergarten teacher says, "there's my nephew."

The boy hits the mini-tramp and does a perfect forward flip in the air over the horse, landing upright and then rolling forward in a somersault.

"Yea, Jack!" she cheers. "No sweat! Yea, Jackie boy!"

The boy trots to the other end of the room and stands with the others; the crowd is applauding. The last of the sixth-graders goes over the horse, and Mr. Clayton says into the microphone that the fifth-graders are next. It's Brenda who's next. She stands in the doorway, her cheeks flushed, her legs looking too heavy in the tights. She's rocking back and forth on the balls of her feet, getting ready. It grows quiet. Her arms swing slightly, back and forth, and now, just for a moment, she's looking at the crowd, her face hiding whatever she's feeling. It's as if she were merely curious as to who is out there, but he knows she's looking for him, searching the crowd for her grandfather, who stands on his toes, unseen against the far wall, stands there thinking his heart might break, lifting his hand to wave.

∽

About the Author

Richard Bausch was born in 1945 in Fort Benning, Georgia. He was one of six children, a twin, in a Roman Catholic family. Before going to college and subsequently becoming a writer, he worked as a singer, songwriter and stand-up comedian.

Married and the father of three children, he is now a college professor in Virginia. "What Feels Like the World" appears in a collection of short stories called **Spirits,** which was published in 1987.

Like the grandfather and grandaughter in "What Feels Like the World," all the characters in the **Spirits'** stories suffer from a failure of spirit. That is, they fail, for whatever reasons, to connect at critical points in their lives with those they love. Moreover, they are haunted by dreams, events or persons in the past — spirits that are alive and working in the problems of the present.

Questions for Thought and Discussion

1. To review some of the facts of the story, place the story in terms of Brenda's life: what grade is she in? How old was she when her parents divorced? How long ago did her mother die? How long has she been living with "Pops"? How old is he?

2. What might happen if she made it over the horse? If she didn't?

3. Why does Brenda's grandfather not tell her about his job? What do you think about this?

4. What are some of the other things Brenda's grandfather does which show that he cares for her a great deal?

5. During the gymnastics demonstration, Brenda's grandfather protests this kind of pressure on children "with a passion that surprises him[self]." Does it surprise you, the reader? Do you think he is too involved with her struggles?

6. Brenda's grandfather senses that she has feelings about her mother's life and death that need to be talked about. To the neighbor, Mrs. Eberhard, he says, "She keeps it all to herself — all of it. All I can do is try to be there when she wants me to be there. I don't know — I don't even know what to say to her." How do parents get their children to talk about the things that are troubling them? Could he do any more?

7. Brenda's grandfather initiates the topic of her mother in a

conversation by saying that she (Brenda) has her mother's eyes. But instead of responding by talking about *her* feelings, Brenda responds by asking him questions about *his* feelings, about *his* relationships. His answers to her questions are evasive. "There are regions of his own sorrow that he simply lacks the strength to explore, and so he sits there watching her restlessness . . ."

Why don't they talk? How important do you think parental expressiveness is?

8. How common is the sense of inadequacy he experiences at this moment? Do you think he is poorer than most parents in confronting feelings like grief? Or do you think he is better than most since he is aware of this inadequacy?

9. Compare his relationship with his daughter in the past (at least, what we know about it) with his relationship with his granddaughter in the present. If different, how do you account for the differences: in terms of his aging? His grief? His singleness in (grand) parenting Brenda? His sex, in that as a male he formerly relied on his wife, a female, to do the "feeling work" for both of them? Individual differences between his daughter and his granddaughter?

10. When Brenda is at school, "it comes to him more painfully than ever that he can't protect her. Not any more than he could ever protect her mother." To what extent can/should parents protect their children from painful experiences? What are the goals of parenting strategies which are used when children encounter problems?

11. What advice would you give Brenda's grandfather? Brenda?

12. What does the title of the story mean to you?

Parenting Issue:

Correcting Misbehavior of Children

All children misbehave from time to time and need to be corrected. Their correction is an important part of the parenting role. (The correction role is what most people have in mind when they speak of "discipline," but discipline happens in many other ways, too. See the introduction to "Birthday Party" by Shirley Jackson.)

"The Boy on the Train" consists of memories of adult children about their father's efforts to correct their misbehavior when they were younger. Although they regard him with "grudging respect," they remember his lectures, warnings and demonstrations to have been largely ineffective and slightly comic.

Edward, one of the sons (and the character through whom the author reveals his own perspective), speculates on why their father was the way he was, tries to parent in a different manner, but still finds himself using some of the same methods with his children which their father used with them.

10.
The Boy on the Train
Arthur Robinson

ᘯᔍ

In 1891, at the age of five, Lewis Barber Fletcher traveled alone from Jacksonville, Florida, to the little town of Camden, thirty-one miles northwest of Utica, in upstate New York. Fifty years later, his wife, children, and friends heard about his trip for the first time when this item appeared on the editorial page of the *Utica Daily Press* under a standing head, "50 Years Ago Today in the Press": "Lewis B. Fletcher, 5, arrived in Utica yesterday on a New York Central train on his way to join his mother in Camden. He was traveling alone from Jacksonville, Florida." A friend spotted the item and phoned Mrs. Fletcher, who called her husband at his office and read it to him. She had to read it twice before he got it straight; he was hard of hearing and even with an amplifying device on his telephone often had trouble understanding, mostly because he became tense when he had to use it. When he understood what she had read him, he gave an embarrassed "Ha!" and said he had forgotten about the trip. There was no further discussion — he disliked talking about personal matters at his office, possibly suspecting that all work stopped while the help listened for material for gossip. When he came home that evening, he had already read the item at work, clipped it, stuck it in his billfold, and developed an attitude toward it — a sort of amused, self-conscious pride that seemed to say yes, he had traveled nearly fourteen hundred miles by himself when he was five, with two changes of train, one of them involving a ferry from Jersey City to Manhattan, and had managed the whole thing, as he had everything else in his life, by strict application to business.

The item was a sort of one-day sensation. Two clippings were put away in a photograph album, and the subject was pretty much forgotten. Sarah, the youngest child, occasionally resurrected it when the family was together at Christmas or, in later years, during vacations at the elder Fletchers' place outside Utica. In the evening, when their parents had gone to bed and the children stayed up talking, Sarah might say in a reverential tone, "Can you imagine him traveling alone from Jacksonville to Camden when he was five?" The two others—Howard, the oldest, and Edward —would say they could imagine it, that it was the easiest thing in the world to imagine. The picture they'd then conjure up was of a five-year-old old man with white hair, steel-rimmed bifocals, and a hearing aid that he kept turned off to save the flat, half-pint-shaped battery. (Edward and Howard had never thought of him as anything but an old man, even when they were small and he was in his thirties.) He would have dickered, they'd say, with the railroad until it agreed to give him a ticket in exchange for some worn-out toys, and he would have worked a deal in the dining car for his food, perhaps agreeing to polish silver. He would have brought along candy, fruit, and tattered copies of old newspapers to sell on the train. When he wasn't busy selling, or polishing silver, he'd be doing his bookkeeping. At every stop, he'd buy more stuff to sell, and at Jersey City he'd trade some of his inventory for the ferry ride to Manhattan. He'd be too busy to see the Hudson River or the Mohawk Valley, and when there was nothing else to do he'd make notes for the lectures he'd someday give his sons on How to Get Ahead and Be Somebody. "You don't get anything in this life without working . . . You'll never get anywhere until you learn to apply yourselves . . . How do you suppose we got this nice home? Nobody handed it to us. I worked hard for everything we've got . . . If you don't develop some get-up-and-go, you'll never amount to anything or have any-thing." He'd write a note to himself to mention the horrible example of Uncle Reggie, who was two at the time and showing unmistakable signs of having no get-up-and-go.

Edward did wonder that his father seemed to have forgotten about a trip that should have been a momentous experience for a five-year-old. He decided that his father may have felt there was something shameful about it and the shame had caused him to repress the memory. The children were dimly aware that their paternal grandparents had separated in Jacksonville and were later divorced, and that their grandmother had brought up Lewis and Reginald in Camden, her home town, but they didn't know any details, a divorce in a churchgoing family was a matter of some embarrassment. What Edward learned later was that right after the separation their grandmother had returned to Camden with Reginald, leaving Lewis with their grandfather. The grandfather, who wasn't much good, had apparently decided that he didn't want Lewis and had put him on a train for the two-day trip to his mother's. It was not an amusing picture: a five-year-old had been left behind by his mother and then sent off alone by his father — abandoned by one, rejected by the other. Edward would try to imagine him without white hair, hearing aid, or steel-rimmed bifocals, a small boy with brown hair and a grave face, being taken to the train by his father, so dumb with misery and fright that he couldn't cry, knowing only that he was going somewhere out there into unknown space. A train would thunder into the station, all smoke and steam. He had seen trains from a distance, and this one was all the more terrifying for being seen from three feet above the platform. His father would take him aboard and stow a bag in the rack. After reminding him when to eat the food he had brought along, his father would embrace him and leave, possibly waiting on the platform to gesture and smile until the train moved, and then walking a few steps with it and waving. Lewis would sit there, keeping a toy close to him, putting off as long as he could going to the toilet, because so many people would be watching him walk through the aisle and because he wouldn't be sure he could undertake such a project without help. Maybe two days of sitting there and sleeping in a berth, if his father had bought him a Pullman ticket — long enough for the railroad car to become his world — and then Jersey City, the end of the line. A conductor or Pullman porter who had been tipped would take him across the river on a ferry to a horse-drawn cab and instruct the driver to take Lewis to Grand Central and see that someone put him on a train for Utica. Then the train out of New York and up the Hudson and through the Mohawk Valley. At Utica he would change trains for Camden. Edward supposed Lewis's mother would be at the Camden station to meet him.

Edward went over the trip from time to time, adding details, trying to get inside the boy to experience his anxiety and despair and very likely his distrust of people on the train, whose brief, unctuous kindnesses betrayed their fear of ending up with him on their hands.

This was the image of his father that could move Edward, and it seemed to bear no relation to the anxiety-ridden old man in his early forties who sat all evening with a *Saturday Evening Post* in his lap, his hands clasped over his stomach and his thumbs revolving first one way and then the other while he went over and over whatever was worrying him — whether his sons would turn out like Reggie or his own father, whether there'd be enough profit at the end of the year to enable him to meet his bank loan, whether the new Jewish family in the neighborhood meant more to come. In 1928, a pressing worry was whether a cocky Irish Catholic from New York City would defeat Herbert Hoover and succeed in destroying business and the country — Hoover, surpassed in wisdom and ability only by his great predecessor, Calvin Coolidge.

What upset their father as much as anything else was the attitude of his sons, particularly Howard's. They had done nothing to earn their good life, and yet they took it for granted, with never a word of gratitude or any acknowledgment of what he had done for them. He tried to teach them that it all came hard, that at eleven he supported his mother and Reggie by taking care of the fire in the Camden library stove, carrying the morning and evening Syracuse papers, delivering telegrams, shoveling walks in winter and doing yard work in summer, working in the hardware store on Saturdays, and pumping the organ in the Presbyterian church on Sundays. As he explained the importance and the rewards of work and the seriousness of life, Edward would stare past his head, glassy-eyed, and Howard would wear a bored smirk. At an age when their father was supporting his mother and Reggie, his sons were coasting on their Flexible Flyers, skating, building snowhouses and forts, riding bikes, exploring in a nearby woods, or playing baseball or football in vacant lots. He would come home to find the driveway unshoveled and be forced to park in the street, or the lawn unmowed, or the garage or attic uncleaned. There was always agitation for more things — for skis, pack baskets, hockey skates, hockey sticks, a double-bladed ax, new or more golf clubs, punching bag and rings for the attic, or a stay in the Adirondacks in summer. They were establishing attitudes that would be lifelong unless he succeeded in persuading them that life was more than play.

Dinnertime was lecture time. The speeches flowed right past both boys in a meaningless litany they knew by heart. Conversation at the table was on two levels: one, loud, between their parents, who were both slightly hard of hearing and left their hearing aids turned off to save the batteries, and the other among the children, who could carry on a protracted quarrel without their parents' knowledge until Sarah—it was usually Sarah—raised her voice to alert her parents that she was being picked on. Then both parents would set about adjusting their hearing aids to get tuned in. Sometimes, with heads bent, Howard and Edward would recite their father's speeches along with him, occasionally commenting on omissions ("He forgot money doesn't grow on trees"). Howard refined a talent for rephrasing their feisty mother's numerous sayings, turning them into nonsense. At the end of one of their father's speeches, Howard commented, "I always say you can lead a horse to drink but you can't make him water." All three children were convulsed; it was far and away Howard's most successful effort, and they were helpless with laughter. Their father, red-faced, demanded to know what was funny. Sarah, still shaking, said it was something Howard had said. Their father ordered Howard to tell him what it was. The thought of Howard's having to repeat the saying set them off again. Their mother, who loved a good laugh and was always on their side, joined them, although she didn't know what was funny. When Howard finally got it out, their mother gave a delighted shriek. Their father was left out of it altogether, a red-faced spoilsport.

"Reggie all over," he said.

"Don't be such a stick-in-the-mud," their mother said.

Their father's attitude toward Howard grew harsher and he often predicted Howard would amount to nothing, like Uncle Reggie, unless he changed. Howard, near tears, would fight back and was sometimes sent away from the table. Their mother, tears streaming down her face, would say their father was always picking on Howard. "I don't see why you can't leave him alone," she'd say.

"He thinks life's a joke. Well, it isn't, and it's time he learned it isn't. Believe me, I know what I'm talking about."

"Maybe you'd be better off if you loosened up a little."

"Loosen up. Loosen up. I like that."

He'd say Howard wasn't a Fletcher, he was a Davies. Their mother's name was Davies, and her father, a carpenter, had come from Wales. Her maternal forebears were farmers who had settled in central New York.

"Howard inherited a mean Welsh temper, just like your father's," he'd say.

He'd try to eat—he couldn't bear to waste food—but would have to give it up. He'd lay his napkin on the table, breathe deeply, and put his hand on his chest; these scenes brought on heartburn. A little later he'd mix a glass of Citrocarbonate, then sit in the living room with the *Saturday Evening Post* in his lap and a worried expression on his face.

Howard had a bagful of tricks with which to annoy his father. At the table he'd pour himself milk, starting with the pitcher close to the glass, then moving it higher and higher until it was a couple of feet in the air, all the time being careful not to spill. His expression throughout was one of intense concentration, as though he were performing some difficult but necessary task. It was a performance that Edward loved, partly because they both knew what was coming.

Their father would strike the table with the flat of his hand. "We're not going to have such goings on at our table," he'd say.

Howard would look incredulous. "You mean I can't drink milk?"

There'd be no reply.

"You can't do anything around here, Percival," Howard would say.

"Don't call me Percival," Edward would reply.

With the handle of his spoon, Howard would depress the tablecloth to form a crease where the pads under it came together; the crease marked a boundary between his and Edward's territories and was necessary, Howard insisted, because of Edward's habit of encroaching on Howard's territory with his elbow. It was really needed to annoy their father. By Howard's decree, territorial violations were punishable by a hit on the upper arm, administered with a flick of the wrist and the knuckle of the middle finger extended. Edward, who liked living on the brink, kept his elbow as close to the crease as he could and tried to find excuses for crossing. There were disputes in an undertone over whether his elbow had actually crossed and he had a hit coming. Howard always found him guilty and passed sentence, and for a few seconds, while Howard explained how sorry he was to have to do it, Edward tingled with suspense. Then Howard hit him. The pain was excruciating, and Edward would double over, laughing hysterically and weeping from pain.

Hearing aids came on. There were warnings, and their father would ask rhetorically if they couldn't have one dinner in peace. Edward carried a permanent bruise.

If everything else failed, Howard could often get things started by calling Edward Percival, or Archibald. Then he discovered a wonderful term, "poop deck," which sounded indecent but wasn't.

"Poopdeck, hand me the butter."

"What did you call him?" Sarah asked.

"Poopdeck."

Sarah, loud: "Howard used a nasty word."

Hearing aids were adjusted and there was debate about whether "poop deck" was a nasty word. Their mother didn't think so; she'd seen it in novels and, she thought, in the *Press* crossword. Their father said Howard wasn't to use it. Howard said he had a right to use it — it was part of a ship — and Edward didn't mind being called Poopdeck, did you, Poopdeck? Their father said Howard was only calling Edward *that* to get something started and he was not to call him *that* again at the table and that was final.

"Percival, the butter."

"Please."

"Poopdeck, you want your arm in a sling?"

Sarah, loud: "He's using that word again."

Howard was sent away from the table.

Their father seemed to get a new hearing aid every year or two as improved models came out. Their mother got the old one. They were bone-conducting devices, held in place behind one ear with a narrow band of spring steel that fitted over the head. A cord ran from the bone-conducting unit behind their father's ear down inside his collar and emerged from his shirtfront to connect with a microphone, which clipped to a vest pocket. Another cord led from the microphone to the battery pack in his hip pocket. A switch and volume control were on the microphone. Sometimes, after their father had fumbled with the control and still couldn't hear, Howard would suggest that maybe he was sitting on the cord. The possibility that current couldn't get through a wire because their father was sitting on it was one of their standing jokes. Whenever their father had trouble getting tuned in at the table, Howard would trot out the idea: "I think you're sitting on the cord." It amused them even more that their father would always reply, "What? What?" and feel around under him.

Their mother was self-conscious about having to wear a hearing aid and did her hair so as to conceal it; one had to look closely to see the cord that emerged from her hair at the back of her neck and disappeared into her dress. She didn't want anyone to know about the embarrassing gear she wore under her clothes. Doctors found nothing organically wrong with her hearing; her impairment, they said, was "sympathetic." The children referred to the hearing aids as speakers, and before saying anything to either parent would ask, "Is your speaker on?"

Edward — thin and small-boned — had more passive ways than Howard's of resisting their father. He was rarely hungry, and at dinner invariably became nauseated halfway through the meal. The nausea always came suddenly, usually when he had food in his mouth. He'd park it (a family expression) in a cheek and wait for the nausea to pass, meanwhile dangling his fork between two fingers and batting it between thumb and little finger, daydreaming. Their father was as distressed about seeing Edward's cheek packed with food he wasn't even chewing as he was about Howard's tricks — and it was food bought with his hard-earned money, the only kind of money he ever had.

"Chew," he'd exhort Edward. Edward would chew a couple of times experimentally and give up.

"Watch me chew," his father would say. He'd lean above Edward and solemnly chew. The sessions of chewing instruction were frequent, and Edward came to know every pore on the shiny plane at the tip of his father's nose. The image of his father's big face above him, his gray eyes peering down through steel-rimmed bifocals, was often what he remembered when he thought of his father, the jaw going in a slightly circular fashion, like a cow's. He was fully grown before he discovered pleasure in food, that things he thought he hated — peas, for example — were really rather good. He was never able to eat rice. It evoked a picture of his father at lunch, about to pour cream into a bowl of steaming rice mixed with brown sugar and butter, saying, "Oh, boy!" which was his way of expressing perfect contentment. Years later, Edward would feel the old nausea rising. He was surprised to discover that Howard, in his fifties, still became emotional on the subject of Boston baked beans. Their father, who adored them — their mother baked them all day until they were, as their father said, nutty — once forced Howard to eat them when he was very small. Howard threw up. Edward rather liked Boston baked beans.

Their father never merely liked or disliked something; he felt compelled to impose his opinions on his family. These opinions involved everything from his view of life to the food he ate, the Republican Party, the make of car he drove. Not eating the food that he believed in was subversive. Every meal that Edward couldn't finish represented a stalemate, or even a defeat, for his father.

In prepubescence, Edward gazed at his face in the mirror a great deal and studied the effects he could get with it. Once he discovered that a strip of toothpaste artfully placed just below a nostril produced an effect that could easily turn his father's queasy stomach. The result was more than he could have hoped for. He waited until everyone was at the table before joining them. Sarah, sitting opposite, was the first to notice. In a loud voice she announced that Edward was making her sick. Their father looked, and a few moments later rose, napkin over mouth, and left the room.

Curious about how he'd look without eyebrows, Edward shaved one off with his father's razor. His father was always conscious of the image that the family presented, and Edward could sense his discomfort at having to sit in church with a son who had only one eyebrow. After Howard persuaded Edward that the new eyebrow would grow in bushier than its mate, he shaved off the second one so that they'd match.

When Edward had become a conspicuously unsuccessful father, who quarreled with his children over their pot smoking, their rock music, their language, their clothes, until they had become alienated, he'd think with some respect and sympathy of his father's ability to survive, particularly as he and Howard grew older. Howard was addicted to strange projects, some of them involving firecrackers. When he was about thirteen, to see what would happen he dropped a lighted firecracker into an empty ink bottle and quickly put the stopper in the bottle. What he learned was that the bottle blows up and sprays the experimenter with bits of inky glass. For days, Howard's face was flecked with dark blue freckles. He and Edward decided Howard must have blinked at the instant of the explosion, since they could find no glass in his eyes and since he could still see. The walls of his room were speckled with the glass.

Impressed by a contortionist he had seen in vaudeville, Howard spent a few weeks trying to get a foot behind his head by tightening a belt that was looped around head and foot. He abandoned the project when he had a heel within a couple of inches of his forehead. He was strong, and proud of his muscles, and often scuffled with their ninety-five-pound mother, who had never quite grown up. Once, as they wrestled for some object — a ball, a report card — without intending to he tossed her over his hip. There was an audible crack as she hit the floor. "Howie," she said as she lay there, "I think you broke my ankle." She was on crutches for more than a month.

Howard had nearly perfect teeth, with one slight imperfection — a minute hole between the two upper front teeth, through which he could squirt a tiny water jet. He'd take a drink of water at the table and sit smiling, to uncover the hole. His mother, seeing him looking at her with a foolish grin and knowing what was coming, would say, "Howie, don't you dare!" At which he'd give her a small squirt. She'd no sooner get her glasses wiped off than he'd squirt her again. She'd laugh with delight. Howard would have enough water left to give Edward a shot or two on the ear. Their father, outnumbered as usual, would be silent. He may have thought it was funny.

There was a series of four or five automobile accidents that started when Howard was fourteen. His father had made the mistake of showing him how to drive. Edward was eager to have Howard teach him, and at the first opportunity, when their parents were out playing bridge, they pushed their father's car out of the garage and got in. Howard started the engine and they roared into the garage, crushing the Easy Washer against a laundry tub and knocking the tub off its supports. Howard made the first of the reports that came close to becoming a habit. He phoned the house where his parents were, asked for his father, and said, "Dad, I just had an accident." Accidents usually took place at night. They'd wake their father to break the news, and he'd sit on the edge of his bed, trying to comprehend through the fog of half sleep and saying in a singsong, "Oh, oh, oh, oh, oh, oh, ohhh." In the last and worst of them, in daylight, when he was through school and returning home from his first job, Edward collided at an intersection with an old Reo Speed Wagon, whose driver, a short bald man who worked on a W.P.A. project and was the father of four children, was pitched out the door on his head. He lay on his back in the roadway, dead.

Edward lived with a jumble of images of his father; some of them in time became moving, including that worried face hovering over him, showing him how to chew. Another was of his father sprawled flat on his face on Genesee Street, in New Hartford, while a car skidded to a stop a few feet from him. It was a Sunday, and the children wanted ice cream cones. Their father, of course, said they didn't need ice cream cones, but their mother shamed him, as she always shamed him: "Honest, Lewis, you're so tight you squeak." So he was crossing the street, red-faced and mad, to get cones for the children, who were waiting in the car with their mother. Seeing a car bearing down on him, he started to sprint. He tripped, or slipped, on a streetcar track and fell flat. They all watched, horrified. Their mother screamed. The driver managed to stop. Their father got up, picked up his glasses and cap, and completed his mission. He handed the children their cones and got into the car without a word. As they drove home, their mother wept quietly on the front seat and the children, in back, licked their ice cream without pleasure.

There was their father the golfer with the flossy waggle, and the skier with the strange posture. Occasionally, on a Sunday in winter, wrapped in blankets, the family drove in their 1922 Buick open touring car with isinglass curtains to the village of Sauquoit, south of Utica, where a farmer waited with a sleigh and a team of horses. They rode on straw under heavy blankets that smelled of a cow barn for the two miles uphill to the little house they owned overlooking the Sauquoit Valley. The unpaved road was snowed in, and the sleigh went through barnyards and across fields. They had a fire in the dining room stove and ate a hot meal that their mother had put up in aluminum containers that fitted into an insulated cylinder with a heated flat stone at the bottom — slices from a leg of lamb, mashed potatoes, gravy, and cauliflower. They used a privy inside a woodshed attached to the house. They skied through a planted pinewood to a snow-covered cornfield with a steep slope, and spent the afternoon there, their father standing straight up on his skis, feet together and arms extended from his sides like a tightrope walker. He said that was the correct form, and he liked to get the form right. (He had played high school football and baseball in Camden and church league baseball in

Utica, and had a rather showy throwing motion; when they played catch with him, Howard and Edward called him, in an undertone, Joe Form.) Using their skis, they pushed up a mound of snow and compacted it to make a jump. The farmer returned with the sleigh in the late afternoon, lighted a lantern, hung it from a hook beside his raised seat, and jovially tucked them in—except for tireless Howard, who insisted on skiing down.

There was their father the competitor, who had to be taking on someone at something every day to keep his juices flowing. He always drove home for lunch to have a half hour of cards with their mother. For years the game was Russian bank, a two-handed form of solitaire; later, it was cribbage; still later, canasta; and, after he retired, Scrabble. He kept a running score in a little notebook, and could tell her at any time how many points he was ahead. There were often arguments over who was cheating whom, she joshing, he dead serious. He loved bridge—it challenged his ability to keep track of the cards played, and tested his ingenuity in making difficult contracts. He didn't like playing with people who took the game less seriously than he did, who talked and didn't pay attention, or, as he would say, didn't apply themselves. Howard, who didn't like to play when his father was in the game, was occasionally dragooned into making a fourth when no one else was available. His father may have suspected there was some justice in his wife's criticism that he was too hard on Howard. As Howard went about making himself comfortable, hauling up an easy chair and settling into it sideways to the table, his legs over an arm, his father would try to restrain himself, but several deep breaths gave him away. Howard kept up a silly chatter guaranteed to annoy his father, who couldn't abide silliness. Howard had become fond of the words "nicely" and "extremely," possibly from reading Damon Runyon stories in *Collier's*. "That's very nicely" and "That's extremely," he'd say, and sometimes he'd combine them: "That's extremely nicely." If the game lasted long enough, he might wind up with one leg on the back of the chair and his head almost under the table. He would finally succeed in provoking a confrontation. Once, his father told him sharply that he couldn't pass. "Your partner bid two no-trump," he said. "You have to say something."

Howard, not wanting to take a chance on getting stuck with the bid, stalled. "How do we get out of this, Poopdeck?" he said. "How about three no-spades?"

"What's your bid?" his father asked.

Loud, defiant: "Three no-spades."

His father threw down his cards. "Lord help us," he said. The game was over.

Howard raised his head and looked innocently around. "Something the matter, Poopdeck?"

As a lover, their father was unusual, and even playful. When courting their mother (both worked for a wholesale building-supply firm, she as a stenographer, he as a salesman), he'd call on her in the evening with a ball glove and ball, she once told the children, and they'd play catch in her parents' side yard, he gallantly letting her use the glove. Even in their sixties they'd occasionally chase each other out of the kitchen with a water pistol they kept there, laughing like schoolchildren. They became hysterical once when the hot-water bottle they were throwing at each other in their bedroom broke and soaked a bed. Another night, unable to restrain herself when she saw him praying on his knees beside his bed, she took the Bible, kept on a nightstand between their beds, and threw it, hitting him on the shoulder. He thought that was hilarious. Although for much of the time he carried the weight of the world on his shoulders, when mightily amused he went all out, laughing uncontrollably, tears streaming down his face. He'd pull himself together, blow his nose, and then have a second seizure.

Their father had given them a good life, a wonderful life, as the appreciative Sarah sometimes said; he worried about them, undoubtedly loved them, and tried to be just. And yet, it seemed to Edward, both sons had withheld affection and given him only grudging respect. Since Edward couldn't believe that he and Howard were mean by nature, he looked for the fault elsewhere. He always came back to the child on the train and the insecurity and despair he suspected the boy had experienced, possibly even before his trip to Camden, until an exaggerated sense of anxiety had become permanently established and was later inflicted on his sons. Almost too late, Edward pitied, if not loved, his father.

Edward wondered why his grandfather, a lawyer and member of a prosperous family, hadn't taken his son to Camden instead of sending him off by himself at age five. The answer seemed to be that he was monstrously irresponsible. He married two more times, left more children around the country, went on the gold rush to the Klondike, and died chasing a rumor of gold in British Honduras (now Belize), where he was buried. Why hadn't the boy's mother met him in New York, or even in Utica? Both parents seemed to have set him up for whatever might have happened to a small child making such a long journey alone.

It may have been inevitable that this touching child, this David Copperfield, metamorphosed into a ponderous apostle of get-up-and-go. His upbringing had taught him about the snares set for the unwary, a lesson made urgent by the example of his own father, and may have accounted for the harsh, bullying tone, for the implication that his sons would turn out like Uncle Reggie (he never mentioned his father) unless they shaped up. It was the implication and the tone that turned them off.

Contemplating his own disaster, Edward wondered why anyone who doesn't have to ever becomes a father. "There is no one right way to bring up children," a therapist once told him, to ease his guilt after he had poured out his own meanness as a father. There seemed to be only wrong ways. He had thought that all he needed to do was to avoid his father's example. No lectures on getting ahead and being somebody. Let the kid park all the food he wanted in his cheek or blow up ink bottles or spend his evenings trying to get his foot behind his head. Keep the hearing aid turned on, and keep smiling.

As it turned out, Edward was unprepared for the reality of the early seventies in southern Marin County. By the time he calmed down and began seeing a therapist, his seventeen-year-old son was living in a shack with a girl, and his fifteen-year-old daughter was scarcely speaking to him. He was shocked and depressed. On the day his son moved out of the house, Edward could barely contain his frustration. "How do you expect to have any kind of life?" he said. "Or have *anything?* Your mother and I work hard so we can live here, and you thumb your nose at what makes it possible — at the whole idea of making something of your life. Believe me, it doesn't come easy." Then he stopped. For a moment, he could hear Howard saying, in an undertone, "He forgot money doesn't grow on trees."

About the Author

Arthur Robinson was born in 1916 in Utica, New York, and was educated at nearby Hamilton College. He is married and the father of two adult children. After a career of writing for newspapers in New York, Indiana and Florida, and for a technical magazine in California, Robinson retired and is now living in California.

"The Boy on the Train," his only published story, was chosen for the collection *The Best American Short Stories 1989* after its appearance in *The New Yorker* in 1988 (when the author was 72 years of age).

Robinson's autobiographical "The Boy on the Train" uses a series of loosely connected, vividly detailed incidents to convey the unsatisfactory nature of his and his brother's relationship with their father. The story grew out of his effort to better understand why they did not feel emotionally connected to him. An item in the *Utica Daily Press* in 1941 about a trip his father had made alone at the age of five led Robinson to a more sympathetic view of his father, and became an important element of the story.

Questions for Thought and Discussion

1. Lewis Fletcher's children speculated that their father was "anxiety-ridden" because of the separation of his parents and the long trip he made alone following their divorce. Do you think this is likely? Do you think the father really had forgotten about the trip he took at age 5?

2. Howard had a "bagful of tricks" with which to annoy his father. Did you? How did your parents respond? Which of their responses were effective in reducing your misbehavior? Which were not?

3. How do you think the misbehavior of Howard, Edward and Sarah was affected by their mother's role in the family interactions?

4. Eventually Edward "pitied, if not loved" his father. Why was loving him so difficult? What was there about Lewis that his sons did not like? What was lacking in his parenting style?

5. Although Edward was determined to do a better job of parenting than his father had done, he became a "conspicuously unsuccessful" father himself. Quarrels with his teenagers led to their alienation from him; he sought help from a therapist and "poured out his own meanness" as a father. What do you think

the therapist could have told him?

6. The adult children remembered that "their father never merely liked or disliked something; he felt compelled to impose his opinions on his family." Think of opinions which you hold today which are similar to those of your parents. How do you explain these similarities of opinion? How do you account for your divergent opinions?

7. What upset their father as much as anything else was the attitude of his sons about material possessions. "They had done nothing to earn their good life, and yet they took it for granted, with never a word of gratitude or any acknowledgment of what he had done for them." Why would he have felt so strongly about this issue? Do you think this is a common conflict between generations?

8. Imagine Lewis Fletcher seated in the living room after an unpleasant meal with his family, suffering from heartburn, a glass of Citrocarbonate in hand, the *Saturday Evening Post* in his lap and a worried expression on his face. What do you think he would be thinking about? If you were with him, what would you say?

9. Imagine Howard, Edward and Sarah, now middle-aged, gathered together for a family reunion at the home of their elderly parents. They share memories about their father late into the night after their parents have gone to bed. If you were present, what advice would you give them?

Parenting Issue:

Providing Information to Children

When parents are bothered by a situation, one of the first means they have for effecting change is to talk about it — to convey facts and reasons and to express personal feelings and preferences. However, the first response of many parents to bothersome situations is to issue orders, without prior discussion of the issues involved. This is especially true when parental anxieties about the situation are high.

In "Mr. Parker," a mother's inability to talk about sexuality with her daughter results in resistance, confusion and, finally, anxiety in her daughter.

11.
Mr. Parker
Laurie Colwin
ও৺

Mrs. Parker died suddenly in October. She and Mr. Parker lived in a Victorian house next to ours, and Mr. Parker was my piano teacher. He commuted to Wall Street, where he was a securities analyst, but he had studied at Juilliard and gave lessons on the side—for the pleasure of it, not for money. His only students were me and the church organist, who was learning technique on a double-keyboard harpsichord Mr. Parker had built one spring.

Mrs. Parker was known for her pastry; she and my mother were friends, after a fashion. Every two months or so they spent a day together in the kitchen baking butter cookies and cream puffs, or rolling out strudel leaves. She was thin and wispy, and turned out her pastry with abstract expertness. As a girl, she had had bright-red hair, which was now the color of old leaves. There was something smoky and autumnal about her: she wore rust-colored sweaters and heather-colored skirts, and kept dried weeds in ornamental jars and pressed flowers in frames. If you borrowed a book from her, there were petal marks on the back pages. She was tall, but she stooped as if she had spent a lifetime looking for something she had dropped.

The work "tragic" was mentioned in connection with her death. She and Mr. Parker were in the middle of their middle age, and neither of them had ever been seriously ill. It was heart failure, and unexpected. My parents went to see Mr. Parker as soon as they got the news, since they took their responsibilities as neighbors seriously, and two days later they took me to pay a formal condolence call. It was Indian summer, and the house felt closed in. They had used the fireplace during a recent cold spell, and the living room smelled faintly of ash. The only people from the community were some neighbors, the minister and his wife, and the rabbi and his wife and son. The Parkers were Episcopalian, but Mr. Parker played the organ in the synagogue on Saturday mornings and on High Holy Days. There was a large urn of tea, and the last of Mrs. Parker's strudel. On the sofa were Mrs. Parker's sisters and a man who looked like Mr. Parker ten years younger leaned against the piano, which was closed. The conversation was hushed and stilted. On the way out, the rabbi's son tried to trip me, and I kicked him in return. We were adolescent enemies of a loving sort, and since we didn't know what else to do, we expressed our love in slaps and pinches and other mild attempts at grievous bodily harm.

I loved the Parker's house. It was the last Victorian house on the block, and was shaped like a wedding cake. The living room was round, and all the walls curved. The third floor was a tower, on top of which sat a weathervane. Every five years the house was painted chocolate brown, which faded gradually to the color of weak tea. The front-hall window was a stained-glass picture of a fat Victorian baby holding a bunch of roses. The baby's face was puffy and neuter, and its eyes were that of an old man caught in a state of surprise. Its white dress was milky when the light shone through.

On Wednesday afternoons, Mr. Parker came home on an early train, and I had my lesson. Mr. Parker's teaching method never varied. He never scolded or corrected. The first fifteen minutes were devoted to a warmup in which I could play anything I liked. Then Mr. Parker played the lesson of the week. His playing was terrifically precise, but his eyes became dreamy and unfocused. Then I played the same lesson, and after that we worked on the difficult passages, but basically he wanted me to hear my mistakes. When we began a new piece, we played it part by part, taking turns, over and over.

After that, we sat in the solarium and discussed the next week's lesson. Mr. Parker usually played a record and talked in detail about the composer, his life and times, and the form. With the exception of Mozart and Schubert, he liked Baroque music almost exclusively. The lesson of the week was always Bach, which Mr. Parker felt taught elegance and precision. Mrs. Parker used to leave us a tray of cookies and lemonade, cold in the summer and hot in the winter, with cinnamon sticks. When the cookies were gone, the lesson was over and I left, passing the Victorian child in the hallway.

In the days after the funeral, my mother took several casseroles over to Mr. Parker and invited him to dinner a number of times. For several weeks he revolved between us, the minister, and the rabbi. Since neither of my parents cared much about music, except to hear my playing praised, the conversation at dinner was limited to the stock market and the blessings of country life.

In a few weeks, I got a note from Mr. Parker enclosed in a thank-you note to my parents. It said that piano lessons would begin the following Wednesday.

I went to the Parkers' after school. Everything was the same. I warmed up for fifteen minutes, Mr. Parker played the lesson, and I repeated it. In the solarium were the usual cookies and lemonade.

"Are they good, these cookies?" Mr. Parker asked.

I said they were.

"I made them yesterday," he said. "I've got to be my own baker now."

Mr. Parker's hair had once been blond, but was graying into the color of straw. Both he and Mrs. Parker seemed to have faded out of some bright time they once had lived in. He was very thin, as if the friction of living had burned every unnecessary particle off him, but he was calm and cheery in the way you expect plump people to be. On teaching days, he always wore a blue cardigan, buttoned, and a striped tie. Both smelled faintly of tobacco. At the end of the lesson, he gave me a robin's egg he had found. The light was flickering through the bunch of roses in the window as I left.

When I got home, I found my mother in the kitchen, waiting and angry.

"Where were you?" she said.

"At my piano lesson."

"What piano lesson?"

"You know what piano lesson. At Mr. Parker's."

"You didn't tell me you were going to a piano lesson," she said.

"I always have a lesson on Wednesday."

"I don't want you having lessons there now that Mrs. Parker's gone." She slung a roast into a pan.

I stomped off to my room and wrapped the robin's egg in a sweat sock. My throat felt shriveled and hot.

At dinner, my mother said to my father, "I don't want Jane taking piano lessons from Mr. Parker now that Mrs. Parker's gone."

"Why don't you want me to have lessons?" I said, close to shouting. "There's no reason."

"She can study with Mrs. Murchison." Mrs. Murchison had been my first teacher. She was a fat, myopic woman who smelled of bacon grease and whose repertoire was confined to "Little Classics for Children." Her students were mostly under ten, and she kept an asthmatic chow who was often sick on the rug.

"I won't go to Mrs. Murchison!" I shouted. "I've outgrown her."

"Let's be sensible about this," said my father. "Calm down, Janie."

I stuck my fork into a potato to keep from crying and muttered melodramatically that I would hang myself before I'd go back to Mrs. Murchison.

The lessons continued. At night I practiced quietly, and from time to time my mother would look up and say, "That's nice, dear." Mr. Parker had given me a Three-Part Invention, and I worked on it as if it were granite. It was the most complicated piece of music I had ever played, and I learned it with a sense of loss; since I didn't know when the ax would fall, I thought it might be the last piece of music I would ever learn from Mr. Parker.

The lessons went on and nothing was said, but when I came home after them my mother and I faced each other with division and coldness. Mr. Parker bought a kitten called Mildred to keep him company in the house. When we had our cookies and lemonade, Mildred got a saucer of milk.

At night, I was grilled by my mother as we washed the dishes. I found her sudden interest in the events of my day unnerving. She was systematic, beginning with my morning classes, ending in the afternoon. In the light of her intense focus, everything seemed wrong. Then she said, with arch sweetness, "And how is Mr. Parker, dear?"

"Fine."

"And how are the lessons going?"

"Fine."

"And how is the house now that Mrs. Parker's gone?"

"It's the same. Mr. Parker bought a kitten." As I said it, I knew it was betrayal.

"What kind of kitten?"

"A sort of pink one."

"What's its name?"

"It doesn't have one," I said.

One night she said, "Does Mr. Parker drink?"

"He drinks lemonade."

"I only asked because it must be so hard for him," she said in an offended voice. "He must be very sad."

"He doesn't seem all that sad to me." It was the wrong thing to say.

"I see," she said, folding the dish towel with elaborate care. "You know how I feel about this, Jane. I don't want you alone in the house with him."

"He's my *piano* teacher." I was suddenly in tears, so I ran out of the kitchen and up to my room.

She followed me up, and sat on the edge of my bed while I sat at the desk, secretly crying onto the blotter.

"I only want what's best for you," she said.

"If you want what's best for me, why don't you want me to have piano lessons?"

"I *do* want you to have piano lessons, but you're growing up and it doesn't look right for you to be in a house alone with a widowed man."

"I think you're crazy."

"I don't think you understand what I'm trying to say. You're not a little girl any more, Jane. There are privileges of childhood, and privileges of adulthood, and you're in the middle. It's difficult, I know."

"You don't know. You're just trying to stop me from taking piano lessons."

She stood up. "I'm trying to protect you," she said. "What if Mr. Parker touched you? What would you do then?" She made the word "touch" sound sinister.

"You're just being mean," I said, and by this time I was crying openly. It would have fixed things to throw my arms around her, but that meant losing, and this was war.

"We'll discuss it some other time," she said, close to tears herself.

I worked on the Invention until my hands shook. When I came home, if the house was empty, I practiced in a panic, and finally, it was almost right. On Wednesday, I went to Mr. Parker's and stood at the doorway, expecting something drastic and changed, but it was all the same. There were cookies and lemonade in the solarium. Mildred took a nap on my coat. My fifteen-minute warmup was terrible; I made mistakes in the simplest parts, in things I knew by heart. Then Mr. Parker played the lesson of the week and I tried to memorize his phrasing exactly. Before my turn came, Mr. Parker put the metronome on the floor and we watched Mildred trying to catch the arm.

I played it, and I knew it was right—I was playing music, not struggling with a lesson.

When I was finished, Mr. Parker grabbed me by the shoulders. "That's perfect! Really perfect!" he said. "A real breakthrough. These are the times that make teachers glad they teach."

We had lemonade and cookies and listened to some Palestrina motets. When I left, it was overcast, and the light was murky and green.

I walked home slowly, divided by dread and joy in equal parts. I had performed like an adult, and had been congratulated by an adult, but something had been closed off. I sat under a tree and cried like a baby. He had touched me after all.

About the Author

Laurie Colwin was born in 1944 in New York City. She attended Bard College and Columbia School of General Studies. Married, with one daughter, she works for a publishing house in New York City and as a volunteer for the homeless.

In addition to three novels, she has written three collections of short stories. "Mr. Parker" is taken from one of them, *Passion and Affect.* Her subjects are romantic love and happiness among the upper middle class of New York City. She is noted for the light touch she brings to her characters' conflicts.

"Mr. Parker" is, however, a story about unhappiness. It chronicles a young girl's coming to an uncertain awareness of sexuality in the world. It focuses on the sadness of this loss of innocence.

Questions for Thought and Discussion

1. To review some of the facts of the story, how old is Mr. Parker? What is his occupation? Why does he give Jane piano lessons? How old does Jane appear to be? What do the lessons mean to her?

2. Why is Jane's mother bothered by the situation? What does Jane understand about her mother's stand against the lessons?

3. How does Jane's mother respond to the situation? Given her discomfort with the situation, how else might she have responded?

4. How did Mr. Parker "touch" Jane? How do you think Jane was affected by this situation and the way her mother dealt with it?

5. What advice would you have for Jane in regard to being "touched?" For her mother?

6. If you were a parent in this situation, what would you do?

Parenting Issue:

Punishment

On no other issue do parents (and parenting experts, too) disagree as much as they disagree about the appropriateness of physical punishment. Some believe punishment to be appropriate provided that it is not physically abusive. Others believe physical punishment is always abusive — abusive of parental power. Misbehavior of children can be corrected, they maintain, in ways which do not rely on the greater physical power of the parent and therefore are less violent than physical punishment is.

In practice, many parents use physical punishment occasionally, even when they prefer not to, depending on how resourceful they feel. When they know of other methods and other methods seem to be effective, they don't punish. But when they don't know of other methods or when other methods don't seem to work, they resort to punishment.

The story "Grass" is about a 1920s father who was dying of tuberculosis. He wanted to teach his son to be responsible and to value work, and he resorted to harsh methods, including frequent whippings, to do so.

It is clear from the story that the son resented the methods of his father at the time it happened. What is not clear is how he felt about it later. The final paragraph seems to suggest that, in retrospect, he valued the summer's impact on his life: he was more serious, quieter and better behaved than before. However, Wheelis's book *How People Change*[1] leaves no doubt that he deeply resented the effects of that summer in the long-term, as well as short-term. Immediately following the "Grass" story Wheelis writes:

My father and I have never parted. He left his mark on me that summer, and after his death that fall continued to speak on a high-fidelity system within my conscience, speaks to me still, tells me that I have been summoned, that I am standing once again before him on that glass porch giving an account of myself, that I will be found wanting, still after all these years a "low-down, no-account scoundrel," and that this judgment will be binding on my view, that I shall not now or ever be permitted to regard myself as innocent or worthy (p. 73).

12.
Grass
Allen Wheelis
∽

It was the last day of school. The report cards had been distributed, and—to my great relief—I had passed. Now at eleven
o'clock in the morning I was on my way home with two friends.
We felt exhilaration at the prospect of three months of freedom
and manifested it by pushing each other, yelling, throwing rocks
at a bottle, chasing a grass snake, and rolling a log into the creek.
Being eight years old, it took us a long time to reach our homes.
Before parting we made plans to meet that afternoon to play ball. I
ran through the tall grass up to the back door and into the kitchen.
My mother was stirring something on the stove.

"Mama, I passed!"

"Not so loud, hon." She leaned over and kissed me, then
looked at the report card. "This is very good. Show it to Daddy if
he's not asleep."

I went through the bedroom to the glassed-in porch where my
father lay sick with tuberculosis. The bed faced away from the
door and I could not tell whether he was asleep or not.

"Daddy?"

"Come in, son."

"I passed," I said, offering the card.

He smiled and I lowered my eyes. I could never bring myself to
face for long the level gaze of those pale blue eyes which seemed
effortlessly to read my mind. He looked over the report. "I see you
got seventy-five in conduct."

"Yes, sir."

"Do you have an explanation?"

"No, sir."

"Do you think you deserved a better grade?"

"No . . . sir."

"Then you *do* have an explanation?"

I twisted one foot around the other. "Yes, sir. I guess so, sir."

"What is the explanation?"

This tireless interrogation could, I knew, be carried on for hours. Mumbling the words, I began to recount my sins. "I guess I . . . talked too much."

"Speak up, son."

"Yes, sir. I talked too much . . . and laughed . . . and cut up."

"Do you find silence so difficult?"

"Sir?"

"Was it so hard to be quiet?"

"Yes . . . sir. I guess so."

"You don't seem to find it difficult now."

I looked up and found him smiling. It wasn't going to be so bad after all. "But the other grades are good," he said. I grinned and turned to look out the window. Heat waves shimmered over the tin roof of the barn; away to the west was an unbroken field of sunflowers. Everything was bathed in, and seemed to be made drowsy by, the hot, bright sunlight. I thought of playing ball and wished dinner were over so I could go now. "Daddy, can I go over to Paul's house after dinner?" Almost before the words were out I realized my mistake. I should have asked my mother first. She might have said yes without consulting my father.

"No. You have to work, son."

"What've I got to do?"

He looked out over the several acres which we called the back yard. "You have to cut the grass."

Through a long wet spring the grass had sprung up until it was nearly a foot high. Now, in June, the rain was over and the heat was beginning to turn the grass brown. As we had no lawn mower, any cutting of grass or weeds was done by hoe, scythe, or sickle. It was with one of these I assumed the grass would be cut, but I was mistaken. After dinner my father gave me directions. The tool was to be an old, ivory-handled, straight-edge razor. The method was to grasp a handful of grass in the left hand and cut it level with the ground with the razor. The grass was to be put in a basket, along with any rocks or sticks that might be found on the ground. When the basket was full it was to be removed some hundred yards where the grass could be emptied and burned.

When the razor was dull it was to be sharpened on a whetstone in the barn.

I changed my clothes, put on a straw hat, and went to work. Unable to realize the extent of the task or to gauge the time required, my only thought was to finish as soon as possible so as to be able to play before the afternoon was over. I began in the center of the yard and could see my father watching from his bed on the porch. After a few experimental slashes an idea occurred to me. I walked to the house and stood under the windows of the porch.

"Daddy."

"Yes, son."

"When I've finished can I play baseball?"

"Yes."

I resumed work, thinking I would cut fast and get it over in a couple of hours. For a few minutes all went well; there was some satisfaction in watching the thin steel cut easily through dry grass. I grabbed big handfuls and hacked away with gusto. Soon my father called. Obediently I walked to the porch. "Yes, sir?" He was looking through field glasses at the small patch of ground that had been cleared.

"Son, I want you to cut the grass *level* with the ground. Therefore you will have to cut slower and more carefully. Take a smaller handful at a time so you can cut it evenly. Also, you must pick up every stone." This referred to the few pebbles left in the cleared area. "Do you understand?"

"Yes, sir."

"Now go back and do that patch over again, and cut it level with the ground."

"Yes, sir."

Walking back I wondered why I had not started in some part of the yard out of my father's view. The work was now harder; for the stubble was only one or two inches high and was difficult to hold while being cut. It took an hour to do again the area originally cleared in a few minutes. By this time I was tired and disheartened. Sweat ran down my forehead and into my eyes; my mouth was dry. The razor could not be held by the handle, for the blade would fold back. It had to be held by its narrow shank which already had raised a blister. Presently I heard my friends; soon they came into view and approached the fence.

"Whatya doin'?"

"Cuttin' the grass."

"What's that you're cuttin' it with?"

"A razor."

They laughed. "That's a funny thing to be cuttin' grass with."

"Son!" The boys stopped laughing and I went to the porch.

"Yes, sir?"

"If you want to talk to your friends, you may; but don't stop working while you talk."

"Yes, sir." I went back to the basket and resumed cutting.

"What'd he say?" Paul asked in a lowered voice.

"He said I had to work."

"You cain't play ball?"

"No."

"How long is he going to make you work?"

"I don't know."

"Well . . . I guess we might as well go on."

I looked up with longing. They were standing outside the fence, poking their toes idly through the palings. James was rhythmically pounding his fist into the socket of a first baseman's mitt.

"Yeah, let's get goin'."

"Can you get away later on?" Paul asked.

"Maybe I can. I'll try. I'll see if he'll let me." The two boys began to wander off. "I'll try to come later," I called urgently, hoping my father would not hear.

When they were gone I tried for a while to cut faster, but my hand hurt. Several times I had struck rocks with the razor, and the blade was getting dull. Gingerly I got up from my sore knees, went to the hydrant, allowed the water to run until cool, and drank from my cupped hands. Then I went to the barn and began whetting the blade on the stone. When it was sharp I sat down to rest. Being out of my father's sight I felt relatively secure for the moment. The chinaberry tree cast a liquid pattern of sun and shadow before the door. The berries were green and firm, just right for a slingshot.

"Son!"

With a sense of guilt I hurried to my father's window. "Yes, sir."

"Get back to work. It's not time to rest yet."

At midafternoon I looked about and saw how little I had done. Heat waves shimmered before my eyes and I realized that I would not finish today and perhaps not tomorrow. Leaving the razor on the ground, I made the familiar trek to my father's window.

"Daddy."

"Yes."

"Can I quit now?"

"No, son."

"I cain't finish it this afternoon."

"I know."

"Then cain't I go play ball now and finish it tomorrow?"

"No."

"When can I play ball?"

"When you have finished cutting the grass."

"How long do you think it'll take me?"

"Two or three months."

"Well, can . . . ?"

"Now that's enough. Go back to work."

I resumed work at a sullenly slow pace. To spare my knees I sat down, cutting around me as far as I could reach, then moving to a new place and sitting down again.

"Son!"

I went back to the porch. "Yes, sir."

"Do you want to be a lazy, no-account scoundrel?" The voice was harsh and angry.

"No, sir."

"Then don't you ever let me see you sitting down to work again! Now you get back there as quick as you can and stand on your knees."

The afternoon wore on with excruciating slowness. The sun gradually declined. The thin shank of the razor cut into my hand and the blisters broke. I showed them to my father, hoping they would prove incapacitating, but he bandaged them and sent me back. Near sundown I heard the sounds of my friends returning to their homes, but they did not come by to talk. Finally my mother came to the back door, said supper was ready. The day's work was over.

When I woke the next morning I thought it was another school day, then remembered the preceding afternoon and knew that school was far better than cutting grass. I knew that my father intended for me to continue the work, but as no specific order had been given for this particular day there was possibility of escape. I decided to ask my mother for permission to play and be gone before my father realized what had happened. My mother was cooking breakfast when I finished dressing. I made myself useful and waited until, for some reason, she went on the back porch. Now we were separated from my father by four rooms and clearly out of earshot.

"Mama, can I go over to Paul's house?"

"Why yes, hon, I guess so."

That was my mother. To the reasonable request she said yes immediately; the unreasonable required a varying amount of cajolery, but in the end that, too, would be granted. When breakfast was over, I quickly got my cap, whispered a soft good-bye, and started out. I had reached the back door when she called. "Be sure you come back before dinner."

"Son!"

I stopped. In another moment I would have been far enough away to pretend I had not heard. But though my conscience might be deaf to a small voice, it was not deaf to this sternly audible one. If I ran now I would never be able to look at my father and say, "No, I didn't hear you." I gave my mother a reproachful glance as I went back through the kitchen. "Now I won't get to go," I said darkly.

I entered the glass porch and stood by the bed, eyes lowered. I was aware of omitting the required "Yes, sir," but did not care.

"Where were you off to?"

"To Paul's."

"Who told you you could go?"

"Mama."

"Did you ask her?"

"Yes."

"Yes *what*?"

"Yes, sir," I said sulkily.

"Didn't you know I wanted you to work today?"

"No, sir."

"Don't you remember my telling you that you could not play until you finished cutting the grass?"

"No, sir." One lie followed another now. "Anyway . . . that will take just about . . . all summer." My mouth was dry and I was swallowing heavily. "James and Paul . . . don't have to work and . . . I don't see why . . . I . . . have to work all the time."

I choked, my eyes burned, and tears were just one harsh word away. After a moment I saw the covers of the bed move; my father's long, wasted legs appeared. The tears broke, flooding my face. My father stood up, slowly, with difficulty, found his slippers, and put on a bathrobe. My ear was seized and twisted by a bony hand, and I was propelled into the bathroom. My father sat on the edge of the tub and held me in front of him. The fingers were relentless, and it seemed that my ear would be torn from my head.

"Look at me, son."

Tears were dripping from my chin, and every other moment my chest was convulsed by a rattling inspiration. Trying to stop crying, I managed at last to raise my head and look in my father's face. The head and neck were thin. The skin had a grayish glint, and the lines that ran down from his nose were straight. His eyes were steady, and on their level, searching gaze my conscience was impaled.

"Do you know why you are going to be punished?"

The pose of injured innocence was gone now. My guilt seemed everywhere, there was no place to hide.

"Yes . . . sir."

"Why?"

"Because . . . I . . . didn't tell the . . . truth." It was terrible to look into those eyes.

"And?" The question was clipped and hard.

"And . . . because . . . . "

I tried to search my conscience and enumerate my sins, but my mind was a shambles and my past was mountainous with guilt. I could not speak. My eyes dropped.

"Look at me, son."

It was agony to lift my eyes again to that knifelike gaze, that implacable accusation.

"You are being punished because you tried to get your mother's permission for an act you knew to be wrong. You were scoundrel enough to do that!" the razored voice said. "Do you understand?"

"Yes . . . sir."

"You are being punished, further, because you were sullen and insubordinate. Do you understand?"

"Yes . . . sir."

I saw the other hand move and felt the old, sick terror. The hand grasped the clothes of my back and lifted me onto my father's knees. My head hung down to the floor. The hand began to rise and fall.

"Do you understand why you're being punished?"

"Ye . . . es . . . sir."

The blows were heavy and I cried.

"Will you ever do any of those things again?"

"No . . . sir."

The whipping lasted about a minute, after which I was placed on my feet. "Now, stop crying and wash your face. Then go out in the yard to work."

Still sobbing, I approached the lavatory, turned on a trickle of water. Behind me I heard my father stand and slowly leave the room. I held both hands under the faucet, stared with unseeing eyes at the drops of water tumbling over my fingers. Gradually the sobs diminished. I washed my face and left the room, closing the door softly. Passing through the kitchen I was aware that my mother was looking at me with compassion, but I avoided her eyes. To look at her now would be to cry again.

All that day I worked steadily and quietly, asked no questions, made no requests. The work was an expiation and my father found no occasion to criticize. Several times my mother brought out something cold for me to drink. She did not mention my punishment but knowledge of it was eloquent in her eyes. In the afternoon I began to feel better and thought of my friends and of playing ball. Knowing it to be out of the question, I only dreamed about it.

That evening when supper was over and the dishes washed my father called me.

"Tell him you're sorry," my mother whispered.

In our house after every punishment there had to be a reconciliation, the integrity of the bonds that held us had to be reaffirmed. Words of understanding had to be spoken, tokens of love given and received. I walked out on the porch. The sky was filled with masses of purple and red.

"Do you feel better now, son?"

"Yes, sir." The blue eyes contained a reflection of the sunset. "I'm sorry I acted the way I did this morning."

A hand was laid on my head. "You said you didn't know why you had to work, didn't you?"

"Yes, sir, but I . . . "

"That's all right, son. I'll tell you. You ought to know. When you are grown you will have to work to make a living. All your life you'll have to work. Even if we were rich you would labor, because idleness is sinful. The Bible tells us that. I hope some day you will be able to work with your head, but first you've got to know how to work with your hands." The color of the ponderous clouds was deepening to blue and black. "No one is born knowing how to work. It is something we have to learn. You've got to learn to set your mind to a job and keep at it, no matter how hard it is or how long it takes or how much you dislike it. If you don't learn that you'll never amount to anything. And this is the time to learn it. Now do you know why you have to cut the grass?"

"Yes, sir."

"I don't like to make you work when you want to play, but it's for your own good. Can you understand that?"

"Yes, sir."

"Will you be a good boy and work hard this summer until the job is done?"

"Yes, sir."

I left the room feeling better. It was good to be forgiven, to be on good terms with one's father.

Day after day I worked in the yard, standing on my knees, cutting the grass close to the ground. There were few interruptions to break the monotony. Three or four times a day I went to the barn and sharpened the razor, but these trips were no escape. If I went too often or stayed too long my father took notice and put a stop to it. Many times each day I carried away the full basket of grass and stones, but the times of my departure and return were always observed. No evasions were possible because nothing escaped my father's eyes.

One day in July at noon I heard a rattle of dishes indicating that the table was being set. I was hot and tired and thirsty. I could smell the dinner cooking and thought of the tall glasses of iced tea. My mother came to the back door. At first I thought it was to call me, but it was only to throw out dishwater. Suddenly I dropped the razor and ran to the back steps.

"Mama," I called eagerly, but not loud enough for my father to hear. "Is dinner ready?"

"Yes, hon."

I came in, washed my hands, sat in the kitchen to wait.

"Son!"

It was my father's voice, the everlasting surveillance I could never escape.

"Yes, sir."

"What did you come in for?"

"Mama said dinner was ready."

"Did you *ask* her?"

"Yes, sir."

"You trifling scoundrel! Get on back outside to work! And wait till she *calls* you to dinner! You understand?"

As weeks passed the heat increased and the grass withered. Had a match been touched to it the work of a summer would have been accomplished in a few minutes. No rain fell, even for a day, to interrupt the work. The grass did not grow, and the ground which was cleared on the first day remained bare. The earth was baked to a depth of four or five feet and began to crack. The only living thing I encountered was an occasional spider climbing desperately in or out of the crevices in search of a habitable place. My friends knew I had to work and no longer came looking for me. Occasionally I would hear them playing in a nearby field, and sometimes in the mornings would see them pass with fishing poles over their shoulders. I knew that I was not missed, that they had stopped thinking of me and probably did not mention my name.

I became inured to the work but not reconciled to it, and throughout the summer continued to resist. Whippings — which had been rare before — were now common, and after each I would, in the evening, be required to apologize. I would go out on my father's glass porch, say I was sorry, and listen guiltily to a restatement of the principles involved. Tirelessly my father would explain what I had done wrong, the importance of learning to work, and the benefit to my character which this discipline would eventually bring about. After each of these sessions I would feel that I was innately lazy, unworthy, and impulsive. Each time I would resolve to try harder, to overcome my resentment, but each time would relapse. After two or three days I would again become sullen or rebellious and again would be punished. Sometimes I saw my mother in tears and knew she interceded in my behalf, but her efforts were ineffective.

Throughout June and July I worked every day except Sundays. As the job seemed endless I made no future plans. Anything that would last all summer was too large an obstacle to plan beyond, any happiness which lay at its end too remote to lift my spirit. About the middle of August, however, my outlook changed. One evening at sundown I noticed that relatively little grass remained standing. For the first time since the beginning of summer I realized that the job would have an end, that I would be free. Surveying the area remaining to be cut, I attempted to divide it by the area which could be cleared in a single day and reached an estimate of five days. I felt a surge of hope and began visualizing what I would do when I was through. During the next several days I worked faster and more willingly, but found that I had been too sanguine in my estimate. I did not finish on the fifth day or the sixth. But on the evening of the seventh it was apparent to my father as well as to me that the next day the job would be done. Only one or two hours of work remained.

The following morning — for the first time since May — I woke to the sound of rain. I wanted to work anyway, to get it over, but was told I could not. Then I asked if I could go to Paul's house to play until the rain stopped. Again the answer was no. About nine o'clock the rain let up and I hurriedly began to work, but the lull was brief and after a few minutes I had to stop. I stood under the awning which extended out over the windows of my father's porch and waited. After a while I sat on the ground and leaned against the house. A half hour passed. The rain was steady now, seemingly would last all day. It dripped continuously from the canvas and formed a little trench in the earth in front of my feet. I stared out at the gray sky in a dull trance.

"I wish I could go to Paul's house."

I spoke in a low, sullen voice, hardly knowing whether I was talking to myself or to my father.

"It's not fair not to let me play . . . just because it's raining. It's not fair at all."

There was no comment from above. Minutes passed.

"You're a mean bastard!"

A feeling of strangeness swept over me. I had never cursed, was not used to such words. Something violent was stirring in me, something long stifled was rankling for expression.

"If you think you can kick me around all the time you're wrong . . . you damned old bastard!"

At any moment I expected to be called. I would go inside then and receive a whipping worse than I had known possible. A minute passed in silence.

Could it be that my father had not heard? That seemed unlikely, for always I spoke from this place and was always heard.

The windows were open. There was nothing to prevent his hearing. Oh he had heard, all right. I was sure of that. Still, why wasn't I called? The waiting began to get on my nerves. Feeling that I could not make matters worse, I continued. This time I spoke louder and more viciously.

"You're the meanest man in the world. You lie up there in bed and are mean to everybody. I hate you!"

I began to feel astonished at myself. How incredible that I should be saying such things—I who had never dared a word of disrespect!

But why didn't he call? What was he waiting for? Was he waiting for me to say my worst so as to be able to whip me all the harder? The rain drizzled down. The day was gray and quiet. The whole thing began to seem unreal. The absence of reaction was as incredible as the defamation. Both seemed impossible. It was like a bad dream.

But it's real! I thought furiously. I *had* said those things, and would keep on saying them till I made him answer. I became frantic, poured out a tirade of abuse, searched my memory for every dirty word I knew, and when the store of profanity was exhausted and I stopped, breathless, to listen . . . there was no response.

"You goddamn dirty son of a bitch!" I screamed, "I wish you was dead! I wish you was dead, do you hear? Do you hear me?"

I had finished. Now something would happen. I cowered and waited for it, but there was no word from the porch. Not a sound. Not even the stir of bedclothes.

The rage passed and I became miserable. I sat with arms around my knees, staring blankly at the indifferent rain. As the minutes went by I became more appalled by what I had done. Its meaning broadened, expanded in endless ramifications, became boundless and unforgivable. I had broken the commandment to honor thy father and mother. I had taken the name of the Lord in vain, and that was the same as cursing God. I thought of my mother. What would she say when she learned? I pictured her face. She would cry.

For another half hour I sat there. I no longer expected to be called. For some reason the matter was to be left in abeyance. Finally, unable to endure further waiting, I got up and walked away. I went to the barn and wandered about morosely, expecting momentarily to see my mother enter to say that my father wanted me, but she did not come, and the morning passed without further incident.

On entering the house for dinner my first concern was to learn whether she knew. When she smiled I knew that she did not. Now that I was indoors I knew something would happen. I stayed as far from the porch as possible and spoke in low tones. Yet my father must know me to be present. I could not eat, and soon left the house and went back to the barn, where I felt somewhat less vulnerable.

I spent the afternoon there alone, sitting on a box, waiting. Occasionally I would get up and walk around aimlessly. Sometimes I would stand in the doorway looking out at the rain. Though unrestrained I felt myself a prisoner. I searched through my small understanding of my father but found no explanation of the delay. It was unlike him to postpone a whipping. Then it occurred to me that what I had done might so far exceed ordinary transgression as to require a special punishment. Perhaps I would not be whipped at all but sent away from home, never be permitted to come back.

When supper time came I sneaked into the house and tried to be inconspicuous, but was so agitated that my mother was concerned. She looked at me inquiringly and ran her hand affectionately through my hair. "What's the matter, son? Don't you feel well? You look haggard."

"I feel all right," I said.

I escaped her and sat alone on the back porch until called to the table. When supper was safely over my situation was unimproved. It was too late to go outside again, and I could not long remain in the house without meeting my father. At the latest it could be put off only till family prayer. Perhaps that was the time when my crime would be related. Maybe they would pray for me and then expel me from home. I had just begun drying the dishes when the long-awaited sound was heard.

"Son."

It was not the wrathful voice I had expected. It was calm, just loud enough to be audible. Nevertheless it was enough to make me tremble and drop a spoon. For a moment it seemed I could not move.

"Your daddy wants you, dear."

I put down the dishtowel and went to the door of the porch.

"Yes, sir."

"Come out here where I can see you."

I approached the bed. My hands were clenched and I was biting my lip, trying not to cry.

"Your mother tells me you haven't been eating well today. You aren't sick, are you?"

"No, sir."

"You feel all right?"

"Yes, sir."

"Sit down, son. I just called you out here to talk for a while. I often think we don't talk to each other enough. I guess that's my fault. We'll have to do better in the future. I'd like to hear more about what you're interested in and what you think, because that's the only way I can get to know you." He paused a moment. "Maybe you think because I'm grown up I understand everything, but that's not true. You'll find as you get older that no matter how much you learn there's always much you don't know. For example you're my own son and I ought to know you pretty well, but every now and then something'll happen that'll make me realize I don't understand you at all."

I choked back a sob and tried to brace myself for the coming blow.

"I don't think I ever understood my own father," he went on presently, "until it was too late. We were very poor—much poorer, son, than you can imagine. From year in to year out we might see only a few dollars in our house, and what little there was had to be saved for essentials. When we sold our cotton we'd have to buy a plow or an ax. And there were staple foods we had to buy like flour and sugar. We bought cloth, too, but never any ready-made clothes. Until I was a grown man I never had any clothes except what my mother made. I got my first store-bought suit to go away to medical school in, and I don't believe my mother ever had a store-bought dress. My father worked hard and made his boys work hard. We resented it and sometimes even hated him for it, but in the end we knew he was right. One of my brothers never could get along with Daddy, and he ran away from home when he was fifteen. He turned out to be a no-account scoundrel, and the last I heard of him he was a saloon keeper in New Orleans.

"In the summer we hoed corn and picked cotton, and in the winter we fixed rail fences and chopped wood and hauled it home. And always there were mules and pigs to take care of. It was a very different life from yours . . . and in some ways a better one." He looked at me affectionately. "At any rate, we learned how to work, and there's nothing more important for a boy to learn. It's something you haven't yet learned, son. Isn't that right?"

"Yes, sir."

"You will, though. If you ever amount to anything you'll learn. You're learning now. I wish you could understand, though, that I wouldn't be trying to teach you so fast if I knew I would live long enough to teach you more slowly." He paused a moment. "Do you have anything to say?"

"No, sir."

"Then I guess you'd better see if your mother needs you."

I stood up, hardly able to believe that this was all.

"Son."

"Yes, sir."

"Come here a minute."

I went to the bed and my father put a hand on my shoulder. "Remember, son," he said in a husky voice, "whenever it seems I'm being hard on you . . . it's because I love you."

Late that night I woke in terror from a nightmare. For several minutes I lay in bed trembling, unable to convince myself that it was just a dream. Presently I got up and tiptoed through the dark house to the porch.

"Daddy?" I whispered. "Daddy . . . are you all right?"

There was no reply, but soon I became aware of his regular breathing. I went back to bed but almost immediately got up and knelt on the floor. "Dear God, please don't let anything happen to Daddy. Amen."

Still I could not sleep. I lay in bed and thought of many things and after a while began worrying about the razor. What had I done with it? Was it still on the ground under the awning? Perhaps I had left it open. Someone might step on it and get cut. I got up again and went outside looking for it. In the dark I felt about on the ground under my father's windows but did not find it. Then I went to the barn and found it in its usual place, properly closed.

The next morning before noon I finished the job. The last blade of grass was cut and carried away and the back yard was as bald as a razor could make it.

"Daddy," I said, standing under the porch windows, "I've

finished. Is it all right?"

He looked over the yard, then took his binoculars and scrutinized it in more detail, particularly the corners.

"That's well done, son."

I put away the basket and razor and came inside. After dinner I began to feel uncomfortable. It seemed strange not to be working. Restless, unable to sit still, I wandered about the house, looking out the windows and wondering what to do. Presently I sought and obtained permission to go to Paul's house, but somehow felt I was doing something wrong.

During the next two weeks I often played with my friends but never fully lost myself in play and was secretly glad when school started and life settled down to a routine again. I was more quiet than before and better behaved, and when next the report cards were distributed I had a nearly perfect score in conduct.

About the Author

Allen Wheelis, born in 1915 in Louisiana, was educated at the University of Texas, Columbia University and the New York Psychoanalytic Institute. He is a psychiatrist and psychoanalyst practicing in San Francisco. He is the father of three children by two marriages.

Wheelis has written several books on psychology, many scientific articles, one novel and several short stories which he uses to illustrate various points in his psychology books. The autobiographical story "Grass" was used in **The Quest for Identity** (1958) and again in **How People Change** (1973) to show how he came to acquire character traits he doesn't like, especially a sense of guilt and inadequacy.

Questions for Thought and Discussion

1. If Wheelis was born in 1915, in what year did the story take place? Do you think his father's treatment of him that summer would have been considered child abuse at the time? Do you think it would be today? What constitutes child abuse?

2. What were the father's goals for that summer? Why did he require Allen to use a razor when other tools were available?

3. Do you think his goals were appropriate? If so, what other means did he have for reaching them?

4. How have goals of parents changed since this story took place?

5. Why do you think the father never responded directly to the son the day the son sat under the window and vented his anger and resentment towards his father? How do you think the father was affected by the son's attack? And how do you think the son was affected by the events of that particular day?

6. Using information from the introduction to the story as well as the story itself, list the "lasting lessons" of that summer. Which are positive and which are negative? Which are most important?

7. How do you react to the role the mother played in the events of that summer? What else could she have done?

8. What methods do you think parents use today which, years from now, are likely to be judged as negatively as this father's methods are judged today?

---

[1] Wheelis, A. (1973). *How People Change.* New York: Harper Colophon Books, p. 73.

Parenting Issue:

Use of Rewards

From the perspective of behavioral psychology, parents and children "train" each other how to behave. They use material things, privileges and affection as positive reinforcers to "shape" the behavior they desire in each other. Some parents do this systematically by applying the methods of behavior modification. More commonly, however, parents are not aware of the ways family members reward each other. They take good behavior for granted and often they train each other to misbehave by rewarding misbehavior inadvertently.

13.

Bless Me, Father

Andre Dubus

At Easter vacation Jackie discovered that her father was commit-
ting adultery, and four days later—after thinking of little else—
she wrote him a letter. She was a dark, attractive girl whose brown
eyes were large and very bright. She would soon be nineteen, she
had almost completed her freshman year at the University of
Iowa, and she knew, rather proudly, that her eyes had lost some
of their innocence. This had happened in the best possible way:
she hadn't actually done anything new, but she had been exposed
to new people, like Fran, her roommate, who was a practicing
nonvirgin. Fran's boy friend was a drama student and sometimes
Jackie double-dated with them, and they went to parties where
people went outside and smoked marijuana. Jackie had also
drunk bourbon and ginger at football games and got herself
pinned to Gary Nolan. Being pinned to Gary did not interfere with
her staying in the state of grace; every Sunday she went to the Folk
Mass at the chapel, and she usually received Communion, approaching the altar rail to the sound of guitars. It had been a good
year for growing up: seven months ago she had been so naive that
she never would have caught her father, much less written him a
letter.

Before writing the letter, she talked to Fran, then Gary. The
night she got back from vacation she told Fran; they talked until
two in the morning, filling the room with smoke, pursing their
lips, waving their hands. As sophisticated as Fran was, she agreed
with Jackie that her father was wrong, that her parents' marriage
was in danger, and that her mother must be delivered from this
threat of terrible and gratuitous pain. Again and again they
sighed, and said in gloomy, disillusioned, yet enduring voices that

something had to be done. The next night she talked to Gary. There was a movie he wanted to see, but she asked him if they couldn't go drink beer. I have to talk to you, she said.

They sat facing each other in a booth at the rear, where it was dark, and using fake identification cards they drank beer, and she watched his eyes reflecting the sorrow and distraction in her own. Her story lasted for three beers; then, as she ended by saying she would write her father a letter, her tone changed. Now she was purposeful, competent, striking back. This shift caught Gary off guard, nearly spoiling his evening. He had liked it much better when she had so obviously needed his comfort. So he nodded his head, agreeing that a letter was probably the thing to do, but he looked at her with compassion, letting her know how well he understood her, that she was not as cool as she pretended to be, and that a letter to her father would never ease the pain in her heart. Then he took her out to his car, drove to the stadium and parked in its shadow, and soothed her so much that, on the following Saturday, she went to confession and told the priest she had indulged in heavy petting one time.

By then, she had written and mailed the letter. It was seven pages long, using both sides of the stationery, and she had read the first draft to Fran, then written another. Five days later she had heard nothing. When she mailed the letter, she had thought there were only two possible results: either her father would break off with the woman and renew his fidelity to her mother, or he would ignore the letter (although she didn't see how he could possibly do that; the letter was there at his office; her knowledge of him was there; and—this was it—his knowledge of himself was there too: he could not ignore these things). But after a week she was afraid: she saw other alternatives, even more evil than the affair itself. Feeling trapped, he might confront her mother with the truth, push a divorce on her. Or he might bolt: resign his position at the bank and flee with the other woman to California or Mexico, leaving her mother to live her life, shamed and hurt, in Chicago. She thought of the awful boomerangs of life, how the letter—written to save the family—could very well leave her a scandaled half-orphan; as the last unmarried child, she saw herself bravely seeking peace for her mother, taking her on trips away from their lovely house that was now hollow, echoing, ghost-ridden.

Then, at seven o'clock on a Wednesday morning, exactly one

week after she had mailed the letter, her father phoned. He woke her up. By the time she was alert enough to say no, she had already said yes. Then she lit a cigarette and got back in bed. From the other bed, Fran asked who was that on the phone.

"My father. He's driving down to lunch."

"Oh Lord."

When he arrived at the dormitory she was waiting on the front steps, for it was a warm, bright day. He was wearing sunglasses, and he smiled easily as he came up the walk, as though — trouble or not — he was glad to see her. He was a short man who at first seemed fat until you noticed he was simply rounded, his chest and hips separated by a very short waist; he kept himself in good condition, swimming every day in their indoor pool at home, and he could still do more laps than she could. Jackie rose and went down the steps. When he leaned forward to kiss her, she turned her cheek, receiving his lips a couple of inches from hers.

He followed her to the Lincoln, opened the door for her, and she directed him to the bar and grill where she and Gary had talked, then led him to the same booth, where it was dark even in the afternoon and people couldn't distinguish your face unless they walked past you. He wanted a drink before lunch, and Jackie ordered iced tea.

"Nothing stronger?" he said.

"They won't serve me."

She thought now he would wait until his Scotch came.

"You said you saw her at the train station," he said.

She nodded and put her purse on the table and offered him a cigarette; he said no, they were filtered, and she lit one and looked past his shoulder.

"When I was getting off I saw you nod your head to somebody, and I looked that way and saw her getting into a taxi."

Then she tried to look into his eyes, but the best she could do was his mouth.

"She's a blonde," she said.

"A lot of blondes nowadays. When I was a kid — before TV, you know — the blondes in movies were always bad. If a woman was blonde and smoked, you knew right away she was bad."

The drinks came and she told the waiter she'd have a hamburger with everything but onions; her father ordered a salad, then winked and patted his belly, and she thought of him naked with that blonde, whom she would see forever in a black coat stepping into a taxi.

"Then you heard me on the phone. On Holy Saturday, you said."

She nodded and sipped her tea. She was smoking fast, deeply, knowing she would need another as soon as she finished this one, while he sat calmly, drinking without a cigarette, and it struck her that perhaps he was a corrupt, remorseless man. She tried to remember the last time he had received Communion. Of course at Easter he had stayed in the pew while she and her mother went to the altar rail; returning to the pew, she had kept her head bowed, hoping he was watching her. She didn't know about Christmas because, while she was on a date, her parents had gone to midnight Mass. She couldn't remember the Sunday of Thanksgiving vacation, but she knew he had received last summer, kneeling beside her. So apparently he still had the faith, but he sat calmly, enclosing a mortal heart, one year away from fifty: the decade of sudden death when a man had to be careful not only about his body but his soul as well. Now she was shaking another cigarette from her pack.

"How much do you smoke?" he said.

"A pack." It was a lie, but one she also told herself.

"I should have paid you not to, the way some parents do."

"Or set an example," she said quickly, but then she flushed and lowered her eyes. She wasn't ready to fight him and, looking into her glass of tea, she thought if her own husband was ever unfaithful, she didn't want to know about it.

"I suppose that's best," he said. "What if you made a mistake?"

"Did I?"

"No, I just wanted to see if you'd be disappointed."

"That's sick," she said. "It really is."

"Suppose your mother had seen that letter."

"I sent it to the bank."

"Letters get seen. Suppose I was sick or something, and they'd sent it home?"

"People get heard talking on the phone too."

"That's right, they do. And I sounded like a — wait a second."

He took her letter and a pair of glasses from his inside coat pocket, put on his glasses, and scanned the pages.

"Here it is: 'That voice on the phone was not yours. I might as well be honest and say it was the voice of a silly old man. I was so ashamed that I couldn't move' —"

"Daddy—"

"Wait: I would think at least your respect for Mother would keep you from making a phone call to your mistress right in our home."

"Well it's true."

"True? What's true?"

He took off the glasses and put them and the letter in his coat pocket.

"What you just read."

"You think I don't respect your mother?"

"I'd think if you did you wouldn't be doing what you're doing."

His smile seemed bitter, perhaps scornful, but his eyes had that look she had seen for years: loving her because she was a child.

"So you want me to stop seeing this woman before your mother gets hurt."

"Yes."

"And go to confession."

"I hope you will."

"Just like that."

"Don't you still believe in it?"

"Sure. Do you?"

"Of course I do."

"Are you a virgin?"

"Me!" She leaned toward him, keeping her voice low. "Oh, that's petty. That's so petty and mean and perverted. *Yes,* I am."

"What, then? Semivirgin? Never mind: I didn't come for that. Anyway, I went to confession."

"You did?"

Now the waiter was at their booth, and she was thankful for that, because she felt she ought to be happy now, but she wasn't, and she didn't know what to say next. She watched her hamburger descending, then looked over her father's shoulder, blinking as though looking up from a book: a group of boys and girls came in and sat at a long table in the front. When the waiter left, she said: "That's wonderful."

"Is it?"

"Well, of course it is."

"*I* don't feel so good about it."

"I won't listen to that. I'm not interested in how *hard* it is to break up with some—"

"Wait—I didn't feel good while it was going on, either. You

think I *like* being involved with this woman?"

"But you're *not* involved, Daddy. Not if you've been to confession."

"You sound like the priest. I told him the first mistake was sleeping with her. He bought that, all right. But he wouldn't buy it when I told him I felt just as sinful about leaving her. She's alone, you know. She didn't cry when I broke it off, she's too old for that, but I know she hurts now. It's not love, it's—"

"I should hope not."

"It's a lie. Don't you know that?"

"What is?"

"Adultery. A sweet lie, sometimes a happy lie, but a lie. You know what happens? We'd see each other for an hour or two, and that's not real. What's real is with your mother. The other's just a game, like you and that boy in a car someplace."

"Would you *please* get over this compulsion of yours? Accusing me of what *you're* doing?"

"Compulsion—that's a good word. Now I'm compulsive, old, and silly. Is that right?"

"Well, you have to be old, but you don't have to be silly."

"That's absolutely right. And you don't have to be selfish."

"Selfish?"

"Sure. Why did you write a letter like that and hurt your father?"

"I didn't want to hurt you."

"Come on."

"I was worried about Mother."

"Come on."

"I *was*."

He finished his salad and pushed the bowl away; then, smoking, he watched her eating, and now the hamburger was dry and heavy, something to hurry and be done with.

"You did it for yourself," he said.

"That's not true."

"Sure it is. It's okay for Richard Burton but not your father."

"It's not okay for him either. I think they're disgusting."

"Not glamorous and wicked? Not silly, anyway. Or old. You think your mother doesn't know about it?"

"*Does* she?"

"Probably. The point is, we've been married twenty-five years and you can never know what we're like, mostly because it's none of your business. You know what she said two nights ago? After dinner? She said: You must have broken up with your girl friend; you're not being so sweet to me anymore. Joking, you see. Smiling. So I smiled back and said: Sure, you know how it is. That's all we said. Last night I took her out for beer and pizza and a cowboy show —"

In her confusion Jackie thought she might suddenly cry, for she knew the story was sentimental, even corny, but it touched her anyway. She looked at her watch: she had missed gym.

"I'll tell you this too, so you'll know it," he said. "I don't know one man who's faithful. Not in here anyway." He tapped his forehead. "Or whatever it is." His dropping hand gestured toward his chest. "Some don't get many chances. Or they're afraid to see a chance."

"That letter didn't do a bit of good, did it? Come on, I've already missed one class."

"I told you, I broke it off. And you know why? For you and me."

"Sorry," she said. "I'm not one of those daughters."

"Jesus — don't they teach anything but psychology around here? Listen, Jackie: we'll have a good summer, and I don't want suspicious looks every time I walk out of the house."

"I don't believe you anymore. I don't think you even broke it off."

"That's right: I drove two hundred and fifty miles to lie to an eighteen-year-old kid."

"All right. You broke up with her."

"But I'm not saying it right. I should be happy, I should be thanking you and blowing my nose. Right, Peter Pan?"

"What?"

"You used to read Peter Pan, over and over. That's what you were playing: Peter Pan, make everybody happy, save Wendy and Tiger Lily. Or maybe you were Tinker Bell. Remember? She flew ahead because she was jealous and she wanted the boys to shoot Wendy."

"Oh *stop* it."

"Okay. That was mean."

He reached across the table and touched her face, then trailed his fingers down her cheek.

"It just happens that I don't like to tell people goodbye, especially if it's a woman I've slept with. It reminds me of dying."

"I have to get back," she said. "I have a class."

He signalled the waiter, paid, and left a two dollar tip on the table. She slipped out of the booth and walked out, feeling him behind her as though she were being stalked; on the sidewalk she stopped, blinking in the sun. Then his hand was on her arm and he led her to the car. As they rode to the dormitory she watched students on the sidewalks, hoping to see Gary, for she could not be alone now and she could not go to math, which was the same as being alone, only worse. They passed the classroom buildings and, looking ahead now, she saw Fran climbing the dormitory steps; when her father stopped, she opened the door.

"Wait," he said. "Sit a minute and cool off."

He shifted on the seat, hitching his right leg up, and faced her. At first she thought she would look straight ahead through the windshield but she didn't really know what she wanted to do, so — sitting straight — she turned her face to him.

"When you come home you'll have to carry your load, the same as Mother."

"Meaning what?"

"Meaning don't look at me that way anymore. Mother doesn't."

"She must be terribly hurt."

"The difference between you and your mother is she knows me and you don't. Here: take this."

Now the letter was out of his pocket, crossing the space between them, into her lap.

"Read it over tonight and see who you wrote it for."

"For *her*," she said, looking down at her own handwriting of a week ago.

"Think it over. And take this."

Raising himself, he got his wallet; she was shaking her head as, barely looking at them, he pulled out some bills and pressed them into her hand. She left her fingers open.

"Get a dress or take your boy friend to dinner. Go on, take it."

The top one was a five, and it was a thick stack; she folded it and dropped it in her purse.

"I'm not buying you, either. It's just a present."

"All right."

She was looking down, her warm cheek profiled to him, knowing it was a humble posture, but she could not lift her eyes.

"I want you to be straightened out by June."

"Maybe I shouldn't come home."

"Yes you will. And you'll be all right too. Now give me a kiss."

She leaned toward him and kissed his mouth, then she was hugging him and, closing her eyes, she rubbed them quickly on his coat. He got out and came around her side, held the door open, and walked with her up the sidewalk and dormitory steps.

"Be careful driving back," she said.

"Always." Then he was grinning, shrugging his shoulders. "What the hell, I've been to confession."

She smiled, and held it while he got into the car, put on his sunglasses, waved, and drove off. Then she went inside and took the elevator to her floor. Fran was lying on her bed, wearing a slip.

"What happened?"

Jackie shook her head, went to the window, and looked down at the girls walking to class.

"What did he say?"

"He broke up with her."

"Great! So it's okay now."

Jackie left the window and lay on her bed.

"I'm going to cut this afternoon," she said. "Do you think we can find Dick and Gary?"

"Sure."

"Let's go someplace. Maybe to a movie, then out for dinner. It's on me."

"How much did he give you?"

"I don't know, but it's enough."

"Okay," Fran said. "We won't tell the boys how you got it, though."

"No," Jackie said, "we won't."

She closed her eyes. When Fran was dressed, she got up and they went down the elevator and out into the sunlight to find the boys.

About the Author

Andre Dubus was born in 1936 in Louisiana. After graduating from college, he spent six years in the Marines, then earned an M.F.A. from the University of Iowa. He is the father of three children.

Dubus is considered one of the best short story writers in

America today. "Bless Me, Father" was published in 1983 in his collection *The Times Are Never So Bad* which, like his other collections *Separate Flights,* and *Adultery and Other Choices,* received critical praise.

Dubus's characters generally are men and women or parents and children in disintegrating relationships. Unlike many of his contemporaries, however, Dubus's characters do not experience total alienation. They remain connected, if only in a perverted way, as in the case of the father and daughter in "Bless Me, Father," and are possessed of will and passion.

Dubus is Roman Catholic and the church serves as a moral touchstone in some of his works. One of his most famous stories, "A Father's Story," is about a father who goes to disturbing lengths to cover the sin of his daughter. In "Bless Me, Father" it is the father who has sinned but the daughter seeks his blessing nonetheless. Note that the title is the beginning of the Catholic confessional "Bless me, Father, for I have sinned."

Questions for Thought and Discussion

1. How do you react to the father in this story? What kind of person is he? Do you think he ended the affair? Why did he give Jackie money?

2. What is the significance of the verbal exchange regarding Jackie's cigarette smoking?

3. Why was Jackie willing to kiss and hug her father before he left, when she was so angry with him shortly before? What do you think the kiss meant? Why did she take his money? What did the money mean?

4. How do you explain the power the father seemed to have over his daughter (and apparently, over his wife, as well)? What are the similarities between the family in this story and families enduring sexual abuse?

5. In terms of behavioral psychology, what behaviors were being rewarded in this story and by whom? What were the reinforcers each used? In more general terms, what did each of the family members need from each other? What were they giving up in an attempt to get (or maintain) what they wanted?

6. Do you think Jackie was selfish, as her father charged?

7. What meanings do you see in the story title?

8. How do you think this series of events will affect relationships among family members? What options did Jackie have after discovering her father's adulterous relationship?

Parenting Issue:

Balancing Togetherness and Separateness

In a parent-child relationship which is too close, individual identities are lost. In such a fused relationship, the feelings of individuals are obscured for the sake of togetherness. In order to react as one person, parent and child become emotionally manipulative and too involved in each other's lives.

In the ideal parent-child relationship, on the other hand, the feelings, wishes, beliefs, desires and preferences of both parent and child are clarified and, since each person is valued for qualities which are unique, the relationship is able to tolerate some conflict. This clarity of individual identity is called *differentiation* in family systems theory. Differentiation is the opposite of *fusion* and is a prerequisite to parent-child relationships which successfully balance the desires to be both close and separate.

"Going Ashore" illustrates a parent-child relationship which is too close. An emotionally immature mother makes inappropriate demands of her daughter and impedes her daughter's development; the daughter, in turn, is too dependent on the mother since she, too, is immature.

14.
Going Ashore
Mavis Gallant
ॐ

At Tangier it was surprisingly cold, even for December. The sea was lead, the sky cloudy and low. Most of the passengers going ashore for the day came to breakfast wrapped in scarves and sweaters. They were, most of them, thin-skinned, elderly people, less concerned with the prospect of travel than with getting through another winter in relative comfort; on bad days, during the long crossing from the West Indies, they had lain in deck chairs, muffled as mummies, looking stricken and deceived. When Emma Ellenger came into the breakfast lounge barelegged, in sandals, wearing a light summer frock, there was a low flurry of protest. Really, Emma's mother should take more care! The child would catch her death.

Feeling the disapproval almost as an emanation, like the salt one breathed in the air, Emma looked around for someone who liked her—Mr. Cowan, or the Munns. There were the Munns, sitting in a corner, frowning over their toast, coffee, and guidebooks. She waved, although they had not yet seen her, threaded her way between the closely spaced tables, and, without waiting to be asked, sat down.

Miss and Mrs. Munn looked up with a single movement. They were daughter and mother, but so identically frizzy, tweedy, and elderly that they might have been twins. Mrs. Munn, the kindly twin, gazed at Emma with benevolent, rather popping brown eyes, and said, "Child, you'll freeze in that little dress. Do tell your mother—now, don't forget to tell her—that the North African winter can be treacherous, very treacherous indeed." She tapped one of the brown paper-covered guidebooks that lay beside her coffee tray. The Munns always went ashore provided with books, maps, and folders telling them what to expect at every port of call. They differed in every imaginable manner from Emma and her mother, who seldom fully understood where they were and who were often daunted and upset (particularly Mrs. Ellenger) if the people they encountered ashore were the wrong color or spoke an unfamiliar language.

"You should wear a thick scarf," Mrs. Munn went on, "and warm stockings." Thinking of the Ellengers' usual wardrobe, she paused, discouraged. "The most important parts of the—" But she stopped again, unable to say "body" before a girl of twelve. "One should keep the throat and the ankles warm," she said, lowering her gaze to her book.

"We can't," Emma said respectfully. "We didn't bring anything for the cruise except summer dresses. My mother thought it would be warm all the time."

"She should have inquired," Miss Munn said. Miss Munn was crisper, taut; often the roles seemed reversed, and it appeared that she, of the two, should have been the mother.

"I guess she didn't think," Emma said, cast down by all the things her mother failed to do. Emma loved the Munns. It was distressing when, now, they failed to approve of her. They were totally unlike the people she was accustomed to, with their tweeds, their pearls, their strings of fur that bore the claws and muzzles of some small, flattened beast. She had fallen in love with them the first night aboard, during the first dinner out. The Munns and the Ellengers had been seated together, the dining-room steward having thought it a good plan to group, at a table for four, two solitary women and their solitary daughters.

The Munns had been so kind, so interested, asking any number of friendly questions. They wondered how old Emma was, and where Mr. Ellenger might be ("In Heaven," said Emma, casual), and where the Ellengers lived in New York.

"We live all over the place." Emma spoke up proudly. It was evident to her that her mother wasn't planning to say a word. *Somebody* had to be polite. "Most of the time we live in hotels. But last summer we didn't. We lived in an apartment. A big apartment. It wasn't our place. It belongs to this friend of my mother's, Mr. Jimmy Salter, but he was going to be away, and the rent was paid anyway, and we were living there already, so he said—he said—" She saw her mother's face and stopped, bewildered.

"That was nice," said Mrs. Munn, coloring. Her daughter

looked down, smiling mysteriously.

Emma's mother said nothing. She lit a cigarette and blew the smoke over the table. She wore a ring, a wedding band, a Mexican necklace, and a number of clashing bracelets. Her hair, which was long and lighter even than Emma's, had been carefully arranged, drawn into a tight chignon and circled with flowers. Clearly it was not for Miss or Mrs. Munn that she had taken such pains; she had expected a different table arrangement, one that included a man. Infinitely obliging, Mrs. Munn wished that one of them were a man. She bit her lip, trying to find a way out of this unexpected social thicket. Turning to Emma, she said, a little mildly, "Do you like school? I mean I see you are not in school. Have you been ill?"

Emma ill? The idea was so outrageous, so clearly a criticism of Mrs. Ellenger's care, that she was forced, at last, to take notice of this pair of bumps. "There's nothing the matter with my daughter's health," she said a little too loudly. "Emma's never been sick a day. From the time she was born, she's had the best of everything — the best food, the best clothes, the best that money can buy. Emma, isn't that right?"

Emma said yes, hanging her head and wishing her mother would stop.

"Emma was born during the war," Mrs. Ellenger said, dropping her voice. The Munns looked instantly sympathetic. They waited to hear the rest of the story, some romantic misadventure doomed by death or the fevered nature of the epoch itself. Mrs. Munn puckered her forehead, as if already she were prepared to cry. But evidently that part of the story had ceased to be of interest to Emma's mother. "I had a nervous breakdown when she was born," Mrs. Ellenger said. "I had plenty of troubles. My God, *troubles!*" Brooding, she suddenly dropped her cigarette into the dregs of her coffee cup. At the sound it made, the two ladies winced. Their glances crossed. Noticing, Emma wondered what her mother had done now. "I never took my troubles out on Emma," Mrs. Ellenger said. "No, Emma had the best, always the best. I brought her up like a little lady. I kept her all in white — white shoes, white blankets, white bunny coats, white hand-knitted angora bonnets. When she started to walk, she had little white rubbers for the rain. I got her a white buggy with white rubber tires. During the *war*, this was. Emma, isn't it true? Didn't you see your pictures, all in white?"

Emma moved her lips.

"It was the very best butter," Miss Munn murmured.

"She shows your care," Mrs. Munn said gently. "She's a lovely girl."

Emma wanted to die. She looked imploringly at her mother, but Mrs. Ellenger rushed on. It was important, deeply important, that everyone understand what a good mother she had been. "Nobody has to worry about Emma's school, either," she said. "I teach her, so nobody has to worry at all. Emma loves to study. She reads all the time. Just before dinner tonight, she was reading. She was reading Shakespeare. Emma, weren't you reading Shakespeare?"

"I had this book," Emma said, so low that her answer was lost. The Munns began to speak about something else, and Emma's mother relaxed, triumphant.

In truth, Emma had been reading Shakespeare. While they were still unpacking and settling in, she had discovered among their things a battered high school edition of *The Merchant of Venice.* Neither she nor her mother had ever seen it before. It was in the suitcase that contained Mrs. Ellenger's silver evening slippers and Emma's emergency supply of comic books. Emma opened the book and read, "You may do so; but let it be so hasted that supper be ready at the farthest by five of the clock." She closed the book and dropped it. "It must have come from Uncle Jimmy Salter's place," she said. "The maid must have put it in when she helped us pack." "I didn't know he could read," Mrs. Ellenger said. She and Mr. Salter had stopped being friends. "We'll mail it back sometime. It'll be a nice surprise."

Of course, they had never mailed the book. Now, at Tangier, it was still with them, wedged between the comic books and the silver slippers. It had never occurred to Emma's mother to give the book to a steward, or the purser, much less take it ashore during an excursion; the mechanics of wrapping and posting a parcel from a strange port were quite beyond her. The cruise, as far as she was concerned, had become a series of hazards; attempting to dispatch a volume of Shakespeare would have been the last straw. She was happy, or at least not always *un*happy, in a limited area of the ship—the bar, the beauty salon, and her own cabin. As long as she kept to this familiar, hotel-like circuit, there was almost no reason to panic. She had never before been at sea, and although she was not sickened by the motion of the ship, the idea of space, of endless leagues of water, perplexed, then frightened, then, finally, made her ill. It had come to her, during the first, dismal dinner out, that her life as a pretty young woman was finished. There were no men on board—none, at least, that would do—and even if there had been, it was not at all certain that any of them would have desired her. She saw herself flung into an existence that included the Munns, censorious, respectable, prying into one's affairs. At that moment, she had realized what the cruise would mean: She was at sea. She was adrift on an ocean whose immenseness she could not begin to grasp. She was alone, she had no real idea of their route, and it was too late to turn back. Embarking on the cruise had been a gesture, directed against the person Emma called Uncle Jimmy Salter. Like any such gesture, it had to be carried through, particularly since it had been received with total indifference, even relief.

Often, even now, with twenty-four days of the cruise behind and only twenty more to be lived through, the fears she had experienced the first evening would recur: She was at sea, alone. There was no one around to tip stewards, order drinks, plan the nights, make love to her, pay the bills, tell her where she was and what it was all about. How had this happened? However had she mismanaged her life to such a degree? She was still young. She looked at herself in the glass and, covering the dry, darkening skin below her eyes, decided she was still pretty. Perplexed, she went to the beauty salon and had her hair washed by a sympathetic girl, a good listener. Then, drugged with heat, sated with shared confidences, she wandered out to the first-class bar and sat at her own special stool. Here the sympathetic girl was replaced by Eddy, the Eurasian bartender from Hong Kong. Picking up the thread of her life, Mrs. Ellenger talked to Eddy, describing her childhood and her stepmother. She told him about Emma's father, and about the time she and Emma went to California. Talking, she tried to pretend she was in New York and that the environment of the ship was perfectly normal and real. She played with her drink, smiling anxiously at herself in the mirror behind the bar.

Eddy wasn't much of an audience, because he had other things to do, but after a time Mrs. Ellenger became so engrossed in her own recital, repeating and recounting the errors that had brought her to this impasse, that she scarcely noticed at all.

"I was a mere child, Eddy," she said. "A child. What did I know about life?"

"You can learn a lot about life in a job like mine," Eddy said.

Because he was half Chinese, Eddy's customers expected him to deliver remarks tinged with Oriental wisdom. As a result, he had got into the habit of saying anything at all as if it were important.

"Well, I got Emma out of it all." Mrs. Ellenger never seemed to hear Eddy's remarks. "I've got my Emma. That's something. She's a big girl, isn't she, Eddy? Would you take her for only twelve? Some people take her for fourteen. They take us for sisters."

"The Dolly Sisters," Eddy said, ensconced on a reputation that had him not only a sage but a scream.

"Well, I never try to pass Emma off as my sister," Mrs. Ellenger went on. "Oh, it's not that I couldn't. I mean enough people have told me. And I was a mere child myself when she was born. But I don't care if they know she's my daughter. I'm *proud* of my Emma. She was born during the war. I kept her all in white . . ."

Her glass slid away, reminding her that she was not in New York but at sea. It was no use. She thought of the sea, of travel, of being alone; the idea grew so enormous and frightening that, at last, there was nothing to do but go straight to her cabin and get into bed, even if it was the middle of the day. Her head ached and so did her wrists. She took off her heavy jewelry and unpinned her hair. The cabin was gray, chintzed, consolingly neutral; it resembled all or any of the hotel rooms she and Emma had shared in the past. She was surrounded by her own disorder, her own scent. There were yesterday's clothes on a chair, trailing, smelling faintly of cigarette smoke. There, on the dressing table, was an abandoned glass of brandy, an unstoppered bottle of cologne.

She rang the service bell and sent someone to look for Emma.

"Oh, Emma, darling," she said when Emma, troubled and apprehensive, came in. "Emma, why did we come on this crazy cruise? I'm so unhappy, Emma."

"I don't know," Emma said. "I don't know why we came at all." Sitting on her own bed, she picked up her doll and played with its hair or its little black shoes. She had outgrown dolls as toys years before, but this doll, which had no name, had moved about with her as long as she could remember. She knew that her mother expected something from this winter voyage, some miracle, but the nature of the miracle was beyond her. They had shopped for the cruise all summer—Emma remembered that— but when she thought of those summer weeks, with Uncle Jimmy Salter away, and her mother sulking and upset, she had an impression of heat and vacancy, as if no one had been contained in the summer season but Mrs. Ellenger and herself. Left to themselves, she and her mother had shopped, they had bought dresses and scarves and blouses and bathing suits and shoes of every possible color. They bought hats to match the dresses and bags to match the shoes. The boxes the new clothes had come in piled up in the living room, spilling tissue.

"Is he coming back?" Emma had asked once.

"I'm not waiting for *him* to make up *his* mind," her mother had said, which was, to Emma, scarcely an answer at all. "I've got my life, too. I mean," she amended, "we have, Emma. We've got a life, too. We'll go away. We'll go on a cruise or something."

"Maybe he'd like that," Emma had said, with such innocent accuracy that her mother, presented with the thought, stared at her, alarmed. "Then he could have the place all to himself."

In November, they joined the cruise. They had come aboard wearing summer dresses, confident in the climate promised by travel posters — the beaches, the blue-painted seas, the painted-yellow suns. Their cabin was full of luggage and flowers. Everything was new — their white bags, the clothes inside them, neatly folded, smelling of shops.

"It's a new life, Emma," said Mrs. Ellenger.

Emma had caught some of the feeling, for at last they were doing something together, alone, with no man, no Uncle Anyone, to interfere. She felt intensely allied to her mother, then and for several days after. But then, when it became certain that the miracle, the new life, had still to emerge, the feeling disappeared. Sometimes she felt it again just before they reached land — some strange and unexplored bit of coast, where anything might happen. The new life was always there, just before them, like a note indefinitely suspended or a wave about to break. It was there, but nothing happened.

All this, Emma sensed without finding words, even in her mind, to give the idea form. When her mother, helpless and lost, asked why they had come, she could only sit on her bed, playing with her doll's shoe, and, embarrassed by the spectacle of such open unhappiness, murmur, "I don't know. I don't know why we came at all."

Answers and explanations belonged to another language, one she had still to acquire. Even now, in Tangier, longing to explain to the Munns about the summer dresses, she knew she had better not begin. She knew that there must be a simple way of putting these things in words, but when Mrs. Munn spoke of going ashore, of the importance of keeping the throat and ankles warm, it was not in Emma's grasp to explain how it had come about that although she and her mother had shopped all summer and had brought with them much more luggage than they needed, it now developed that they had nothing to wear.

"Perhaps we shall see you in Tangier, later today," said Mrs. Munn. "You must warn your mother about Tangier. Tell her to watch her purse."

Emma nodded vigorously. "I'll tell her."

"And tell her to be careful about the food if you lunch ashore," Mrs. Munn said, beginning to gather together her guidebooks. "No salads. No fruit. Only bottled water. Above all, no native restaurants."

"I'll tell her," Emma said again.

After the Munns had departed, she sat for a moment, puzzled. Certainly they would be lunching in Tangier. For the first time, now she remembered something. The day before (or had it been the day before that?) Emma had invited Eddy, the bartender, to meet them in Tangier for lunch. She had extended the invitation with no sense of what it involved, and no real concept of place and time. North Africa was an imaginary place, half desert, half jungle. Then, this morning, she had looked through the porthole above her bed. There was Tangier, humped and yellowish, speckled with houses, under a wintry sky. It was not a jungle but a city, real. Now the two images met and blended. Tangier was a real place, and somewhere in those piled-up city blocks was Eddy, waiting to meet them for lunch.

She got up at once and hurried back to the cabin. The lounge was clearing; the launch, carrying passengers ashore across the short distance that separated them from the harbor, had been shuttling back and forth since nine o'clock.

Emma's mother was up, and—miracle—nearly dressed. She sat at the dressing table, pinning an artificial camellia into her hair. She did not turn around when Emma came in but frowned at herself in the glass, concentrating. Her dress was open at the back. She had been waiting for Emma to come and do it up. Emma sat down on her own bed. In honor of the excursion ashore, she was wearing gloves, a hat, and carrying a purse. Waiting, she sorted over the contents of her purse (a five-dollar bill, a St. Christopher medal, a wad of Kleenex, a comb in a plastic case), pulled on her small round hat, smoothed her gloves, sighed.

Her mother looked small and helpless, struggling with the awkward camellia. Emma never pitied her when she suffered — it was too disgraceful, too alarming — but she sometimes felt sorry for some detail of her person; now she was touched by the thin veined hands fumbling with flower and pins, and the thin shoulder blades that moved like wings. Her pity took the form of exasperation; it made her want to get up and do something crazy and rude — slam a door, say all the forbidden words she could think of. At last, Mrs. Ellenger stood up, nearly ready. But, no, something had gone wrong.

"Emma, I can't go ashore like this," her mother said. She sat down again. "My dress is wrong. My shoes are wrong. Look at my eyes. I look old. Look at my figure. Before I had you, my figure was wonderful. Never have a baby, Emma. Promise me."

"O.K.," Emma said. She seized the moment of pensive distraction — her mother had a dreamy look, which meant she was thinking of her pretty, fêted youth — and fastened her mother's dress. "You look lovely," Emma said rapidly. "You look just beautiful. The Munns said to tell you to dress warm, but it isn't cold. Please, let's go. Please, let's hurry. All the other people have gone. Listen, we're in *Africa*."

"That's what's so crazy," Mrs. Ellenger said, as if at last she had discovered the source of all her grievances. "What am I doing in Africa?"

"Bring a scarf for your head," said Emma. "Please, let's go."

They got the last two places in the launch. Mrs. Ellenger bent and shuddered and covered her eyes; the boat was a terrible ordeal, windy and smelling of oil. She felt chilled and vomitous. "Oh, Emma," she moaned.

Emma put an arm about her, reassuring. "It's only a minute," she said. "We're nearly there now. Please look up. Why don't you look? The sun's come out."

"I'm going to be sick," Mrs. Ellenger said.

"No, you're not."

At last they were helped ashore, and stood, brushing their wrinkled skirts, on the edge of Tangier. Emma decided she had better mention Eddy right away.

"Wouldn't it be nice if we sort of ran into Eddy?" she said. "He knows all about Tangier. He's been here before. He could take us around."

"Run into *who?*" Mrs. Ellenger took off the scarf she had worn in the launch, shook it, folded it, and put it in her purse. Just then, a light wind sprang up from the bay. With a little moan, Mrs. Ellenger opened her bag and took out the scarf. She seemed not to know what to do with it, and finally clutched it to her throat. "I'm so cold," she said. "Emma, I've never been so cold in my whole life. Can't we get away from here? Isn't there a taxi or something?"

Some of their fellow passengers were standing a short distance away in a sheeplike huddle, waiting for a guide from a travel bureau to come and fetch them. They were warmly dressed. They carried books, cameras, and maps. Emma suddenly thought of how funny she and her mother must look, alone and baffled, dressed for a summer excursion. Mrs. Ellenger tottered uncertainly on high white heels.

"I think if we just walk up to that big street," Emma said, pointing. "I even see taxis. Don't worry. It'll be all right." Mrs. Ellenger looked back, almost wistfully, to the cruise ship; it was, at least, familiar. "Don't look *that* way," said Emma. "Look where we're going. Look at Africa."

Obediently, Mrs. Ellenger looked at Africa. She saw hotels, an avenue, a row of stubby palms. As Emma had said, there were taxis, one of which, at their signals, rolled out of a rank and drew up before them. Emma urged her mother into the cab and got in after her.

"We might run into Eddy," she said again.

Mrs. Ellenger saw no reason why, on this particular day, she should be forced to think about Eddy. She started to say so, but Emma was giving the driver directions, telling him to take them to the center of town. "But what if we *did* see Eddy?" Emma asked.

"Will you stop that?" Mrs. Ellenger cried. "Will you stop that about Eddy? If we see him, we see him. I guess he's got the same rights ashore as anyone else!"

Emma found this concession faintly reassuring. It did not presage an outright refusal to be with Eddy. She searched her mind for some sympathetic reference to him — the fact, for instance, that he had two children named Wilma and George — but, glancing sidelong at her mother, decided to say nothing more. Mrs. Ellenger had admitted Eddy's rights, a point that could be resurrected later, in case of trouble. They were driving uphill, between houses that looked, Emma thought, neither interesting nor African. It was certainly not the Africa she had imaged the day she invited Eddy — a vista of sand dunes surrounded by jungle, full of camels, lions, trailing vines. It was hard now to remember just why she had asked him, or if, indeed, she really had. It had been morning. The setting was easy to reconstruct. She had been the only person at the bar; she was drinking an elaborate mixture of syrup and fruit concocted by Eddy. Eddy was wiping glasses. He wore a white coat, from the pocket of which emerged the corner of a colored handkerchief. The handkerchief was one of a dozen given him by a kind American lady met on a former cruise; it bore his name, embroidered in a dashing hand. Emma had been sitting, admiring the handkerchief, thinking about the hapless donor ("She found me attractive, et cetera, et cetera," Eddy had once told her, looking resigned) when suddenly Eddy said something about Tangier, the next port, and Emma had imagined the three of them together — herself, her mother, and Eddy.

"My mother wants you to go ashore with us in Africa," she had said, already convinced this was so.

"What do you mean, ashore?" Eddy said. "Take you around, meet you for lunch?" There was nothing unusual in the invitation, as such; Eddy was a great favorite with many of his clients. "It's funny she never mentioned it."

"She forgot," Emma said. "We don't know anyone in Africa, and my mother always likes company."

"I know *that*," Eddy said softly, smiling to himself. With a little shovel, he scooped almonds into glass dishes. "What I mean is your mother actually said" — and here he imitated Mrs. Ellenger, his voice going plaintive and high —" 'I'd just adore having dear Eddy as our guest for lunch.' She actually said that?"

"Oh, Eddy!" Emma had to laugh so hard at the very idea that she doubled up over her drink. Eddy could be so witty when he wanted to be, sending clockwork spiders down the bar, serving drinks in trick glasses that unexpectedly dripped on people's clothes! Sometimes, watching him being funny with favorite customers, she would laugh until her stomach ached.

"I'll tell you what," Eddy said, having weighed the invitation. "I'll meet you *in* Tangier. I can't go ashore with you, I mean — not in the same launch; I have to go with the crew. But I'll meet you there."

"Where'll you meet us?" Emma said. "Should we pick a place?"

"Oh, I'll find you," Eddy said. He set his plates of almonds at spaced intervals along the bar. "Around the center of town. I know where you'll go." He smiled again his secret, superior smile.

They had left it at that. Had Eddy really said the center of town, Emma wondered now, or had she thought that up herself? Had the whole scene, for that matter, taken place, or had she thought that up, too? No, it was real, for, their taxi having deposited them at the Plaza de Francia, Eddy at once detached himself from the crowd on the street and came toward them.

Eddy was dapper. He wore a light suit and a square-shouldered topcoat. He closed their taxi door and smiled at Emma's mother, who was paying the driver.

"Look," Emma said. "Look who's here!"

Emma's mother moved over to a shopwindow and became absorbed in a display of nylon stockings; presented with a *fait accompli,* she withdrew from the scene — turned her back, put on a pair of sunglasses, narrowed her interest to a single stocking draped on a chrome rack. Eddy seemed unaware of tension. He carried several small parcels, his purchases. Jauntily he joined Mrs. Ellenger at the window.

"This is a good place to buy nylons," he said. "In fact, you should stock up on everything you need, because it's tax free. Anything you buy here, you can sell in Spain."

"My daughter and I have everything we require," Mrs. Ellenger said. She walked off and then quickened her step, so that he wouldn't appear to be walking with them.

Emma smiled at Eddy and fell back very slightly, striking a balance between the two. "What did you buy?" she said softly. "Something for Wilma and George?"

"Lots of stuff," said Eddy. "Now, this café right here," he called after Mrs. Ellenger, "would be a good place to sit down. Right here, in the Plaza de Francia, you can see everyone important. They all come here, the high society of two continents."

"Of two continents," Emma said, wishing her mother would pay more attention. She stared at all the people behind the glass café fronts — the office workers drinking coffee before hurrying back to their desks, the tourists from cruise ships like their own.

Mrs. Ellenger stopped. She extended her hand to Emma and said, "My daughter and I have a lot of sightseeing to do, Eddy. I'm sure there are things you want to do, too." She was smiling. The surface of her sunglasses, mirrored, gave back a small, distorted public square, a tiny Eddy, and Emma, anguished, in gloves and hat.

"Oh, Eddy!" Emma cried. She wanted to say something else, to explain that her mother didn't understand, but he vanished, just like that, and moments later she picked out his neat little figure bobbing along in the crowd going downhill, away from the Plaza. "Eddy sort of expected to stay with us," she said.

"So I noticed," said Mrs. Ellenger. They sat down in a café — not the one Eddy had suggested, but a similar café nearby. "One Coca-Cola," she told the waiter, "and one brandy-and-water." She sighed with relief, as if they had been walking for hours.

Their drinks came. Emma saw, by the clock in the middle of the square, that it was half past eleven. It was warm in the sun, as warm as May. Perhaps, after all, they had been right about the summer dresses. Forgetting Eddy, she looked around. This was Tangier, and she, Emma Ellenger, was sitting with the high society of two continents. Outside was a public square, with low buildings, a café across the street, a clock, and, walking past in striped woollen cloaks, Arabs. The Arabs were real; if the glass of the window had not been there, she could have touched them.

"There's sawdust or something in my drink," Mrs. Ellenger said. "It must have come off the ice." Nevertheless, she drank it to the end and ordered another.

"We'll go out soon, won't we?" Emma said, faintly alarmed.

"In a minute."

The waiter brought them a pile of magazines, including a six-month-old *Vogue*. Mrs. Ellenger removed her glasses, looking pleased.

"We'll go soon?" Emma repeated.

There was no reply.

The square swelled with a midday crowd. Sun covered their table until Mrs. Ellenger's glasses became warm to the touch.

"Aren't we going out?" Emma said. "Aren't we going to have anything for lunch?" Her legs ached from sitting still.

"You could have something here," Mrs. Ellenger said, vague.

The waiter brought Emma a sandwich and a glass of milk. Mrs. Ellenger continued to look at *Vogue*. Sometimes passengers from their ship went by. They waved gaily, as if Tangier were the last place they had ever expected to see a familiar face. The Munns passed, walking in step. Emma thumped on the window, but neither of the ladies turned. Something about their solidarity, their sureness of purpose, made her feel lonely and left behind. Soon they would have seen Tangier, while she and her mother might very well sit here until it was time to go back to the ship. She remembered Eddy and wondered what he was doing.

Mrs. Ellenger had come to the end of her reading material. She seemed suddenly to find her drink distasteful. She leaned on her hand, fretful and depressed, as she often was at that hour of the day. She was sorry she had come on the cruise and said so again. The warm ports were cold. She wasn't getting the right things to eat. She was getting so old and ugly that the bartender, having nothing better in view, and thinking she would be glad of anything, had tried to pick her up. What was she doing here, anyway? Her life . . .

"I wish we could have gone with Eddy," Emma said, with a sigh.

"Why, Emma," Mrs. Ellenger said. Her emotions jolted from a familiar track, it took her a moment or so to decide how she felt about this interruption. She thought it over, and became annoyed. "You mean you'd have more fun with that Chink than with me? Is that what you're trying to tell me?"

"It isn't that exactly. I only meant, we *could* have gone with him. He's been here before. Or the Munns, or this other friend of mine, Mr. Cowan. Only, he didn't come ashore today, Mr. Cowan. You shouldn't say 'Chink.' You should say 'Chinese person,' Mr. Cowan told me. Otherwise it offends. You should never offend. You should never say 'Irishman.' You should say 'Irish person.' You should never say 'Jew.' You should say—"

"Some cruise!" said Mrs. Ellenger, who had been listening to this with an expression of astounded shock, as if Emma had been repeating blasphemy. "All I can say is some cruise. Some selected passengers! What else did he tell you? What does he want with a little girl like you, anyway? Did he ever ask you into his stateroom —anything like that?"

"Oh, goodness, no!" Emma said impatiently; so many of her mother's remarks were beside the point. She knew all about not going anywhere with men, not accepting presents, all that kind of thing. "His stateroom's too small even for him. It isn't the one he paid for. He tells the purser all the time, but it doesn't make any difference. That's why he stays in the bar all day."

Indeed, for most of the cruise, Emma's friend had sat in the bar writing a long journal, which he sent home, in installments, for the edification of his analyst. His analyst, Mr. Cowan had told Emma, was to blame for the fact that he had taken the cruise. In revenge, he passed his days writing down all the things at fault with the passengers and the service, hoping to make the analyst sad and guilty. Emma began to explain her own version of this to Mrs. Ellenger, but her mother was no longer listening. She stared straight before her in the brooding, injured way Emma dreaded. Her gaze seemed turned inward, rather than to the street, as if she were concentrating on some terrible grievance and struggling to bring it to words.

"You think I'm not a good mother," she said, still not looking at Emma, or, really, at anything. "That's why you hang around these other people. It's not fair. I'm good to you. Well, am I?"

"Yes," said Emma. She glanced about nervously, wondering if anyone could hear.

"Do you ever need anything?" her mother persisted. "Do you know what happens to a lot of kids like you? They get left in schools, that's what happens. Did I ever do that to you?"

"No."

"I always kept you with me, no matter what anyone said. You mean more to me than anybody, any man. You know that. I'd give up anyone for you. I've even done it."

"I know," Emma said. There was a queer pain in her throat. She had to swallow to make it go away. She felt hot and uncomfortable and had to do something distracting; she took off her hat, rolled her gloves into a ball and put them in her purse.

Mrs. Ellenger sighed. "Well," she said in a different voice, "if we're going to see anything of this town, we'd better move." She paid for their drinks, leaving a large tip on the messy table, littered with ashes and magazines. They left the café and, arm in arm, like Miss and Mrs. Munn, they circled the block, looking into the dreary windows of luggage and furniture stores. Some of the windows had been decorated for Christmas with strings of colored lights. Emma was startled; she had forgotten all about Christmas. It seemed unnatural that there should be signs of it in a place like Tangier. "Do Arabs have Christmas?" she said.

"Everyone does," Mrs. Ellenger said. "Except—" She could not remember the exceptions.

It was growing cool, and her shoes were not right for walking. She looked up and down the street, hoping a taxi would appear, and then, with one of her abrupt, emotional changes, she darted into a souvenir shop that had taken her eye. Emma followed, blinking in the dark. The shop was tiny. There were colored bracelets in a glass case, leather slippers, and piles of silky material. From separate corners of the shop, a man and a woman converged on them.

"I'd like a bracelet for my litle girl," Mrs. Ellenger said.

"For Christmas?" said the woman.

"Sort of. Although she gets plenty of presents, all the time. It doesn't have to be anything special."

"What a fortunate girl," the woman said absently, unlocking the case.

Emma was not interested in the bracelet. She turned her back on the case and found herself facing a shelf on which were pottery figures of lions, camels, and tigers. They were fastened to bases marked *"Souvenir de Tanger,"* or *"Recuerdo."*

"Those are nice," Emma said, to the man. He wore a fez, and leaned against the counter, staring idly at Mrs. Ellenger. Emma pointed to the tigers. "Do they cost a lot?"

He said something in a language she could not understand. Then, lapsing into a creamy sort of English, "They are special African tigers." He grinned, showing his gums, as if the expression "African tigers" were a joke they shared. "They come from a little village in the mountains. There are interesting old myths connected with them." Emma looked at him blankly. "They are magic," he said.

"There's no such thing," Emma said. Embarrassed for him, she looked away, coloring deeply.

"This one," the man said, picking up a tiger. It was glazed in stripes of orange and black. The seam of the factory mold ran in a faint ridge down its back; the glaze had already begun to crack. "This is a special African tiger," he said. "It is good for ten wishes. Any ten."

"There's no such thing," Emma said again, but she took the tiger from him and held it in her hand, where it seemed to grow warm of its own accord. "Does it cost a lot?"

The man looked over at the case of bracelets and exchanged a swift, silent signal with his partner. Mrs. Ellenger, still talking, was hesitating between two enamelled bracelets.

"Genuine Sahara work," the woman said of the more expensive piece. When Mrs. Ellenger appeared certain to choose it, the woman nodded, and the man said to Emma, "The tiger is a gift. It costs you nothing."

"A present?" She glanced toward her mother, busy counting

change. "I'm not allowed to take anything from strange men" rose
to her lips. She checked it.

"For Christmas," the man said, still looking amused. "Think of
me on Christmas Day, and make a wish."

"Oh, I will," Emma said, suddenly making up her mind.
"Thanks. Thanks a lot." She put the tiger in her purse.

"Here, baby, try this on," Mrs. Ellenger said from across the
shop. She clasped the bracelet around Emma's wrist. It was too
small, and pinched, but everyone exclaimed at how pretty it
looked.

"Thank you," Emma said. Clutching her purse, feeling the
lump the tiger made, she said, looking toward the man, "Thanks, I
love it."

"Be sure to tell your friends," he cried, as if the point of the gift
would otherwise be lost.

"Are you happy?" Mrs. Ellenger asked kissing Emma. "Do you
really love it? Would you still rather be with Eddy and these other
people?" Her arm around Emma, they left the shop. Outside, Mrs.
Ellenger walked a few steps, looking piteously at the cars going
by. "Oh, God, let there be a taxi," she said. They found one and
hailed it, and she collapsed inside, closing her eyes. She had seen
as much of Tangier as she wanted. They rushed downhill. Emma,
her face pressed against the window, had a blurred impression of
houses. Their day, all at once, spun out in reverse; there was the
launch, waiting. They embarked and, in a moment, the city, the
continent, receded.

Emma thought, confused, Is that all? Is that all of Africa?

But there was no time to protest. Mrs. Ellenger, who had lost
her sunglasses, had to be consoled and helped with her scarf.
"Oh, thank God!" she said fervently, as she was helped from the
launch. "Oh, my God, what a day!" She tottered off to bed, to
sleep until dinner.

The ship was nearly empty. Emma lingered on deck, looking
back at Tangier. She made a detour, peering into the bar; it was
empty and still. A wire screen had been propped against the
shelves of bottles. Reluctantly, she made her way to the cabin. Her
mother had already gone to sleep. Emma pulled the curtain over
the porthole, dimming the light, and picked up her mother's
scattered clothes. The new bracelet pinched terribly; when she
unclasped it, it left an ugly greenish mark, like a bruise. She
rubbed at the mark with soap and then cologne and finally most

of it came away. Moving softly, so as not to wake up her mother, she put the bracelet in the suitcase that contained her comic books and Uncle Jimmy Salter's *Merchant of Venice*. Remembering the tiger, she took it out of her purse and slipped it under her pillow.

The bar, suddenly, was full of noise. Most of it was coming from a newly installed loudspeaker. "Oh, little town of Bethlehem," Emma heard, even before she opened the heavy glass doors. Under the music, but equally amplified, were the voices of people arguing, the people who, somewhere on the ship, were trying out the carol recordings. Eddy hadn't yet returned. Crew members, in working clothes, were hanging Christmas decorations. There was a small silver tree over the bar and a larger one, real, being lashed to a pillar. At one of the low tables in front of the bar Mr. Cowan sat reading a travel folder.

"Have a good time?" he asked, looking up. He had to bellow because "Oh, Little Town of Bethlehem" was coming through so loudly. "I've just figured something out," he said, as Emma sat down. "If I take a plane from Madrid, I can be home in sixteen hours."

"Are you going to take it?"

"I don't know," he said, looking disconsolately at the folder. "Madrid isn't a port. I'd have to get off at Gibraltar or Málaga and take a train. And then, what about all my stuff? I'd have to get my trunk shipped. On the other hand," he said, looking earnestly at Emma, talking to her in the grown-up, if mystifying, way she liked, "why should I finish this ghastly cruise just for spite? They brought the mail on today. There was a letter from my wife. She says I'd better forget it and come home for Christmas."

Emma accepted without question the new fact that Mr. Cowan had a wife. Eddy had Wilma and George, the Munns had each other. Everyone she knew had a life, complete, that all but excluded Emma. "Will you go?" she repeated, unsettled by the idea that someone she liked was going away.

"Yes," he said. "I think so. We'll be in Gibraltar tomorrow. I'll get off there. How was Tangier? Anyone try to sell you a black-market Coke?"

"No," Emma said. "My mother bought a bracelet. A man gave me an African tiger."

"What kind of tiger?"

"A toy," said Emma. "A little one."

"Oh. Damn bar's been closed all day," he said, getting up. "Want to walk? Want to go down to the other bar?"

"No, thanks. I have to wait here for somebody," Emma said, and her eyes sought the service door behind the bar through which, at any moment, Eddy might appear. After Mr. Cowan had left, she sat, patient, looking at the folder he had forgotten.

Outside, the December evening drew in. The bar began to fill; passengers drifted in, compared souvenirs, talking in high, excited voices about the journey ashore. It didn't sound as if they'd been in Tangier at all, Emma thought. It sounded like some strange, imagined city, full of hazard and adventure.

". . . so this little Arab boy comes up to me," a man was saying, "and with my wife standing right there, right there beside me, he says—"

"Hush," his wife said, indicating Emma. "Not so loud."

Eddy and Mrs. Ellenger arrived almost simultaneously, coming, of course, through separate doors. Eddy had his white coat on, a fresh colored handkerchief in the pocket. He turned on the lights, took down the wire screen. Mrs. Ellenger had changed her clothes and brushed her hair. She wore a flowered dress, and looked cheerful and composed. "All alone, baby?" she said. "You haven't even changed, or washed your face. Never mind, there's no time now."

Emma looked at the bar, trying in vain to catch Eddy's eye. "Aren't you going to have a drink before dinner?"

"No. I'm hungry. Emma, you look a mess." Still talking, Mrs. Ellenger ushered Emma out to the dining room. Passing the bar, Emma called, "Hey, Eddy, hello," but, except to throw her a puzzling look, he did not respond.

They ate in near silence. Mrs. Ellenger felt rested and hungry, and, in any case, had at no time anything to communicate to the Munns. Miss Munn, between courses, read a book about Spain. She had read aloud the references to Gibraltar, and now turned to the section on Málaga, where they would be in two days. "From the summit of the Gibralfaro," she said, "one has an excellent view of the city and harbor. Two asterisks. At the state-controlled restaurant, refreshments . . ." She looked up and said, to Mrs. Munn, who was listening hard, eyes shut, "That's where we'll have lunch. We can hire a horse and *calesa*. It will kill the morning and part of the afternoon."

Already, they knew all about killing time in Málaga. They had never been there, but it would hold no surprise; they would make no mistakes. It was no use, Emma thought. She and her mother would never be like the Munns. Her mother, she could see, was becoming disturbed by this talk of Gibraltar and Málaga, by the threat of other ventures ashore. Had she not been so concerned with Eddy, she would have tried, helpfully, to lead the talk to something else. However, her apology to Eddy was infinitely more urgent. As soon as she could, she pushed back her hair and hurried out to the bar. Her mother dawdled behind her, fishing in her bag for a cigarette.

Emma sat up on one of the high stools and said, "Eddy, where did you go? What did you do? I'm sorry about the lunch."

At that, he gave her another look, but still said nothing. Mrs. Ellenger arrived and sat down next to Emma. She looked from Emma to Eddy, eyebrows raised.

Don't let her be rude, Emma silently implored an undefined source of assistance. Don't let her be rude to Eddy, and I'll never bother you again. Then, suddenly, she remembered the tiger under the pillow.

There was no reason to worry. Eddy and her mother seemed to understand each other very well. "Get a good lunch, Eddy?" her mother asked.

"Yes. Thanks."

He moved away from them, down the bar, where he was busy entertaining new people, two men and a woman, who had come aboard that day from Tangier. The woman wore harlequin glasses studded with flashing stones. She laughed in a sort of bray at Eddy's antics and his funny remarks. "You can't get mad at him," Emma heard her say to one of the men. "He's like a monkey, if a monkey could talk."

"Eddy, our drinks," Mrs. Ellenger said.

Blank, polite, he poured brandy for Mrs. Ellenger and placed before Emma a bottle of Coca-Cola and a glass. Around the curve of the bar, Emma stared at the noisy woman, Eddy's new favorite, and the two fat old men with her. Mrs. Ellenger sipped her brandy, glancing obliquely in the same direction. She listened to their conversation. Two were husband and wife, the third a friend. They had picked up the cruise because they were fed up with North Africa. They had been traveling for several months. They were tired, and each of them had had a touch of colic.

Emma was sleepy. It was too much, trying to understand Eddy, and the day ashore. She drooped over her drink. Suddenly, beside her, Mrs. Ellenger spoke. "You really shouldn't encourage Eddy like that. He's an awful show-off. He'll dance around like that all night if you laugh enough." She said it with her nicest smile. The new people stared, taking her in. They looked at her dress, her hair, her rings. Something else was said. When Emma took notice once more, one of the two men had shifted stools so he sat halfway between his friends and Emma's mother. Emma heard the introductions: Mr. and Mrs. Frank Timmins. Mr. Boyd Oliver. Mrs. Ellenger. Little Emma Ellenger, my daughter.

"Now, don't tell me that young lady's your daughter," Mr. Boyd Oliver said, turning his back on his friends. He smiled at Emma, and, just because of the smile, she suddenly remembered Uncle Harry Todd, who had given her the complete set of Sue Barton books, and another uncle, whose name she had forgotten, who had taken her to the circus when she was six.

Mr. Oliver leaned toward Mrs. Ellenger. It was difficult to talk; the bar was filling up. She picked up her bag and gloves from the stool next to her own, and Mr. Oliver moved once again. Polite and formal, they agreed that that made talking much easier.

Mr. Oliver said that he was certainly glad to meet them. The Timminses were wonderful friends, but sometimes, traveling like this, he felt like the extra wheel. Did Mrs. Ellenger know what he meant to say?

They were all talking: Mr. Oliver, Eddy, Emma's mother, Mr. and Mrs. Timmins, the rest of the people who had drifted in. The mood, collectively, was a good one. It had been a wonderful day. They all agreed to that, even Mrs. Ellenger. The carols had started again, the same record. Someone sang with the music: "Yet in thy dark streets shineth the everlasting light . . ."

"I'd take you more for *sisters*," Mr. Oliver said.

"Really?" Mrs. Ellenger said. "Do you really think so? Well, I suppose we are, in a way. I was practically a child myself when she came into the world. But I wouldn't try to pass Emma off as my sister. I'm proud to say she's my daughter. She was born during the war. We only have each other."

"Well," Mr. Oliver said, after thinking this declaration over for a moment or so, "that's the way it should be. You're a brave little person."

Mrs. Ellenger accepted this. He signaled for Eddy, and she

turned to Emma. "I think you could go to bed now. It's been a big day for you."

The noise and laughter stopped as Emma said her good nights. She remembered all the names. "Good night, Eddy," she said, at the end, but he was rinsing glasses and seemed not to hear.

Emma could still hear the carols faintly as she undressed. She knelt on her bed for a last look at Tangier; it seemed different again, exotic and remote, with the ring of lights around the shore, the city night sounds drifting over the harbor. She thought, Today I was in Africa . . . But Africa had become unreal. The café, the clock in the square, the shop where they had bought the bracelet, had nothing to do with the Tangier she had imagined or this present view from the ship. Still, the tiger was real: it was under her pillow, proof that she had been to Africa, that she had touched shore. She dropped the curtain, put out the light. To the sound of Christmas music, she went to sleep.

It was late when Mrs. Ellenger came into the cabin. Emma had been asleep for hours, her doll beside her, the tiger under her head. She came out of a confused and troubled dream about a house she had once lived in, somewhere. There were new tenants in the house; when she tried to get in, they sent her away. She smelled her mother's perfume and heard her mother's voice before opening her eyes. Mrs. Ellenger had turned on the light at the dressing table and dropped into the chair before it. She was talking to herself, and sounded fretful. "Where's my cold cream?" she said. "Where'd I put it? Who took it?" She put her hand on the service bell and Emma prayed: It's late. Don't let her ring . . . The entreaty was instantly answered, for Mrs. Ellenger changed her mind and pulled off her earrings. Her hair was all over the place, Emma noticed. She looked all askew, oddly put together. Emma closed her eyes. She could identify, without seeing them, by the sounds, the eau de cologne, the make-up remover, and the lemon cream her mother used at night. Mrs. Ellenger undressed and pulled on the nightgown that had been laid out for her. She went into the bathroom, put on the light, and cleaned her teeth. Then she came back into the cabin and got into bed with Emma. She was crying. She lay so close that Emma's face was wet with her mother's tears and sticky with lemon cream.

"Are you awake?" her mother whispered. "I'm sorry, Emma. I'm so sorry."

"What for?"

"Nothing," Mrs. Ellenger said. "Do you love your mother?"

"Yes." Emma stirred, turning her face away. She slipped a hand up and under the pillow. The tiger was still there.

"I can't help it, Emma," her mother whispered. "I can't live like we've been living on this cruise. I'm not made for it. I don't like being alone. I need friends." Emma said nothing. Her mother waited, then said, "He'll go ashore with us tomorrow. It'll be someone to take us around. Wouldn't you like that?"

"Who's going with us?" Emma said. "The fat old man?"

Her mother had stopped crying. Her voice changed. She said, loud and matter-of-fact, "He's got a wife someplace. He only told me now, a minute ago. Why? Why not right at the beginning, in the bar? I'm not like that. I want something different, a *friend*." The pillow between their faces was wet. Mrs. Ellenger rubbed her cheek on the cold damp patch. "Don't ever get married, Emma," she said. "Don't have anything to do with men. Your father was no good. Jimmy Salter was no good. This one's no better. He's got a wife and look at how — Promise me you'll never get married. We should always stick together, you and I. Promise me we'll always stay together."

"All right," Emma said.

"We'll have fun," Mrs. Ellenger said, pleading. "Didn't we have fun today, when we were ashore, when I got you the nice bracelet? Next year, we'll go someplace else. We'll go anywhere you want."

"I don't want to go anywhere," Emma said.

But her mother wasn't listening. Sobbing quietly, she went to sleep. Her arm across Emma grew heavy and slack. Emma lay still; then she saw that the bathroom light had been left on. Carefully, carrying the tiger, she crawled out over the foot of the bed. Before turning out the light, she looked at the tiger. Already, his coat had begun to flake away. The ears were chipped. Turning it over, inspecting the damage, she saw, stamped in blue: "Made in Japan." The man in the shop had been mistaken, then. It was not an African tiger, good for ten wishes, but something quite ordinary.

She put the light out and, in the dim stateroom turning gray with dawn, she got into her mother's empty bed. Still holding the tiger, she lay, hearing her mother's low breathing and the unhappy words she muttered out of her sleep.

Mr. Oliver, Emma thought, trying to sort things over, one at a time. Mr. Oliver would be with them for the rest of the cruise. Tomorrow, they would go ashore together. "I think you might call Mr. Oliver Uncle Boyd," her mother might say.

Emma's grasp on the tiger relaxed. There was no magic about it; it did not matter, really, where it had come from. There was nothing to be gained by keeping it hidden under a pillow. Still, she had loved it for an afternoon, she would not throw it away or inter it, like the bracelet, in a suitcase. She put it on the table by the bed and said softly, trying out the sound, "I'm too old to call you Uncle Boyd. I'm thirteen next year. I'll call you Boyd or Mr. Oliver, whatever you choose. I'd rather choose Mr. Oliver." What her mother might say then Emma could not imagine. At the moment, she seemed very helpless, very sad, and Emma turned over with her face to the wall. Imagining probable behavior was a terrible strain; this was as far as she could go.

Tomorrow, she thought, Europe began. When she got up, they would be docked in a new harbor, facing the outline of a new, mysterious place. "Gibraltar," she said aloud. Africa was over, this was something else. The cabin grew steadily lighter. Across the cabin, the hinge of the porthole creaked, the curtain blew in. Lying still, she heard another sound, the rusty cri-cri-cri of sea gulls. That meant they were getting close. She got up, crossed the cabin, and, carefully avoiding the hump of her mother's feet under the blanket, knelt on the end of her bed. She pushed the curtain away. Yes, they were nearly there. She could see the gulls swooping and soaring, and something on the horizon — a shape, a rock, a whole continent untouched and unexplored. A tide of newness came in with the salty air: she thought of new land, new dresses, clean, untouched, unworn. A new life. She knelt, patient, holding the curtain, waiting to see the approach to shore.

About the Author

Mavis Gallant was born in 1922 in Montreal, Quebec, Canada. Although a Protestant, she began her education at a convent. After her father died when she was young, she attended 17 schools in Canada and the United States. She worked as a reporter in Montreal for a few years, then left Canada for France, where she has lived most of her adult life.

Gallant has written three novels and one play, but is best

known for her four collections of short fiction.

A writer of both "Canadian" and "international" stories, she is highly skilled at depicting a sense of place, a social reality, a milieu. Her characters are exiles in class or place, suffering from alienation or dislocation, like the mother and daughter in "Going Ashore."

Questions for Thought and Discussion

1. Use the first few questions to set the story in time and place and to review the facts of the story. During what period of history was Emma born? How old is she when the story takes place? How old do you think Mrs. Ellenger was when Emma was born? How old would she be at the time of the story? Approximately when does the story take place?

2. How long is the cruise to be? How long have they been on the cruise to this point? Where do they go ashore during the story? What port is next?

3. Why are they on the cruise? What do you think happened between Mrs. Ellenger and "Uncle" Jimmy Salter?

4. The mother and daughter in this story illustrate parent-child role reversal. For example, Mrs. Ellenger gets into Emma's bed, whereupon Emma moves to her mother's bed. What other examples of parent-child role reversal do you see in the story?

5. The mother and daughter relationship also illustrates emotional fusion of two identities into one. In what ways is this revealed?

6. Fused relationships tend to be emotionally manipulative because of the need to react in harmony, as one individual rather than two. List examples of Mrs. Ellenger's emotional manipulation of Emma.

7. What does Mrs. Ellenger get out of the over-closeness with her daughter? What price does she pay for it?

8. In what ways is Emma being held back developmentally by the over-closeness with her mother?

9. Why do you think Emma is so drawn to the tiger?

10. Many times a fused relationship becomes increasingly conflicted until the person who is more dominated by the other declares an emotional "breakaway." Do you think this will happen in this case? What lies ahead for them? What does the final

paragraph suggest?

11. "She (Mrs. Ellenger) was at sea." And Emma looked forward to "going ashore." What meanings do you see in the phrases "at sea" and "going ashore" as the author uses them in this story?

Parenting Issue:

Family Patterns of Anxiety

Parents become anxious about such issues as money, work, sex, food, household responsibilities, in-laws and religion. They also become anxious about their relationships with each other and with their children.

When their anxiety is high, parents react in patterned ways, according to family systems theorists. Sometimes one parent pursues emotional and physical closeness in the family and the other parent distances. Sometimes one parent assumes more and more responsibility for family functioning and the other withdraws from responsibility. Sometimes parents react to the tension they feel in each other's presence by competing for alliances with the children. Sometimes parents focus their anxiety on a child, rather than on their own relationship, and the child's problems become exaggerated.

"The Rocking Horse Winner" illustrates a family which is highly charged with anxiety. The issue is money. The son Paul behaves in a bizarre, self-sacrificial manner in his attempt to help the family reduce the anxiety and maintain its equilibrium.

15.
The Rocking-Horse Winner
D. H. Lawrence

There was a woman who was beautiful, who started with all the advantages, yet she had no luck. She married for love, and the love turned to dust. She had bonny children, yet she felt they had been thrust upon her, and she could not love them. They looked at her coldly, as if they were finding fault with her. And hurriedly she felt she must cover up some fault in herself. Yet what it was that she must cover up she never knew. Nevertheless, when her children were present, she always felt the center of her heart go hard. This troubled her, and in her manner she was all the more gentle and anxious for her children, as if she loved them very much. Only she herself knew that at the center of her heart was a hard little place that could not feel love, no, not for anybody. Everybody else said of her: "She is such a good mother. She adores her children." Only she herself, and her children themselves, knew it was not so. They read it in each other's eyes.

There were a boy and two little girls. They lived in a pleasant house, with a garden, and they had discreet servants, and felt themselves superior to anyone in the neighbourhood.

Although they lived in style, they felt always an anxiety in the house. There was never enough money. The mother had a small income, and the father had a small income, but not nearly enough for the social position which they had to keep up. The father went into town to some office. But though he had good prospects, these prospects never materialized. There was always the grinding sense of the shortage of money, though the style was always kept up.

At last the mother said: "I will see if I can't make something." But she did not know where to begin. She racked her brains, and

tried this thing and the other, but could not find anything successful. The failure made deep lines come into her face. Her children
were growing up, they would have to go to school. There must be
more money, there must be more money. The father, who was
always very handsome and expensive in his tastes, seemed as if he
never would be able to do anything worth doing. And the mother,
who had a great belief in herself, did not succeed any better, and
her tastes were just as expensive.

And so the house came to be haunted by the unspoken phrase:
There must be more money! There must be more money! The
children could hear it all the time, though nobody said it aloud.
They heard it at Christmas, when the expensive and splendid toys
filled the nursery. Behind the shining modern rocking horse,
behind the smart doll's-house, a voice would start whispering:
"There must be more money! There must be more money!" And
the children would stop playing, to listen for a moment. They
would look into each other's eyes, to see if they had all heard. And
each one saw in the eyes of the other two that they too had heard.
"There must be more money! There must be more money!"

It came whispering from the springs of the still-swaying rocking horse, and even the horse, bending his wooden, champing
head, heard it. The big doll, sitting so pink and smirking in her
new pram, could hear it quite plainly, and seemed to be smirking
all the more self-consciously because of it. The foolish puppy, too,
that took the place of the Teddy bear, he was looking so extraordi-
narily foolish for no other reason but that he heard the secret
whisper all over the house: "There must be more money!'

Yet nobody ever said it aloud. The whisper was everywhere,
and therefore no one spoke it. Just as no one ever says: "We are
breathing!" in spite of the fact that breath is coming and going all
the time.

"Mother," said the boy Paul one day, "why don't we keep a car
of our own? Why do we always use uncle's, or else a taxi?"

"Because we're the poor members of the family," said the
mother.

"But why are we, mother?"

"Well—I suppose," she said slowly and bitterly, "it's because
your father has no luck."

The boy was silent for some time.

"Is luck money, mother?" he asked, rather timidly.

"No, Paul. Not quite. It's what causes you to have money."

"Oh!" said Paul vaguely. "I thought when Uncle Oscar said filthy lucker, it meant money."

"Filthy lucre does mean money," said the mother. "But it's lucre, not luck."

"Oh!" said the boy. "Then what is luck, mother?"

"It's what causes you to have money. If you're lucky you have money. That's why it's better to be born lucky than rich. If you're rich, you may lose your money. But if you're lucky, you will always get more money."

"Oh! Will you? And is father not lucky?"

"Very unlucky, I should say," she said bitterly.

The boy watched her with unsure eyes.

"Why?" he asked.

"I don't know. Nobody ever knows why one person is lucky and another unlucky."

"Don't they? Nobody at all? Does nobody know?"

"Perhaps God. But He never tells."

"He ought to, then. And aren't you lucky either, mother?"

"I can't be, if I married an unlucky husband."

"But by yourself, aren't you?"

"I used to think I was, before I married. Now I think I am very unlucky indeed."

"Why?"

"Well—never mind! Perhaps I'm not really," she said.

The child looked at her, to see if she meant it. But he saw, by he lines of her mouth, that she was only trying to hide something from him.

"Well, anyhow," he said stoutly, "I'm a lucky person."

"Why?" said his mother, with a sudden laugh.

He stared at her. He didn't even know why he had said it.

"God told me," he asserted, brazening it out.

"I hope He did, dear!" she said, again with a laugh, but rather bitter.

"He did, mother!"

"Excellent!" said the mother, using one of her husband's exclamations.

The boy saw she did not believe him; or, rather, that she paid no attention to his assertion. This angered him somewhat, and made him want to compel her attention.

He went off by himself, vaguely, in a childish way, seeking for the clue to "luck." Absorbed, taking no heed of other people, he went about with a sort of stealth, seeking inwardly for luck. He wanted luck, he wanted it, he wanted it. When the two girls were playing dolls in the nursery, he would sit on his big rocking horse, charging madly into space, with a frenzy that made the little girls peer at him uneasily. Wildly the horse careered, the waving dark hair of the boy tossed, his eyes had a strange glare in them. The little girls dared not speak to him.

When he had ridden to the end of his mad little journey, he climbed down and stood in front of his rocking horse, staring fixedly into its lowered face. Its red mouth was slightly open, its big eye was wide and glassy-bright.

"Now!" he would silently command the snorting steed. "Now, take me to where there is luck! Now take me!"

And he would slash the horse on the neck with the little whip he had asked Uncle Oscar for. He knew the horse could take him to where there was luck, if only he forced it. So he would mount again, and start on his furious ride, hoping at last to get there. He knew he could get there.

"You'll break your horse, Paul!" said the nurse.

"He's always riding like that! I wish he'd leave off!" said his elder sister Joan.

But he only glared down on them in silence. Nurse gave him up. She could make nothing of him. Anyhow he was growing beyond her.

One day his mother and his Uncle Oscar came in when he was on one of his furious rides. He did not speak to them.

"Hallo, you young jockey! Riding a winner?" said his uncle.

"Aren't you growing too big for a rocking horse? You're not a very little boy any longer, you know," said his mother.

But Paul only gave a blue glare from his big, rather close-set eyes. He would speak to nobody when he was in full tilt. His mother watched him with an anxious expression on her face.

At last he suddenly stopped forcing his horse into the mechanical gallop, and slid down.

"Well, I got there!" he announced fiercely, his blue eyes still flaring, and his sturdy long legs straddling apart.

"Where did you get to?" asked his mother.

"Where I wanted to go," he flared back at her.

"That's right, son!" said Uncle Oscar. "Don't you stop till you get there. What's the horse's name?"

"He doesn't have a name," said the boy.

"Gets on without all right?" asked the uncle.

"Well, he has different names. He was called Sansovino last week."

"Sansovino, eh? Won the Ascot. How did you know his name?"

"He always talks about horse races with Bassett," said Joan.

The uncle was delighted to find that his small nephew was posted with all the racing news. Bassett, the young gardener, who had been wounded in the left foot in the war and had got his present job through Oscar Cresswell, whose batman he had been, was a perfect blade of the "turf." He lived in the racing events, and the small boy lived with him.

Oscar Cresswell got it all from Bassett.

"Master Paul comes and asks me, so I can't do more than tell him, sir," said Bassett, his face terribly serious, as if he were speaking of religious matters.

"And does he ever put anything on a horse he fancies?"

"Well—I don't want to give him away—he's a young sport, a fine sport, sir. Would you mind asking him yourself? He sort of takes a pleasure in it, and perhaps he'd feel I was giving him away, sir, if you don't mind."

Bassett was serious as a church.

The uncle went back to his nephew, and took him off for a ride in the car.

"Say, Paul, old man, do you ever put anything on a horse?" the uncle asked.

The boy watched the handsome man closely.

"Why, do you think I oughtn't to?" he parried.

"Not a bit of it! I thought perhaps you might give me a tip for the Lincoln."

The car sped on into the country, going down to Uncle Oscar's place in Hampshire.

"Honor bright?" said the nephew.

"Honor bright, son!" said the uncle.

"Well, then, Daffodil."

"Daffodil! I doubt it, sonny. What about Mirza?"

"I only know the winner," said the boy. "That's Daffodil."

"Daffodil, eh?"

There was a pause. Daffodil was an obscure horse comparatively.

"Uncle!"

"Yes, son?"

"You won't let it go any further, will you? I promised Bassett."

"Bassett be damned, old man! What's he got to do with it?"

"We're partners. We've been partners from the first. Uncle, he lent me my first five shillings, which I lost. I promised him, honor bright, it was only between me and him; only you gave me that ten shilling note I started winning with, so I thought you were lucky. You won't let it go any further, will you?"

The boy gazed at his uncle from those big, hot, blue eyes, set rather close together. The uncle stirred and laughed uneasily.

"Right you are, son! I'll keep your tip private. Daffodil, eh? How much are you putting on him?"

"All except twenty pounds," said the boy. "I keep that in reserve."

The uncle thought it a good joke.

"You keep twenty pounds in reserve, do you, you young romancer? What are you betting, then?"

"I'm betting three hundred," said the boy gravely. "But it's between you and me, Uncle Oscar! Honor bright?"

The uncle burst into a roar of laughter.

"It's between you and me all right, you young Nat Gould," he said, laughing. "But where's your three hundred?"

"Bassett keeps it for me. We're partners."

"You are, are you! And what is Bassett putting on Daffodil?"

"He won't go quite as high as I do, I expect. Perhaps he'll go a hundred and fifty."

"What, pennies?" laughed the uncle.

"Pounds," said the child, with a surprised look at his uncle. "Bassett keeps a bigger reserve than I do."

Between wonder and amusement Uncle Oscar was silent. He pursued the matter no further, but he determined to take his nephew with him to the Lincoln races.

"Now, son," he said, "I'm putting twenty on Mirza, and I'll put five for you on any horse you fancy. What's your pick?"

"Daffodil, uncle."

"No, not the fiver on Daffodil!"

"I should if it was my own fiver," said the child.

"Good! Good! Right you are! A fiver for me and a fiver for you on Daffodil."

The child had never been to a race meeting before, and his eyes were blue fire. He pursed his mouth tight, and watched. A

Frenchman just in front had put his money on Lancelot. Wild with
excitement, he flayed his arms up and down, yelling "Lancelot!
Lancelot!" in his French accent.

Daffodil came in first, Lancelot second, Mirza third. The child,
flushed and with eyes blazing, was curiously serene. His uncle
brought him four five-pound notes, four to one.

"What am I to do with these?" he cried, waving them before the
boy's eyes.

"I suppose we'll talk to Bassett," said the boy. "I expect I have
fifteen hundred now; and twenty in reserve; and this twenty."

His uncle studied him for some moments.

"Look here, son!" he said. "You're not serious about Bassett
and that fifteen hundred, are you?"

"Yes, I am. But it's between you and me, uncle. Honor bright!"

"Honor bright all right, son! But I must talk to Bassett."

"If you'd like to be a partner, uncle, with Bassett and me, we
could all be partners. Only, you'd have to promise, honor bright,
uncle, not to let it go beyond us three. Bassett and I are lucky, and
you must be lucky, because it was your ten shillings I started
winning with . . ."

Uncle Oscar took both Bassett and Paul into Richmond Park for
an afternoon, and there they talked.

"It's like this, you see, sir," Bassett said. "Master Paul would get
me talking about racing events, spinning yarns, you know, sir.
And he was always keen on knowing if I'd made or I'd lost. It's
about a year since, now, that I put five shillings on Blush of Dawn
for him — and we lost. Then the luck turned, with that ten shillings he had from you, that we put on Singhalese. And since that
time, it's been pretty steady, all things considering. What do you
say, Master Paul?"

'We're all right when we're sure," said Paul. "It's when we're
not quite sure that we go down."

"Oh, but we're careful then," said Bassett.

"But when are you sure?" smiled Uncle Oscar.

"It's Master Paul, sir," said Bassett , in a secret, religious voice.
"It's as if he had it from heaven. Like Daffodil, now, for the
Lincoln. That was as sure as eggs."

"Did you put anything on Daffodil?" asked Oscar Cresswell.

"Yes, sir, I made my bit."

"And my nephew?"

Bassett was obstinately silent, looking at Paul.

"I made twelve hundred, didn't I, Bassett? I told uncle I was putting three hundred on Daffodil."

"That's right," said Bassett, nodding.

"But where's the money?" asked the uncle.

"I keep it safe locked up, sir. Master Paul he can have it any minute he likes to ask for it."

"What, fifteen hundred pounds?"

"And twenty! and forty, that is, with the twenty he made on the course."

"It's amazing!" said the uncle.

"If Master Paul offers you to be partners, sir, I would, if I were you; if you'll excuse me," said Bassett.

Oscar Cresswell thought about it.

"I'll see the money," he said.

They drove home again, and sure enough, Bassett came round to the garden-house with fifteen hundred pounds in notes. The twenty pounds reserve was left with Joe Glee, in the Turf Commission deposit.

"You see, it's all right, uncle, when I'm sure! Then we go strong, for all we're worth. Don't we, Bassett?"

"We do that, Master Paul."

"And when are you sure?" said the uncle, laughing.

"Oh, well, sometimes I'm absolutely sure, like about Daffodil," said the boy; "and sometimes I have an idea; and sometimes I haven't even an idea, have I, Bassett? Then we're careful, because we mostly go down."

"You do, do you! And when you're sure, like about Daffodil, what makes you sure, sonny?"

"Oh, well, I don't know," said the boy uneasily. "I'm sure, you know, uncle; that's all."

"It's as if he had it from heaven, sir," Bassett reiterated.

"I should say so!" said the uncle.

But he became a partner. And when the Leger was coming on, Paul was "sure" about Lively Spark, which was a quite inconsiderable horse. The boy insisted on putting a thousand on the horse, Bassett went for five hundred, and Oscar Cresswell two hundred. Lively Spark came in first, and the betting had been ten to one against him. Paul had made ten thousand.

"You see," he said, "I was absolutely sure of him."

Even Oscar Cresswell had cleared two thousand.

"Look here, son," he said, "this sort of thing makes me nervous."

"It needn't, uncle! Perhaps I shan't be sure again for a long time."

"But what are you going to do with your money?" asked the uncle.

"Of course," said the boy. "I started it for mother. She said she had no luck, because father is unlucky, so I thought if I was lucky, it might stop whispering."

"What might stop whispering?"

"Our house. I hate our house for whispering."

"What does it whisper?"

"Why—why"—the boy fidgeted—"why, I don't know. But it's always short of money, you know, uncle."

"I know it, son, I know it."

"You know people send mother writs, don't you, uncle?"

"I'm afraid I do," said the uncle.

"And then the house whispers, like people laughing at you behind your back. It's awful, that is! I thought if I was lucky . . ."

"You might stop it," added the uncle.

The boy watched him with big blue eyes that had an uncanny cold fire in them, and he said never a word.

"Well, then!" said the uncle. "What are we doing?"

"I shouldn't like mother to know I was lucky," said the boy.

"Why not, son?"

"She'd stop me."

"I don't think she would."

"Oh!"—and the boy writhed in an odd way—"I don't want her to know, uncle."

"All right, son! We'll manage it without her knowing."

They managed it very easily. Paul, at the other's suggestion, handed over five thousand pounds to his uncle, who deposited it with the family lawyer, who was then to inform Paul's mother that a relative had put five thousand pounds into his hands, which sum was to be paid out a thousand pounds at a time, on the mother's birthday, for the next five years.

"So she'll have a birthday present of a thousand pounds for five successive years," said Uncle Oscar. "I hope it won't make it all the harder for her later."

Paul's mother had her birthday in November. The house had been "whispering" worse than ever lately, and, even in spite of his luck, Paul could not bear up against it. He was very anxious to see the effect of the birthday letter, telling his mother about the thousand pounds.

When there were no visitors, Paul now took his meals with his parents, as he was beyond the nursery control. His mother went into town nearly every day. She had discovered that she had an odd knack of sketching furs and dress materials, so she worked secretly in the studio of a friend who was the chief "artist" for the leading drapers. She drew the figures of ladies in furs and ladies in silk and sequins for the newspaper advertisements. This young woman artist earned several thousand pounds a year, but Paul's mother only made several hundreds, and she was again dissatisfied. She so wanted to be first in something, and she did not succeed, even in making sketches for drapery advertisements.

She was down to breakfast on the morning of her birthday. Paul watched her face as she read her letters. He knew the lawyer's letter. As his mother read it, her face hardened and became more expressionless. Then a cold, determined look came on her mouth. She hid the letter under the pile of others, and said not a word about it.

"Didn't you have anything nice in the post for your birthday, mother?" said Paul.

"Quite moderately nice," she said, her voice cold and absent.

She went away to town without saying more.

But in the afternoon Uncle Oscar appeared. He said Paul's mother had had a long interview with the lawyer, asking if the whole five thousand could be advanced at once, as she was in debt.

"What do you think, uncle?" said the boy.

"I leave it to you, son."

"Oh, let her have it, then! We can get some more with the other," said the boy.

"A bird in the hand is worth two in the bush, laddie!" said Uncle Oscar.

"But I'm sure to know for the Grand National; or the Lincolnshire; or else the Derby. I'm sure to know for one of them," said Paul.

So Uncle Oscar signed the agreement, and Paul's mother touched the whole five thousand. Then something very curious happened. The voices in the house suddenly went mad, like a chorus of frogs on a spring evening. There were certain new furnishings, and Paul had a tutor. He was really going to Eton, his father's school, in the following autumn. There were flowers in the winter, and a blossoming of the luxury Paul's mother had been used to. And yet the voices in the house, behind the sprays of mimosa and almond blossom, and from under the piles of iridescent cushions, simply trilled and screamed in a sort of ecstasy: "There must be more money! Oh-h-h, there must be more money. Oh, now, now-w! Now-w-w—there must be more money—more than ever! More than ever!"

It frightened Paul terribly. He studied away at his Latin and Greek with his tutors. But his intense hours were spent with Bassett. The Grand National had gone by: he had not "known," and had lost a hundred pounds. Summer was at hand. He was in agony for the Lincoln. But even for the Lincoln he didn't "know" and he lost fifty pounds. He became wild-eyed and strange, as if something were going to explode in him.

"Let it alone, son! Don't you bother about it!" urged Uncle Oscar. But it was as if the boy couldn't really hear what his uncle was saying.

"I've got to know for the Derby! I've got to know for the Derby!" the child reiterated, his big blue eyes blazing with a sort of madness.

His mother noticed how overwrought he was.

"You'd better go to the seaside. Wouldn't you like to go now to the seaside, instead of waiting? I think you'd better," she said, looking down at him anxiously, her heart curiously heavy because of him.

But the child lifted his uncanny blue eyes.

"I couldn't possibly go before the Derby, mother!" he said. "I couldn't possibly!"

"Why not?" she said, her voice becoming heavy when she was opposed. "Why not? You can still go from the seaside to see the Derby with your Uncle Oscar, if that's what you wish. No need for you to wait here. Besides, I think you care too much about these races. It's a bad sign. My family has been a gambling family, and you won't know till you grow up how much damage it has done. But it has done damage. I shall have to send Bassett away, and ask Uncle Oscar not to talk racing to you, unless you promise to be reasonable about it; go away to the seaside and forget it. You're all nerves!"

"I'll do what you like, mother, so long as you don't send me away till after the Derby," the boy said.

"Send you away from where? Just from this house?"

"Yes," he said, gazing at her.

"Why, you curious child, what makes you care about this house so much, suddenly? I never knew you loved it."

He gazed at her without speaking. He had a secret within a secret, something he had not divulged, even to Bassett or to his Uncle Oscar.

But his mother, after standing undecided and a little bit sullen for some moments, said:

"Very well, then! Don't go to the seaside till after the Derby, if you don't wish it. But promise me you won't let your nerves go to pieces. Promise you won't think so much about horse racing and events, as you call them!"

"Oh, no," said the boy casually. "I won't think much about them, mother. You needn't worry. I wouldn't worry, mother, if I were you."

"If you were me and I were you," said his mother, "I wonder what we should do!"

"But you know you needn't worry, mother, don't you?" the boy repeated.

"I should be awfully glad to know it," she said wearily.

"Oh, well, you can, you know. I mean, you ought to know you needn't worry," he insisted.

"Ought I? Then I'll see about it," she said.

Paul's secret of secrets was his wooden horse, that which had no name. Since he was emancipated from a nurse and a nursery-governess, he had had his rocking horse removed to his own bedroom at the top of the house.

"Surely, you're too big for a rocking horse!" his mother had remonstrated.

"Well, you see, mother, till I can have a real horse, I like to have some sort of animal about," had been his quaint answer.

"Do you feel he keeps you company?" she laughed.

"Oh, yes! He's very good, he always keeps me company, when I'm there," said Paul.

So the horse, rather shabby, stood in an arrested prance in the boy's bedroom.

The Derby was drawing near, and the boy grew more and more tense. He hardly heard what was spoken to him, he was very frail, and his eyes were really uncanny. His mother had sudden seizures of uneasiness about him. Sometimes, for half-an-hour, she would feel a sudden anxiety about him that was almost anguish. She wanted to rush to him at once, and know he was safe.

Two nights before the Derby, she was at a big party in town, when one of her rushes of anxiety about her boy, her first-born, gripped her heart till she could hardly speak. She fought with the feeling, might and main, for she believed in common sense. But it was too strong. She had to leave the dance and go downstairs to telephone to the country. The children's nursery-governess was terribly surprised and startled at being rung up in the night.

"Are the children all right, Miss Wilmot?"

"Oh, yes, they are quite all right."

"Master Paul? Is he all right?"

"He went to bed as right as a trivet. Shall I run up and look at him?"

"No," said Paul's mother reluctantly. "No! Don't trouble. It's all right. Don't sit up. We shall be home fairly soon." She did not want her son's privacy intruded upon.

"Very good," said the governess.

It was about one o'clock when Paul's mother and father drove up to their house. All was still. Paul's mother went to her room and slipped off her white fur coat. She had told her maid not to wait up for her. She heard her husband downstairs, mixing a whisky-and-soda.

And then, because of the strange anxiety at her heart, she stole upstairs to her son's room. Noiselessly she went along the upper corridor. Was there a faint noise? What was it?

She stood, with arrested muscles, outside his door, listening. There was a strange, heavy, and yet not loud noise. Her heart stood still. It was a soundless noise, yet rushing and powerful. Something huge, in violent, hushed motion. What was it? What in God's name was it? She ought to know. She felt that she knew the noise. She knew what it was.

Yet she could not place it. She couldn't say what it was. And on and on it went, like a madness.

Softly, frozen with anxiety and fear, she turned the door handle.

The room was dark. Yet in the space near the window, she heard and saw something plunging to and fro. She gazed in fear and amazement.

Then suddenly she switched on the light, and saw her son, in his green pyjamas, madly surging on the rocking horse. The blaze of light suddenly lit him up, as he urged the wooden horse, and lit her up, as she stood, blonde, in her dress of pale green and crystal, in the doorway.

"Paul!" she cried. "Whatever are you doing?"

It's Malabar!" he screamed, in a powerful, strange voice. "It's Malabar!"

His eyes blazed at her for one strange and senseless second, as he ceased urging his wooden horse. Then he fell with a crash to the ground, and she, all her tormented motherhood flooding upon her, rushed to gather him up.

But he was unconscious, and unconscious he remained, with some brain-fever. He talked and tossed, and his mother sat stonily by his side.

"Malabar! It's Malabar! Bassett, Bassett, I know it! It's Malabar!"

So the child cried, trying to get up and urge the rocking horse that gave him his inspiration.

"What does he mean by Malabar?" asked the heart-frozen mother.

"I don't know," said the father stonily.

"What does he mean by Malabar?" she asked her brother Oscar.

"It's one of the horses running for the Derby," was the answer.

And, in spite of himself, Oscar Cresswell spoke to Bassett, and himself put a thousand on Malabar: at fourteen to one.

The third day of the illness was critical: they were waiting for a change. The boy, with his rather long, curly hair, was tossing ceaselessly on the pillow. He neither slept nor regained consciousness, and his eyes were like blue stones. His mother sat, feeling her heart had gone, turned actually into a stone.

In the evening, Oscar Cresswell did not come, but Bassett sent a message, saying could he come up for one moment, just one moment? Paul's mother was very angry at the intrusion, but on second thought she agreed. The boy was the same. Perhaps Bassett might bring him to consciousness.

The gardener, a shortish fellow with a little brown moustache, and sharp little brown eyes, tiptoed into the room, touched his imaginary cap to Paul's mother, and stole to the bedside, staring with glittering, smallish eyes, at the tossing, dying child.

"Master Paul!" he whispered. "Master Paul! Malabar come in first all right, a clean win. I did as you told me. You've made over seventy thousand pounds, you have; you've got over eighty thousand. Malabar came in all right, Master Paul."

"Malabar! Malabar! Did I say Malabar, mother? Did I say Malabar? Do you think I'm lucky, mother? I knew Malabar, didn't I? Over eighty thousand pounds! I call that lucky, don't you, mother? Over eighty thousand pounds! I knew, didn't I know I knew? Malabar came in all right. If I ride my horse till I'm sure, then I tell you, Bassett, you can go as high as you like. Did you go for all you were worth, Bassett?"

"I went a thousand on it, Master Paul."

"I never told you, mother, that if I can ride my horse, and get there, then I'm absolutely sure — oh, absolutely! Mother, did I ever tell you? I'm lucky."

"No, you never did," said the mother.

But the boy died in the night.

And even as he lay dead, his mother heard her brother's voice saying to her: "My God, Hester, you're eighty-odd thousand to the good and a poor devil of a son to the bad. But, poor devil, poor devil, he's best gone out of a life where he rides his rocking horse to find a winner."

About the Author

D(avid) H(erbert) Lawrence was born in 1885 in Eastwood, Nottinghamshire, England, the son of an illiterate coal miner and a former schoolteacher. (The conflict between his earthiness and her refinement became a central theme in Lawrence's fiction.) Lawrence was educated at Nottingham University College and taught school for a short while, until contracting tuberculosis. He married Frieda von Richtofen Weekley and together they traveled and lived in many countries, including the southwestern U.S. He died in 1929 at the age of 44.

Lawrence is one of the literary giants of the modern age. In just two decades he wrote 10 novels (*The Rainbow,* and *Women in Love* are two of the best), nearly 60 novellas and short stories ("The Rocking Horse Winner," published posthumously in 1934, is one of many "bests"). Lawrence wrote excellent poetry (*Birds, Beasts and Flowers*), essays, ("Psychoanalysis and the Unconscious"), literary criticism ("Studies in Classic American Literature"), travel sketches, even plays. A twentieth century prophet, he was sharply at odds with the values of the modern age.

In "The Rocking Horse Winner," the mother represents conventional religious, sexual and materialistic middle class values which for Lawrence were a destructive force on the individual and society. The father's abdication of his "natural" role in the family allows the mother to impose "destructive" values on the rest of the family. The mother's substitution of the "false" value of materialism for the "natural" bond of love between parent and child results in tragedy.

The fairy tale opening and the use of the supernatural heightens the fable-like nature of the story, which is intended to teach its readers moral truths.

Questions for Thought and Discussion

1. The story takes place in England, probably in the 1920s. To review the story's setting, make a list of terms which are unique to that time and place.

2. Why do you think there was never enough money? What effect did Paul's anonymous gift have?

3. Why was it so important to Paul that he be lucky? How did Paul's mother respond to him when he first told her that he was lucky? How did you feel, later, when he asked her, "Mother, did I ever tell you? I'm lucky."

4. What are the clues that this family was repeating patterns of previous generations?

5. The father is barely mentioned by the storyteller. What role did he play in the family system?

6. What are the similarities between Paul's family and the contemporary, North American family? The differences?

7. If you could give Paul's sisters some advice, what would you tell them?

8. How do you react to the final statement by Uncle Oscar? What is tragic about Paul's life? His mother's?

9. What have you observed to be the effects of parental anxiety on children?

Readings and Sources

Bruner, J. (1986). **Actual minds, possible worlds.** Cambridge, MA: Harvard University Press.

Campbell, J. (1984). **Myths to live by.** New York: Bantam.

Coles, R. (1989). **The call of stories.** Boston: Houghton Mifflin.

Cousins, N. (1979). **Anatomy of an illness.** New York: W. W. Norton.

Cousins, N. (1989). **Headfirst: The biology of hope.** New York: E. P. Dutton.

Osborne, P. (1989). **Parenting for the '90s.** Intercourse, PA: Good Books.

Postman, N. (1989, December). Learning by story. **The Atlantic,** pp. 119–124.

White, M., & Epston, D. (1990). **Narrative means to therapeutic ends.** New York: W. W. Norton.

Wiggins, J. (Ed.) (1975). **Religion as story.** New York: Harper.

About the Editors

Philip Osborne has taught in the Psychology department of Hesston College since 1971 and has served there as Associate Academic Dean since 1978. His Ph.D., received from George Peabody College in 1974, is in Educational Psychology and Education. He is the author of **Parenting for the '90s,** (1989, Good Books), a companion book to this one. Osborne and his wife Lorna are the parents of three grown children.

Karen Weaver Koppenhaver earned an M.F.A. in Creative Writing at Wichita State University. She is a writer/editor in the publications department of Hesston College. She considers herself a great parent to her four grown children.

Both Osborne and Koppenhaver are natives of Hesston, Kansas. During their grade school and high school years, they were neighbors and classmates. This is their first collaboration.